I0771655

PSYPHER

Psypher
Copyright © 2024 by Joshua Mejia

Cover art by Johny Prayogi

Printed by Axiom Publishing, in the United States of America.
www.axiompublishingllc.com
inquiry@axiompublishingllc.com

Library of Congress Control number: 2024906351

ISBN: 979-8-9903754-0-6 (paperback)
ISBN: 979-8-9903754-1-3 (hardcover)

10 9 8 7 6 5 4 3 2 1

PSYPHER

JOSHUA MEJIA

Axiom Publishing

CONTENTS.

I
Purge

Chapter 1
Audio log No. 27.

I could remember hearing the stories as a child, of what life had been like on the surface, long before the bombs ever hit. You could talk about the surface more freely then; it hadn't yet been considered dangerous. I don't remember when that was exactly, but at some point, while growing up, conversations about the surface were harder to come by, until they had vanished altogether. Though no one tells the stories anymore, I never once stopped thinking about them, and in truth, they're all I ever think about. I could spend hours imagining, almost reminiscing, about a life I never lived, in a time I never knew, a time which now seems worlds apart from ours. It's hard enough to remember my own past, but to picture a life so different from my own, despite what little I've been told, I find it comes so naturally to me. Regardless, it's not the idea of the surface that amazes me, but the thought of what society then had once been. Is that really how things were like before?

Some people today choose to ignore the stories; others outright deny them. But, as for me, I want to believe in them, more than anything this city has to offer. It would give me such peace to know that the world hadn't always been this way, that at some point in time, I and the rest of mankind, used to share the same ideals, and to think that perhaps someday humanity can achieve a world like that. And who knows, maybe even something better. But as much as I want to believe in them, I find it every day more difficult to, because how could we have ever abandoned that for this?

I unlock the door to my apartment, open it quickly, slip in. I've been anxious to get home all day. It's dark, but I avoid turning on the lights; I prefer to be left alone this evening. As I make my way towards my closet, I carelessly toss my briefcase on the kitchen counter and hurriedly begin unbuttoning my coat. It's too muggy in here. I switch on the television set just in time to hear the five o'clock news. From the screen, I can hear the faint voice of the anchorman beginning his address. I turn the volume up, just high enough to have it playing in the background as I prepare.

"Good evening, Acolytes," the voice says, overly optimistic as usual, "currently, in Liberty Plaza, the oxygen levels are at a critical low and will be under lockdown till further notice. Later this evening, this month's Purge Rally is scheduled to take place in Freedom Square—"

I fling my coat onto my bed, and after clumsily taking off my shoes, I eagerly open my closet door to reach for an old storage box that sits neatly tucked away on the highest shelf. I place the box down on my desk and lift the lid to find, lying amongst a pile of shredded paper, an antique tape recorder. As is customary, whenever I finally get the chance to use my tape recorder after being separated from it for so long, I first take a moment to fully admire what wondrous piece of machinery I have before me. I'd bought the tape recorder many years ago from an old junk shop down in Liberty Plaza for five Apocrypha. It was rather lucky of me to have bought it for so cheap, considering what good condition I found it in. And I would have gone back to the junk shop, which from what I last remember sold a great many other interesting finds, had it not been burned down many years ago during a Peace Parade for harboring traitorous artifacts.

I look up. Before me, on the wall above my desk, is a small air duct, about an inch away from the ceiling—too high for anyone alone to reach. And being such a small and trivial thing, no one would even suspect it of being used for any other purpose. I quickly pull out my chair, climb on top and, with one foot on my desk, carefully stretch myself forward, giving me just enough range to reach it. I begin to gently unhinge the grill, struggling at first to get it loose, but eventually managing to detach it from its frame. Inside the air duct lie, wrapped in parchment, the cassette tapes I use for my recorder. My last cassette tape has nearly run out of space and will soon need to be replaced, as I've already used up the other side. I grab the cassette tape, climb back down off my desk, and begin setting up the recorder for today's session.

Should the time arise once more when my mind can't bear the silence any longer and needs to be free, I find recording these audio logs to be the best way for relieving my thoughts. The short, and often rare period in which I have the privacy to speak my mind is, to me, one of the most fulfilling uses of my time. Finn, my roommate, won't be back from work for another hour or so, and this, I find to be an ideal time to hear myself speak. But these are also some of the deadliest hours of my life, as speaking to oneself in private, away from the attentive ears of others, and under the wrong pretext, can be a leading indicator of possessing some of the most dangerous thoughts of all: Unthoughts.

Once I finish setting up the tape recorder, I switch off the television, abruptly ending the anchorman's speech, as even the light from the screen could signal to someone—or something—outside my apartment that someone is home. I lean over the edge of my chair and open the lowest drawer of my desk to retrieve a small packet of cigarettes and a lighter. I open the pack. There's only one cigarette left. Good. Now I won't have to deal with the temptation of smoking another.

I take the cigarette from the pack, put it to my lips, then, with my other hand, bring the lighter forward, flip it open, and light the cigarette. I take one long drawn-out breath in, savoring the Exodus, breathe out, then just as quickly crush the end of the cigarette in the ashtray. That's it, that's the last one. I hold the receiver up to my mouth and hit record.

"Audio log number 27," I say, "during lunch hour today at the Bureau of Operations there was this woman who stood up in the middle of the lunchroom from her seat and suddenly began violently screaming. As far as I could tell, she hadn't been screaming at anyone in particular. The Exodus must've made her mind react in a way that forced her to speak her thoughts just as they were being conceived. She might've been trying to address the rest of us in the lunchroom, but most of what she said was either too inaudible to understand or just pure nonsense. Though at one point, even among her rambling, I could hear her say quite clearly, 'We're going to suffocate down here,' and 'Thought Blockers are poison.'

"These kinds of incidents remain a rather uncommon occurrence, with only a few cases having ever been recorded since the inception of Exodus. But as rare as these episodes are, they've gained enough attention from the Engineers to have been worthy of being given a name: Mental Escapade.

"A Mental Escapade is a brief episode of psychosis set off by the resulting factor of three linked causes. First is not taking our daily prescribed dose of Thought Blockers: the mandatory prescriptive drug Primaries are expected to take twice a day. The drug's core purpose is to numb down our minds to prevent us from pursuing any new desires we might have throughout the day. Everyone is advised to always carry some on his or her person, in case we ever feel at any moment the urge to do something even remotely unorthodox, and are always given out during lunch hour at the Bureau.

"The second cause is consuming an excessive amount of Exodus. Exodus, however, is not prescribed but can be taken whenever one feels the need to experience some sort of emotion, as Primaries are advised to use most of our energy at work. Everything in Apocalypse is always 'advised,' never ordered, you could very well not do the things you are told, but no one really ever has that choice. Soon enough, a Recall

Officer will come along and eradicate you of your existence, as you would no longer hold any importance to the city."

I break off into silence, listening patiently to the distant sounds of footsteps steadily approaching from the hall.

No, please. Not now.

I pull away from my desk, staring intently at the door, my finger over the pause button. The footsteps come closer. They don't sound like they're coming this way. Whoever it is, they're moving too fast, they would've slowed down by now. But as soon as I finish this thought, I feel my heart plummet inside my chest.

"Hello? Acolyte, are you there?" says a voice, followed by knocking, the sound ringing in my ears.

I hit pause. I don't answer, but remain in my chair, afraid to move. Which one of them is it this time? Arthur? Leonard? Or maybe Douglas?

"Hello? Acolyte?" he calls out again.

It's Sylis, my next-door neighbor. Could he have seen me enter the building? What does he want?

"I just wanted to make sure you weren't planning on missing out on this month's Purge Rally," he says.

Does he know I'm here? Maybe not. Still, I have to be quiet.

Some more knocking. "Hello?" he calls out once more, and this time he calls me by name.

That doesn't mean anything. He knows Finn wouldn't be here this early. I shut my eyes, forcing myself to block out the noise.

This goes on for several more moments before he finally gives up. I hear as his footsteps slowly continue past my apartment, followed by the distant sound of his own apartment door shutting, and only then do I finally open my eyes.

I take a brief moment to quickly regain my bearings before starting again.

"Sorry," I say, "where was I? Oh yes. The third and final cause is reaching a high enough level of stress, which will eventually set off the person's mind to warrant the hysteria. But why it happens is a far more important question than how.

"As for what will happen to the woman in the lunchroom, once the Exodus leaves her body so that she is left fully conscious of her efforts, they will first need to conduct an investigation to determine whether she stopped taking her Thought Blockers as an act of defiance or just pure negligence. If they do end up discovering what she did was done with even the slightest hint of rebellion, they'll waste no time in getting rid of her. A Mental Escapade incited by an Unthinker isn't enough to get one Pacified, but she will be tried and subsequently Purged for her transgressions.

"There have been some cases though, where it turns out some people will experience prolonged episodes of apathy due to a natural tolerance built towards Exodus, which would, in turn, lead someone to stop taking their Thought Blockers and allow the Exodus to take its full effect. This could very well have been the cause for this woman's sudden outburst, but based on what she said, and the fact that there were multiple witnesses to hear her, she most likely won't be coming back."

I take a brief pause to steal myself before proceeding.

"I've only ever witnessed Mental Escapade happen a few other times before in my life, but never did I once see it happen this close, and not to this degree. I didn't know the woman, or what exactly prompted her to behave in such a way. It was obvious her mind had escaped on Exodus; I don't doubt that. But what I really want to know is how something like that can truly happen to a person. How are we able to resort to a state of such savagery? It's as if the drug is capable of tapping into the mind and setting off some animalistic impulse deep within the human brain, just beyond our range of thought. Sometimes I wonder if something like that could ever happen to me."

I pause again.

Keep it together, you don't have time for this.

"As you know by now," I say, "I haven't taken my Thought Blockers in years. So, there have been moments when I knew that if I continued to let myself be consumed by Exodus, I would have ultimately suffered the same fate as her.

"The Recall Officers were immediately alerted, of course, and arrived within a matter of moments. I don't think she intended to hurt anyone, even in the state she was in. Still, they weren't taking any chances. They had to shut her up, and fast. The officers didn't want to draw any further attention to the scene by beating and tasing her right there, with all of us watching. Instead, they managed to hold her down and inject her with a sedative before hauling her away as quickly as they came. Everybody else in the lunchroom continued on with their lunches as if nothing had happened, while I was still in shock just thinking about it. I tried my best to ignore the whole incident, but I couldn't help myself. That's when I noticed another woman, one whom I'd recognized as being from my department, just staring at me from across the lunchroom. I don't know how long she had been looking at me, but I knew whatever she could read in my face was enough to call for suspicion. This took me so much by surprise that I didn't know what to do. I could tell she obviously didn't care that I'd caught her staring either, so after a moment, she simply looked away.

"I've had oddly similar encounters with this same woman before, where on occasion, we'll unexpectedly run into each other, either in or out of work, and always meeting eyes with one another, but never once speaking. She has short curly red hair, and large down turned green eyes, which make her always look mournful, or tired. She's an editor, I don't know her name.

"I want to believe there exists a deeper meaning in all this. I know it must sound strange, but if I'm wrong, then this is far more dangerous than I thought. What if she's a Psi-Op?"

I lift my head towards the far wall of my apartment, now faced with the enormous glass screen that inhabits this one ominous and inscrutable side of my room. The window spans most of the end wall of my apartment, giving a clear panoramic view of the street below, but in return, a clear view inside the apartment as well. There are no curtains; they're not allowed. I'm nearing the end of my time now, and I'll soon need to bring this recording to a close.

"I don't know how long I've got left till I have to go," I say, "but there's one last thing I want to talk about before I do. I don't expect anyone to hear this message, and as of now, I have only been speaking to myself. But, if by chance, someone else happens to come upon this, I hope to God that you are not one of them, and that my only hope from you is that you don't forget me. However long I have left to live, it won't be enough, a year, two years. I can't see myself living past the age of thirty.

"Waking up every day is enough of a challenge in itself. It's gotten harder to exist in this sort of world, and I know things won't get any easier. Of course, no one can ever be too certain of their time; there isn't a set date, no clock counting down to zero, the length varies. How long, or however much time I've got left all depends according to me and my choices. There have been some instances where I've had my brush with death because of these choices. When it will happen, I won't know, not until it's too late. So, if this turns out to be my final entry, I just want to tell you that I—"

Just then, out of the corner of my eye, I spot a shimmer of light peering in through the window. I turn my head to look, but before I know it, my apartment suddenly becomes engulfed in an enormous beacon of light. The searchlight sweeps steadily across the room, making a direct route towards me. I think fast and hastily double over to hide under my desk, accidentally knocking over the ashtray in my effort to escape, nearly being caught in its gaze. Glass shatters on the floor. I sit, my body bent at an awkward angle, trying desperately to hold my position, watching as the light carefully passes over everything in the room. Though I know the drone can't hear me from in here, out of instinct, I refrain from making any noise. I don't even let my mind have a chance to process any of this, with only one thought now running through my head: don't get caught.

After a moment, the light finally disappears. Is it really gone?

Chapter 2
Surrogate.

Once a surveillance drone has concluded its search, there is always the looming possibility that it will return or be followed by another drone just as it left. Paralyzed by fear, I wait, refusing to move. What if it saw me, and it's just out there waiting for me? They want me to feel safe, to think I escaped getting caught, only for the searchlight to suddenly beam down upon me as soon as I leave the safety of my hiding place. After sitting for what felt like an eternity, though must've only been a few minutes, I manage to convince myself that it's safe to come out and slowly begin to withdraw my body from underneath my desk. I try to make as little noise as possible, carefully avoiding stepping on any broken glass, before finally standing in full view of the window. It really is gone.

I realize that I had accidentally left the tape running this whole time and quickly go to stop the recording, making sure to rewind it back exactly where I had left off. I know there's little chance a drone will come by again today, but I don't feel comfortable enough to continue. I think it might be best if I finish it some other time. I quickly make work of restoring the room exactly to how it was before: the tape recorder into the closet, the cassette tape behind the vent, and doing my best to clean up as much evidence of broken glass as I can. By now, I've managed to calm down enough that I can actually hear myself think and decide that I should just rest until it's time to get ready for the Purge Rally.

I go over to the side of my bed and sit, trying to collect my thoughts. Finn still isn't home from work yet; if he doesn't come back soon, he'll be too tired to go to the rally. Though being him, he wouldn't let such a simple thing as being fatigued stop us from attending. Of course, a true Acolyte wouldn't think of missing an event like this, not even if he were dying, but Finn is no true Acolyte, and yet how does he do it? Finn and I have known each other for nearly all our lives; we were brought up in the same assembly line back in Surrogate and have remained to this day the closest of friends. We may even go as far as to call ourselves brothers.

Surrogate is the name of the private institution to which all Primary children are surrendered come the night of their fifth birthday. I haven't thought about that place in years. I'd been so eager to leave it all behind that the moment I left, I never once looked back. I can remember myself as a young boy having all my lessons authorized by the Operator, even then, and how dangerous it was for us to believe in anything other than what the Mothers had instructed us. I also remember how if any one of us questioned the accuracy of their teachings, the child would be sent off to be disfigured in some way, an ear, a nose, a toe, a finger, or even an eye if it came to that, would be removed from the child. This was done as a sort of ironic lesson to being alive, because if our old mothers—our real mothers—had decided they didn't want to keep us for the five years in which they were allowed to nurse us, we could've been shipped off at any time to the Organ Banks to be Harvested. Luckily, I was never one of these children.

These forms of disfigurement were prone to happen, as most, if not all, lessons taught in Surrogate are of a collection of fashioned truths. Meaning some aspects of a lesson may very well apply to one part of history without fault, but not another.

In that case, a new timeline would have to be invented to relieve one's confusion in the matter. There was never one direct form of "truth." In other words, there was no meaning to any of it, it was all meaningless, and even as a young child, I knew this wasn't right. So as one can imagine, it was very difficult to determine anything from fact to fiction, and especially when everyone else around you seemed to believe in the opposite of nearly everything you thought was right.

And then there were the Unlessens. I remember those. One day in our later years at Surrogate, all the assembly lines were forced to undergo a period of what they called "deprogramming," where we had to unlearn a large majority of the things we were once taught, and without question. At one point, they even made us take these specialized tests where we couldn't select the correct answers, or else they'd know we weren't complying. It's not like we had much of a choice in the matter; we couldn't avoid it. We would've been called Unthinkers.

"It was nuclear bombs," Mother Sylvia said, "the air is full of poison, and the earth is dead. We were reduced to living underground, we are safe now, but we can never go back, or else we will die."

Yes, I remember, it's all coming back now. But there's something missing. I don't feel as if I lived these memories, only witnessed them. When recalling the past, one can also remember what it felt like, now being projected into the present. What separates a memory from the imaginary is the ability to relive those former emotions as they begin to resurface. But had I really managed to let so much of my past go? These memories to me feel only like something I conjured up on my own, to fill in the empty space of my forgotten past. I did not live this. But if I didn't have as much confidence in my own memory as I do now, I probably wouldn't believe in them myself.

Despite this, the past and I did not part ways without leaving a piece of itself behind, and likewise, not without taking something else in return. So I know these memories must hold some truth in them because of this, and after all these years.

We were around the age of ten, and all the children in my assembly line had gone on a day trip to the history museum to visit a synthetic tree reserve as part of an earth ecological exhibit. This was because none of us, nor has anyone else in the entire city in all our lives seen a real tree, as trees, like many other things now, no longer exist. I remember most of the children being frightened by the trees, as they were so vast in size. Some avoided going near them, thinking they would at any moment reach out at us with their long branches and grab us. But Finn and I were of the few children who found them to be quite fascinating. Even now, I can remember how I felt when I found myself thinking almost as if I somehow managed to return to the surface, at a time before the bombs hit, and was now walking through a real forest. And what a pleasure it was to see something that had long since been extinct, simulated so beautifully that my mind couldn't believe it wasn't the real thing. That was until I had been broken out of my reverie by something so small, that I could have ended that day never seeing it, and yet it chanced to catch my eye. I came nearer and realized what it was. On a leaf of one of the trees, there was imprinted on it a sort of code, a serial number. This was to indicate the type of plastic used to make the trees. It had been printed on the wrong side. At that moment, all hope in me vanished, and I knew it was impossible. I'm never going to reach the surface, and I'm never going to walk through a real forest, and I'm never going to see a real tree.

But then the terrible day came a few weeks later. Mother Sylvia stood in front of the classroom, heels clicking, hands neatly clasped. "I've got very important news for you children," she said, "it has been decided that all future lessons about the surface have been terminated, as well as requiring your full participation in liquidating the lesson from your memory." Later I found out that the tree reserve had been shut down because the word "tree" had been deemed too dangerous and declared an Unword.

I hadn't known it at the time, but Finn later told me what they did when this happened. Every book, film, news article, journal, and documentation that contained the word "tree" and other words of that nature were immediately hunted down and collected, most of which were recycled or destroyed. But of the few that weren't, they were either edited or taken and locked up in the Library of Unbooks in the Records Department at the Bureau of Operations.

After being brought up in Surrogate for five years, I'd become well versed in the school's psychotic methods of teaching. But this was something I'd not been prepared for, and especially not for what came next. To my horror, most of the children openly abided by this sudden change almost instantly and without question; some were even glad to hear this news. I couldn't believe it; how could anyone not see the fault in this? At that moment I felt vulnerable. I knew that if I didn't hold fast to what was true, my mind would become susceptible to tampering. Out of the children who wondered how such a decision could be made, Finn was the only one who spoke up and asked: "Why do we have to forget?"

Mother Sylvia told him something along the lines of: "It isn't our place to ask that sort of question," as it didn't matter what the answer was. In the end, we still had to obey.

"Well, what's wrong about knowing?" Finn went on. Even then, he knew there was something deeply wrong in this. Mother Sylvia and Finn kept going back and forth on the matter, but neither of them would give it up. Eventually, Mother Sylvia stopped replying to him and quickly paged for a Protector to come and remove him from the room. At the time, I remembered thinking I might never see him again. Finn returned a few days later with the right side of his head all bandaged up. It wasn't until a week after they finally removed the bandages that I realized what they'd done. They'd cut off his ear and cauterized the wound so that it left an ugly scar. I'm not sure if they'd done the procedure while he was still conscious; I never asked, and he never talked about it. But if I could make guess, I'd say, he was. And the fact that Finn's ear remains missing to this day is how I know this was all real and did not make it up.

Chapter 3
Finn.

The hours lapsed over me, as I sat back idly waiting, absorbed in thought, the silence a perfect backdrop for composing my ideas on, when, out of the stillness, I hear the sounds of someone unlocking the door and stepping inside. I sit up, it's Finn, he's finally come back from work. Finn's posted in the Records Department of the Bureau of Operations as a Record Keeper, so he often is forced to stay and work longer shifts in order to keep up with the endless amounts of edits tasked to his department. His hair is a platinum blond, spiked at the tips from the moisture in the air. He has tired blue eyes. And there, on the right side of his head, is his scar.

"You're back," I say, "how was work?"

"It was alright," he says, removing his coat, "I heard what happened."

"What?" I say. How could he have found out?

"You know…" he says, "in the lunchroom, the woman in the lunchroom."

For some reason, I thought he was referring to the incident

with the surveillance drone, as if he would know such a thing.

"Oh, that," I say, noticeably relieved.

"Well… did you see anything?" he says, half expecting me to break into another one of our end-of-the-day debriefings.

"No, I—I couldn't get a good look at her," I say quickly. "I didn't even notice what was happening until the Recall Officers came into the room, but by then, it was too late."

"Oh," he says, a bit dismayed, "so, how was your day?"

"It was fine I guess." I don't want him to find out about the drone; he already goes through enough trouble having to worry for the both of us.

"Are you alright?" he says.

"Yes, why?" I reply. I've never been good at lying, and especially to Finn.

"You just seem bothered," he says, "did something happen to you at work today?"

"No," I say, "it's just… today's the Purge Rally."

He lays his briefcase on the kitchen counter, comes forward, stops, stares at me. I look back at him, worried, trying to act indifferent. His stare suddenly focuses on the floor near my desk, then quickly shifts back, shooting me a nervous look. What is it? What did he see? He reaches down and picks something up off the floor.

"You were taking Exodus," he says, holding out what remains of the cigarette I smoked earlier today.

How could I have missed it?

"It was only one puff," I say, "I didn't think it'd be that bad."

"Did you forget what happened last time?" he says, "I don't want to have to repeat that night again."

"You're right," I say shamefully, "I'm sorry. I should've just thrown it away."

He resists the urge to speak. He's trying his best not to let out his frustration on me. By now, he must think I find him irritating from all the other times he's warned me, but he's not the one in the wrong here. Then, suddenly, he looks down again.

"What is this?" he says, looking back up at me, "is this…

glass on the floor?"

Did I really do that poor of a job at cleaning up? I suppose there's no use in lying about it now.

"I was recording another one of my audio logs," I say, "and a drone came by."

"What!" he yells out.

"It didn't see me," I quickly add, as if this would ease his concern, "I knocked over the ashtray trying to hide under the desk. I waited until I was sure it was gone."

"That makes it three times that you were almost seen," he says, breathing heavily, the thought of what might happen running through his head. "What did I tell you about making those? You can only make them when you're sure it's safe."

"I know," I say, "you're right. I'm sorry."

"I don't think you should make those anymore," he says.

At this, I feel a tightness in my throat. "Don't do this to me," I say, my voice breaking, "you know how hard it's been for me. I'm not like you."

"What if something happens?" he says, "you can't keep putting yourself at risk."

"Those recordings are the only other escape I have," I say raising my voice. "You have your Undocuments, and I have my audio logs, don't make me give this up."

He takes a moment to breathe before speaking again. I notice his hands shaking a little. "Alright," he says, "alright, please just try to be more careful next time."

What I really wanted to say to him in that moment was that I didn't care anymore and that I'd given up. If they find me out now, then so be it. At least I'd finally be free from this miserable place. But I knew I was only being selfish. If it wasn't for Finn, I wouldn't have lasted as long as I have. So many times, I could have stopped fighting, lied down, accepted my fate. But then what would happen to him? I couldn't bear being alone here, so why should he?

"It was my last one," I say, "the cigarette, it was my last one."

"It's alright," he says, "I'm not mad."

He's always been so patient.

"I know you don't think I mean it," I say, "and I don't blame you, but it was my last one."

He puts his hand to the back of his neck, debating this in his head. "Alright," he sighs. "So, are you ready to leave for the Purge Rally?"

"Oh, I didn't think you wanted to go," I say, "you came back really late."

"I know," he says, "but if we both don't show up, someone might notice."

"Alright," I say, "I suppose we can always skip the next one."

"We'll see," he says.

Chapter 4
Rally.

We exit the doors of the Habitat, descend the stoop onto the street. We don't bother using the sidewalk, it's already become too crowded with other Primaries also on their way to the rally. The air outside has strangely become dry, which is rare on Purging Days. Usually, the Operator schedules the heating and cooling beforehand so that when it's time for us all to come out, we have no choice but to stand huddled together in the saturated air. But not today.

As Finn and I walk, we make sure to distance ourselves from one another, just far enough so that we won't lose sight of each other in the crowd, but not too close, so that no one will mistake us for being friends. Having friends isn't forbidden by any means, but the fact is, if people know that we're close, then we won't be able to avoid association from the other, in case they ever find one of us out.

All across our district, more and more Primaries gradually stream in from various sectors, together, mindlessly in pursuit of this one singular destination. Eager chatter fills the streets. Everyone's anxious to find out who this month's guest speaker will be. After a few blocks, we pass under a large television hung from a building, the screen displaying the digitally rendered image of a man's floating head, something like that of a hologram over a black three-dimensional landscape. The head hovers eerily from above, its colorless eyes casting a sharp glare down upon the crowd, glowing in an aura of bright light. The head's geometry gives it the appearance of being carved from a glittering white crystal, with the man's visage a perfect portrayal of masculinity. This is as close as it gets to having a sun.

The image has a sort of fuzzy film grain to it. Words run across the bottom of the screen; it reads:

THE OPERATOR KNOWS EVERYTHING

We pass under several more buildings with televisions on them, each displaying that same looming white face and piercing stare.

THE OPERATOR KNOWS EVERYTHING

Keeping with everyone else, we continue pass several more blocks until we come to the entrance of the square, where they've set up a security check in conjunction with today's rally. There are no lines, and with too many people trying to go through all at once, nobody can seem to get in. We merge with the rest of the horde, the collective movement of the mob directing our steps, becoming one with the crowd, until finally it's our turn to be screened. I give the Protector my card, he scans it. Another Protector comes forward, this one carrying a handheld metal detector, and carefully waves it over me before flagging me through. On the other side of the security check Finn and I subtly rejoin in the same way as before, pretending not to notice each other, then file in with the rest of the attendees as we try to get as close to the front as possible.

Towards the very front of the square, they've erected a platform where today's speakers will take turns giving their usual speeches. We advance together in unison, rapidly filling in the open space, an enormous crowd of figures dressed in all white, waiting in anticipation for the Purging to begin.

The audience is divided into two sections, with the front half of the crowd closed off from us by two rows of cage-linked fences topped with barbed wire, the fences traveling horizontally through the middle, with the empty space in between creating a long narrow path that breaks off into alleyways on either side. The fences had been set up prior to the rally's admittance, only leaving a small opening for people to pass through, which by now has been sealed, as the first section has already reached capacity.

Finn and I manage to come to the very front of the second section, directly behind the fencing, which most consider lucky since it's the best view to have for a Purging.

This is good for us. less suspicious.

What I can truthfully tell you from my experience after coming to these rallies, for however many years they've been holding them, and listening to the same thought-provoking speeches, is that despite the immense amount of time and energy the Operator puts into them, they still remain to be among one of the most meaningless things Apocalypse has ever conceived. And yet it is the highest witnessed event in the entire city. A Purge Rally's only purpose is to incite fear among Unthinkers and invoke hatred towards them.

As soon as the event is at full capacity, the checkpoints are closed, and the rally begins. Peering through the two layers of fences, my vision partially obscured by wired netting, I can just barely make out three men in white suits stepping up onto the platform. One of the men goes directly up behind the podium, while the other two sit in chairs placed at the back. Above the platform are three large projecscreens that display the speaker's face.

The event is being televised throughout the whole city for those who couldn't attend the rally in person. Viewings of the rally itself have practically become impossible to miss, as one would simply need to find a television screen, which is not hard to come upon, as they can easily be found throughout the city: plastered on the sides of buildings, fixed upon pillars in the metro station, conveniently placed through the display cases of shops, and in the homes of every single citizen.

Looking at the projecscreens, I can tell this man is in his late forties. He has a fixed stern look molded onto his face, which is square and angular. Brown slicked back hair, rough facial scarring. I can even make out the greasiness of his face from the sweat dripping from his forehead. But he's not nervous, on the contrary, he's eager to begin. Finally, the crowd goes silent, and he begins his speech.

"Good evening fellow Acolytes!" he says, vigorously without delay, "we gather here today to celebrate yet another glorious feat! It is my great honor to announce that as an institution, we have made tremendous strides to better ourselves, not only in the present age but for the ages to come!" He shakes his fist in the air as he speaks. "As we continue to progress further in our fight for mental liberation, we must never forget that to oppose the Unthinker is not enough to counteract the actions of one if we wish to succeed in this war!"

There's a soft cheer among the crowd, and Finn takes the opportunity to play along, though I don't feel like starting this early.

"We must stand together as a people against these psycho-terrorists who wish to wreak havoc upon our righteous city! We left the surface to protect ourselves from the actions of those who wish to hurt us, and now they reside here with us! It is our duty to protect and uphold our rights as citizens because this is all we have left!

"It is an infestation, an epidemic! If they take control here, then we will never be free from the wicked bonds of our enemies!"

Another cheer.

"They will creep into our homes, our workplaces, they will pretend to be our friends! Why, there may very well be traitors among us now! But before they can get us, we will smoke them out, we will rip them from our streets, De-psypher them, tear them apart!"

This man is not an important figure. He was hired simply for his voice work. Of all the people in the city, he needed to be the one to make this speech. He didn't write it though; that's evident in itself, but he definitely has the right voice for such speeches. He knows how to speak with an air of great passion, enough to easily invoke even the smallest of crowds. This is a very large crowd.

"And for those of you who may be suffering from Unthought!" he goes on, spit flying out of his mouth, "turn yourself in now! It is not too late! We can help you! But if you indulge in those thoughts, and continue to hide, then when you are finally De-psyphered, we will show no mercy!"

This time, the whole crowd cheers, and I have no choice but to participate.

"Now, I am pleased to welcome this evening's honored guest, Primary: 6-079 Sebastian, the first ever recovered Unthinker!" As the speaker finishes his sentence, the audience suddenly bursts into a frenzy, the square enthralled in cries of triumph and victory.

The men sitting in the chairs at the back stand up. I notice one of them has a limp and is too weak to walk on his own so that he needs help from the other man, whose only purpose I see now is to assist him as he makes his way up to the podium.

I recognize this man all too well, his face was in the newspapers, *The First Test Subject to Successfully Complete the Assimilation Program*, and I should know, I took his photograph at the obedience showcase.

News of his recovery broke headlines. It had awoken something in the people of Apocalypse, it was their idea of hope, and to think they were even capable of having any. Everywhere in the city people spoke of the man who freed himself from Unthought, a condition once deemed terminal now curable. In the newspaper, Dr. Nimdok, head doctor of Neo Synapse, gave a statement to the press describing it as: "a breakthrough in Unthought recovery," and would forever be marked as a pivotal moment in Apocalypse history. Weeks passed, and still, their vigor showed no signs of slowing down. The city couldn't get enough of him. It got to a point where everyone saw this man as some kind of savior, come to lead the way for more future recoveries. Finally, a hope that not just

Unthinkers but Unthought itself will be eradicated, once and for all. They even have a name for him, they call him the "Ataraxia." Poor guy. This is the first public appearance he's ever made since being officially discharged from Neo Synapse about a month ago.

Chapter 5
Ataraxia.

What sets this man apart from the rest of the test subjects is that he wasn't De-psyphered. No. He turned himself in. I remember his name appearing in the newspapers about a year ago, *Unthinker Reports Himself to the Operator*. He's a special case.

Most prisoners never have the chance to escape a Purging or Pacification, but in the rare instance where they do, they offer them the choice to prove their worth. The Operator has a covert team of specialists whose job is to go through and carefully review every prisoner's case file before they're sentenced. What they hope to find from these investigations is what the Operator calls "vestiges," unique characteristics in Unthinkers that indicate them as potential candidates for the assimilation program. As a final preliminary before the fates of these prisoners are ultimately decided, the Operator presents them with the offer to volunteer as test subjects at the recently constructed psychological manipulation and reconditioning facility: Neo Synapse. And if those select few agree, test subjects will, in practice, inevitably be relieved of their dangerous thoughts. They will become nothing more than walking husks of what some may have once called humans. Though this man is the only person who's ever been sent there and come out alive. And all this to set him up as an example for other Unthinkers, to show what they can become if only they'd surrender. Though the chances of being chosen are slim to none, and even then, who could ever choose to become like this?

He looks to be around the same age as me. He has short light brown hair, a thin face, sickly pale skin, and round glasses that sit neatly on the top of his nose. I note the white gloves on his hands. What did they do to him in there?

"Good day, Acolytes," he begins meekly, "for as long as I can remember, I had been terrorized by the sickening thoughts that were prohibiting me from becoming the free man I am today. I'd allowed myself to be at the will of these thoughts, even when I knew somewhere deep down what I was doing was wrong. I believed I was the only sane person in the world. That everything the Operator said was a lie. I tried so hard to fight against the truth that I found myself living in a world of my own making. And perhaps for a time, I found happiness in this, but it was only a false sort of happiness. None of it was real. I was a prisoner, trapped in my own psyche. For over twenty-five years, I was held hostage by the very thoughts that still reside within the minds of some people today.

"My perception of reality had quickly begun to deteriorate. I was sick. It was as if I escaped reality on my thoughts alone. Finally, it was too much for me. I knew I had to do something before it was too late, before I would completely let my mind go. So, I turned myself in and had myself committed. I was lucky enough to seek help when I did. If I'd held off even a moment longer, I would not be standing here today."

There's applause.

What strikes me most of all about this speech is not the things he is saying, but how he is saying it, which makes it all the more terrifying. His words seem to effortlessly flow out of his mouth, with the expression on his face having changed not once since he began, speaking in the same monotone voice the whole way through, showing no emotion or purpose behind any of the things he's saying. Not even the Operator's voice sounds like that.

"The person that walked into Neo Synapse," he goes on, "did not just have the freedom of thought, but the urge to do evil things with that freedom. I would rather die than return to living a life like that; I was already dead in thought. Let me be an example for the rest of them. I am not a victim; I am a survivor. I was in Neo Synapse for only a year. I was another man before, but now he is dead. My name is Sebastian, and I am free."

At this, the crowd issues one last rapturous applause, and the Purging commences. I watch as from one end of the fenced pathway, swarms of men and women pour out of the alley, with their hands bound together and mouths locked shut. Protectors equipped with tactical shields keep the prisoners from running through, herding them slowly down the narrow path, and slamming them back if they push too hard.

Together, the two audiences rush upon the fences, violently thrusting those of us at the front up against it, then in another motion, drawing us out from our places, our bodies toppling over one another. The people nearest to the fence begin viciously seizing it, with even some of the audience members trying to climb it before quickly being shot down. The crowd carries on as they begin shouting obscenities towards the prisoners, spitting through the fences to try to hit one of them as they pass through. I notice one red-faced woman in the crowd who has even begun to froth at the mouth.

I participate in the shouting and screaming, though not as passionate as some of the other people in the audience, with their deep bellows and high-pitched shrieking. One man to the left of me begins shouting the usual chant of: "THIS IS YOUR FREEDOM!"

I notice Finn some distance away from me, completely immersed in the yelling and cheering, almost as if he really did contain a deep hatred for the prisoners, more than enough to convince anyone that he wasn't an Unthinker himself.

I don't quite know what happened to him within the time

he was gone, back when he had his ear removed. I'm sure they'd done more to him than that. But what? He was gone for a week after all. Whatever they did, it set off something in him, which I can understand to a certain degree. At any rate, it didn't quite produce the outcome they intended. He knows there is nothing he can do about who runs this city. The shouting, the screaming, I thought it was just an act, but no, he's expressing genuine hatred, though not of any kind towards the prisoners, but to the Operator, and who he represents.

The Operator, as we've been told, is the artificial super intelligence in charge of controlling the various workings and mechanics of the city's infrastructure, effectively thinking for the needs of every citizen. Created by a team of Engineers, the Operator is capable of processing data at "the speed of thought," with an intellect far beyond that of the minds of humans, and is the sole being in charge of running Apocalypse. The only trouble is, none of this is true. The Operator is nothing more than an elaborate computer program: ones and zeros, along with the unknown man whose voice and likeness they've used. Who the actual people behind the Operator are, I will never know; though if you pay attention, during one of his many public addresses, which play throughout the city, you can hear, just audibly, the sound of someone typing in the background as he goes on with his announcements.

So that's it. Finn hates the Operator, and yet he's willing to obey almost every rule without fault. He's no longer taking chances. If we wish to survive, we must be willing to look the part. Finn's also managed to acquire for himself a few skills over the years. He knows how to tell a lie and believes he's actually telling the truth. Only, he lies for my and his own benefit, a talent he learned in order to keep us safe. He embodies the image of a true Acolyte, but has become the perfect enemy of the Operator. He will never get Recalled, he will never get Pacified, he will never get Purged. But in return, he has sacrificed his freedom.

Before the Purging started, the prisoners were first unloaded from the buses into the alleyway. Once it was time, they were rushed out by dogs on chains, trained to tear away and mutilate those unlucky enough to get too close. It's common knowledge that the last few prisoners always get bitten, so as expected during Purgings, every one of them makes it a practice to try to be the first one through, which only adds to the havoc.

The prisoners in the middle jostle about one another, screaming and groaning from the constant back-and-forth movement, getting scraped against the fence as they tumble about. By now, a few of the prisoners have either been crushed or trampled to death in their struggle to get through, with one woman having already been mauled away by the dogs. I'm not sure which is worse.

At last, the first couple of prisoners make it to the end of the path into the proceeding alley, where the prison shuttles await. At the end of Purgings, once all the prisoners who survive are eventually rounded up, they are then loaded securely into the back of the prison shuttles and immediately shipped out to the mines. Meanwhile, as these last few prisoners begin squeezing their way up the path, the crowd starts chanting: "PURGE! PURGE! PURGE!" the chant getting faster the closer they get, until at last, all the prisoners are processed through, whereupon the whole crowd delivers one last final cry, as the Purging comes to a close.

Even after everything I've seen, what all these people have endured, and the knowledge of what they will continue to go through, once they arrive at the mines, you'd think it would be enough to destroy one's sanity, make me go permanently insane. And how can it not? Especially to the mind of an Unthinker. And yet, why do I feel nothing?

None of this is my own doing. I am not lying to myself, nor do I lack in any form of understanding; I am entirely aware of the events which have just taken place. So then the question remains, how is it that I've become like this?

To feel emotion is not just a psychological sensation, but also a physical one. Whenever one's mind centers its attention on something, it has learned through past experiences to react by telling the brain how to respond in order to determine the most appropriate course of action. In other words, this is your conscience. But you mustn't always rely on your conscience, because your conscience can always be wrong.

I've been forced to exist for so long in this ambiguous state of constant doubt, that it's come to a point where I can't even trust in myself. What if that's it? What if this place has already destroyed my sanity, and after all this time, I've been trying to hold on to something I've already lost—the very thing separating me from everyone else: my humanity. Does Finn feel the same way?

Within the compass of my psyche, I am trapped, perpetually desensitized by the unending violence around me. Nothing could have prevented this, it was inevitable. I've become this way simply by existing in this sort of world, subject to the only emotion I know, and forced from all other feelings.

But to be constrained in this condition for so long, I've merely become accustomed to it. I've lost all sense of pain because I can't remember what it's like living in a time without it, even though I know there must have been one, once. I understand this plainly. I have no questions about that. What I don't understand is what then will it take to feel something again.

What if Finn was there? What if he was Purged? Would that finally break me out of it? But I already know there's no point in trying, because no matter how much I want to cry, I remain, nevertheless, empty.

Though the Purging has concluded, and we are now allowed to leave, the audience's energy doesn't appear to be slowing down. Actually, now that the crowd has my attention, it almost sounds like they're getting louder. Yes, I can hear it more clearly now. Their screams and shouts have gradually become more aggressive. Beneath the mob's cries now lies a desperate plea of urgency. But the prisoners are long gone. They're going to live out the rest of their lives in agony. What more can they want? Something's happening. I think I should look for Finn.

As I begin to look around, I spot a group of people taking turns attempting to smash the windows of the surrounding buildings. What are they doing? Quickly, more and more audience members are becoming increasingly hostile towards one another. All around me, small pockets of people have begun fighting each other, with some now even retaliating against the Protectors.

The audience had built up such an outpour of anger towards the prisoners that, even after the Purging, it's reached a point where it simply wasn't enough. And now, to fully satisfy their hatred, they've turned to themselves. This is exactly what they want. They incite outrage and violence in us, so that once there's no one left to hate, we begin to hate each other. They enjoy seeing us tear ourselves apart.

I can sense the hatred boiling all around me; everything's happening too fast. If I don't leave now, I might not have the chance to later. I need to find Finn, and fast. I begin looking franticly about the crowd, peering through the field of bodies, but finding it nearly impossible to tell anyone apart among such confusion. I'm wasting too much time. Where can he be? I begin calling out his name, but I can't even hear myself over the noise, my voice completely lost among the torrent of screams. Then the yellow trucks start pulling in.

One by one, large men in the yellow hazmat suits of the Exterminators begin dismounting from their trucks, equipped with gas masks and brandishing their heavy-duty vaporizers. I don't believe it; they actually called the Exterminators on us. I watch as they quickly station themselves around the square, then begin deploying their toxic gas upon the crowd, causing even more of a panic. I feel someone grab my arm. I turn my head. It's Finn.

"RUN!" he yells, "RUN!"

We make a break for the security check, desperately tearing our way amidst the havoc, the square rapidly becoming engulfed in fumes. All around me, I watch as those who fall behind are immediately swallowed up by the large, rolling clouds of noxious smoke. I can hardly breathe, my eyes and chest burn, and my vision is blurry. Finn and I are coming up to the checkpoint now, we're among the only few people who've managed to make it this far. The checkpoint is open for us to freely pass. And with that, Finn and I cram our way through and out of the square.

We did eventually make it back to our apartment, having survived without suffering any major injuries. Later that evening, when the news reported on the rally, there was no mention of the Exterminators or the ensuing chaos with the crowd becoming hostile, instead choosing to describe it as: "going off without a hitch." I later found out that they'd also cut the live feed as soon as the Purging had concluded. No one else mentioned it at work the next day either, or the day after that. It was as if everyone had come to an unconscious, unspoken agreement to act like none of it even happened.

When will it end? When will it all stop? It can't go on like this forever, it just can't. I might just have my sanity after all; though it weakens, all is not lost. I still have a fighting chance. I must not lose focus, allow an opening, resist every thought, to keep this world from destroying my sanity. But in the end, I must be careful not to let my sanity destroy me.

II

Pacify

Chapter 6
Mother.

A few months ago, I had a dream, but when I woke up the following morning, I could barely remember having dreamed of anything at all. It would have meant nothing to me, and I may as well have left it at that, if I hadn't been so completely overwhelmed with the burning desire to find out what I'd seen in my sleep the second I opened my eyes. I could feel that the dream wasn't too far gone either, that I hadn't lost it forever, if only I kept looking. Nothing else mattered, I knew that whatever I'd dreamt about that night was somehow important to me, and that I needed to find it. I tried to make sense of what things I could recall, which wasn't much. There were sounds, voices? No, not voices, just the one voice. And streams of indefinite shapes, which could either have been a person, I think, or perhaps a place? At any rate, it was familiar, in some undefinable way.

Weeks went by, and it was all I could think about. Though I couldn't understand what I was looking at, I knew that if I only focused hard enough, I would eventually make out the scene clearly in my head. But no matter how long I kept trying to piece it together, I never got any closer. There was this one time though, I remember feeling like I was closer than I had ever been to unscrambling the image, but then it suddenly slipped away again. You wouldn't understand the amount of frustration I was in. It was like catching a glimpse of something momentarily at the edge of your vision, only for it to dematerialize as soon as you looked at it—vanish without a trace—while wondering the whole time if there had been anything there in the first place.

Though it was gone, I knew that somehow it never left. There was still some part of it clinging to me, and all I needed to do was bring it into the light.

It wasn't until a few days after that something in my head finally clicked, and it all just came flooding back. Only this wasn't just an ordinary dream, it was a memory, one I'd long forgotten. A piece of my past that I'd managed to shut out for over twenty years, only for it to resurface under the mysterious pretense of my subconscious. But why now? Why must I remember?

To put it more truthfully, it wasn't one singular memory that occurred to me that night, but a series of memories from a past that, for months, had been trying so desperately to be remembered. They were about my mother, not that sad excuse of a Mother they assigned to me in Surrogate, but my own real mother, the one who saved my life.

These memories came to me one after the other, and in fragments, like flashes, or like a damaged film, or a series of photographs taken one after the next. I'm not even sure if this is all of it, but this was as much as I could recover for now.

The first one that came to me was of us sitting at the window in our old apartment. I don't remember much about what the apartment looked like, but what I do remember is that from our view of the window, you could see the abandoned clock tower that stood at the head of Freedom Square, which at the time of this memory, was still in Operation. She was teaching me how to read a clock, "analog" was the word, how do I remember this? The big hand marked the minutes, and the little hand marked the hours. I don't know anyone who can read this sort of clock, I suppose that's why it was abandoned, but the clock tower still stands today as tall as ever in Freedom Square. And that's all for that memory.

The next memory I had was of us taking the metro to Liberty Plaza. We'd gone there to walk around and look in the shops. I remember there was a little bookstore, and we decided to stop in. No one else was inside except for us and the shop keeper who was behind the counter. She was an elderly woman. I remember she had a kind face, not at all like the deranged faces of Mothers you see in Surrogate.

Most of the things sold in the store were relics, items left behind from the past, she even sold films, but we didn't buy any of those. My mother bought me a book instead.

I'm sorry there aren't enough details in this memory. It's hard. I don't recall much, like I said, only images. What I do remember is what the book was about. It read the adventures of a little boy and his journeys in the woods.

What I'm going to tell you next wasn't in my dream, at least not as far as I know, but I remember now that the next time we went to the bookstore, it was gone, and I mean the whole building. It was a Peace Parade. They burnt it down from the inside out. That was the first time I heard about them. I never knew what had happened to the old woman. She's probably dead.

My mother and I didn't go out as much after that, and then she stopped taking me altogether. But one day, she told me we were going on a walk. I can remember being so excited. It had been so long since I was last allowed out. We walked around Liberty Plaza for hours; we didn't buy anything though, which I can still remember being upset with her for. I remember that as we stopped to have lunch at the eatery, she kept anxiously looking behind her as if she was waiting for someone. After our walk, we took the metro to Freedom Square, and I got to see the clock tower for the first time up close and in person. Little five-year-old me was amazed to be there, though my excitement was soon short lived. My mother suddenly began leading me away, and we were now walking hastily down an alleyway. She kept telling me to hurry up or we were going to be late.

We took the metro again but didn't get off for a long while. I was getting tired by this time, and I told her I wanted to go home. "We'll go home soon," she said, stroking my hair as I lay at her side. Little did I know I'd never see my home again.

The carriage was empty now, and this was when she finally decided we should get off. She pulled me up again by my arm and rushed me out of the carriage and onto the platform. There was no one else there apart from us, but as we continued towards the exit, two men in the usual Primary attire stopped in front of us and tried to grab me. My mother picked me up and held me firmly in her arms; out of all the things I can still vividly remember, it was how tight she held on to me. When she turned around, there was another pair of men, and my mother tried to run. One of the men grabbed me, and my mother screamed for him to let me go. At this point, I was also screaming, and two of the men grabbed her, held her down, and began handcuffing her. I began to cry.

I didn't know it then, but these men were Psi-Ops: Psycho Operatives. It turned out that my mother was scheduled to surrender me to Surrogate that day as it was my fifth birthday, but when we didn't show up, they sent Protectors to collect me from the apartment. When they didn't find us, they dispatched a team of Psi-Ops to scout us out. She didn't want to let me go. Was she trying to run away with me? Did she even know where we were going? Either way, I'm just as grateful. She tried to save me. She doesn't know it, but even though we were caught, she did save me after all. If she followed protocol and surrendered me, I would have gone my whole life hating her. I never did find out what happened to her. She's probably dead too. I don't even know her name.

Chapter 7
Apocalypse Now.

Finn wakes me up as usual. He's always the one to get up first. It's his way of keeping pace with the ever-constant moving present. We're up earlier than normal, though you can't tell solely by looking out the window. From our view of the world beyond our apartment, nothing about the city's dark appearance suggests that any time has elapsed; but since when, or from what era in the past, I can't say. As far as I know, there doesn't exist a point in history from which I can distinguish this perpetual lack of change. It may as well have always been like this. But I want you to understand, I'm not saying that we're stuck reliving the same day, no. It has always been the same day, today has never ended. This city is trapped, forever frozen in time, damned to live in an eternal haze.

We're just about ready to leave for work. Finn starts for the door, and I hurry to join him. On my way, I pass by the kitchen counter to grab my briefcase, but almost immediately after picking it up, I watch helplessly as one end of the handle suddenly snaps right out from its rivet. I begin awkwardly fumbling with it for a moment, trying my best to get a proper hold of it, before hurrying over to my desk, Finn following in tow. I set the briefcase down, anxiously examining both broken ends, seeing if there's any hope of fixing it. The leather around the handle is worn down, but other than that, it doesn't look too badly damaged, all I need to do is fasten the loop back around the rivet.

"You should get that fixed before it gets worse," says Finn.

"I'll have to stop by the repair shop after work then," I say, "but it should hold for now."

We leave for work, down the crowded street, past the Habitats, where other men and women are also on their way to work, all of us donning the standard plain white outfits of the Primaries. Some carry clear vinyl briefcases, and some the cheaper nylon mesh handbags. Since Finn and I both work at the Bureau of Operations, we are of the few Primaries in our district who've been granted the privilege of having been issued our special detailed solid black briefcases.

We continue down the street towards the metro station, the urge to cover my nose growing stronger with every breath. The air in this district has become severely polluted with the pungent stench of rotting waste. It permeates through the streets. Thankfully, today we've decided to wear our long, vapor-resistant overcoats, or else, the scent would seep into our clothes. Sadly, if it ever did get to the point where I had to cover my nose, I couldn't; Primaries aren't allowed to obscure our faces in any way. They need to be able to identify us at all times. There are some exceptions for those who've developed respiratory issues, but even with these provisions, the Operator is very selective about who can be eligible for oxygen masks.

A chill draft is coming in now. So far, the temperature has remained relatively cool today, this is rare. Some days they allow the air to become freezing, forcing us to wear our thick plastic overcoats, which don't do much to keep us warm, as most of our clothing is synthetic. And on other days, they crank the temperature all the way up, leaving us with no other choice but to bear the heat. And what's more, due to these constant shifts in temperature, most of our districts have been ruthlessly plagued with the foul presence of an ominous mist. It hovers around us, almost watching us, as though some omnipresent being, observing our every move. Carried by the air, it lazily drifts along the current, seeking out even the remotest places of the city to inhabit.

The air in our districts is supposed to be filtered out only once a week, for energy preservation. The only other time the Operator does something about it is when the oxygen levels become dangerously low, mostly due to the high carbon emissions from smoke caused by Peace Parades. By that point, it's no longer just our problem but theirs as well.

The sound of faint coughing fills the background. We enter the metro station, file in line. I give the Protector my card, he scans it. I move ahead into the next line where they search my briefcase and have me walk through a metal detector. When I'm through, I meet back up with Finn and head towards the platform, where we wait for the train to arrive. Above me, there's a television fixed to a pillar airing an advert for Thought Blockers. Words dart across the screen:

THE NO.1 ENEMY OF THE PUBLIC IS
UNTHOUGHT

Then it shows the image of a woman swallowing a pill.

The train soon arrives. We enter the carriage and take our seats. It isn't long before the car becomes crowded with other passengers, though today seems much busier than usual. It must have been the cool air that brought them out. Standing opposite me is a woman, turned at her side, one hand on the guardrail, and the other carrying her mesh bag, which hangs directly in front of me. Inside the bag, I can see her wallet, which is made of a transparent vinyl, three large tins of tuna, and an almost empty bottle of Thought Blocker.

Above on the wall of the car is another television, only this time, it's broadcasting one of the Operator's public address announcements: an advert for Cyber-Op terminals. The picture simply displays the glimmering image of the Operator's persona, with the words: "Do you have a question? Ask the Operator, the Operator knows everything," across the bottom.

And then the subtext which reads: "Remember, three questions a day."

When the train comes to our stop, we get off the carriage and leave the station, exiting through the turnstile gate. Finn and I don't usually talk as much on our way to the Bureau, there's not much to talk about, and even if there was, they're usually never things we would speak openly about in public.

I try not to look about myself too much; to show curiosity is an early sign of Unthought. But if I begin to turn my head as though I don't know where I'm going, it'll look suspicious. We walk only where we are permitted to walk; if you look lost, then chances are you shouldn't be here, and someone will notice.

"Stop right there!" we hear a Protector shout close behind us. Although we aren't sure if he's calling specifically for us to stop, we do so anyway as to proper protocol. I don't react fast enough and Finn has to put his arm in front of me to get me to stop. We don't move; we don't even turn around to look at him. I hear the Protector walk up beside Finn to my left, and even then, we still don't look at him. At the edge of my vision, I can make out the dark blue silhouette, the gas mask, and the tip of his machine gun.

"Good day Acolytes," he says.

"Good day," we say.

I try not to show too much emotion in my face, and Finn does the same, though he's far better at doing this than me.

"Cards," is all the Protector says. We give him our cards. He begins verifying them, taking great care to thoroughly examine our faces, to make sure we are who we say we are. "Headed to work?" he asks.

"Yes sir," Finn says.

The Protector turns to me.

"Yes sir," I say. He's only stopping us because of our briefcases.

The Protector looks at us for a moment before speaking again. "Show me your briefcases."

Was there something about us that looked suspicious? Or is he just performing this search because he can? We each take turns giving him our briefcases for inspection, though he struggles with mine for a moment.

"The handle on yours is broken," he finally says, "did you notice it?"

"Yes sir," I say, "I'm getting it fixed at the repair shop after work."

"This is not up to standard," he says, "I'll have to report it."

"Yes sir," I say.

He takes one last long look at us from behind his tinted goggles, then says, "as you were Acolytes," and continues with his patrol.

We enter through the Primary's entrance of the Bureau and wait in line. As we come nearer to the front, I overhear some commotion up ahead and look to see the man next for screening arguing with the Protectors. His card must be malfunctioning, could just be his first day. The Protectors quickly dismiss the man's cries and quietly pull him aside and into the security room. They're not taking any chances. It's my turn now. The Protector scans my card, it works. I proceed down to the next line, where I have my briefcase searched for the third time today, another metal detector, and this time they pat me down.

Those done with screening head up to the airlock for decontamination. It's a simple mandatory procedure, they don't want us tracking in the bad air. We enter the gate and quickly assume the standard position in our rows of five. When we're ready, the doors shut behind us, the lights turn red, and the alarm sounds as valves from the ceiling spray us in a disinfecting mist. The process only takes a few seconds before the air is then filtered out, where blasts of wind shoot at us from all sides, pumping in new detoxified air and vacuuming out the old. Once our decontamination is complete, the lights flick green, and we exit through the proceeding doors into the main atrium.

As soon as we exit the airlock, there's an instant almost tangible shift in the atmosphere. I take one long breath in of the clean, crisp air, reveling in the rushing stimulation of my senses. The change in air quality is so sudden and foreign to my lungs that as soon as it reaches my bloodstream, I can hardly handle myself. I take a moment to adapt to this new feeling of awareness. If I wasn't awake before, I am now. It pleases me to know that I've never fully gotten used to this after all this time. It's one of the only good things about working for the Bureau. This must be the cleanest air in the entire city, no, the entire world. There's no smoke or mist, no stench of decaying flesh. Instead, the air is relatively odorless, with just a slight hint of fresh sanitizer and cleaning chemicals.

Finn and I head to our respective departments, the shared scrambled urgency of the crowd forcing us to take separate elevators to our floors. I work as a photographer for the newspaper division of *Apocalypse Now*, the last surviving news network in the entire city. I enter the Newsroom and walk down the rows and rows of cubicles, where other staff members busily work from their desks, writing and answering telecalls through their clunky wired headphones. The collective sound of typing fills the air, accompanied by the faint mingled voices of copywriters using the vox-types on their Cyber-Op terminals. The soft electric hum of the conveyor belt runs in the background, the low din of the Newsroom occasionally broken by the random whooshing of canisters shooting up and down the pneumatic tubes.

From the aisle, I turn off in another direction and proceed towards the darkroom. Once inside, I lock the door behind me, and switch on the *Darkroom In Use* sign. I open my briefcase, remove the canister of negative film, and begin the lengthy process of developing the photos, which will take up the rest of my morning.

During lunch hour, I decide not to eat in the lunchroom with everyone else, instead choosing to have lunch at my desk. On my tray are a Soylent tablet, a tin of raw tuna, a clump of brown mush, a vitamin D capsule, a Thought Blocker, and a pouch of filtered water.

As I begin switching through the channels on the television, I feel the strange urge to look up. I lift my head to see the same woman from before with the red hair staring at me from within her cubicle. She sees me looking, and we lock eyes, peering at one another from across the room. At first glance, I'm not sure how to react. What do I do? Then I notice something peculiar. What I feel at this moment isn't any sense of fear or danger from this woman, but remarkably, what I feel instead is at one with her. It's as though through this meeting of eyes, we have somehow become aligned in thought. She knows what I am thinking because she is thinking the exact same thing.

What is it about us that we should even recognize the other's existence? Out of everyone else, why do we seem to be equally drawn to one another? Neither she nor I know anything about the other, not even our names, and yet there still remains a firm indefinable connection between us, which doesn't appear to be going away any time soon. This looking of ours only lasts a few seconds before she then calmly turns away.

I could be imagining all this; it wouldn't be the first time I've conjured up such scenarios. But if what I think is happening is really happening, and not only in my head, then I ought to take this more seriously. To begin with, why would there be a link between us? There is perhaps a small chance that she might also be an Unthinker. The possibility hasn't entirely escaped my mind. Apart from Finn, I've never met another Unthinker. It would be nice to have someone else to talk to for a change without having to pretend to be someone I'm not. There are only a few other people left in the Newsroom now. I think I should go up and talk to her, try to get to know her. That would be nice, but I don't entertain this idea any further. It's too dangerous. I need to give up whatever plans, whatever thoughts I may have about a potential future involving this woman. She could be my one and only chance, if she really is an Unthinker, which is too bad, because I'll never know.

I find a channel airing a live telepro of *We Think,* a popular talk show, which is being broadcast from a studio somewhere within the Bureau. The host Felix Fitzpatrick has just welcomed his first guest, Dr. Savant, a clinical psychologist who specializes in the study of patients at the Recall Clinic. She's there today to address the matter of inter-caste relationships. The Operator's not as strict on Secondaries regarding Unthoughts as he is compared to us, although you think he would. Instead, he allows small public displays of rebellion as a way to give rise to false hope, until he decides he's had enough of their nonsense before quickly shutting them down.

This is how their conversation goes:

"Perhaps one of the most deliberated topics among Secondary societies today poses the rather threatening position of allowing the existence of inter-caste relationships," says Fitzpatrick. "Now, this philosophy isn't new by any means, seeing as there was no rule against the act, being that the caste structure hadn't yet been created before it was later decided that relationships should remain isolated from within one's own caste. But strangely enough, small pockets of *avant-garde* thinkers have increasingly humored the idea, with the question having quickly resurfaced amidst the growing need for change by defying the very social order in which we operate. Here I have joining with me today is Dr. Savant. Now I will admit, doctor, that when you asked to be on the show, I was a bit reluctant to let you on at first when I found out what we were going to be talking about today. Still, I want to give you the fair opportunity to speak, and perhaps see if you're open to changing your mind."

"Well, thank you for having me," says Dr. Savant, visibly taken aback by his remarks but still trying to remain composed.

After watching this show for many years now, I've figured out the way these kinds of interviews generally play out. The moment his guests finish stating their position he wastes no time bombarding them with absurd and outlandish questions, all of which hold no real standing on the argument as a whole. He rigs the interview right from the start with the aim of making it difficult to have a genuine discussion about the topic at hand. Then once he's managed to embarrass their credibility, he'll abruptly end the interview on a cynical note, leaving no time for any of his guests to redeem themselves before being labeled a fool. But will he manage it this time?

"As we know," says Dr. Savant, "for a time, Primaries and Secondaries were allowed such freedoms, but due to health reasons, it was later ruled that all forms of inter-caste relationships were deemed dangerous and therefore outlawed. Children born of inter-caste couples were sterilized and later Recalled when the official caste structure was finalized. And today, if a Primary is caught having relations with a Secondary, he or she will simply be Purged. However, records have shown that the spread of generational birth defects in children has declined immensely over the past few decades as far back as half a century. Even at the time this ruling was made, we haven't had the need for these kinds of restrictions."

"May I just interrupt you for a moment," he says, "aren't you married Dr. Savant?"

"Yes," she says, "I am."

"Why then would you involve yourself in a matter that doesn't or at the very least shouldn't concern you," he says.

"I'm a psychologist," she says, trying to keep her demeanor, "I know what is best for the people, even if they don't themselves."

"Is that right?" he says, "then what about Primaries? They certainly don't want to have anything to do with the Secondary populace, or else they wouldn't have tyrannized us for so long," the audience cheers. "Do you know what they did to us, we weren't allowed to have children because they deemed us too genetically impure, let alone with a Primary. They were hoping we would die out, but it was their fault we were contaminated to begin with."

"Don't you find it ironic," says Dr. Savant, "that the Primaries from sixty years ago, the ones you so proudly hate, were pushing the same ideas as you are today?"

"My, aren't you just funny," says Felix. The invisible crowd laughs. "What say if a child is born from two parents of a different caste," he goes on, ignoring her previous comment, "where then would the child fit into the structure of our city? How can the castes coexist if we begin to destroy ourselves?"

"I agree," she says, "that's why I propose it's time we finally dismantle the caste structure, once and for all."

Suddenly the channel cuts to static, and then the adverts begin to play. When the telepro comes back on the air, the woman is no longer there, but Felix continues to talk to the audience as if nothing had happened.

There have been others before her, though they've never been forced off the air like this, this was a first. The producers knew the risk of inviting her, and they paid for it. Even with what little screen time they gave her, she was still able to get a fair amount of truth out; and they obviously couldn't allow that. They ended the interview the moment they realized she wasn't going to fall victim to their little game.

Chapter 8
Pacification.

I'm back in the darkroom. As I'm rinsing off the last finished print of the day, I hear a knock at the door, and then the voice of Mr. Freeman's secretary saying, rather carelessly, "he wants to see you in his office." I try to tell her through the door to give me a moment, but before I can, she's already gone.

When I'm done, I head towards the back staircase, and onto the upper level walkway which runs along the top of the first floor. The upper level is mostly comprised of offices for the Secondary staff and Engineers, with Mr. Freeman's office located directly above the entrance, overlooking the entire Newsroom.

As I round the corner, I can tell by the loud yelling coming from down the hall that Mr. Freeman's already busy attending to other people, all of them engaged in what sounds like a highly heated debate. I pass the retractions room, come to his office door and stop. His personal Protector stands guard, machine gun at the ready, no gas mask. We both stand here quietly listening as the commotion next door drags on, anxiously waiting for them to finish. After a minute or two of awkwardly standing around, a sudden banging comes at the door. The Protector opens it, and a man and woman, both in the black uniforms of the Engineers, emerge from the room. It's the advert executive and associate editor of the newspaper. That's funny, it sounded like there were a lot more people in there.

"Come in," the voice of Mr. Freeman says. I step in. The room is dark, lit only by the light from the Newsroom, which peers in through the partially open blinds from the window behind him. Mr. Freeman stands at his desk, looming over the stacks of paperwork he has yet to finish. Small traces of smoke rise from the smoldering red tip of his cigarette burning away in his ashtray. The only reason I can see him is because the screen on his Cyber Op terminal is on. Why does he insist on always keeping the lights off?

His face is a strong saturnine, both in manner and color, with short greying hair. He too is an Engineer, a low-ranking one, but even a low-ranking Engineer has more power than every single Primary combined. But above all, Mr. Freeman is the editor-in-chief of *Apocalypse Now*: Mr. Frank Freeman.

"I've got a new job for you," he says.

His voice is deep but sounds friendly enough, though the clear juxtaposition between this and the fact that he's an Engineer is unmistakable. It was only a few seconds ago that I heard him involved in a vigorous exchange between two other Engineers, and now all of a sudden, he's speaking to me in a calm manner.

"There's going to be a Prisoners' Pacification tomorrow," he says, "and I need you to take photos of the children in the audience. It's at eight o'clock in the morning. After tomorrow you've got the day off, so once you're done, leave your camera at your desk."

"Yes sir," I say.

"Here's your Press Pass," he hands me a badge, "don't lose it, and don't be late, alright?"

"Yes sir," I say.

"Good," he smiles. As I go to take up my pass I fix my attention on his teeth. He has a charming smile, but it's also uncanny. Are they his real teeth? Must be dentures. He has the right look for an Engineer. His demeanor suggests that he likes to get things done and done the right way. But that voice of his, does he force himself to sound like that? He's always so unbelievably kind. And yet there's something about the way he conducts himself behind closed doors that hints at a more private side to his personality. He is, after all, one of the many people who take part in running this city.

He says nothing more, and I leave his office. Despite his good nature, it's this contradictory behavior between who he is and how he acts that makes me all the more apprehensive towards him. The brighter the picture, the darker the negative.

It's the following day, and Finn and I are getting ready for work. I slip into my vapor-resistant overcoat, reach for my briefcase, then, without warning, as I go to turn towards the door, I suddenly become unbalanced, causing me to jerk forward and almost fall before immediately regaining my footing. I turn my head just in time to see my briefcase hit the floor and all my camera equipment bursting out. I picked up my briefcase so fast that the handle—which I'm still holding on to—had torn completely off from its rivets.

"You didn't get it fixed yesterday?" Finn says.

"I forgot," I say, instantly dropping to the floor to recover my things.

"Is it broken?" he means my camera.

"No," I say with a sigh of relief, after a quick examination of the lens, "it's not, thankfully." But what about my briefcase? Its damages are too severe. I can't simply reattach the handle like before, this is my last briefcase, and today's the Prisoners' Pacification, I can't be late.

"Can I borrow one of your spare briefcases?" I ask Finn.

"But they're not registered under your name," he says, "they might think you stole it."

"Just don't report it missing then," I say, "if I get caught, and as long as I have your permission, there shouldn't be any trouble. Besides, they don't check at the Bureau."

He ponders at this for a moment, then lets out an

exhausted sigh. "Alright then," he says.

Finn and I walk together down the sidewalk. When we come to the street corner, I stop, wait for the cross signal. Finn instead turns right and continues in the other direction, towards the metro station. Neither one of us acknowledges the other as we part. We know better than to address each other when we're out in public. Finn says it's for our protection. "We don't want to look like we're close. If one of us gets into trouble, the other won't want to be held accountable for his actions. It's safer this way." This is how we survive, we become strangers, and it must remain this way if we hope to outlive one another.

As I wait, huddled at the corner where other Primaries are also waiting to cross, a Recall Wagon drives by, blaring its emergency sirens. The Recall Wagon is red, its windows tinted. It's the same model of vehicle used for ambulances. I focus my eyes on it till it's out of sight. Someone experiencing Unthought symptoms, maybe? Or perhaps a Mental Escapade?

It's warmer out today. Water has begun to trickle down from the firmament, the roads glistening with a slick oily sheen. A thin cool mist brushes through the streets, the damp air clinging to my face and hair. I'll have to bring my umbrella tomorrow. The cross-signal lights up, and we begin to walk. Suddenly, a beam of light shines on me from overhead, scattered by the vapor and dust particles suspended in the air. It's a surveillance drone, but I ignore it, as does everybody else.

The searchlight traces over the crowd, scanning indiscriminately as we cross, until we come to the other side, where we disperse. The drone hovers for a moment, turns, aims its light through the windows of a suspended train carriage passing by, and follows it briefly before quickly whizzing off down another street.

It's interesting, the way light holds such a prominent role in shaping the city's environment. We must make do with what artificial lighting there is. There are the large glowing television screens, playing their endless series of adverts, occasionally interrupted by a news bulletin. The flashing red and white signals of the Recall Wagon. The colorful neon signs displayed in the windows of stores and above shops: orange, green, and purple. The flickering white bulbs of the streetlamps and cross signals. And the beaming searchlights of the surveillance drones.

When I arrive at the Prisoners' Pacification, I'm seated in the first row of the center aisle. From here, I have a direct view of the stage. I can look about myself more freely now. Prisoners' Pacifications are usually for Sub-Circuits, or psycho-terrorists trying to destroy social order. So practically any Unthinker who acts out against the Operator, more than just in thought.

The center audience is comprised only of Primaries; Secondaries don't attend such events, not to say that they're not allowed, but that they'd far rather be doing something else than interfere with the affairs of Primaries. To either side of the hall are the upper galleries for children brought from Surrogate to witness the Pacification of these prisoners. They're accompanied by their Mothers, with Protectors stationed at each corner, all brandishing sub-machine guns and wearing gas masks.

I can remember the first time I attended a Prisoners' Pacification; I must have been fifteen then, and even at that age, I was still too young to attend such an event, exposing someone to this level of violence. No one should ever be too young to attend such events because there should never be such events in the first place. However, these children are no more than eight years old, the youngest group in history to witness a Pacification. Over the years, they've gradually lowered the age at which children can be allowed to watch. Soon enough, they'll make it mandatory for children, even those before being surrendered to Surrogate, to come and spectate. But why the children?

There is something so deeply heinous, not only in the fact that these sorts of things exist, but that they've embraced forcing the children to participate in them as well. The urge to cover their faces, take them away from this place, burns within me. But I can't. There's violence everywhere you look. And where would I go? All I can do is sit back and watch as their innocent eyes become witness to the horrors that lie ahead of them. My mother must have thought this when she decided to run away with me. They're sowing their seeds in the minds of these children; now they'll never have a chance for a real life.

The hall is dimly lit, soft whispers fill the room, the crowd ever becoming more anxious. Then the speaker appears, takes his place on the platform, situated between the gallows, underneath the large spotlights. He begins with the usual introductions: a thought-provoking speech about the dangers of Unthought, which is met with rapturous applause, then he reads off a list of the committed Unthinkables. As he's still speaking, the Pacifists emerge from behind, escorting the first round of prisoners onto the scaffolding, their hands zip-tied behind their backs. Their faces look severely beaten. Some have bulging lips or swollen eyes, and some have broken noses, with blood and pus leaking from their wounds. I wouldn't be surprised if some have missing teeth.

As always, once the prisoners make their appearance, the shouting starts up immediately, and I have no choice but to join in. Some of the prisoners are crying. I notice most of them are of the older generation, between the ages of forty and sixty. The Pacifists slowly begin looping the nooses around their necks, two at a time, which are made of a thick steel cable. The Pacifists wait a moment before putting the plastic bags over their heads to rouse up the crowd. They aren't for hiding their faces though. The bags are creased and semi-clear, so the prisoners' expressions are still left partially visible but warped in the light, like one's reflection in a shattered mirror, or like the ghostly photos of people's faces captured in motion. From the prisoners' perspective, confined beneath the bags, it must look just as horrifying.

Once everything is prepared, there is a long period of waiting to be done; it keeps the crowd in anticipation. I look at my hand. It's completely still. I'm calm.

Just before the audience becomes absolutely ravenous, the trapdoors suddenly give out, and the bodies are suspended.

From the way the floor collapses beneath their feet, their chests instantly thrust forward, throwing their legs back, and the weight of their bodies causing them to bob from the neck down, like a pendulum, taut on the cord. Some of the prisoners have already started urinating themselves, the bottom half of their white jumpsuits turning yellow. Everybody instantly gets up from his seat, including the children, clapping, and cheering, trying to make as much noise as possible. It's too late; now these children belong to the Operator.

I aim my camera and begin taking pictures.

Chapter 9
The Exchange.

The Prisoners' Pacification lasted for another two hours, long after the final round of prisoners had expired. It would've looked suspicious of me if I left right away, so I forced myself to stay as long as I could before leaving. I'm sitting in my cubicle in the Newsroom. I'd just finished developing the photos I took of the children from Surrogate; they're out drying in the darkroom. Right now, I'm eating lunch. On my trey are the same things as yesterday, with the only exception being that this time I'm eating a pinkish clump of mush instead of brown. It's supposed to be a type of artificial meat. The woman with red hair is not at her cubicle today, and I didn't see her as I came in either. I must have just missed her. She probably decided to eat in the lunchroom instead.

I turn on the television to the same program as yesterday. I don't know why I force myself to watch these kinds of things. I certainly don't find them entertaining, but what else is there to watch? I guess you can say I find a special kind of enjoyment criticizing these sorts of shows, it's easy for me not to feel bad for doing it.

Before the show starts, however, a content warning displays on the screen. That's odd. I keep watching. Felix begins with his usual address to the audience, and right away, I can see there's something different about him. His demeanor has changed. He's more composed, as compared to his usual flamboyant self, and this catches my attention even more. I listen, then the shot switches to another camera, and to my disbelief, sitting opposite Felix is the same woman from yesterday's program: Dr. Savant. I never expected to see her face again after she disappeared halfway through the interview. She looks disturbed and slightly disheveled, though there was some clear attempt to make her look presentable for the cameras. But how could they ever allow her back on the air? She was obviously exhibiting signs of Unthought. Was not calling for the abolishment of the caste structure proof enough? How is this even possible?

"Now Dr. Savant," says Felix, "after much consideration, I've decided to allow you back on the show because I hear you have a very important message you'd like to share with the audience of yesterday's program, don't you?"

The camera changes so that Dr. Savant is the only one visible on the screen. She doesn't answer right away, but looks off for a moment, and takes a deep breath. "Yes," she says breathlessly. She pauses, turns, and looks directly down the barrel of the camera, "I wanted to say that I sincerely apologize for putting everyone through such a traumatic experience yesterday. I've taken the time to educate myself since I was last here. I know what I said was careless of me, I made a huge mistake, and I take full responsibility for any of the harm I may have caused. And to show that I am truly sorry, I have willingly volunteered to undergo social communications training."

"Is that all, Dr. Savant?" says Fitzpatrick.

"And…" she goes on, "and I had myself sterilized so that I can no longer have children of my own. I thank you for listening and will take this as a valuable learning moment—"

This is why. This is what they wanted her for. She is a warning. Not just a warning, a threat. It doesn't matter how high you are in status or rank. It doesn't matter how much we do to fight for better change, there is no point in trying, because no matter what, we will never win.

I'm heading home to my apartment. I stand on the platform waiting for the train to arrive. I didn't plan on taking the metro back, I would've much rather enjoyed the walk, but I'm tired. At least I have the day off. Conveniently enough, above on one of the television screens is an advert for Exodus. I can hear the energetic voice in my head now: "Feeling tired and deprived of emotion, take Exodus." This is what the drug does; it makes you feel energized. If you're feeling lackluster or trapped in a stupor, it offers you an escape from the world. But what they don't warn you about is what happens if you take the drug to escape from yourself.

The advert goes on to show all the different ways you can take Exodus. First, there are the ExoPens, a hypodermic needle that administers Exodus through the skin. ExoPods, the regular kind of cigarettes. ExoInhalers, a spray that gets Exodus directly into the lungs so you can take as many doses as you like. And then the Digestibles, Soylent tablets laced with Exodus. Though it doesn't matter which way you take it, in the end, you'll still go into escape.

"Exodus," a strange name for it, isn't it? It means a departure of a large number of people. Everyone in Apocalypse takes Exodus. Together we escape this world in pursuit of the one we create in our minds. I'm surprised the Operator doesn't consider it an Unword. One can just as easily use the word to refer to all of us escaping to the surface, which fits much closer to the original meaning. But I suppose the word no longer holds its original meaning anymore. A lot of things nowadays don't hold their original meaning anymore.

I can imagine it now, all of us leaving Apocalypse on an exodus back to the surface. It pains me to think about such things. I don't like to ponder too much on the impossible. I must come to terms with reality. The earth is dead, and I mustn't attempt to grab at things I cannot reach, or else I will die as well.

The train arrives on schedule. I walk into the carriage. It's crowded, but I manage to procure a seat for myself from someone getting off. I place Finn's briefcase between my legs to make room for the people around me. Suddenly, just before the carriage doors close, the woman with red hair rushes into the carriage, rather clumsily and out of breath. She quickly walks past without noticing me, looking for somewhere to sit. There are no more empty seats, so she stands in the middle of the car, one hand on the guardrail, and the other keeping a strong hold of her briefcase, making such a tight fist with how firm of a grip she has on it. I can tell she's trying to act calm, but she's clearly distressed, and I can't help but stare. I don't think she realizes how much she stands out. She suddenly shifts her gaze towards me, and our eyes meet. I quickly look away, and I assume she does the same. In that brief exchanging of eyes, I could feel the terror on her face. It was so strong that it left a searing impression on me. What has she gotten herself into?

When the train comes to the next stop, the person beside me gets off, and the woman with red hair takes this opportunity to sit down. She wastes no time trying to have a conversation with me.

"Hello there Acolyte," she says, trying to sound cheery.

She's gotten herself in some sort of trouble, I can see that now. I want to help her. "Hello Acolyte," I say back.

This is not what I wanted our first official meeting to be like. At least I know she does want to talk to me after all. Now, how are we going to do this? It should go without saying that we know exactly why we're talking to each other; we just have to try to keep this conversation discreet.

"Haven't we met somewhere before?" she goes on, acting unwitting. I see what she's doing.

"I'm afraid not," I say, going along with it, "but I have seen you around the Bureau."

"That's right," she says, "you work in the same department as me. You're a photographer, right?"

"Yes," I say, "and you're an editor." We know well enough not to introduce ourselves or ask each other our names. "I can't remember, were you the one who co-wrote that very interesting piece about the fish hatcheries and aquaponic farms—"

"You know I heard a few Primaries are organizing a Peace Parade later today," she says, completely disregarding my last comment, "I'm trying to find out where it's taking place, any idea?"

"No, sorry," I say, "I haven't heard anything about it."

"Oh, well if you do find out anything," she says, "you should really make the effort to go when you can."

"Alright," I say. What is she trying to tell me?

There's an awkward silence between us as we each try thinking of what to say next. I'm trying to let her lead the conversation.

"I hear the Operator's been working on a new treatment of thought reform at Neo Synapse," she says, by way of keeping conversation.

"Oh, really?" I say, "I didn't know, what is it?"

"It involves a procedure," she says, "the removal of half the brain."

This conversation is going in a strange direction. What is she trying to do?

"How… fascinating," I say. I have a feeling she's just making stuff up now.

"Oh, this is my stop," she says nervously.

"Well, it was nice talking to you, Acolyte," I say.

"Yes," she says, "well, take care Acolyte." She reaches down for her briefcase, "I'll see you back at work then." She gets up, then turns to me one last time, that fear still in her eyes, and says: "*Compos Mentis.*"

"What?" I say. Just then I look down and realize she's taken Finn's briefcase and left me hers by mistake. She hurries out of the carriage, and as I look up to call for her to come back, she's already gone.

Now I've lost Finn's briefcase to some stranger and her briefcase to me. I am also a stranger to this stranger. When the train comes to my stop, I get off and walk to the metro station's bathroom. Finn's going to be annoyed with me. I should have gone after her. At this point, I don't mind if I know what her name is, if it means not disappointing Finn again. I need to see if I can find some kind of identification so that I can return it and get his briefcase back. A prescribed pill bottle with her name on it, signed work documents, something like that.

I walk into the stall, lock the door behind me. Hopefully, I can recover Finn's briefcase without him ever knowing I lost it. I take a seat on the toilet, open the briefcase, and stop. What I find instead is something I never would have thought. What I find instead is this: a small handwritten note, a gun, a key, and a plant.

III

Briefcase

Chapter 10
The Plant.

I sit, paralyzed, unable to look away. I don't know how to react. For one, I'm speechless. So, it isn't true then; plants haven't become extinct. If this one survived, could there be more just like it? I feel, for the first time, genuine solace. Then I hear the bathroom door slam open and the sounds of someone entering. I begin blinking the world back into existence as my heart starts up again. I hadn't realized it, but I'd been holding my breath this whole time. I'd been stuck in such a tranced, hypnotized state, I completely forgot where I was.

The door shuts. There are footsteps. Now he's washing his hands in the sink. As I come to, the adrenaline hits me. It feels like I just took Exodus. I'm awake. I'm more than awake. I'm conscious. I lean back against the stall wall, trying to make as little noise as possible. I know what will happen if they find this on me. I wait until the man leaves to finally catch my breath. I need to get home, now. I don't think twice; I put the plant back inside the briefcase, unlock the stall door, make my way out of the bathroom, and exit the metro station.

*　　　*　　　*

I walk at a fast pace, my upper body steady in movement. I don't think to look around me. I can't afford to. I need to focus on where I'm going. I'm only a few blocks away from my Habitat; I should be able to make it there in no more than five minutes, as long as there are no interruptions.

I stop at the crosswalk, waiting for the light to change. I look at the signal, watching it with immense fixation, refusing to break my focus. Its picture is of the red hand, surrounded by a fuzzy outline of glowing light. I can see them now, the Recall Officers in their red uniforms, seizing me all at once and dragging me into the back of the Recall Wagon. God no. I'm going to get caught. Just don't worry too much; if you begin to falter now, you will get caught. The light switches to the white cut-out silhouette of a person walking. You can do this, now walk.

I try to moderate my breathing, restrain my facial muscles, but it's hard. Anyone looking my way will notice, see it in my face, as if it were written all over, it may as well be written a hundred times: Unthinker. I must not look worried; I must not show it. Now I know why the woman with red hair stood out so much, and like her, I too am standing out, displaying myself for the world to see. I try to collect my thoughts, one piece at a time. Don't lose your nerve now.

I'm walking too fast; someone is going to notice. I slow down, breathe. I've begun to sweat under my arms and on my forehead, but it's not as noticeable, it blends in with the humidity. I suddenly feel something strange. I look down at my hand, it's shaking, that's never happened before.

I can see my Habitat from here, it's not too far.

"Stop right there!" a Protector sharply calls out behind me. I feel the blood seep from my face. I've been found out. I think to run, I think to pull the gun out, but it's easier if I don't. If I go quietly, it will hurt less. But if I run, he will shoot me, and no one will come to help me. I've seen it before; they'll leave you on the ground bleeding out, sometimes for hours, just to bring in a crowd. And if they're quick enough, they'll even call over a news reporter to film live on the scene, just another example of how desperate they are for public engagement.

He's going to search my briefcase.

I stop, look straight ahead, as I've been taught to do. I hear him approach me, his footsteps heavy in his boots. This is it; he's going to De-psypher me. I feel my hand slowly inching its way to the briefcase, aiming for the gun.

"Cards please," he says, not to me, but to someone else. I wasn't the one he was calling then. I hear him talking to other people just a few feet away. I hesitate, slowly turn my head to look. His back is to me. He'll come to me next if I don't move. Without time to spare, I start towards my Habitat, not looking back. I hope no one's seen what I've done.

I turn, enter through the glass doors, ascend the stairs to my floor, and down the hall till I reach my door. I unlock it, walk in, and shut it. A wave of relief flows through me. Though I am relieved, the fear doesn't subside. I am safe here, for now.

I put the briefcase on the kitchen counter and begin hastily removing my clothes, which have become drenched with sweat. I wash my face, drink some water, and put on a new pair of clean clothes. I can feel my lungs inflate with air. I'm exhausted.

I stare at the briefcase; it looks like any ordinary briefcase, the same black leather with buckles and singular strap. No one would suspect a thing. I think to myself for a moment, I must have imagined it, this can't be real. But I know it is. I sit, my back to the window, concealing the briefcase with my body. I take another deep breath. I open it, reach inside, and pull out the plant. Is it real? Or is it a fake?

The plant itself is contained inside a glass capsule, like those used in the Newsroom to send papers up and down in the pneumatic tubes. The dirt is held in place by a fabric gauze. I hold the plant up into the light. Inside, tiny water droplets cling against the glass, some sliding down past the gauze into the dirt. There are five leaves, all very small in size. I absorb the color with my eyes. I haven't seen this kind of green in a very long time. I want to open it, to touch it, more than just with my eyes, but I don't want to hurt it. It's real. It's alive.

Now I'm confused more than anything. I want to know

what that woman was doing with this, walking around with it in her briefcase. How did she ever manage to get this in the first place? We were told plants no longer exist, of course, I should have known this was a lie; it's what I've come to expect. That means they must be holding plants somewhere in the city, away from the public eye, a secret farm. I rummage inside the briefcase for the note, a small slip of paper. It simply reads:

Soma Bar 6:47

The Soma Bar is the name of a sex club down in the Fourth Sector, located in the next district over, a Secondary district. It's instructions. She must have been going to meet someone there to deliver the plant. So, my suspicions were correct. She is an Unthinker, but not just any Unthinker. She's a member of the resistance. There have been talks of a rebellion in the news, "psycho-terrorists" is the word they use, she must be one of them, but she's no terrorist. I rifle through the briefcase for the key, it's a room key, and tied to the end of it is a small label marked: Room 101. This is the room where they're meeting.

What now? I can try to take it there for her, but I can't take the metro—it's the fastest way to travel between districts, but they'll search the briefcase as soon as I enter it. How did she manage to bring it in without getting caught? There's no way she could've been cleared through, yet somehow, she was.

If I walk, I'll be stopped at the checkpoint, maybe even before that. Why did this have to happen to me? She would've been at the Soma Bar by now if she'd only picked up the right briefcase. I wonder if she's realized it yet. What if she took it on purpose? Was that conversation just to distract me? And what was that thing she said to me just before she left the train? *Compos Mentis.* I think it's a different language. This is all too much. I don't know what to do. If I leave now, I have a little more than an hour to get there. An alleyway, maybe? There must be some alternate route around the checkpoints.

Suddenly there's a knock at the door, and I grow worried again. I know it's not Finn. He's not supposed to come back for another two hours. Besides, he has a key. Did someone report me? Notice something in my face? Dispatch a Protector to come check up on me?

I yell at whoever's on the other side of the door to give me a moment as I hastily begin putting everything back inside the briefcase, frantically looking for a place to hide it.

"Oh, that's alright Acolyte," the person on the other side of the door says.

I recognize that voice. I open the door. It's Sylis. "Oh, hello Acolyte," I say.

"Good evening," he says cheerfully, completely oblivious to the dire circumstances I've currently found myself in, "I thought I heard you come home, how are you today?"

"I'm well, thank you," I say, "and you?"

"Oh, just fine," he says, "listen Acolyte, there's going to be a Peace Parade at the east end of the district. We're burning a canteen, the one near the checkpoint."

"Oh, what for?" I ask, by way of sounding interested.

"One of the workers there is a suspected Unthinker," he says.

"Why, what did he do?" I say.

"Someone overheard him making a snide remark about the Operator," he says, "he was reported this morning and they'd been interrogating him ever since."

I don't know what to say, it sounds too absurd. They're burning a canteen because someone made a snide remark about the Operator, not even one of the owners, but a worker.

"Well, anyways Acolyte, will you be going?" he says.

"Perhaps later," I say, "if it's not over by then."

"What are you doing now?" he says, trying to peak into the apartment.

"I was actually just about to head out myself," I say, "I hear they're having another sale on handheld radios."

"Oh, alright then," he says, "well, goodbye Acolyte."

"Goodbye," I say, and he leaves.

This couldn't have happened at a better time. I know which canteen he's talking about, I've eaten there before, it's right next to the checkpoint which leads into the Secondary district, the one where the Soma Bar is located. And on some occasions, checkpoints are left open during Peace Parades as a safety precaution, so people can freely pass through. I won't be searched. The woman with red hair must have known this too, that's why she mentioned it back on the train. This is my chance, my only chance. If the checkpoint is closed, then that is it, but if it's open, then there is hope. There is no room for mistakes. If I am to go, I must leave now.

Chapter 11
Peace Parade.

I walk along the street, past the stores and shops. The air is much warmer now, but the smell still lingers. I try to block out the foreknowledge of my possible death. I don't want my head clouded with fear, but the thought persists. I know there is no way to escape it. I suppose I ought to accept it when the time comes, when I'll be caught. It will arrive like the snuffing of a flame. Whether it will happen years from now or in a matter of moments, I can't say. Nevertheless, it is inevitable. I won't last much longer. But for now, I attempt to ease myself away from the subject. Don't worry. It will be alright. I hope.

As I continue walking, I suddenly become aware of the sounds of distant screaming, only faint at first, but gradually becoming louder the farther I progress. This is how I know I'm headed in the right direction. As soon as I turn the corner to the next street over my nose is instantly hit with the harsh scent of chemical fumes, and then I see it: the Peace Parade.

They've set fire to the building occupying the canteen, the first floor already engulfed in an orange blaze, reducing it to nothing but a hollow shell. The fire's become too strong.

Enormous flames shoot out the windows. Plumes of thick black smoke fill the air. From behind a barricade, a crowd of people stand yelling and throwing things into the fire to burn. What they're burning are the former possessions of Unthinkers who've been Recalled. They don't even consider them worth being sold. They want absolutely no trace of their existence left. Afterwards, they'll force themselves to forget, and then finally be at peace.

A fire truck sits parked next to the crowd, waiting to put the fire out, but not yet, not until the crowd is satisfied with their level of destruction. If they put it out too early, they'll just start the fire up again, probably in one of the neighboring buildings. They want to destroy as much of it as possible and get away with it. The other shops to either side of it have been blocked off and emptied.

The Recall Wagon is there as well, with the Recall Officers standing just outside of it in their red leather uniforms, wearing their half caps and visors, keeping watch in case anything happens during the parade; something always happens. As I pass, I focus my eyes on the electric batons strung from their belts, no guns: their purpose is to sedate, not kill.

It puzzles me to think why anyone would deliberately start a fire when the air down here is as bad enough as it is. Primaries, as well as those in the lower Secondary districts, suffer the most from the poor air quality, and yet are the ones who make it worse. The woman from the lunchroom was right, we're going to suffocate down here, if not killed first.

The street's blocked up by the mass of people who've come to see the parade, with only a small section towards the back of the crowd just spaced out enough to pass through. Even from this distance, the heat of the flames burns my skin. Soon the whole district will have to suffer from the rising temperatures. The people continue to cry out in ovation as the fire roars on, creating such a horrific scene. I don't know how they can use up so much energy, or oxygen for that matter, without fainting.

I make it clear of the Peace Parade and continue down the street, but it only takes me a few paces before I suddenly stop in place. The checkpoint's still in routine operation, I won't get through, not without being searched first. What do I do now? Any alleyways? No, there aren't any. I can't walk into a store, all the nearby buildings are closed. There's no escape, none. I walked halfway across the district. If I go back, someone will stop me for sure.

I've already been standing still too long. I look lost. Someone must have noticed me by now. Then I feel it, a pair of eyes snag on me. I turn my head slowly over my shoulder and see him, a man at the edge of my vision, a Protector. He stands, his head turned to me, holding his machine gun. He sees my briefcase, shifts his position, begins walking towards me. I don't think he knows I've spotted him. Fear rises within me, and like the fire of the burning building, I won't be able to contain it. I decide to keep moving forward towards the checkpoint. I'm trapped. Where else can I go? Turning around now will only make him even more suspicious of me. He'll think I'm hiding something. I am hiding something.

What am I even doing? Maybe they'll let me pass somehow, but this is wishful thinking; I know they won't. What will it be first? Will I reach the checkpoint, have them search, and pull me aside? Or will the Protector stop me before I can make it? Either way, I'm just as dead.

I sense him close behind me now. "Stop right there!" he shouts, but I don't. Dread begins to take over me. I act as if I don't hear him, could be calling for anyone, and I continue walking. "I said stop!" he shouts, now directly behind me. In that instant, I make the split-second decision to break into a sprint, but feel his hand suddenly seize my shoulder, and only then do I finally come to a stop. Now I'm ashamed. I risked my life for this, and for what? If only Finn was here, he's always here when I need him. If he was here, he'd find a way to get me out of this, he's good at that, but he's not here now. I ought to have left him a note before I left. He's going to wonder why I never came back. "If I don't come back, don't forget about me," it would say. If I could write to him now, I'd say I'm sorry, sorry I had to leave you, all alone, in this place. I chose to put myself in this position. I came here of my own free will, or what's left of it. It was silly of me to think I could make it, even this far. I was lucky, but my luck's run out. Now it's time.

But before the Protector can say anything, a sudden loud blast of noise shakes the air. I instantly drop to the floor, cover my head, overcome with shock. I hear what sounds like thousands of shards of broken glass sprinkling the street, followed by a cacophony of screams.

After a moment, I regain the strength to lift my head and look back. The building now has an enormous hole in it, with large flames jetting out in all directions. It was the canteen, it exploded. Fragments of broken concrete and glass scatter the floor. Dust and smoke fill the air. The blast of the explosion caused the windows in the nearby buildings to burst outwards. Several bodies lay on the street in front of the canteen where the parade had been, with all the survivors running about, many of them badly wounded. It's absolute chaos. There must have been a gas leak. I realize the Protector's gone. I look at the checkpoint to see people scrambling through it, they're letting everyone pass. Now's my chance. I take up the briefcase, clumsily start to my feet, take one last look back, and run.

Chapter 12
Fourth Sector.

The adrenalin only lasts me a few blocks before my lungs can't take it anymore and have to stop to catch my breath. My eyes are stinging. I'm crying a little, out of fear, but mostly out of relief. That was too close. I feel like vomiting. At least the Protector didn't get a clear view of my face. I wait for some minutes, trying helplessly to convince myself to keep moving. You made it past the hard part, don't quit now, you're almost there. I steady my posture, breathe in, sweating now more than ever. Alright, move your legs. I lift my head, slowly ease myself into taking a step, and then another. Some good better come out of this, or I'm wasting my time.

I hadn't noticed when, but it started drizzling. You would think the climate in a Secondary district, even if it is a lower-quality one, would be better considering their status, but I'm not surprised. The Engineers and powerful Secondaries always enjoy promoting help to their fellow caste members, now if only they had actually acted on their words.

It's not long before the familiar white outfits of the Primaries begin to fade out into the background, overshadowed by the vibrant multi-colored clothing of the Secondaries. It's only the Primaries who are free to wear white. It distinguishes us, marks us off. The white symbolizes our genetic hygiene, the only ones who've never suffered from the radiation sickness. From their perspective, they see me only for what I am on the outside: a man in white. But whereas they see me as vapid and dull, I see a blank canvas of possibilities, reduced now to nothing more than my genetic code.

The Secondaries aren't allowed to be defined by a single color and are instead authorized to wear anything they want, at which they make every effort to dress themselves in the most fashionable attire. Though, unlike the more powerful Secondaries, these Secondaries are also subject to the drastic shifts in atmospheric conditions and, as a result, have to incorporate synthetics in their clothes for practical purposes. But in their attempt to dress luxuriously, their clothes end up looking like gritty imitations of the real thing.

They utilize every kind of shade, pattern, and color in their designs—some I've never even known existed—along with their large assortment of accessories: theatrical hats, tinted glasses, and solid handbags. They even have face masks. Though rather than wear them, some prefer to show off their makeup instead, which for most, has become dewy from all the mist. Down here, they've created their own style of fashion.

It's not uncommon for Primaries to wander about the lower Secondary districts since they're always interconnected in some way. As long as I keep to myself, I shouldn't get into trouble with the Operator. The lower Secondaries tend not to pay much attention to what goes on around them, ignoring everyone else in pursuit of their own desires. They have every immediate pleasure available to them; why shouldn't they live in their heads in place of the real world? They might have thought about things beyond the extent of their minds once, but not anymore. Now they're like how I once thought other people were mere extensions of my reality, that I was the only real person in the world, having my own individual thoughts, my own experiences. I believed everyone else existed simply to fill in the landscape of my existence. I guess you could say this is what they must think of their own existence. That is, of course, if they're not an Unthinker in secret.

As I pass a storefront, I notice the televisions in the window airing a news bulletin. I think nothing of it at first but quickly double back to watch the broadcast. It's of a journalist reporting live on the scene of a street somewhere in this district. Text runs across the bottom of the screen, it reads:

WE INTERRUPT THIS PROGRAM TO BRING
YOU A SPECIAL NEWS BULLETIN:

A WOMAN WAS SHOT AND PACIFIED FOR
ATTEMPTING TO RUN FROM A PROTECTOR
AFTER HAVING BEEN DISCOVERED
CARRYING A DEADLY WEAPON.

I recognize that street. I'll be passing through it on my way to the Soma Bar. By the time I get there, it'll be swarming with people trying to get a glimpse of the body. I could try to reroute directions to find another path around it, but all other ways will take longer to get there, and I've already wasted enough time as it is.

I turn and continue down the road, navigating several stretches of populated streets. Unlike in the Primary districts, the roads here are brimming with cars, so the sidewalks are always busy. I bend a corner down the next street, where towards the end of it, a horde of people are blocking off traffic.

Steadily, the more I move closer, the more uneasy I become. I don't know what's the matter with me. It's as if I'm about to come upon the very scene that will take place once this story ends, a premonition of my own death. It's not me, but it could just as easily have been me, lying there dead on the street, with everyone huddling around, hoping to get a chance to see me bleed out in pain.

Surrounded by oddly dressed people, I weave my way through the throng of onlookers crowding around the small open space where someone has recently been shot. I'm closer to it than I intended. I might even manage to catch a glimpse of the woman. I'm not going to look; that's the last thing I want. But why? It's not like I've never seen a dead body before. It was only a few hours ago that I attended a Pacification where I witnessed the mass hanging of fifty Unthinkers, and I couldn't even care. And yet why does this feel so much worse? There's something different about this.

As I come to the edge of the crowd towards the inner space, every part of me begins screaming for me to look. I don't know whether it's just some form of twisted curiosity, or if my subconscious is trying to tell me something. Either way, I make every effort in my mind to keep my eyes averted. But I just can't take it anymore. I trick myself into stealing a look. From between the moving heads, I manage to catch a glimpse of it. The first thing that stands out to me is all the red, not just of blood, but of hair. Is that? No. The crowd's moving too fast; I can't get a good view. As soon as I get the chance, I take another look, this time from a better angle, and I can see her now; there's no denying it. There displayed out in the middle of the street, lies the lifeless body of the woman with red hair.

I gasp out of shock. Her eyes are wide open, she's staring right at me, but these are not her eyes, they can't be. Of all the things I remember about her, I will always remember the feeling I get when her eyes lock into mine. But these look as if they're made of glass, and this time, as we lock eyes, whatever connection, whatever bond had previously been there no longer exists.

What is this? What am I feeling? I think I'm going to pass out. It's too much. They must have been looking for her then; that's why they shot her. They knew what she was doing, what she had, what she was carrying. Now she's dead.

I pull away quickly and continue down the street, cautious of my surroundings. If they know about the plant, then they must still be looking for it. I can't keep stalling. In the meantime, the crowd will provide me with just enough cover to make it to the Soma Bar undetected.

If I get caught, I'm far more terrified of being found with the plant than with a gun.

Chapter 13
The Soma Bar.

This part of town isn't buzzing as much with foot traffic. If the Psi-Ops are lurking near, my presence will be noted. I know not to chance the front entrance. Not only will I immediately be turned away, but by doing something as stupid as that, I may as well be begging to get their attention.

I enter the building through a side entrance in the alleyway. I figured they weren't too concerned with security, and I was right. What's more, no one even seems to notice a random Primary wandering about. At least with the briefcase, those who do notice will dismiss my being here as on an official assignment from the Bureau. Who are you fooling, is anyone really thinking that? Just keep telling yourself this. You might even look more convincing.

There's no law against Primaries going into Secondary establishments, who would ever dare, so I'm technically not breaking any rules. Then again, I don't think the interrogators will simply disregard this irregularity of mine without further questioning my intent.

I arrive at the scene of what looks to be some sort of

backstage dressing room, where scantily clad men and women festooned in costumes hurriedly walk to and fro down the corridor. Many of the costumes have parts that poke out from every which way, and I have to stoop several times as I pass to avoid getting hit.

I emerge into the main lounge area, which is swarming with guests. There's a bar, a dance floor, and a stage full of performers. On the ceiling, strobe lights hung from fixtures bathe the room in fading multicolor. Smoke and music fill the air. I've never been to this kind of establishment before. I can't imagine this sort of thing ever being allowed to happen in a Primary district; they're too work-based oriented. I press my way through the club amidst the glitz and glamour. It's funny, really; in a place where everyone dresses so eccentrically, I'm the one to stand out. Though, the further I go, the more it slowly begins to weigh on me that, just beneath the surface of it all, there also lies a heavy sense of depravity. It's unsettling to see how these people allow their desires to consume them so completely.

I near the check-in desk but move ahead past it, down a separate corridor where there are elevators to either side. I try some of the buttons, but none of them seem to be working. Are they all out of service? I head further down the corridor, aiming for the back stairs instead. I enter the stairwell and begin to ascend. The stairwell is just as busy as the lounge area; I keep having to squeeze my way through just to get by. It's getting harder not to get noticed. I'll occasionally receive a few side glances, many out of bewilderment or disgust, and others blatantly trying to look either intimidating or seductive. Most people here are just standing around smoking, keeping to themselves. Some are in hysterics, completely psyched out of their minds, mumbling about nothing. A few lay on the steps, either passed out or dead from overdose, foamed at the mouth. There are even a couple of them engaging in some form of sexual intercourse; they couldn't wait to get to the room, I suppose.

I don't want to be here.

* * *

I tour the halls, glancing swiftly from left to right as I walk down the middle, looking from door to door. This place would have been beautiful once, in another time, in another era. It isn't grand by any means, but it would have looked better than it does now. This place wasn't always a sex club, before I think it was a hotel, it doesn't match the architecture in the rest of the city. They could have burnt it down a long time ago for simply looking the way it did, but instead, they repurposed it for what it is today. And ever since then, its looks have begun to wear. The elegant gold molding no longer brightly polished. Bits of the magnolia wallpaper peeling from the walls like dead skin.

From behind the doors, I can hear the loud moaning, the rhythmic knocking against walls and floors, the creaking of beds. I turn down the hall, counting off the room numbers one after the next until I find it: room 101. I take the key out from the briefcase, making sure there's no one around. I unlock the door, go in, and shut it behind me.

It's empty. Am I early? I was expecting to see my contact. I look at the alarm clock, 6:50, I'm not too late, but I guess he wouldn't be on time either. I take a few steps, quietly examining the room. What if this is a trap? They knew about the plant, could they know about the room too? There's someone else in here, isn't there? Stop that. You need to calm down. There's nobody here. But I can't stay. I'll only wait a few minutes. If my contact doesn't show up soon, then I guess I'll just have to leave the briefcase here. I don't want to be anywhere near this room if the Psi-Ops are coming. But I'll leave it up to faith that that won't be the case.

As I wait, I begin to explore the room, making sure to keep the lights off. The room is small but lavish, yet also decrepit, and smells vaguely of mildew. There's the bed which has a velvet cover with satin sheets, a glass bedside table, and a fur sofa with matching rug. There's an ivory marble dresser with a small television set on top, doors for the closet and bathroom, and at the end of the room, a window. The window even has curtains; they're mesh, but at least I'll have some privacy for once.

Coming in through the window, light from the neon signs radiates the room in a faint glow of flashing colors, with the muffled sounds of music and moaning occupying the void of audible space. On the bedside table is a body catalog. All you'd have to do is call the front desk and tell them which one you'd like from the available list, then the person selected would be sent off to your room within a matter of minutes.

How strange. Of all the places, why here? To think, the meeting place of the resistance, a sex club? It seems highly out of character for something this serious. But I suppose that's why it's the perfect place for performing this transaction—less conspicuous.

I sit in the bed, mindlessly flipping through the catalog, when, without warning, I hear the floor creak directly behind me. My eyes widen. I'm suddenly stricken with the realization that someone else is in this room.

"Don't move," a voice says.

My skin crawls, and I go cold. It can't be. All of this for nothing?

"Put your hands up," says the Psi-Op, "and turn around slowly."

I do as I am told. I don't bother to fight. I always thought if I found myself in this exact scenario that I would have enough will to resist, but now that I am, I realize I'm not as strong as I thought I was.

My eyes meet with the long barrel of a gun aimed point-blank between my eyes. I focus my vision, and bearing the gun, I see, is a woman. I'm suddenly taken aback by her dazzling appearance. She has long, thick black braids interlaced with purple tinsel, wearing a mauve cropped leather jacket, dressed in a skin-tight black romper over an iridescent mesh top, black net stockings, and black leather knee-high boots. But none is more striking than her makeup and her enchanting silver eyes. She's absolutely gorgeous. Seeing her I never would have thought she was a Psi-Op, it's a perfect disguise; she blends in with everyone else here. She must have been hiding in the closet.

"Listen to me carefully," she says, "and you won't get hurt, put the briefcase on the bed there."

I nod and follow her orders, slowly placing the briefcase on the bed closer to her, trying not to make any sudden movements.

"Now stay over there, and just wait." She carefully takes up the briefcase, still keeping a close eye on me, pulls it towards her, and opens it. "Sorry about that, but I had to make sure you weren't one of them."

I don't say anything but remain silent, still petrified. She isn't a Psi-Op, she's my contact.

"Listen," she says, "I'm sorry, but I really can't stay. The lines are backed up enough as they are, you'll just have to wait here longer than usual," she closes the briefcase, and turns away to leave, "*Compos Mentis.*"

"Wait," I say, and I rush over to grab her hand, "there was a woman before me, she was supposed to bring the briefcase here, but she left it to me. They were looking for her, for that plant. Now she's dead."

She looks at me for a moment, then pulls her hand away, almost offended. "Did you… know her?" she says.

"No," I say, "I didn't, not really." I want to explain to her about the strange connection me and the woman with red hair had, even though we'd never spoken to each other, not up until that moment on the train, but she might not understand.

"And she just trusted you with this?" she said with fear in her voice.

"She could see it in me," I say, "that I wasn't like them, I saw it in her too."

She gives me a nasty glare, as if I tricked her somehow. She hesitates to say anything. She's struggling to trust me; I can see that. She must be wondering who I am, and why I didn't just report it instead. What are the chances of something like this happening?

"Tell me, are you a member of the resistance?" I say, "what's going on?"

"You're not one of us?" she finally says, somewhat reserved of herself.

"'Us?'" I say.

"Those of us on the televox," she says, "it's how we communicate with one another in the resistance."

I was right after all. I have a thousand questions running through my head now. I want to know more.

"Where—where did that plant come from," I say, "was it stolen from some secret hydroponic farm?"

"No," she says, "it came from outside."

"What do you mean?" I say. She just stares, and then it hits me, "the surface?"

The outside. There isn't an outside, not anymore. That's what we've been told. I don't know what to say, they said the earth was dead, killed by the actions of wicked men, but it's alive. And this whole place, everything, all lies. Why did they do this? It's been eighty years since the bombs hit, if the history's correct, they could've lied about that too. It could have been one hundred years, and I'd never know it, or if there were ever bombs. I don't know what to believe anymore. There is no truth here, never was.

"But how—how is that possible?" I finally say.

"It's true," she says, "there are ways people have been able to leave. It wasn't safe before to help people. We tried hiding them away, there are places, but our efforts are growing smaller. But this, this is proof, living proof, that we can leave, that there's a way out."

"A way out," to hear these words, it's almost too good to be true. It's too much for me; I have to sit down,

"What happens now?" I say.

"There isn't much we can do right now," she says, "they want to start moving people out of the city. They have safe houses, but not until it's confirmed, till the rest of them have seen the plant with their own eyes. For now, all we can do is wait."

"What about me?" I say, "what do I do?"

"Well, if you know any others, tell them the news, and we'll get in contact with you somehow. I need to go now. I've already been here too long. Wait here an hour after I leave. There are Psi-Ops everywhere." She turns, walks towards the door.

"Will I ever see you again?" I say.

"I don't think so," she says, "perhaps someday, but not for a long while yet. Till then, try to stay safe," then she leaves.

So that's it then. There is hope after all, and people out there who are willing to help. It may not look like it now, with all that's in the news, you wouldn't believe it, but it's true. Even now, people are fighting. It feels so unreal.

I waited an hour, like she said, before leaving. It's safe for me to take the metro back home. It's late, there's no one else in the carriage besides me. I can't wait to tell Finn. He won't believe it. Maybe for a couple of days, he'll attempt to coax me into telling him I'm only lying, or that I've finally lost it, but I know he'll come to believe it soon enough. I have no reason to lie. Some day we will finally leave this place, all of us, I don't know how long it will be by then, but I have hope it will be soon. I can't contain myself and begin to cry. I've never felt so happy before in my life.

I enter my Habitat and take the elevator to my floor. Finn should be coming home now; if not, then perhaps he's already here. I'll have to explain to him why I've been out so late; I'll explain it all, even if he doesn't believe me, he wouldn't want me leaving out any details.

I come to my apartment, unlock the door, walk in, stop. Sitting at the end of Finn's bed is a man I've never seen before, about a foot shorter than me and very thin. He looks to be about eighteen years old. For a moment I think I might have entered someone else's apartment by mistake, but I haven't. As soon as I come into view, the boy notices me and quickly gets up to introduce himself.

"Oh, hello Acolyte," he says, reaching his arm out to shake my hand. Though puzzled, I shake his hand without question.

"Hello," I say in return, trying my best not to sound confused. Who is this? And where's Finn? Why isn't he here?

"My name is Curtis," he says, "I'm your new roommate."

IV

Unthinkable

Chapter 14
Audio log No. 28.

I stand alone at the crosswalk, waiting for the light to change. I'm going back to my apartment. It's much colder out now, I can see my breath, but the smell is worse, especially today. Once a month on these days, any garbage, along with the corpses collected from the Pacifications and the mines, are sent off to the waste facility to be incinerated, where the resulting ashfall is exhausted directly into Primary districts. It covers the streets, like a thin blanket of grey snow. I haven't forgotten what snow is. I brought my umbrella today, which is made of a clear vinyl—no chance of hiding my face. But even from underneath the umbrella, I watch as a speck of ash lands on the back of my hand. I try to rub it off, accidentally leaving behind a grey smudge.

There wasn't much for me to do today at the Bureau of Operations. Yesterday, there was a Prisoners' Pacification, and I wanted to go in hopes that I might know what became of Finn after being Recalled, but I couldn't bring myself to do it. The worst of it isn't knowing what happened to him, it's not knowing that makes it even more terrifying, to be withheld the comfort of knowing whether he is dead or alive. If I knew he was dead, I'd at least be relieved to know that he's no longer suffering. It's as if a large part of me has been hollowed out, and what remains now is left helplessly waiting to become whole again. Perhaps I may never become whole again, and soon this emptiness of mine will begin to sink upon itself in attempts to fill up on its own, only for it to grow deeper.

Whether he'll be Purged or Pacified, I do not know. All I am left with is the knowledge that he is gone. And for what reason? What Unthinkables must he have committed to have earned his immediate arrest? I later found out what it was, why he had been Recalled. It was because his briefcase was found on the dead body of the woman with red hair; I never did know her name. To even be affiliated with the resistance would be reason enough. Guilty by association. I don't blame her for what happened, she was desperate, and I was her only hope. She wanted to help the resistance, even if it meant putting others at risk.

Being Finn, he must have known that if he didn't confess to whatever he was being accused of, I would've been the one Recalled, and so took the blame for me instead. He protected me, and now he's gone. It's all my fault. If I'd only got my briefcase fixed in the first place like he told me to, and didn't borrow his, I'd be the one gone, not him. He'd still be here, and I'd be off to wherever he is now, which feels like nowhere. Perhaps it's best I don't know what's become of him, not knowing would be easier, I'd just have to stop trying.

The light changes, and I walk.

I enter my apartment, lock the door. It's barely any warmer in here than out there. Even then, the window shows signs that the glass is beginning to fog. Good, just as I had hoped. I switch on the heat lamp, which is fixed to the wall above my desk, its fluorescent tube glowing a blazing orange hue. I'll have the window completely fogged up in no time. I turn on the television to the five o'clock news and set it to high volume, just high enough that anyone who might be listening won't hear what I'm doing.

"Today marks exactly one month since the disappearance of forty-year-old Primary: 1-330 Rachel," says the anchorman, "she was last seen leaving her Habitat on a Tuesday morning and hasn't been seen since. Her neighbors and current roommate have organized a district watch to aid in her search. If you have any information that could help locate her, please report it to the Operator."

I open the closet door, reach for the old tape recorder, and set it down on my desk. So that's it, they've started it, moving people out of the main city, to whatever hiding places they've set up. I've never been out of the main city before, it's forbidden, why would we ever want to leave? Everything beyond the main city perimeter consists of the abandoned city districts, remnants of where the surges on rebels took place during the war. Years ago, the Operator declared this vast network of deserted streets as one giant exclusion zone.

The decommissioned areas surrounding the main city are too hazardous for public access, so entry through them is strictly controlled. There's nothing left there except dilapidated buildings and corridors, but I make a note not to believe this, not fully. I must be skeptical of such things. It's strange to think there's more to the city, apart from what I've only seen. The world feels so small.

I pull out my chair, climb on top of my desk, unhinge the grille from the vent, and take out the cassette tapes. When I finish setting up the tape recorder, I turn off the television, hold the receiver up to my mouth, and hit record.

"Audio log number 28," I begin. I'm unsure what to say next. I stay silent for a few moments, thinking where to start. So many unexpected things have happened lately, it would be too difficult for me to explain everything, and all in one session. "Sorry," I finally say, "it's just that I don't know where to begin." I take another long pause. I don't want to make this too complicated, so I'll just let my mind do the talking. "They got Finn. I always thought I would be first. Our plan worked after all, the Psi-Ops left me alone, in more ways than one. When they did eventually bring me in for questioning, lying itself wasn't the hard part, it was forcing myself to betray him that nearly got me to confess the truth. It was the most difficult thing I ever had to do in my entire life. It didn't go on as long as I thought. By then I'm sure they already decided I wasn't involved. We did hold a Peace Parade for him though, when news spread around my Habitat that Finn was among those who had been Recalled, Sylis and the others asked if I would come to bring his things, there wasn't anything of his that I could burn, since he didn't possess any personal items of his own, so I only brought his clothes. Though there was a moment when Curtis was convinced that this tape recorder belonged to Finn and questioned why I didn't burn it. For some reason, he had trouble understanding that it was in fact mine and to this day still suspects me of lying.

"Oh, I have a new roommate now, his name's Curtis. This wasn't one of the things I had anticipated. Not only was Finn Recalled, but he was replaced, and by some scrawny kid fresh from Surrogate. You can imagine what torture it is to live with someone like that, it's like living with a drone, or a Mother. He always watches me, what I'm doing, waiting for me to step out of line just to have an excuse to berate me. They enjoy making themselves feel like they have the superior mind. They must be stricter with the newer generation of children; I can't believe what they're doing to them in there.

"Also, the woman with red hair is dead. They shot her. Not only was I right about her being an Unthinker, but she was also a member of the resistance. In the news, they lied about her concealing a 'deadly weapon,' when she was only carrying Finn's empty briefcase. Not even the dead can escape being propped up as symbols of fear and hatred. It's how they distort people's view of us. They make them hate us, even those of us who are already dead.

"There's something else, I can't say much, but I can tell you this, for the first time, my life here has been given meaning. Before then, I was nothing. I'd wake up, go to work, come back home, go to bed, and repeat the same meaningless routine. But now I have a reason to live. I have hope that someone might be listening, even in this place. But I can't continue making these as often as I used to. Before then, I was already dead, I was just waiting to get caught, sometimes, I used to wish for it, I was stupid. I could have ended this story a long time ago, but I'm glad I didn't, because now I've been given a chance to change the ending.

"We can leave. I won't go into great detail right now, but I came in touch with the resistance. The earth isn't dead after all. They brought back proof, a plant. Deep down I always knew there was something more to this existence, and now I know the truth, there really is a way out. We can actually go back to the surface." I take a moment to calm myself down. "If only Finn were here," I pause again, "I got my briefcase fixed. The handle won't snap off like last time," another pause, "why did you have to go? I'm not strong enough for this. You'd be better off if it were me. It's not fair to either of us." I begin to feel a pain in my throat, like the urge to yell, but I don't. A tear rolls down my cheek. "You know, I haven't taken Exodus since you left, will you come back now, wherever you are—" suddenly the recorder stops and there's a click. The cassette has finally run out of space. I begin to cry.

He never did come back.

Chapter 15
Exclusion Zone.

I can't remember what today is. For a long time, the days
have begun to merge. I feel trapped, caught in a never-ending
length of time, stuck in a state of perpetual motion, the
everlasting now. Even the weeks have begun to merge. I'm not
sure when the simple task of keeping time became such a
chore. It's hard to keep track.

It's Friday, and Curtis and I are walking along the sidewalk
on our way to work, the air humid and slightly foggy as usual.
I'm not sure if the smell is gone or if I've begun to get used to
it; either way, that's one less thing to complain about.

Around us, every television screen has started broadcasting
a missing persons advert of that woman Rachael, plastering her
pixelated face all throughout the city. Those of us who are
cognizant enough to understand what really happened to her
have realized by now what an amazing thing she's managed to
accomplish. Her disappearance has become a symbol of hope
to us Unthinkers. If she can survive being Sub-Circuit as long
as she has, it won't be long before one day we can be free too.

"Still no sign of that missing woman?" says Curtis, trying

to make conversation as we wait at the crosswalk.

"No, nothing yet," I say in a dispassionate voice.

I can see him watching me from the side. He senses my disinterest. I'm not used to having these kinds of casual conversations when out in public. It feels strange to be openly sharing my thoughts, much less with someone like Curtis: Finn's new replacement. He even replaced Finn's position in the Records Department. It's unnerving how quickly he's settled in, like Finn never existed. I try not to hold it against Curtis, it's not his fault, he's just following protocol. The moment the Psi-Ops found Finn's briefcase on the body of the woman with red hair, they made sure to get rid of him as quickly as possible, even if it had been a misunderstanding. None of us is worth more than the other, the moment they discover a defect, they'll find no difficulty in replacing us. We are all expendable. I suppose the same thing will happen to me when I get Recalled. If I get Recalled.

"In the news," Curtis says, trying again to make small talk, "they suspect she was abducted by those psycho-terrorists. They say they're going to torture her until they've successfully converted her to their ways."

I don't respond. Does he really believe this is what the resistance is capable of?

"You shouldn't worry," he goes on, "the Psi-Ops will find her and bring her back safely."

"Oh, I'm not worried," I say.

Actually, now that I think about it, it might be Tuesday.

As soon as the light changes, I start for the other side of the street, walking at a slightly quicker pace than Curtis, leaving him to catch up.

I'm sure by now he knows I don't appreciate his company. It would be in my best interest to at least try to befriend him, but I'd risk too much for that. It's not like he can report me anyhow, it isn't against the rules to dislike each other, but it can be suspicious, though of what, I'm not sure.

I step into Mr. Freeman's office. He's sitting at his desk listening to the radio: more news about the missing woman.

"Mr. Freeman sir," I say.

"Good morning," he says, lowering the volume on his radio, "I've got a really important assignment for you today."

"Of course, sir," I say. Can't be too important.

"You're going on a trip today," he says, with a slight childish banter.

"A trip, sir?" I say. What does he mean by this?

"The Operator is soft launching an open information initiative," he says, "he's finally permitting *Apocalypse Now* to conduct expanded news coverage on previously classified prisoner and Unthinker affairs."

"That's amazing sir," I say, not entirely sure of what I'm commending. They've decided to let the public see how they handle Recalled Unthinkers behind closed doors; I got that much, but what does this mean for Apocalypse? The Operator's planning something.

"Yes, and it's about time too," he says, "but only via highly selective and highly controlled media access. He wants us to build a gradual focus while disclosing this information, to build public interest. It's for a more 'transparent-oriented' campaign. But at least it gives us a broader range of editorial content."

I take a moment to really process this news. This just opened the door for a barrage of untapped hatred towards Unthinkers. At any rate, even with all this information, I still don't know what my assignment is for today.

He stands up, takes a small stack of papers off his desk, and walks towards me. "You're going to the mines today," he says, handing me what I see now is a long series of approval forms, the pages covered in stamps and signatures.

He can't be serious. The mines are outside of the main city perimeter. Are they actually allowing me to travel through the exclusion zone?

"I need you to take photos of the prisoners in the housing facilities," he continues, walking back to his desk, "there's a private shuttle waiting for you now at loading dock B, give that to the driver, and he'll take care of the rest. The trip is about a three-hour drive each way, if you're lucky enough."

"Yes sir," I say. I don't know what else to say, I thought he said we were starting off slow, I didn't realize that this is what he meant.

I leave Mr. Freeman's office, collect my camera equipment, and head down to the designated loading dock. I enter the shuttle and give the driver the approval forms. As he skims through the pages, I realize no one else is on the shuttle, not even a Protector. We'll be driving unsupervised then. He finally finishes and I take my seat, deciding not to sit directly behind the driver, but instead choosing to sit towards the back. I take my privacy where I can find it, even the privacy to think alone. I'm not sure whether I should feel excited about leaving the main city or frightened.

The shuttle departs, and we begin our trek through the city. I look out the window, watching the people go by, their clothes alternating between casual white civvies and elaborate colorful costumes with each district we pass. The drive is slow, lots of time to spare for thinking. The hum of the engine reverberates through the seats, it's relaxing. Wherever that woman is, Rachel, I hope she makes it out safely.

The shuttle continues for a long while, passing through one district after the next, until finally coming to the checkpoint bordering the main city perimeter where no one, not even Secondaries, are allowed. I counted eight checkpoints. This is the farthest I've ever been away from my district, and it only gets farther from here. The shuttle pulls up into the toll booth, and the driver stops and begins talking to the Protector at the window. I can't hear what they're saying. I peer my head over the seats to try to see what they're doing. After a minute or so, the shuttle doors slide open, and two Protectors walk in, aiming their flashlights down the back. I don't move. One of the Protectors walks over to me while the other begins searching under the seats.

"Show me your card," he says, holding his hand out. I give him my card, he looks at it, then proceeds to search inside my briefcase. "What are you doing sitting all the way back here?" he says, shining his light in my face. I don't know what to say. Even when I'm not presently doing anything against the rules, it still feels like I'm guilty of something. If you have nothing to hide, you have nothing to fear. Everyone has something to hide.

"Move closer to the front," he says, without waiting for an answer. I get up and sit in the seat directly behind the driver.

When both Protectors finish searching the shuttle, another Protector walks in and sits next to me. He doesn't say anything or even look at me. He's wearing his gas mask, so I can't see his face. He's about a head taller than me and is carrying a heavy machine gun. Is he here as my minder? Or maybe he's my temporary personal Protector? Either way, I don't feel safe. They finally give the driver the green light. The shuttle clears the toll booth, and we are now officially out of the main city.

I wasn't prepared for how dark it would be here. There aren't any televisions, or neon signs. Instead, they've managed to keep the streets lit with large floodlights that have been placed periodically along the roads. The buildings here are old and dilapidated. Imagine, this place was once an active part of the city, people used to live here, but now no one does, at least not officially. This is just one of many places affected by the war. Now the resistance uses the buildings as hideouts.

I shift my eyes towards the Protector, I don't want to make it obvious I'm looking at him. It's uncomfortable. I think if I move too suddenly, the Protector might say something, tell me to stop. How can he sit still for so long? It's like he's concentrating all of his energy on it.

I sit, glaring out the window, watching the buildings go by. Right away, I notice these buildings have a stylized look to their architecture, very different compared to the clean geometric designs of buildings today. It's as if we've entered a temporal interlude, a part of Apocalypse still existing in the past. It's a shame these buildings are scheduled to be demolished soon.

The window has begun to fog up, but as I wipe away at the glass, I notice something on the road up ahead. There's a team of Exterminators in their yellow rubber suits fumigating a building. They're trying to smoke out any resistance members who might be hiding in there. This role was what the Exterminator division of the Protector program had originally been created for. But ever since the riots started getting out of control, the Operator has had to regularly deploy them as the city's official riot response unit. As we drive, the shuttle passes through a screen of smoke. I go into a short coughing fit, and so does the driver. The Protector doesn't react.

Finally, we come to a large arched tunnel that goes on for a long way. As we travel down it, the light from the shuttle reflects off the glossy walls of the tunnel, like the shadows of rippling water when light shines through it.

Finally, the shuttle stops. We've arrived.

This site is just one of many in a system of forced labor compounds in Apocalypse, where Unthinkers are sent to work in the mines until they die, either from exhaustion or asphyxiation. They don't give them much protection, and it's much worse for those prisoners stuck working in the uranium mines. Once Purged, there's no coming back, banished to a lifetime of servitude, sentenced to roam the bowels of the earth.

Once inside the compound, I undergo a lengthy screening process where they search me, my briefcase, then after verifying and filling out all the proper paperwork, they finally take me to another room where they begin briefing me on all the rules, what to do and what not to do. Now I'm being escorted by a Protector down a corridor, the walls lined in clear plastic drapery. It's surprisingly well-ventilated down here. We enter a door into another corridor and keep walking until we come to the entrance of a large room. Instantly, my nose is hit with the putrid smell of something I can only describe as bodily. The room is divided into smaller units by fences laid out in a sort of grid formation, tarped with transparent vinyl sheets that have fogged up from all the humidity. All I can make out from behind the sheets are the fuzzy outlines of what I can only assume are the prisoners' shadows, cast by the ugly yellow-beaming overhead lights. At first glance, I'm not sure what to make of this, it's all rather disturbing. It hasn't hit me until now exactly where I am, and even then, not having fully grasped the severity of my surroundings.

I first take a few photos from where I stand, then come

nearer to the entrance of one of the cages, feeling myself growing weaker the closer I get. What am I expecting to see behind the curtain? From behind the sheet, I can hear the weak collective groans of the prisoners, trying helplessly to gasp for air. I reach over and slowly draw back the curtain strips. I stop and freeze in horror. The prisoners huddled together on thin mats placed about the floor, wrapping themselves in foil blankets. They lay naked, heads shaved, their bodies severely underweight. It's as if their flesh were sealed tightly around their skeletons, then hardened in place, tough cracks overlaying the surface. The prisoners have turned grey from all the dust and grime embedded deep within the creases of their skin. It's hard not to believe these people aren't already dead.

I feel myself go numb. This can't be real, I'm hallucinating this, you've gone into escape. No, you haven't, this is what they've turned them into. I look at these prisoners, inside their faces, to see nothing left behind their eyes, but the empty shells of men.

Once all the haziness clears, I realize these men don't seem conscious of my presence. They must think I'm also an illusion, that I'm not really here. That is, if they can think at all. I've intruded upon a scene, one that has escaped the bounds of reality, never meant to be witnessed by human eyes.

I step into the room; I'm not allowed to talk to them or touch them. I've never seen so many old people before, but then I think, what if these men aren't old at all, but are in fact younger than me. They've worked them down to the bone, deprived them of their lives, their futures. It's impossible to tell their real age. And I think, is this where Finn is? What he'll become? Do any of these faces belong to him? Will I be able to even recognize him? How much can he possibly change in a few months?

I start back, horrified at what's become of these men, and begin to cry. There's that pain in my throat again. Finn isn't here, he wouldn't be, this group of prisoners has been here for decades. Then perhaps he's already dead.

I raise my camera and begin taking pictures.

Chapter 16
Rescue.

We're about an hour away from the city. So far, the drive back has felt much quicker than the drive out. I can't wait to get home. After a day like this, all I want to do now is go to bed, sleep forever, never wake up. I want to gouge my eyes out, squeeze them until they pop. I want to scrub away the memory of today, no, of the last twenty years. There's nothing I can tell myself that will convince me I won't just end up like those men in the mines. And I'm supposed to keep tolerating this existence? I don't want to think about it, I don't want to think about anything. You just need to hold out long enough until you can get yourself home. For now, try your best to remove yourself entirely, at least that way you won't feel anything.

I look out the window. The mist here has thickened tremendously since we last drove through this section. This is around the same place where we passed that group of Exterminators. They've been busy with their vaporizers I see; they must be working themselves over to smoke out resistance members. I stare out at the fog when it suddenly strikes me that something about it doesn't feel right. The more I let this thought linger, the more I'm filled with a heavy sense of uneasiness; the driver and Protector feel it too. It finally occurs to me that the mist has a grimier tinge to it than usual, giving off a strange metallic smell. It's not until we travel further on do we realize that this isn't smoke from the fumes at all, but a fire. We all suddenly become alert. Looking up from my seat, I notice an orange glow gradually materializing from the mist. The driver slows down as we approach, stops, and we see what it is. All three of the Exterminator trucks have exploded, the smoke from the flames causing the air to become full. But there aren't any Exterminators around, what's going on?

Suddenly, we spot from amidst the smoke a large yellow shape steadily approaching the shuttle. The Protector positions his gun. It's an Exterminator, he's bleeding, he looks like he's been shot. The Protector lowers his aim and gets out of the shuttle to help him up. I listen to their conversation.

"What happened here?" says the Protector through his mask.

"We were doing our usual rounds when we stumbled across a group of those psycho-terrorists hiding out in that old construction site," points the Exterminator.

The resistance? Here? Now?

"We pacified some of them," says the Exterminator, "but they managed to sneak by us and planted explosives under our trucks. We tried calling for help and that's when they blew up. They have that missing Primary with them, my men are out looking for her now as we speak. They'll find her alright, those brain jobs got nowhere else to run."

My throat goes dry. They found Rachel. This isn't how it was supposed to happen, she was meant to escape. It's not too late, she can still make it. The resistance is fighting back, she's in good hands.

"Where are they now?" says the Protector.

"They're still somewhere in the building," says the Exterminator.

I stare, wide-eyed, as the Protector approaches the shuttle and slides open the door.

"Both of you need to get back to the main city!" shouts the

Protector, "it isn't safe here! I'm going to stay and help! Get on that radio and call for backup!"

"Yes sir," says the driver. The driver does as the Protector says and quickly connects with the emergency line, requesting backup as he tries to explain the situation. I watch anxiously as the Protector slams the door shut and hurries away with the Exterminator into the darkness towards the construction site.

My whole life there's never once been a moment where I felt like I had even the slightest chance of escape, not until now.

Every hair on my body begins to stand on end, I examine my surroundings, in absolute shock of how I've suddenly been granted this perfect opportunity. The moment I realized the Protector was going to leave us I could feel the wheels in my head beginning to turn. I know what I must do. You'll die if you try.

The shuttle starts up and we begin to drive. I can't stop myself, my mind's made up, I've had enough of this place. If the resistance is still here, I might just be able to escape with them after all. I've gone crazy, how can I not, after the things I've seen. I don't want to end up like them, the people in the mines. They're not people anymore. I won't sit here and let this moment go to waste. I'll never have another chance like this again. It truly is now or never.

I look at the door handle, then back at the driver, he's too busy talking to the Protector on the radio, that'll give me enough of an opening before he can react. It won't be hard to outrun him, and I can easily lose him in this fog. I already know how I'll manage without a flashlight. Everything's planned out, but I need to act quickly. The car's moving faster than I hoped. I can't stay here any longer, I must do this now.

I stare at the driver, wait, take a deep breath. In an instant, all the muscles in my body activate. I lunge from my seat and throw myself at the door, bursting it open, my briefcase still in hand. My body tumbles out onto the road, then in one unbroken motion, I roll back to my feet and into a sprint, without a moment's pause for injury.

"Hey! Stop!" I hear the driver yell as I run out into the fog. It's not long before I reach the old construction site, I don't even hear him coming after me. I take a moment to catch my breath. My eyes sting a little, but I'll manage, I can't stop now, not while I still have the energy.

I come to an empty room on the first floor of the building, it's practically pitch black. I quickly open my briefcase, and solely by touch, begin assembling my camera, handling this without much effort. I quickly hold my camera before me and take a picture, the flash allowing me a momentary glimpse of the room. Within my split-second view of the space around me, I notice what I think is a large hole in the wall to my left. I take another picture; a section of the wall appears to have collapsed. I begin to feel my way towards the hole and squeeze through it, emerging into a separate hall, completely enshrouded by darkness. I need to find the resistance before the Exterminators find them first.

I travel deeper and deeper into the building, guided solely by the use of camera flash, and all the while listening to make sure that no one else is near to see it. Sound seems to travel effortlessly here. In such a quiet place, it's very easy to pick up on noises coming from the other side of the building. The Exterminators' voices echo through the halls, their footsteps stomping overhead and underfoot, along with the occasional gunfire—whether from the resistance or the Exterminators, I don't know—but most audible of all is the sound of my own heartbeat.

I underestimated the size of this place, it's like a maze, I don't know how I'll ever find the resistance at this rate.

Some more time passes and my hope for freedom quickly begins to fade. What have I gotten myself into? I enter another hall, take a picture, within the brief moment of the flash going off, I catch sight of a gruesome image before me as it momentarily flickers across my vision. I let out a horrified gasp, accidentally dropping the camera in my panic. I step back, not making any noise. I'm afraid to admit what I saw, because it might just be what I think it is. I slowly bend down, pick up my camera. I hesitate, look in the direction where I saw it, and take the picture. It's an Exterminator, but he's lying against the wall on the floor, blood seeping from his gut. He's dead.

I hear commotion up ahead further down the hall, then several lights pass by from a different corridor. There's a sudden hurrying of footsteps somewhere both on the floor above and below me. Something's happening, and left without any other direction, I have no choice but to follow.

Trailing along the corridor, I see more light moving up ahead. I can hear shouting, but I'm too far to make out what they're saying. Is it the resistance? I move closer.

"She's over here!" a voice yells.

"We found her!" shouts another.

I become anxious and begin moving quicker, I already know what awaits me on the other side. How could they have found her? She was supposed to escape, this was her chance for freedom. They couldn't have found her. Who else could it be?

I emerge into a large open area somewhere in the center of the building, from a second-floor balcony. The room looks like it was meant to be some kind of atrium. In the middle of the hall, I see a man holding Rachel around by the neck, pointing a gun to her head. He's taken her hostage? She clings to the man's arm, sobbing uncontrollably. A ring of spotlights encircles the two as the Exterminators slowly close in on them. I look around the hall and realize what events have transpired here. There's been a massacre. Scattered about the room are the shredded bodies of resistance members. They've torn them to bits; they didn't stand a chance against the Exterminators.

"Drop your weapon!" one of the Exterminators shouts.

I crouch behind a mound of rubble and watch as this scene unfolds. What's going on? What is that man doing? As I try to make sense of all of this, another Protector yells, "put the gun down, now!"

The man is slowly attempting to drag Rachel away, but he's cornered. It finally occurs to me that this man is a resistance member trying to help Rachel escape. He's sacrificing himself to make it look like she was abducted after all, by pretending to take her hostage. They've run out of options. This is their last resort, but will this work? They've got nowhere else to go, they're surrounded. This has to work.

"Get back!" the man says, waving the gun towards the Exterminators, "get back!" Rachel is crying hysterically, her eyes puffy, and her face flushed. She isn't acting, she's genuinely terrified, afraid to go back. A month Sub-Circuit just to get caught.

The loud blast of a shot rings out, and I drop to the floor. My body jolts, I feel a ripple in my nerves, and I become paralyzed. I can't move. You're only human, meat and bones. I've forgotten how fragile I've always been, how delicate the human body is, one bullet to end it all. For a moment I thought I'd gotten hit, but no, it was only the one gunshot, and it did not miss its target. I look up, the man now a limp mass of flesh, sprawled on the floor in a puddle of his own blood and brain matter. He was shot in the head. Rachel lies next to him, her face in the ground, shaking in terror. She couldn't escape after all. We couldn't escape after all. Someone comes up behind me, it's the Protector. He grabs me by the shoulder and begins dragging me away.

Chapter 17
Cyber-Op.

I lie awake in bed, staring up at the ceiling—though not the ceiling of a cell, but of my apartment. I don't understand. Today I tried to escape with the resistance, but when that Protector found me, he simply confiscated my camera and had me brought straight home, no questions asked. I sat here in the apartment waiting for hours, but nobody ever came for me. I don't understand, why wasn't I immediately Recalled then and there? How could I've been free to go, just like that? None of this makes sense. Every time I hear footsteps walking in the hall past my apartment, I brace myself for the door to suddenly burst open as a team of Recall Officers comes rushing in to drag me out, but this hasn't happened yet either. Maybe they aren't coming for me after all, if they were I'm sure they would have done it by now. But why haven't they? I don't want to be kept in suspense any longer, if they're coming for me, let it happen already.

I can't sleep either. The thought of everything that's happened today is too painful to ignore, the scenes replaying in my head as a constant reminder of the brutality of Apocalypse.

They were caught trying to escape, like how my mother and I were caught all those years ago. I feel uneasy now, nauseous even, I want to throw up. Why must my mind race to these conclusions?

News of Rachel's rescue has already spread throughout the city, as well as the rise in hate against Unthinkers. She and her courier tried to escape, but when they were cornered, he pretended to take her hostage as a last resort. It fits with the abduction claims. They still had a chance to escape without the Exterminators immediately arresting them. Now that she's been rescued, she will simply resume her rightful place back on the Circuit.

The Operator has a complex system of tracking methods used to monitor our every move, it's what ultimately determines our existence in Apocalypse. If the Operator doesn't see it, then it doesn't exist. But that's not true. Sometimes I even find it hard to believe we can still exist beyond the Circuit. We learn what goes on in Apocalypse solely by word of mouth, so I can only hear rumors about the resistance and must leave it up to faith to accept that these stories are true. But sometimes, I can't help asking myself if it's actually happening. Living on the Circuit, I've learned there is one place the Operator can't see me—not unless I let him, a place just beyond his peripheral: my mind. So, it's true then, we still exist apart from the Circuit, and as for the part of me he can't see, it exists freely within the Operator's subliminal.

I don't want to go to sleep anymore. Even the thought of sleep sounds like a waste of time. What do you want then?

What I want is to know how we let this happen.

I turn my head to look at Curtis, he's in his bed asleep. Sometimes I think he can hear my thoughts, just as clearly as I hear them in my head. I wouldn't be surprised if they started training the newer generation of children to recognize certain facial patterns to read what people are thinking. Considering how loud my thoughts are, I constantly worry whether someone can hear me in here, purely from the sheer volume with which I think, face or no face. There isn't a day that goes by where I have to tell myself to shut up for thinking too loud.

Maybe Curtis is listening now, or maybe I'm just crazy. Lately, I've begun to lose touch with reality. A little late for you, isn't it? This place has already lost that, it's about time you caught up. Here, reality is what the Operator makes of it.

I'm tired now, tired of waiting for something to happen. I sit up, get out of bed, trying to make as little noise as possible. I walk over to my desk, pull out my chair, and turn on the Cyber-Op terminal. The monitor is a big white box, similar in design to the television set. The machine takes a moment to boot up, making a low humming sound. I hear a noise behind me and look back to see Curtis turning in his sleep. I have to make this quick. I press reset, and small green text skims audibly across the dark glass panel. I begin by addressing the Operator, and this is how it reads in the dialogue box:

```
]PRINT HELLO OPERATOR
HELLO, WHAT WOULD YOU LIKE TO ASK?
REMEMBER, THREE QUESTIONS A DAY.

]|
```

I think for a moment, wondering where I should start. First of all, this isn't a real person, it's a computer program, it's not going to understand complicated questions, so I'll have to keep things simple, which is unfortunate, I tend to have complicated questions. I also need to be cautious of what I type. I have to assume they're monitoring everything I ask. I suppose that's why it's called a "monitor." The thought of asking what happened to my mother had never crossed my mind before until now. It would look suspicious, but not enough to have a Psi-Op stop by. At least, I don't think so. But I can't ask this too directly, I don't even know her name, so I ask for it first:

```
]PRINT WHAT IS MY MOTHER'S NAME?
MOTHER SYLVIA

]|
```

I roll my eyes. I should've been more specific. Why do I even bother? It'll tell me only what it will allow me to know, just another dead end. But the Operator does know what happened to Finn. I could ask where he is, if he's dead or alive. I type in the question but hesitate to press enter. Do I really want to know? Will it even tell me the truth? I click the button, and the screen changes:

```
]PRINT SHOW ME STATUS FILE OF PRIMARY:
1-138 FINNEAS
ID NO LONGER AVAILABLE

]|
```

How disappointing, I should have expected this. Officially, Finn no longer exists. He's been erased. The Operator has no record of him, therefore, it must be true, Finn has never existed. Did a machine always determine one's own existence? I should probably try to forget about him, before it's too late. If I don't, I'll just end up disappointing myself.

I still have one question left, and I already know what I'm going to ask, but it might be risky, because it could mean something dangerous, it could be an Unword. Before the woman with red hair got off the train, she said something to me I didn't understand. And then later again, when the woman with braided hair was about to leave, she said the same thing. This is the question then:

```
]PRINT DEFINE COMPOS MENTIS
?SYNTAX ERROR

]|
```

I suppose the Operator doesn't know everything after all. That was a waste of time. But I'm not giving up. I need to satisfy my thirst for knowledge. There must be something else I can do.

I look over my shoulder. Curtis is still asleep. Just then, I notice his work briefcase sitting on his bedside table, and I have an idea. I get up and slowly begin making my way across the room to his briefcase, one step at a time. He works in the Records Department, so he must have something that can help me. I take up the briefcase, crouch on the floor just out of view in case he wakes up, and steadily start to unbuckle the straps. I open it and quickly make work of carefully removing its components one at a time, being cautious not to knock anything over. I don't see anything of use at first—just a few drafts, some proof copies, early manuscripts, his bottle of Thought Blocker—nothing of interest to me. But then I find something. In the dim light of the apartment, I'm unsure what it is. It feels like a small flimsy piece of plastic. It's a card, but not just any card, it's a clearance pass to the Library of Unbooks.

The Library of Unbooks is a highly secure archive used for storing documents/materials containing information that goes directly against the Operator's authority. None of the information in those records has been tampered with in any capacity and therefore considered dangerous; that is to say, the only place where truth still exists. But the card is a one-time use only, Curtis would have to register to get a new one after he used it, which wouldn't be often. Would he notice if it were missing? Should I risk it? If I have questions, I'll find my answers there. I know this because if the Engineers tried so hard to bury this knowledge deep within the Bureau, where no one else could access it, then the books in there must be true. I pocket the card, then begin putting everything else back in his briefcase, making sure to set it down exactly as it was before. I quietly return to my side of the room, and into bed once more. I roll over towards the edge, reach my arm out, and slip the card into my shoe.

Chapter 18
The Library of Unbooks.

It's the next day. Curtis and I are getting ready for work. So far he hasn't noticed that his pass is gone, that's a surprise. It doesn't usually take long for him to realize when something's amiss.

"Don't you think it's great they found that missing woman," Curtis says.

"It's… wonderful," I say, smiling. I didn't tell him what happened yesterday, he has no idea what I did. I watch him as he opens his briefcase and begins rummaging through it.

"I'm sure it would have been exciting," he says, "to see those brain jobs get what they deserve."

"Oh, definitely," I say, feeling a little disgusted with myself.

He pulls out his bottle of Thought Blocker and quickly gulps down one of the pills. "Here, take one of mine," he says, holding out a single white tablet in the palm of his hand.

At the end of every week, I always make sure to flush about five or six Thought Blockers down the toilet, to maintain the illusion that I've been taking them. It would look suspicious if I didn't, and I always remember to get a new bottle at the end of every month, to have it on my record.

"No thank you," I say, "I've already taken one." I'm starting to feel like Mr. Freeman, with all this smiling and lying.

"Well, take another," he says, "can't be too careful."

"I'm good, thanks," I say nonchalantly.

He watches me quietly as I continue getting ready, the pill still in his hand. I've left him confused, but most of all, disappointed. This was a clear attempt to gain my friendship, and I simply pushed him away.

I stand, waiting in the darkroom, preparing myself for what's to come. It's lunch hour, but I'm going to have to skip out on lunch today. I have something more important to take care of. I step out of the darkroom, walk down the long aisle of cubicles, exit the Newsroom, and out of my department wing. The infrastructure of the Bureau consists of a series of interconnected rooms and corridors, with elevators running up and down along the main atrium. I don't really know how big the Bureau is, I hear it goes on for miles, and anyone can get lost quite easily if you don't know where you're going. But I know where I'm going. I walk down the corridor and stop in front of the landing doors to call the elevator. Once inside, I tell the Protector attending the elevator to stop by the Records Department. He instantly cranks the control lever, and we ascend the shaft. When the elevator reaches my stop, I don't recognize it at first, and the Protector has to remind me to get out. I quickly play it off as being distracted, and step out into the hall, trying my best to act natural.

I've been to the Records Department a few times before, but it was always for official business. I'm not authorized to be here now; I have to be careful. There are more Protectors here than in the Newsroom, patrolling the floor. I have to look like I belong. Stay calm, I tell myself; you haven't done anything wrong, nothing worth getting stopped for, at least not yet. Just try not to get yourself into any unwanted trouble, alright?

I make my way down the corridor, past other departments on the same floor, and into the Records Department. The Records Department is an extensive archive of every single piece of documentation ever recorded: diaries, photographs, maps, music, artifacts, films, recordings, literary works, it's all here. I'm looking for the Historical Section, that's where the Library of Unbooks is. And from what I remember, it should be somewhere right around here.

I walk a little farther down, focusing on the movement of every limb—the sway in my arms, the stride in my legs, the rate of my breath—making sure to keep a consistent pace with everyone else around me. I turn off down another corridor and emerge into a large room.

The space is divided into four columns, each with twenty rows of steel bookcases lined down the middle, spanning from one end of the room to the other, with even more placed all along the walls, and all filled to the brim with books and boxes. This is the Historical Section. Every historical document ever recorded, real or fake, is here. And there, at the far end of the room, is the entrance to the Library of Unbooks.

I enter the Historical Section and move along the columns between the bookcases, towards the back of the room. Most of the information in the Records Department, including the Historical Section, is open for occupational use to the rest of the Bureau. These books have all been "corrected" prior to their publication, as well as stamped with their authentic seal of approval, and therefore pose no threat; though the seals don't usually hold up very long before the books themselves are replaced with the newest edition.

Here and there, Record Keepers are busily working, taking inventory, putting books back on their shelves, and endlessly updating information to fit the current standard of truth. However, the name doesn't seem to quite suit them: Record Keepers. They're constantly changing one record after the next. Just down the hall is where the Engineers hold their board meetings to decide what history they should come up with next. "History Writers," they're called, and each one is responsible for writing a new history every week.

I made that up. I don't actually know what the Engineers do during their meetings, though I don't blame myself for thinking this way. If this turns out to be true, I wouldn't be surprised at all.

Now that I think about it, "Historical Section" doesn't seem to fit either, Historical *Fiction* it ought to be called, for all the countless lies they've made up to keep us in submission. No record today exists that has not been altered in some way, none except those locked up in the Library of Unbooks. They remain, after all these years, in their true original state. That's why they're so dangerous, and that's why I need to get in there.

As I make my way nearer to the back, the reality of what I'm doing finally starts to set in. I'm about to break into one of the most restricted areas in the entire Bureau.

When I come to the security window, a woman sits behind the glass, typing something on her Cyber-Op terminal. She notices me.

"Yes?" she says through the window intercom, "how may I help you?"

"I require entry into the Library of Unbooks," I say with a hint of arrogance and slightly pitching up my voice. I think that sounded like how Curtis would say it.

"You're pass please," she says.

I take out the pass, not my pass, and slide it through the little slit underneath the window. She takes it, reads the numbers, and begins typing them into the Cyber-Op terminal, no questions asked. She must think I work here in this department. When she finishes, she places the card into a machine that burns a series of holes into it and throws it away. Then she slides me a ticket in the little opening. "Your five minutes starts once the door closes," she says.

I nod, take the ticket, move towards the door, and she buzzes me through. Five minutes? That's not enough time to do anything. What good could I do with five minutes? She might as well not have let me in at all. I'll have to be quick, ration my time, think three steps ahead of my next move. I step into the room, stop, and stare in shock. Every book is individually packaged in foil bags, unmarked: no names, no titles, only serial numbers and barcodes. Like the prisoners in the mines, wrapped in foil, no longer addressed by a name but a number. How am I to know where anything is?

I quickly move along the rows of steel bookcases, peering down one aisle after the next, desperately searching for some clear designation as to which section I'm in. I don't believe it, there's no way to tell what documents are what. I could try opening a few bags, but that'll take too much time. What makes this worse is that I never even knew what I was looking for in the first place—answers, of course. But where do I even begin? I was hoping that I could at least use the signs as some sort of basis to start my search, and work my way from there, but I can't even do that. I should have done more research, prepared for this moment, scoped out my options. This is my one and only chance I'll ever get to be here, and I've wasted it. I can't ask for help, and I don't have much time left either. I aimlessly walk down one of the aisles, carefully looking at the packages to see if I've missed something, a stamp, or a label perhaps, but nothing. In my panic, I grab the first package I see, and without thinking, I stuff it into the rim of my pants, beneath my jacket, and walk out of the library through the turnstile.

I can't believe I just did that. I'm already risking so much just being here. Why do I always have to put myself in even more danger? I'm desperate for any information I can get my hands on, even if I don't entirely know what that information is. It's too late to turn back now, I have to be careful.

I move hastily through the Historical Section, back up towards the exit, trying my best to blend in. It suddenly becomes apparent to me that a low crinkling sound can be heard coming directly from inside my jacket. I attempt to steady my stride in an effort to reduce the noise of the foil bag rubbing against me, now stuck walking at an excruciatingly slow pace. Why must you do this to yourself? You're only asking to get caught.

I'm nearly out now. But as I approach the exit, a short man pushing a trolley of books turns out from one of the aisles ahead of me, blocking my path. I move to go around him when I quickly realize that it's Curtis. But before he notices me, I pull myself away into another aisle, walking briskly but calmly down it to the other end. What's he doing back so early from his lunch break? I haven't been here that long, have I? I wouldn't be surprised if he never went in the first place. Finn told me that most Record Keepers often have to go without lunch for days, using the time they would waste eating to catch up on their work instead. Either way, he can't know I'm here.

I stand, my back against the bookcase, pretending to be looking for something on the shelves in front of me. I slowly steal a look behind me, down the same aisle I came from, trying to be as inconspicuous as possible. I don't see Curtis. I turn, look down the aisle to my left. There he is. He's putting books away back on their shelves. I wait for a moment, thinking of what to do next. If he sees me, I'll have to make something up, tell him I'm doing research for Mr. Freeman. I could just run. He won't know it's me. He'll only see a blur of white, could be anyone. I take a deep breath and make a rush for the exit. If someone finds out I have this, I won't get into trouble, as long as what's in the package remains unknown.

I make it back down to my department, with the halls now gradually becoming crowded. People are starting to return from their lunch break. I keep my eyes lowered to the ground, not wanting to meet them with anyone else's. I'm almost there, I just need to get back to the Newsroom. I turn down another hall, but just as I round the corner, out of nowhere, a large man lumberingly comes rushing forward. Neither one of us has time to react and we collide, the force knocking me clean off my feet. It takes me a minute to realize what's even happened, but as I come to, I notice the package is gone. I look up to see it on the floor in front of me, with everyone around staring, and my heart begins racing. The man who bumped into me walks over to the package, bends down, and picks it up, while the other people around me help lift me respectfully back on my feet.

"I'm so sorry Acolyte," he says, handing me back the package, "I didn't see you coming around the corner."

I'm stunned for the first few seconds, forgetting that no one knows what's inside the package, that I don't say anything right away in reply.

"Oh, it's alright," I finally say, "thank you Acolyte," and quickly turn away down the hall.

I enter the Newsroom and move down the aisle of cubicles towards the darkroom. I open the door, step in, shut it, and lock it behind me.

I let out a long sigh of relief, then take a few more deep breaths. I did it. I look at the package in my hands, I want to open it, see what's inside, what I risked my life for. But I decide against it. Lunch break is over, perhaps tomorrow, when I have more time, and my mind is clearer. I walk over to the other side of the room and climb onto the developing table. No chance of getting this out of the Bureau, not without the proper clearance, and there's no way I'm getting that now. So here it shall stay, hidden away in the darkroom. No one else comes in here except for me and the other photographers. I lift one of the ceiling panels, slide the package in, and close it. It'll be safe here, I tell myself, no one knows I took it. Then comes a loud banging at the door.

I turn my head and stare intently at the door. It can't be. Did someone see me? Recognize the package? I've been stupid, selfish even, greedy for knowledge, for answers. I was wrong to seek the truth, it was too much to ask. Another series of bangs, even louder than before, I can feel the room shaking from the force. I get off the table, slowly make my way towards the door. Is this it? Am I walking into my own death? I reach my hand out to unlock it, the blood rushing to my head. I can hear my heartbeat, its pulse rapidly rising to a stop. Sometimes I forget that one day there'll be no pulse left, just one long empty pause, infinite and endless. End.

I turn the door handle slowly. My hands have begun to sweat. I could have done something remarkable, something worth dying for. I did, and I survived that—but not this time. I take another deep breath, swing open the door, and just as I expected, standing before me is a man all in dark blue, a Protector, and I know this is it, this is my end.

Chapter 19
The Invitation.

"Come with me," says the Protector in a deep voice. I step
out of the darkroom, out of the shadows, and into the light of
the Newsroom, exposed for all to see. Everyone's looking at
us, with some of the writers even poking their heads out of
their cubicles, but I don't turn to look at them, I don't break
my focus. When the body knows it's going to die, it will
provoke the urge to fight, do anything it can so that it can go
on living. This is what I feel right now. I want to yell, lunge at
the Protector, reach for his gun. I want to run as fast as I can,
see how far I'll get. But there'd be no use in this. I wouldn't
make it out of the Bureau alive. And even then, to make a scene
would prove to be equally as useless. So, I swallow the urge to
fight, run for my life, go on living, because I know there's no
point in trying.

The Protector signals me to step forward, and I do as I am
told. I don't hesitate, I don't question him, but obey his orders.
I already know where he's taking me. I walk ahead and turn
down towards the exit as he follows close behind, but then he
stops me.

"This way," he says, nodding in the other direction, towards the upper level staircase. Is he taking me to Mr. Freeman's office first? Maybe he thinks there's a story in this worth writing. *Unthinker Breaks Into Library of Unbooks, Caught Stealing Deadly Records.* He'll have it published within the hour.

I turn around, move between the aisle of cubicles, ascend the steps to the second floor, and continue towards Mr. Freeman's office. Is he going to perform his own private interrogation? Try to get as many answers out of me as possible, while we wait for the Recall Officers to come and take me away? As we approach, I see Mr. Freeman waiting there, in his black suit, just outside the room. How strange. I've never seen him outside his office before, it's unnatural, even if he's just outside the door. He holds his hand out to invite me in, and I enter.

"Thank you Martin," I hear him say behind me to the Protector, "close the door please."

I stand here awkwardly, my heart seconds away from exploding. I can't bring myself to look at him, shame fills me, but I know whatever he thinks of me isn't true.

"Please, sit," he says, walking behind his desk. I sit in the chair opposite him, facing forward, staring out into nothingness, into my future. I know what will happen to me. I've seen it first-hand. There is no point in trying to fight once they catch you, it's too late. At this moment, I may as well no longer exist.

I hear him walk over to his liquor cabinet to my left, take something off it, walk back. I don't attempt to turn my head. He's going to ask me where I've hidden the book, what I know, if I know anything. Ask me who've I been talking to, and what about. And I'll tell him the truth. I'll tell him everything, maybe even more. After a few beating sessions, I'll begin to say *yes* to every accusation they throw at me. They'll try to blame me for any faults they can find, and it wouldn't be a difficult thing to do, because I am not faultless. By the end of it all, they'll have turned me inside out. There would be nothing left, I'll have become hollowed, emptied, void of hope, of anything. And finally, I'll be thrown away, down into the mines, discarded as waste. So, I may as well tell him everything now.

"How are you today?" he says, pouring himself a glass, "are you well?"

Please, don't make this any more difficult than it has to be, this endless game. Just get on with it, there's no use in trying to make small talk, I've waited long enough.

"I was shocked to hear what you did yesterday," he says, "when you were on your way back from the mines."

I sit up, look at him. I've been so worried about the book I completely forgot about yesterday. They're not even going to bother with the mines now. They're just going to Pacify me.

"When you realized that Protector left you," he continues, "several thoughts must have flashed across your mind in that moment. You saw the perfect opportunity, and you took it."

What is this supposed to be? Is he just toying with me?

"To think, you were willing to risk your life," he pauses, "chasing a story."

Within a fraction of a second, this single remark seemed to have the power to drain my head of all other thoughts. I sit, mindlessly staring back up at him, too stupid to think.

"I'm sorry, I don't follow," I finally say. What in the world is he talking about?

"Here," he says, "look at this," he hands me an envelope.

Confused, I take it and open it. Inside is the developed photo of the Exterminator's dead body I found back in that old construction site. I look back up at Mr. Freeman. What does this all mean?

"Now that is fine photojournalism," he says, "you might've even turned out to be a great investigative journalist, if only those roles weren't exclusive to Secondary interns."

I see now. The reason he thinks I ran out of the shuttle was to take photos of the Exterminators hunting down the resistance. So that's why I was never Recalled, they didn't realize I was trying to run away.

"I also heard that you witnessed the rescue of that Primary, Rachel," he says, "is that right?"

Mr. Freeman's been keeping tabs on everything that happened last night.

"I just want you to know that I'm impressed," he says, "although you did get me into some trouble."

That's one thing out of the way, but what about the book?

"By now I guess you've been wondering why I sent for my Protector to bring you here," he goes on, pouring the other glass, "sorry about that, but this was important." I wait until he speaks again. "Listen, I have a proposition to make."

A Proposition? What sort of proposition? This is nowhere near the direction I thought the conversation would be going. So many things aren't adding up.

"I'm attending a small party over at the Excelsior," he says, "it's sort of like an informal business gathering. And I would like you to accompany me."

"Sir?" I finally say, confused as ever.

"Don't worry. I won't force you to come along if you don't want to. It's more like a favor," he continues, coming round the front of his desk to hand me the glass. "So, what do you say? Would you kindly accept the offer?"

This isn't about the book at all. He has no idea. I sit, thinking for a moment, the fear slowly seeping from my body. I have not been caught. I've been cleared of all charges. No one knows, at least not yet. But to be sure, I think of something to say.

"Is—is that all you needed to tell me, sir?"

"Well, I could get you something in return," he says, "if you like."

"You could… get me something?" I repeat, looking up at him astonished. I can't quite explain it, but despite his friendly demeanor, he's rather intimidating. Or maybe it's the thought of death still residing within me. "Like what?" I say.

"Anything," he says.

I stop for a moment, taking in the situation. I'm speechless. So many things are running through my head. I want to ask him why, and why me of all people, but I know my questions won't be answered here, so I give into the offer. "Alright," I finally say.

"Wonderful," he says, "well, what would you like me to get you?"

"I—I don't know," I say.

"Don't worry, you'll think of something," he says, pulling me up off the chair and taking the drink and photo out of my hand, "in the meantime, try to stay safe. It's getting more dangerous these days." He knocks on the window of his office door; the Protector opens it. "The party's in a week. I'll send for my driver to stop by and pick you up." He rushes me out, and the Protector shuts the door behind me.

I stand for a moment outside his office, frozen, in complete shock. I'm relieved. I'm alive, I'm still here, still in existence, I have not become disposable. Don't do that again. Don't risk your life trying to find the truth, it won't end well for you if you don't. This whole ordeal was a sign of some kind—a glimpse into my possible future. This is what it will feel like if I don't get my act together. I need to be more careful from now on. But right now, I am grateful that I am still here. Thank you.

But here comes the strange part: he wants me to go with him to the Excelsior suites? Why there? And why me? That building is only for the Engineers and powerful Secondaries. Would they even allow me inside? What's Mr. Freeman got planned for me? Then a sudden thought enters my mind, but I brush it aside, for the thought alone is too foolish to even consider, much less possible, especially for an Engineer. But perhaps maybe, just maybe, he's an Unthinker.

V

Excelsior

Chapter 20
Liberty Plaza.

The air in here is the cleanest it's ever been. For the first time in my life, I don't feel like my lungs are slowly strangling me from the inside out. There isn't any smoke or mist, no dampness in the air, there isn't even the hint of a smell. It's nice. It's more than nice. It's liberating. Of course, this won't last very long. To have clean air is a privilege. A few months ago, it got so bad that they had to put this place under lockdown until Climate Control could get the air quality back to a breathable level. Even with the large open passageways, it's still too enclosed to tolerate a fire, unlike in the streets. Naturally, it was a Peace Parade that caused the lockdown, though I can't remember what they were burning at the time, another canteen perhaps, or a record shop, for selling the wrong kind of music, "Unmusic" it's called. As long as a song doesn't contain any Unwords or Unmeanings, it doesn't matter what genre of music one sells or listens to.

I sit alone at my table, eating lunch at the automat eatery. Around me, other people sit as well, eating and talking with one another, unabashedly themselves. Sometimes I imagine how much kinder life would treat me if only I weren't an Unthinker, to accept my preordain role as a Primary, and to do as I am told without question. To see the world through my eyes is a very difficult thing. While everyone else's view of the world has become blurred by the Operator, I see it for how it truly is. If I could look through the eyes of anyone else here, I would see nothing, I may as well be blind. They all have it so easy. They don't have to live in fear of being mislabeled a threat to the new society. But even with how much pain comes with seeing, I must remind myself to be grateful that I am not one of them.

It's sad to know that I still doubt whether this sort of life is even worth living, contemplating just giving in to all the lies for my own satisfaction. This is not the first time I've had this discussion. Every day I'm faced with the same two choices: do I keep going? Or do I give up? And every day, I make the choice to keep going. I won't give up, not if it means letting them win.

You can't keep letting these moments of loneliness get to you. Yes, even now, among this crowd of people, I am alone. I'm sick of not having someone to talk to. I want to have a genuine conversation with like-minded people for a change, not just with myself or the tape recorder, but other Unthinkers. It's a confusing truth to admit, but sometimes I forget I'm not the only sane person in the world. We have to hide, even from ourselves, so it's no wonder why I feel this way. I need to accept that this isn't going to change anytime soon. I won't deny that it might someday, but for now, all I have to keep myself company is the thought of being alone.

On my tray is a Soylent tablet, still in its foil wrapping, two pills: a Thought Blocker and a vitamin D capsule, a pouch of filtered water, a tin of raw fish—what kind of fish, I can't quite say, it's a dead fish at that—and three servings of different colored paste. Though I'm sure they're all the same thing, just with different colors and added flavoring.

I'm not hungry. Too often, I find myself filling up my time performing menial activities that I can accomplish very quickly and without much difficulty, rather than focusing all my energy on pursuing one overall goal. What else could I do? What goals can I accomplish? There are no goals to accomplish here, no underlying objectives. So then, do I have no purpose? Have I too, like everything else in Apocalypse, become meaningless? No, I haven't. I do have one underlying objective: don't get caught and wait until the resistance can help me escape. Though when the day comes of my escape, will I be ready for it? Or is there anything I need to do to prepare in advance? If anything, I'm just looking for a reason to worry.

In the meantime, there are many things I can do so as to fill in the gaps of my waiting. I could go to an Insemshop, do my duty to the Operator, and reproduce, have a child that I will never know. There are the Purges, the Prisoners' Pacifications, the Peace Parades. I could do a lot of things, truly I can, but I know none of those things are worth doing. Right now, I am filling my time with lunch that I do not want.

I stomach as much food as I can so as not to let it go to waste and end up finishing it all. Afterward, I take up the vitamin D capsule and swallow it. Now all that remains on my tray is the Thought Blocker. I know someone is watching, someone is always watching, so I won't risk throwing it away. I take the Thought Blocker, pop it into my mouth, then grab the pouch of water and put it to my lips. When I finish, I take the aluminum tray and pouch, drop them into the recycling bin, and continue on my walk. I didn't actually take my Thought Blocker. Instead, as I took a sip of my drink, I carefully slipped the pill through the rim of the pouch into the water where it will dissolve, leaving no trace of it behind. Finn taught me this trick, said if I ever needed to hide the fact that I don't take them. Sometimes I think those pills do nothing at all, placebos, and instead, they're just one of the many ways to keep track of those who are obedient and those who are defiant.

I move across the walkway onto the escalator, descending to the lowest level of the plaza, gazing up at the facades emblazoned with fluorescent numerals and neon adverts as I pass. I didn't come here intending to buy anything in particular, I just wanted a reason to get out of the apartment. I have my cheap clear vinyl briefcase with me today. As I approach the bottom of the escalator, the Operator's jingle echoes through the intercom system, changing all the televisions to display his image as the prerecorded message of a man's voice begins playing throughout the district:

REMEMBER, ALL CHILDREN MUST BE SURRENDERED TO SURROGATE BY THE AGE OF FIVE. ANY UNCHILDREN WILL BE DISPOSED OF AT THE ORGAN BANKS FOR HARVESTING.

The man speaks in a calm, almost hypnotic sort of voice, which has slightly been edited, giving it the effect of sounding robotic, though is undoubtedly the voice of a real man. Once in a while, the audio glitches, causing his voice to slow down or stutter, and I have to wonder how anyone can take the Operator seriously. It doesn't help either when the audio comes off as sounding tinny through the speakers.

Suddenly I remember something Mother Sylvia said to me. "If she didn't want to keep you," she meant our old mothers, "you may as well have been better off dead." This was the sort of thing all the Mothers said to the children to guilt us into behaving well. "I'd never wish for a child to grow up suffering knowing it was unworthy of being nursed by its old mother," she goes on, "at least at the Organ Banks, you would have been worth something to the Secondaries. But since you were worth something to her, you are worth something to us. Dead or alive, anyone can be of use to someone."

I reach the bottom, step off the escalator, and proceed down an open corridor, past another automat. I don't remember the last time I'd gone out for a walk; I don't often go on walks like this. I suppose I just needed to clear my head. I move along the crowded walkway, past the shops, glancing through the storefront windows to see if what they're selling is worth the trouble of buying. This store is selling telex machines—little typographs that print the words of the anchorman as he speaks, like the vox-types in the Newsroom. I already have one, so I advance on to the next store.

This one is selling handheld radios—the little ones you can hold up to your ear. That way, if you're ever out doing the shopping and still want to catch up on the news, you can bring one with you, so you'd never miss the latest report. This is not something I'd be interested in buying.

I continue in this manner for some time, peering hastefully through the windows, gazing at the festive signs—not reading them, what the signs say doesn't matter, as long as they look nice enough to consider going in; that's how they catch people, but I am not tempted by the colors—and thinking of every excuse not to step in and look around.

As I move forward, my legs suddenly lock in place as I watch in shock the familiar scene before me: a woman walking hand in hand with her child, a little boy. Instantly I'm reminded of my mother and me on our walks, how we used to do this sort of thing when I was young, and when it was more common. You don't see many children out with their old mothers these days, their real mothers of course. It's a rare sight. It's one of those things that has become sociably unacceptable: to be seen caring for a child, motherly affection, it's a sign of some kind, someone might get the wrong idea.

Her son doesn't have much time left; his next birthday must be any day now. To think that his mother will surrender him to Surrogate soon, and willingly. She's brought him out to go shopping, not intending to give him any gifts, but an experience. Whatever she buys him, in any case, isn't allowed to go with him to Surrogate; they don't want any remnants from his nursing stage to accompany him. She's just trying to spend as much time with him before he's gone.

Anxiety begins to fill me. The sight of them is too much for me to handle. I draw back in some alarm, almost stumbling on my feet. You need to get away from them, I tell myself. I quickly turn in the opposite direction, away from the pair, down another open corridor, trying to gain as much distance from the two. I find a small, secluded passageway, and begin looking for somewhere to sit as I've started to feel dizzy, but there aren't any seats here. I spot a telephone box nearby and hurriedly step inside and shut the door behind me. I rest my body against the Cyber-Op terminal, pretending to be on a phone call. I feel nauseous, I think I'm going to throw up. I can't tell if I'm actually shaking or if it's only in my head. I shut my eyes, take a long deep breath, hold it for a moment, let go, desperately waiting for this feeling to pass.

It takes several more rounds of controlled breaths before the feeling can even begin to fade. Eventually, my heart returns to a natural pace, and I finally open my eyes. Did anyone see me? I was too busy trying to get away to care if anyone noticed me acting odd. This sort of thing has happened to me before, in the past, but not like this. This was worse. I can't remember when it first started. One day it just became another impulse of mine. I didn't even know what was happening until it was too late for me to react. But why now?

The whole reason I decided to go for a walk was to clear my head, yet my head's been so full of thought all this time. I should've known this wasn't a good idea. I step out of the telephone box, shut the door, look around, wondering where I've ended up. There are no people in this corridor, and the stores here don't have as many flashy signs. Then I notice something familiar at the far end of the hall, sitting in the display window of one of the shops. I slowly walk towards it to get a better look at the thing, gradually feeling the excitement grow within me as I realize what it is. It's a clock, the same kind as the clock tower in Freedom Square, only smaller. I never would've expected to see something like this here at all. How can an artifact such as this have survived for so long just to end up here? I look up to see that the store is an antique shop. I'm surprised I've never heard about it before. They must have recently just added it here. I look at the placement of the clock's hands, and if my memory serves me correctly, the time on it reads 4:51. It's sad to think that no one else can read this sort of clock but me, like a forgotten language. But whoever is selling it must also know how to read it. I grab the door handle, pull it, and step inside.

Chapter 21
Antique Shop.

The shop bell rings as the door shuts behind me, alerting my presence to anyone nearby. But there isn't anybody else in the store—I'm alone. I look around in great wonder to see the room crammed full of all manner of things, some of which I've never even seen before. There's a wide array of old-fashioned furniture, a strange assortment of artistic home décor, an eccentric collection of jewelry, hundreds of tattered books, there's even a whole section entirely dedicated to tiny glass figurines. Packed all along the walls hang paintings, placards, tapestries, and many other things I can't even begin to tell you the names of. This is how I imagine what the past looks like, this place is like a walk-in time capsule.

I come to the counter at the far end of the room, but the shopkeeper is nowhere to be found. That's strange; the sign outside says it's open. Behind the counter is a doorway that leads directly to the second floor. Whoever owns the shop must live up there. I look up it, expecting to see someone coming.

"Hello?" I say, but I get no response. I continue exploring, looking from item to item, when something on the other side of the room chances to catch my eye. Hung on the wall between a set of velvet armchairs is an old painting, neatly mounted within a large gold frame. I walk over to it. The painting is of an extremely beautiful woman on a black backdrop, with smooth pale skin and one large pearl earring. Her clothes aren't white. So the woman was a Secondary. A thin coat of dust covers the canvas, and I run my hand across it to get a clearer view of her face. I stare at it for a moment, observing its finer details. Thin cracks layer the painting's surface. On looking closer, I realize that you can even make out where each individual stroke of the brush was made through the paint, like the tiny dots of white as the reflection of light in her eyes. I never thought such a form of history could be preserved so well.

"Hello there," I hear a voice behind me say.

I turn around, startled. An old man emerges into view from the doorway behind the counter. It's the shopkeeper.

"I didn't think anyone was here," I say as if that were an excuse for touching his things.

"Sorry about that," he says in a low gentle voice, slowly making his way towards me from behind the counter, "it's just that I wasn't expecting anyone to stop by today, or at all, for that matter."

The man stands hunched with his walking cane, wearing a white wool cardigan and large round glasses. Attached to his face is a rubber mask hooked up to a small portable oxygen tank, which he carries slung over his shoulder. How quaint. He's probably older than most of the people in Apocalypse, maybe even older than Apocalypse itself.

"I saw the clock in at the window and decided to come in," I say. I feel a strange sense of comfort from this man and find myself talking to him as if we know each other. "I was surprised to see you were selling it."

"Ah yes, the grandfather clock," he says, moving towards it. As he passes, I get a whiff of his scent. He smells faintly of cigarette smoke and talcum powder: the traces of aftershave. I stand, listening to the soft tapping of his cane, watching how his body struggles to move about.

It puzzles me to think that I'll ever become an old man someday. I try to imagine what I would look like, with my hair no longer a mousey brown but a patch of thin, silvery grey, and my face all gaunt and sunken in, sagging jowls, wrinkled skin, and struggling to accomplish basic tasks. I have all the right parts, but I can't seem to make out the picture entirely in my head—this blurred image of my older, frail self. Partly because I've only ever seen a handful of old people in my life, but mostly because I'm unsure of what my future will entail. Where will I be? What would the world be like? Who would I become? Would I have escaped by then? All of my waiting finally paying off? Or will I end up looking like one of the prisoners in the mines?

I don't like to think about my future too much. Too often, I find myself dreaming up this false perception of reality—a reality with no certainty of ever happening, where things are better off, and I tell myself this is what my future holds. But it's not. None of it is real. It's not a bad thing to have these thoughts, they are, after all, what give me hope. But if I begin to obsess over these thoughts as my only source of comfort, believing them to be true, they are no longer thoughts but delusions, and will slowly begin to lose touch with the present. So, I push these thoughts away and save them aside for later, when I will need them.

"Not many people know how to read these types of clocks nowadays," he continues, "or even know what they are."

"It says 4:51, I'm sure, though I think it's broken," I say, following behind him, "my real mother taught me how to read them and—" I stop, halt in place. I was too late. I let a piece of myself slip out. I couldn't catch myself quickly enough. And all I said was "my real mother." He turns back, looks at me, puzzled at this remark. I shouldn't have said this. I've only just met this man, and already I've begun to let the cracks show. I don't know him well enough to be holding these sorts of conversations, knowing whether or not they will end in my arrest. One wrong remark is all it takes. He may very well just be an old man, the sole owner of a forgotten antique shop. But he is still a stranger. There could be more to him than meets the eye. He could be a Psi-Op for all I know. This place could all be one giant ambush, a setup of some kind, with hidden cameras and microphones placed about the room. I wonder who's waiting upstairs, if there even is an upstairs, probably just a vacant room. Or what if that's where they're watching me right now from their cameras with screens, capturing my face from every angle. A trap to lure unsuspecting Unthinkers, and I've just walked right into it. Of course, this is all pure guesswork, mixed with a hint of paranoia. But there is some sense in what I'm saying. I can't rule anything out.

I stand, staring back at him, recovering my senses. This could go either two ways. I could pretend as if I haven't realized the severity of what I said, in case he isn't a Psi-Op, so that the conversation can continue. Or I could show that I'm aware of my mistake and confess with my eyes that I'm sorry. I take the risk and just stare blankly back at him as if nothing's happened, though I can tell that I'm not doing a very good job at it.

"Is that right?" he finally says, after a long period of silence, "what good memory you must have to remember such a thing. Why, I wish I had half as good a memory as you do."

I wasn't expecting this response at all. For him to say this is a relief. I wait for him to say something else, but he doesn't, and continues towards the window. He didn't seem bothered by my remark, but even then, I can't put my trust in him that easily. Trust is something I must ration. It must be saved up and handed out in portions, over time, and to the right people. If I wish to find a friend within him, I must test him somehow.

But then he turns around again and says: "God knows how forgetful I am," then he chuckles.

I feel the life seep from my body. God, God. God is an Unword, one of the deadliest words one can say. If ever caught saying it, they'll make sure you'll never say it again. Who knows what would happen to you? God knows.

He's trying to hint at something, a signal of some kind, but of what exactly I don't know. Maybe I can trust him. Would he risk committing an Unspeakable if he weren't a Psi-Op? Or perhaps now he's testing me, seeing how I'll react. If he were a

Psi-Op, he'd want me to say something, call him out for his illicit use of an Unword, but I can't tell if he is or not. He could be tricking me, playing me for a fool, and I am. I take another chance and say nothing. How many chances have you got left to spare? At this rate, soon there'll be none left, I'll have run out. I wouldn't be in as much trouble if I didn't report him, a couple of weeks of counseling in the Recall Clinic is all, not much to risk there. But still, I have to be careful around him.

"Were you thinking of buying it?" he says, "the grandfather clock."

"No," I say, "I mean, I would like to, but it's too large."

"Oh, is that so?" he says, "then I have something else you might like." He hobbles slowly towards a small table in the corner of the room and takes something out from a little tin box. I come to him, and he places the object in my hand. I look at it for a moment, feeling it with my fingers, wondering what it is. It's something like a clock, only it's small enough to fit in the palm of my hand. Its casing is made of a dull brass, and at the top is a ring linked to a thin metal chain. I turn it over and rub my thumb across the engraving on the back to feel, rather than see, the details of the elaborate etchings in the metal. Its texture seems to give it a sense of dimension, a quality of life. No machine could have created such a thing. On the other side of time, I see the person who made this delicately hand-carving these designs.

"It's beautiful," I say, "what's it called?"

"It's called a pocket watch," he says, "do you know how to use it?"

"No," I say, "how does it work?"

"You have to set the time first," he says, "and then you wind it up." He takes the pocket watch from my hand and shows me how to do this. The time right now is 1:00 so this is what he sets it to, and after a few sharp turns of the crown, the watch begins ticking away, like the engine of a tiny machine.

"No electricity?" I ask, curious to know how something like this would only need to be wound up.

"Of course not," he says, "it's all clockwork, little springs, and cogs, all working together, making it tick."

"It's brilliant," I say, "how many Apocrypha is it worth?"

"One Apocryphon is all," he says, "but it's such a low price, I may as well give it to you for free."

Free? Nothing is ever truly free. There's always a price that must be paid, and those who pay it, perhaps not by me, but someone will have to, sooner or later.

"Thank you," I say, looking back at the old man, before he turns and walks away.

Out of nowhere, my body is taken over by a rush of strange emotions, the sudden change in mood startling me, but I soon find myself embracing these feelings. I feel such an immense sense of peace, so much so that I begin to cry and have to blink away the tears from my eyes. What I really ought to feel is ashamed. How could I have ever suspected this man of being a Psi-Op?

Then the realization of what this man is finally occurs to me, what great importance he possesses. This man is a national treasure, a traveler through time. He's a link between the past and the present, a human history book. He should be recognized for all the pain he's been through. If there's anything even remotely worth knowing, it lies within his mind, the only person in living memory to have seen firsthand what brought this world to where it is now. His knowledge alone holds greater value than anything the news or the Operator can offer, because he has something they don't: the truth.

I want to ask him a question, more than that, I want to ask him a million questions. If anyone has the answers, he's bound to have them. But where do I begin? What do I ask? If there is one thing I'd like to know about the past, it's how all of this came about in the first place. How could we have let something like this happen?

I don't know how old he is. Once someone lives past the age of sixty, it's hard to tell how long anyone's lived. You don't often see old people outside of their homes nowadays. The older ones are more likely to have been Recalled during the Great Purges of the Revolution.

He has a full head of wiry silver hair that sticks up untidily, heavy pink bags under his eyes that almost seem to pull his lids shut, and a scruffy beard and mustache, giving him an aged look.

I want to say he's about eighty years old, maybe ninety, meaning he was born on the surface, a Surfaceborn. But if that's true, then he shouldn't even be allowed to be alive. He ought to have been Recalled for simply existing as long as he has. He's an unwanted liability. He's seen too much.

I can just imagine all the hours I would spend listening to him talk, all the stories he has to share, to finally understand. But not today. It's best I come back another time.

"Was there anything else you wanted to see?" says the old man.

I quickly wipe away my tears before turning to look at him. "Yes, actually," I say, "I was wondering, by any chance, do you sell cassette tapes?"

"Cassette tapes?" he says, "I'm sorry, but if there's one thing I can remember, it's that I don't have any more of those. They're very hard to come by these days."

"It's alright," I say, "thank you anyway."

Chapter 22
Suspect.

I hear the voice of the anchorman from within my apartment, muffled behind the door. Curtis isn't supposed to be home for another three hours; something must've happened at the Bureau. I unlock the door, turn the knob, and pull it open, releasing a sudden burst of sound from the room into the hall. I fumble to free the key, and already I'm annoyed. I step in and shut the door behind me. I see Curtis in the middle of the room, nervously pacing back and forth, his arms crossed. I've caught him at a strange time. He's deep in thought. Something's clearly troubling him, probably just another one of those "abduction" cases. He doesn't even notice me. Though as I come closer, I startle him.

"Where were you?" he says, as if I'd done something wrong.

"I just went out for a walk," I say, confused. Ever since what happened in the exclusion zone during the hostage situation, Curtis has been stricter about leaving home unless absolutely necessary. He thinks he's looking out for me, but because of this, he's become increasingly more annoying, which I didn't even think was possible.

"A walk?" he says, almost disgusted at the notion. Who goes out for walks? Someone that's up to no good, that's who. Why leave your Habitat if you've got nowhere to go? "So, you left for no reason?" he continues.

"Well, I did stop to have lunch in Liberty Plaza," I say, "and while I was there, I also got this," I take the watch out of my coat pocket and show it to him. He begins eyeing the thing for a moment, puzzled, wondering what I've got in my hand.

"What is it?" he says, looking up at me.

"It's called a pocket watch," I say, glad to have found the chance to show it off, "it's a sort of clock, you see."

"A clock?" he says, "looks more like a decoder to me, how do you tell what time it is?"

"Right now, it says 4:00," I say, "notice how that one hand is pointing at the four like that. You see, the little hand tells what hour of the day it is, and the big hand tells—"

"What a waste," he says, cutting me off, "you should return it, and ask for something more useful, like one of those handheld radios. But never mind that, have you seen the news bulletin?"

"I heard," I mumble, putting away the watch, "another abduction."

"No, not that, the one they just aired," he says, pointing at the screen, "if you had a radio, you wouldn't have missed it." I look at the screen. "They De-psyphered another one of those Unthinkers," he goes on, "he tried to get away, but they shot him alright, that filthy no-brainer. That's one less problem to worry about."

"Can you lower that down?" I say with a noticeable hint of disdain. "You can hear that thing from all the way down the hall."

Curtis's expression slowly shifts into a menacing stare. I must have really upset him. He can't seem to wrap his mind around why I don't listen to him. He thinks his ideas are superior to mine and therefore expects me to care what he has to say. I hope now he understands that I couldn't care less about what he thinks.

He holds his stare. I can feel the irritation radiating off of him, like the heat of a heat lamp. He's trying to intimidate me, but I don't feel the least threatened. I stare back at him, unfazed. I don't want to give him the satisfaction of even reacting, so after a moment, I simply turn away, further showing how little his opinion affects me. I hear him slowly walk over to the television set, adjust the volume, and prop himself in front of the screen. Who does he think he is?

I make my way over to the closet door, open it, and place my empty briefcase next to the others, two clear, and one solid black.

"Did you take my clearance pass?" I hear Curtis say.

I stop, my body tenses up. There's a sudden delay in my muscles, but I just as quickly manage to snap myself back in control. So, he finally checked his briefcase. I was wondering when he'd noticed the pass was missing. Possibly he's known for a while but hadn't suspected me until now. He was eventually going to bring it up. There's no way he wouldn't mention something like this to me. But how he would bring about the subject, I wasn't sure. Straight away, he's accusing me of stealing it. He thinks I'm willing to put myself in danger for a card, and he's right, but I don't want him to know that. If he finds out I took it, he's going to report me. It's a good thing I've been preparing for this exact scenario.

I stand up, shut the closet door, and turn to look at him, his face stone cold.

"Your… what?" I say, acting as if I don't know what he's talking about. If I'd immediately just said no, it wouldn't have sounded as convincing.

"My clearance pass," he repeats in the same contempt voice.

"No," I say, "why? Did you lose it?"

"I can't find it," he says.

This is easier than I thought, he's already beginning to doubt himself. I just need to sound genuine enough to discredit his suspicion of me, pretend to be considerate. Saying the wrong thing won't get me into trouble, it's what I don't say that will.

"Well, where did you last have it?" I ask.

"It was in my briefcase," he says.

"What does it look like?" I say.

"It's a clear plastic card, with large green text," he says, "have you seen it?"

"No, I haven't," I say, "but I'll keep an eye out for it."

He looks down, thinks for a moment. "I'm sorry," he says, "it's just that... I had a stressful time at the Bureau today."

By now his temper has died down. I suppose he was only angry because he suspected me of stealing from him. But now I'm curious, what could have happened to him at work? I come closer. "Why? Did you get in trouble or something?" I say.

He looks at me, I sense the hesitation in his eyes, and immediately I know something is off. He isn't at all the kind of person to be uncertain of himself, it's strange to see him like this.

"I shouldn't even be telling you this, but..." he turns around as if to make sure no one else is in the apartment.

What? Telling me what? Spit it out already.

He leans in. "During inventory today," he says in a low voice, "they found that one of the Unbooks was missing. They think someone stole it. They questioned all the Record Keepers, and afterward made us turn the whole place inside out looking for it, but we couldn't find it. Then they decided to send all of us home early. It was one of those high-risk ones too: an Unreadable. I don't even know why we still have those."

My eyes widen. A flicker of panic ignites within me, but I put out this feeling before it catches. So that's what happened, and all that trouble over a missing book. I think for a moment about what to say. I don't want to come off as too concerned.

"An Unreadable?" I repeat, "that sounds dangerous, well, I'm sure it'll turn up soon."

Chapter 23
Patient.

The Protector, whose name I now know is Martin, opens the door to Mr. Freeman's office, letting the other Engineers out first, before inviting me in. As soon as I enter the room, Mr. Freeman hastefully gets up from his chair to greet me at the door.

"Hello there," he says, shaking my hand with both of his, cuffing mine in between, he did the same thing yesterday, "how are you today?"

"I'm well, sir," I say, forcing a smile, one reminiscent of his.

"Good," he says, patting me on the shoulder.

I'm not stupid; I mind each of his gestures and understand he's planning to use me for something. Why else would he suddenly be friendlier to me? Ever since he first invited me to the party, he treats me like we're old friends who rarely get to see each other anymore, even though I'm nowhere near that level of earned respect. I hardly even know anything about him regarding his personal life, and yet he's willingly taken a strange liking to me. He isn't supposed to do this; he's an Engineer, and I a Primary. It's forbidden to form friendships with one another, much less socialize, apart for work-related reasons. Though he continues to favor me. Why is that?

Whenever people are friendly to you, when they usually aren't, it's often because they want something from you that they can't get on their own. If that's the case, then what can he possibly want from me? There's nothing I can give him that he can't already get himself, he's an Engineer after all. Then what? What does he want? I try to think of all the things I might have to offer, but nothing of great value comes to mind.

"Have you decided what you'd like me to get you?" he says with that unnatural smile on his face. Immediately, I direct my eyes on his teeth, as they're the only things that seem to stand out, given little effort. They're too perfect, too clean, too white. There's no way they aren't dentures.

"No," I say, "not yet."

I find it so bizarre that it's somehow reached a point where Mr. Freeman is offering me bribes just to get me to go along with whatever idea he's got planned. I never imagined I would find myself in this situation. As for what I want him to get me, I haven't really given it much thought. The idea in itself seems simple enough. One thing is all, but where do I even begin?

"Oh, it's no rush," he says, "you've got time."

Sadly, this is true. I've got plenty of time, too much it seems. I don't know what to do with it all. Of course, nothing is guaranteed, especially for me, so I shouldn't complain. I'd rather have too much time on my hands than not enough.

"In the meantime," he continues, walking back to his desk, "I've managed to arrange for you a special sort of job, and I can't have us passing off an opportunity like this. Can you promise me that you'll take care of it?"

"Yes sir," I say, though a bit hesitant. What's so special about this one?

He doesn't tell me what the job is but just stares at me, preparing me for what he's about to say. This is serious. Before he says it, I take the opportunity to try to guess what the job might be. I hate when life becomes too unpredictable. If I can just accurately imagine what tomorrow will be like, it makes me feel that I at least have some control over my future.

Maybe I'll be sent off to the uranium mines to take pictures of the prisoners working; that's possible. Or perhaps I've been assigned to join the Exterminators on an expedition through the exclusion zone to take photos as they smoke out resistance. No, they probably think that's too dangerous for me, so I digress.

"You know that Primary they rescued a few days ago? Rachel. Well, she's in the hospital right now under protective custody, and I need a photo of her."

I say nothing but stare back at him. At this moment, my body suddenly becomes frail; if I move the wrong way, I'll fall apart. I don't know why, but of all the jobs it could have been, this one feels the most personal. It's all so frustrating. Why me?

"Though, it's just so that we can have it on file," he adds, "we're not making any further reports on this story just yet. In the meantime, we've also prepared a series of questions we need you to ask her."

"Alright, sir," I finally say. This sounds more like a personal errand than a real assignment. They're not making any further reports?

"Good," he says, showing off that artificial smile of his, "then I'll see you later."

I enter the metro and wait in line. The lines here aren't as long as they were on my way to work this morning. I give the Protector my card, he scans it. Next, I walk to the baggage search lane and pass through the metal detector. Nothing comes up of course. What would they be looking for? What would they expect to find? Some sort of weapon, a bomb perhaps. Who'd be stupid enough to try to sneak something like that in? Though the woman with red hair somehow managed to sneak her briefcase past security, but how? A Protector, working in secret for the resistance, maybe? Let her sneak right through. That's the only possible explanation, but it sounds too absurd. There's no such thing as a Protector Unthinker, they do simply as they are told, nothing more. Then how did she do it?

I stand alone on the platform, waiting for the train to arrive. I'm nervous. This will be like any other job, I remind myself. I will neither lose nor gain anything from this, nothing will change, and I will do as I am told. Why oppose now? Besides, I've done worse. Compared to everything else, this job will be easy. Just because it'll be easy, doesn't mean it won't be hard.

I feel a small gust of air push up against me; the Operator has turned on the cooling for this week. Above me, to my left, is a television fixed to a pillar, airing the usual adverts. I try to ignore it, but the sound is turned up on high volume, the voice of the Operator reciting the familiar mantra:

THE NO.1 ENEMY OF THE PUBLIC IS
UNTHOUGHT

With how much the city cries about the dangers of Unthought, you would think they'd come up with a proper definition for it. Naturally, Unthoughts are any thoughts the Operator deems dangerous. What can be a harmless thought today, the Operator can declare an Unthought the next, and vice versa, it's left up to him to decide. Still, there is one major flaw in this logic. It makes it so that anyone can be at fault at any moment for whichever Unthinkable the Operator accuses them of, even if the thought itself is objectively harmless. They attach the name "Unthought" to the opposing idea and think it suddenly becomes as dangerous as they believe it to be, when in fact it doesn't. But how can that be? It has to, the Operator says so. Why else would he tell us this? It's hard to challenge a perfect immortal machine. But in a sense, I guess you can say Unthoughts are dangerous after all, maybe not to those who call it such, but to an Unthinker, because of what they will do to us if they find out we have them.

I don't often go by the suspension railway, but it's a change, a departure from my usual routine. In Apocalypse, life can get awfully repetitive. I make it a practice to switch things up every once in a while, as a means to break away from the monotony of life, even if the act itself is small. Though I must limit how often I can do this, or else I'll eventually run out of things to do. Sometimes I'll take a different path home from work, or have lunch at a place I rarely ever eat, even if the food is the same everywhere else. It's a risk, change of any kind is, but what I hope to obtain in these small acts of change is variety, which is exactly what this place lacks.

The train pulls into the station, stops, its double doors slide open, and I step in. There are only a few passengers in the carriage, most of whom are seated at the front. I take my seat at the back, away from everyone else, and the train departs the station. I sit, resting my head against the window, watching the buildings go by as the carriage drifts through the city, awaiting the arrival of my final destination.

I watch how the lights from the glittering neon signs shimmer through the window, as a kaleidoscope of colors dances across my face. I can almost feel it. This is certainly a far more scenic route compared to my usual forms of transportation.

I like to think of myself as being a part of one great big machine. I am a cog, one of thousands, carefully cut and fitted to turn in unison when wound by a key. We all have a role to play in powering this machine. Some of us, of course, don't fit as well as the others do, which in that case, we are either fixed or replaced. The machine must keep running without delay, interference of any kind won't be tolerated. And if at any time we show signs of slowing down, the machine will need to be wound up again and again until it fulfills its intended purpose.

But what is its purpose? For there to be a need for a machine in the first place, there must be a purpose. What other use is there for one if it has none? It's like operating a train that leads nowhere. As far as I can tell, this machine doesn't have a purpose. There is no final destination.

I don't know why I think of myself in this way: a cog in a machine, degraded to a piece of disposable metal. In retrospect, this is a perfect way to describe my role in this world, but I suppose it's because it simplifies, for me, a very difficult situation. When something is difficult to understand, it's usually more difficult to handle.

*   *   *

The train stops. I've arrived. I didn't think I'd ever make it this far. Even now, I'm still a long way off. It's going to get a lot more painful from here, this, this is nothing.

I didn't understand why, but between her failed escape and being placed under protective custody, something about Rachel's sudden tragic circumstances had seared me with this strange affinity for her. What I mean is that I don't think of myself as a stranger to her at all. We've known each other long enough so that everything that's happening to her couldn't possibly hurt anyone any more than it has hurt me. The problem is, I don't actually know her, and yet I feel deeply for Rachel in a way only a person close to her can. And what's more, I don't think I'm the only one who shares in this feeling either. How could I be? No. For such a devastating loss to befall the resistance, it has inevitably caused an emotional shockwave of widespread torment to the rest of us. We Unthinkers all grieve in this terrible tragedy for the resistance, because a defeat on them means a defeat for all of us, and our combined efforts are waning. This assault on the resistance was a direct and personal attack on all of our lives. How could I have ever thought I was suffering alone?

I can't bear to watch her hurting inside. I hope they've done nothing to her. The Psi-Ops could've known all this time, pretended to go along with her lie, eased up on her, made her feel safe, until they decided it was time to pull back the curtain. It's another one of those mind games they like to play: false hope. It allows her to give up on her own, willingly come clean. They're the ones in charge, always have been. Or by now she's given something away, her story didn't add up, some of the details were out of place. They'll definitely be keeping a close eye on her now.

Once I'm done filling out the proper paperwork, I'm escorted by a Protector to the elevator. We get off on a private floor, and I follow closely behind him as we make our way down the corridor to her room. On either side of the door, Protectors stand guard, facing front, guns at the ready. They think she's in danger of being abducted again, that she's somehow become a target of the terrorists. Or maybe the protective custody part is just another gimmick. They're here to keep watch to ensure she doesn't try to escape. Either way, no one goes in or out of that room without prior authorization, which I've so fortunately been granted.

I step up to the door. One of the Protectors asks to see my pass, I give it to him. He glances at it quickly, hands it back, and steps aside while the other Protector unlocks and opens the door for me. I look into the room, and I grow cold. The fact that she's here awakens me to the realization that you can put so much time and effort into your escape and still have it amount to nothing. I don't want to end up like this, my chance for freedom so close, to then have it suddenly ripped away from me, just like that.

I enter; the Protector shuts the door behind me. Rachel's bed is in the back corner of the room, with the curtain pulled out. I walk over to meet her, the only sound in the room coming from my footsteps. As I come closer, I'm suddenly stricken with a profound sense of complete and utter failure. I can feel her hopelessness. Being in hiding for so long, she probably never thought they would find her and bring her back. This would destroy me. More than anything, I'm sure she would want someone to confide in, but I can't risk doing that. And even if I did, what could I possibly say to someone in her situation? I know there's no chance of things getting better for her anytime soon. They're never letting her out of their sight.

I come around from behind the curtain. She's sitting at the side of her bed, looking out from what little she can see through the window, which has been plated with metal shutters. She has short blonde hair, covered partially by a white handkerchief tied around the back of her head behind her neck.

"Hello," I say, breaking the silence.

She doesn't move. She's become disconnected, not only from her surroundings, but herself. She has left the confines of her body, while her consciousness is off floating away somewhere else, deep within the annals of her psyche. This is where the mind goes when it wanders.

"I'm a photographer for the *Apocalypse Now Newspaper.*" I pause, to make sure she understands me. I don't want to go too fast, considering her condition. "I'm here to take your picture," she still doesn't acknowledge my presence. I don't know if they told her I would be coming. "I'm also here just to ask you a few questions, if you don't mind." I begin by taking out the camera and dictaphone from my briefcase.

"I already told the Psi-Ops everything," she says without looking, "I'm not sure what else you want me to tell you." Her voice sounds hollow, empty even. She's not gone, but she's not all there either.

"It's alright," I say, "I won't be too long."

"If you must," she says.

I set up my camera and take a photo of her as she is. This already feels so wrong. I place the dictaphone on the bed, take out the list of questions Mr. Freeman gave me, and hit record. I don't want to be inconsiderate of her by making this sound like an interrogation, so I'd rather just talk.

"How are you?" I say, "are you feeling well?"

She takes a moment to answer, though I can tell that she just doesn't feel like talking. "I'm malnourished," she finally says, "that's all."

A moment of silence.

"Could you tell me what you saw," I say, "when your… abductors hid you?"

Another moment of silence.

"No," she says, "I can't, I didn't see anything. They had my head covered the whole time."

"And did they do anything to you," I say, "tell you anything?"

"It's hard to remember," she says; her voice has begun to crack, "they used all sorts of mental manipulation tactics trying to get me to turn into one of them." She turns away to hide her face.

I still remember what it was like when I betrayed Finn the day they brought me in for questioning—so I can imagine how she feels, how difficult it must be for her to be forced to lie about the resistance, the people who died trying to help her, giving the Operator another excuse to label us as terrorists. How can I choose to take part in any of it? I can't go through with this anymore. I don't want to be a cog in a machine.

I stop the dictaphone and place it back into my briefcase. I can't stand back and watch myself do this to her. This is the only chance I have to help someone in her position, so just this once, I'll risk my job.

I come forward, sit beside her on the bed, and put my hand on hers. "I'm sorry," I say, "I don't know what I was thinking, making you go through this, you don't need to lie. I know you weren't abducted. You tried to escape. I can't help you, but I just want you to know that it isn't over. I know with how the way things are looking right now this might be hard for you to believe, but even through this, you still have another chance. You can't give up."

She slowly turns to me, I see her eyes for the first time, they're a deep blue. She's crying. Is this the face of someone who's lost all hope?

"There's no escaping this place," she says, "we're trapped down here."

"The resistance has a plan," I say, "they'll find a way to get everyone out."

"Are you even listening to yourself?" she says, "what makes you so sure they have that kind of power?"

"I trust that they know what they're doing," I say.

"I did too," she says, "and look where that got me. It's hopeless, they're never going to let us go."

I stare back at her, feeling my muscles tighten. "No!" I snap, "I won't accept that. This can't be it; this can't be all this world has to offer. We don't exist just to suffer. There's more to life than Apocalypse. You have to find a way to keep going."

She turns away to hide her face, pondering this for a moment, then gives a slight chuckle. "You know, you almost sounded believable," she says, then: "It won't be long until it's your turn."

"What?" I say, taking a step back. What the hell is wrong with her?

"Oh, I'm sorry," she says, surprised even of herself, "I—I

didn't mean to."

"It's fine," I say, quickly reassuring her.

"No, don't," she whimpers, "I don't need your sympathy, I'm not worth it. You think you can save me, but you can't. Just go, please."

I don't understand, has she actually given up trying? If I can't convince her to change her mind now, then she will have to do that herself. I've done all I can.

"If that's how you feel," I say with understanding. I get up, and head towards the door. These sorts of things you just can't force, she will decide later for herself.

Just as I reach the door I stop and look back at her once more. I suddenly feel guided to say this one last thing to her before I leave, even though I'm unsure of what it means myself, but I have a feeling she's heard it before.

"*Compose Mentis.*"

Although I may not know what it means, in the moment, I knew somehow it was the right thing to say.

Chapter 24
Revelation.

I once again return to the privacy of the darkroom, the only place I am ever truly free from the watchful eyes of others. A blind spot in the Operator's peripheral. It doesn't get better than this. I'm not even safe within the boundaries of my own apartment, with the surveillance drones patrolling aimlessly and unannounced, peaking through the windows of the Habitats. But here, no one is allowed in here while I work. As long as I don't forget to turn on the *Darkroom In Use* sign, I will not be disturbed. This room is my only escape from Apocalypse.

I'm just about done developing the photo I took of Rachel. The safelight is on, its light engulfing the room in deep shades of red. I finish off the developing process by rinsing the film in water, making sure to remove every drop of fixer solution, and pinning it up on the drying line. All that's left for me to do now is wait. But unlike all the other times, this time I finally have something to do. I walk over to the other side of the room, climb onto the developing table, press my hand against the ceiling panel, behind which I've hidden the package, and push.

The whole time leading up to this moment, I tried my best

not to think about the package. I thought if I tricked my mind into forgetting about it, I could somehow absolve myself of any trouble that might befall me. I reach my hand inside and feel the package. It's still here, exactly where I left it. Well of course it is, why wouldn't it be? It just seemed too good to be true. I didn't want to get my hopes up in case something happened.

I take it out, lower myself off the table, and sit. Finally, I'm alone. It's just me and the package, no one else, there will be no interruptions. I begin eyeing the package with great curiosity, turning it over in my hands, consumed by fear and wonder of its presence. But it's not the package I'm interested in, it's what's inside it that has me so in awe. What great secrets do I hold before me, knowledge so deadly, so challenging to the authorities of this world, it needed to be hidden away, deep within the archives of the Bureau? How dangerous can a book possibly be?

I waste no time unwrapping the book from its foil encasing, making sure not to damage it in my hurry to get it open, then carefully slide it out its metallic sleeve. I hold the book out before me, admiring its full glory. It's an average size book, not too big, bound in a dark faux leather. In the red of the room, the book's binding is a harsh solid black, a material so completely absent of color that no light can escape its surface. It's as if a hole has been cut into the fabric of reality. I stand now staring face to face with the abyss.

I slowly rub my thumb across the cold leather, its pebbled surface like the skin of a human. The page edges are gilded with a gold foil which shimmer in the light. The pages themselves are made of a delicate, crisp parchment—paper so thin it's practically see-through. I turn the book over to read the title on the spine, the words too are gilded in a gold foil, and I know what this book is.

I hold in my hands the last surviving copy of its kind. There are no other records of any sort, as all other renditions have been destroyed. The only other remaining vestiges of its existence, if there are any, would be left amidst the minds of those who only wish to remember. If I were caught with this, no punishment would ever be deemed sufficient enough for such a crime as I have committed, because I would deserve so much worse. What I hold in my hands is the Bible.

I think it's best if I get rid of it while I still have the chance. But for now, I finally have something useful to do with my time. I open the book and begin to read.

Chapter 25
Unspeakable.

Time seemed to pass over me, and it wasn't long before I was finally summoned to Mr. Freeman's office. I hid the Bible back behind the ceiling panel, for later when I would return, and exited the darkroom.

I know what I want him to get me. On looking it over, I can't see how I didn't think of it sooner, it seems so obvious. The only trouble now is whether he will be angry with me for not going through with the rest of the interview.

Martin opens the door, I enter the room, file and dictaphone in hand. Mr. Freeman stands over the liquor cabinet, pouring himself a drink, and a cigarette in his mouth. He looks up and is thrilled to see me. He stops what he's doing and begins walking towards me.

Please don't be angry with me.

"There you are," he says, "have you got the photo?"

"Here you are sir," I say, handing him the file, the air under my suit growing hot, "though I'm not sure if it's what you wanted," I quickly add.

"Oh, don't worry," he says without even taking a look, "if

there's anything wrong, we can ask the Film Doctors to fix it."
He says this rather carelessly, which I hadn't anticipated. "Now,
what about the interview?"

"I have it," I say, holding out the dictaphone, "but I should
tell you, I really couldn't record much. There's about a minute
of audio on the tape." He takes a moment to think about this,
he looks concerned. I disappointed him after all. "I'm sorry, sir.
It's just that she didn't want to talk about it."

He turns to me. "Well, if she didn't want to talk," he says
sympathetically, "I suppose you could continue the interview
some other day. In the meantime," he continues, taking up the
dictaphone, "we can try to salvage whatever dialogue you've
managed to record." Then he smiles, his signature gesture. I
can tell by the look in his eyes that he had much more on his
mind. I let him down.

"The party's tonight," he says, "you should go home and
get some rest."

"Yes, sir," I say. He walks back to his desk as I stand here,
stupidly defeated yet again. I missed my chance, I have to wait
till tonight at the party to bring up what I want him to get me,
and even then, I don't know how long it will take for him to
actually get it.

"You may go now," he says, noticing I haven't left yet.

I turn around, about to knock for Martin to open the door,
when I stop. I'm done waiting. I turn back, fix my posture,
straighten my face. "Sir," I say.

He looks up, and glares at me for a moment without
speaking. "Yes?" he finally says.

"I've decided what I would like for you to get me," I say.
He lifts his head with interest. There's no question about it, I
know what I want. "I want to know what happened to my
mother," I say, "my old mother." He did say *anything* after all,
and he was rather insistent on it too.

He looks at me surprised, but unbothered by the request.
"I'll see what I can do," is all he says.

"Thank you," I say, and I leave.

It's the night of the party. I'm riding in the passenger

compartment of Mr. Freeman's car, Mr. Freeman in the seat opposite me, facing my direction, while Martin sits beside me, taking up most of the space. I've never been in a vehicle like this before. The car's interior is lined in a soft black fabric, nothing like the interiors of buses or train carriages. The seats are also black, upholstered in a glossy leather, I try my best not to shift as much to keep my seat from squeaking. The windows are tinted of course, so that no one can see in, but we can see out. This car definitely belongs to an Engineer.

It isn't long before we come to the Engineer's district. I never realized how close it was to the Bureau. Even with what little I can see from my view of the window, the quality of life here compared to the Primary—or even the lower Secondary districts—is vastly superior. It's much brighter here, and the air is clear too. Even the buildings' architecture is better, it reminds me of the outer city. None of the people here dress in white, in fact, they avoid it. Secondaries do everything they can to set themselves apart from us, which is why most of what they wear is festive and full of color. They hate us, and yet they need us. Everyone needs something to hate, it's what keeps the wheels of this machine turning, so they've chosen us. Of course, there's nothing a Secondary hates most of all than a Secondary who's an Unthinker: a *Desaturated,* one of their "own kind," if you can put it that way. But you'll rarely ever see one, though not for the reasons you might be thinking of. "Desaturated" is the name Secondaries and even some Primaries use to call them by, it's meant to be used as an offensive term.

In case you haven't noticed by now, Primaries aren't allowed to own a car. It would make it much easier to smuggle things between checkpoints that way, so it's forbidden; for our safety, of course, the same excuse they always give. During our drive, however, this car hasn't been searched once. It bothers me to know how much freedom comes with being an Engineer. As long as the chauffeur shows the Protector his pass, we're free to come and go as we please. I'll try to remember this fact, if and when the circumstances ever call for it. What have I been thinking of to consider this thought at all?

In my lap is my camera. Mr. Freeman said that they

wouldn't allow a Primary in the building as a guest, but I already knew that. So, he plans to sneak me in as a hired photographer. He said everything would be alright as long as I stayed close to him. But why? Why go through all the trouble of bringing me there in the first place, what does he intend to do with me?

"We're here," he says, "I have a couple of friends who'd like to meet you."

Friends? Meet me? Who would want to meet me? This remark alone brings about more questions than answers. But I suppose I'll have my answers soon enough.

The car stops, his chauffeur gets out, opens the door, and we exit the vehicle, Mr. Freeman first, followed by Martin, then me. The moment I step out into the open, I feel my body withdraw the desire to go further. I watch as other Engineers and Secondaries enter the Excelsior, and already I feel unwelcomed. What if I get into trouble? Or worse, what if someone finds out we're lying? Mr. Freeman won't have enough power to defend me, nor himself.

I suspect he notices my sudden change in behavior, because afterward he comes up close beside me and whispers, "just stay calm, I'll do the talking."

Even though the climate here feels fresh, my body feels hot. As we reach the front entrance, the Protector at the door stops us, no surprise there, I'm the only one here dressed in white.

"He isn't allowed to enter," says the Protector. He didn't even bother asking to see my card, he took one look at me and knew I didn't belong.

"I hired him as my personal photographer," Mr. Freeman says rather seriously in his deep voice.

The Protector turns, looks at me, almost studying me, as if I am something that needs to be understood.

How embarrassing. I feel debased, which is something I hardly ever feel, and all it took was one look. Quickly I think to change something about myself, straighten my back, fix my posture, smile maybe. It doesn't matter what I do, as long as it's not whatever I'm doing now.

"I'm sorry sir," continues the Protector more assertively

now, "he's not allowed to enter with the rest of the guests."

Mr. Freeman has an annoyed look on his face. This is the first time I've seen him even remotely angry. Whenever I'm around him, he gives the impression of being happy all the time. It surprises me to see him like this, even if it's something so small as a look of irritation, I'm not used to it. But ever so slightly, he's beginning to let the cracks show.

Mr. Freeman doesn't argue with the Protector any further but instead pulls Martin aside and begins whispering something to him in his ear, just far enough that I'm unable to hear. I was expecting him to try to persuade the Protector some more, even going as far as to bribe him like he did me, but no. This is a surprise too. Has he actually conceded? Well, that didn't go as planned. This is the part where he apologizes for wasting my time and will ask Martin to escort me safely back home.

After Mr. Freeman finishes speaking to Martin, he briefly glances at me, as if checking if I'm still here, then casually turns away, and enters the building alone without saying so much as a "goodbye." I'm taken aback by this, so much so that I even feel offended. This isn't like him at all. Was he that upset?

Martin approaches, grabs me by the shoulder, and orders me to get back in the car. The chauffeur had been waiting for us with the car the whole time. Mr. Freeman must have told him beforehand not to leave until we were inside in case this happened. It was inevitable. The Chauffeur holds the door open for me as Martin pushes me back into the car. He tells the chauffeur something before he enters through the other side, and we drive off.

Well, that was a disappointment. Nevertheless, I had little faith in this plan to begin with. I won't let this bother me, as it is, I've enough things in my life to worry about.

We don't even drive half a block away when the car suddenly veers off the main road and parks into an alleyway. Martin opens the door, then, without saying a word, seizes me by the arm and, nearly dropping my camera, begins dragging me out of the car. There's a split-second late reaction, but once my mind realizes what's happening, my immediate instinct is to fight against him with all my might. For a brief moment, I'm completely consumed by the object of releasing Martin's grasp and find myself wrestling with him over ownership of my arm. But seeing as I don't have any other choice in the matter, I just as quickly give in, letting him take me, deeper into the alleyway.

In my state of complete and utter disbelief, I find it difficult to understand why this is happening to me and what Martin even intends to do with me. We quickly converge down another passage into a back alley when the realization finally hits me. This is beginning to get more serious than I thought. If Mr. Freeman is willing to risk smuggling me into the Excelsior, I've yet to truly recognize my full worth.

We continue in this way, Martin lugging me along by the arm until we come to a receiving dock with a small set of concrete stairs. We advance up the stairs to a thick metallic door where another Protector stands guarding this entrance. Martin and the Protector glance at each other briefly, then nod, a signal of some kind, and the Protector opens the door to let us in. So, this is how we enter the building, through the servants' quarters.

The door leads into a small vestibule, then into a kitchen. The kitchen itself is large, spanning multiple rooms on the first floor, and is lit by old white fluorescent lights that have faded. It's quiet enough in here that you can even hear a slight hum coming from the bulbs.

And then there are the servants in the kitchen.

Now, I wasn't sure when or how I was going to explain this to you, but I didn't want to leave you wondering about it, being that for a long time I didn't know the answer myself. Part of me still wishes I never found out, but there would be no use, because if I didn't know then, I would definitely know now.

"What do they do to Secondary Unthinkers?" I asked Finn. Like most things, it had been a mystery to me, and not by accident. What reason is there for Primaries to know the business of a Secondary? As always, Finn was the one who told me. But this, this was the first time I had seen it in person. There was no point in bringing it up any other time in this story, so I have no choice but to tell you now.

"They don't get Purged to the mines or Pacified," said

Finn, "they don't punish them the same way they would a Primary."

"What do they do instead?" I asked.

What they do instead is something far more humiliating, to make them regret for ever conceiving a traitorous thought. What they do is turn them into Librivoxes—the permanent servants of the Engineers. Of course, it's not as simple as that, it never is. For a long time, they used to cut their tongues off too, rip them right out of their heads. But new rules were set in place, so now they just cover their mouths, so that they can't speak, along with the electronic tags affixed to their ankles. They've stolen away their voices, silenced them. Why give a voice to an Unthinker?

But that's not the end of it. The cutting of the tongues is reserved strictly for any further Unthinkables committed while under servitude, nor are they limited to just this punishment. They can have their lips sewn shut, their voice box cut out, their jaw wired close, and in some cases, they'll even have the whole jaw removed.

They don't represent the Secondaries, not anymore. How could a Secondary ever agree with those such as the terrorists? God forbid they utter a word. "It only takes a little convincing," is what they say, "until they've got you, whatever you do, don't give them a chance." They figure that if even a Secondary is susceptible to becoming an Unthinker, then there would be no hope of curing them, they are beyond help. They've willingly chosen not only to turn their backs on their own caste but to give up the powers and freedoms granted as a Secondary. Deranged. If you want to be a slave, be a useful one. Now they are a class of people completely removed from society. They don't belong anywhere.

As we make our way across the kitchen, Martin and I steady our pace to move in the same fashion as the Librivoxes, in an effort to keep to ourselves. I try not to move my eyes too much, for fear of meeting them with someone else's, I don't want one of them to catch me staring. But I know that they must also want to stare. Who is this strange man in white? I am as much of a mystery to them as they are to me. I don't know where to look, this room is full of faces, or better yet, eyes without faces, for it's the eyes that are the only discernible feature about them. I give up trying and decide to keep my head down.

Although I don't see it, I can tell that a few of the Librivoxes have started looking our way, as the sounds of movement—either from the clanking of metal pots or ceramic plates—have stopped, all of them pausing to stare as we pass. All the time we're in the kitchen it's quiet, too quiet, I feel as if I've gone deaf. You walk into a room full of people staring at you, expecting to hear voices, at least a whisper, but not here. It's all the more disturbing. Not a single mouth in here has been left uncovered.

There's this phenomenon that happens, whenever your surroundings don't seem to align with the sounds your mind thinks it ought to be hearing. In this case, it's the sounds of voices. Your mind will attempt to recreate the sound by memory, like filling in the gaps, giving the illusion of noise. But that's all it really is, an illusion, I hear nothing.

Suddenly from somewhere in the kitchen—I don't dare to turn my head—I hear the voice of a woman, a Protector, yell: "Get back to work!" which confirms my suspicion.

Oddly enough, I think to look among this room of eyes, but what would be the use of that? No one I know would be here, no one except that woman, the one with braided hair, but I don't think she'd be here either; even from our brief meeting in the Soma Bar, I could tell she's too cunning to let herself get caught.

We exit through a door at the other end of the kitchen, the door leading directly into a corridor. The lighting in here feels just as lifeless, a few of the bulbs flickering overhead. More Librivoxes stare as we pass. Further down the corridor, we stop in front of a service elevator. Its doors slide open, and we step in. Martin pushes the button for the floor, and I notice him press the highest number in the building. Finally, we begin our slow ascent up the elevator shaft, rising ever so steadily to the top. But even in this, I feel myself begin to sink. A ripple of uneasiness moves over me, like a tremor deep within the earth. What is waiting for me on the top floor?

Chapter 26
Penthouse.

The elevator comes to a sudden halt. We've reached the top. The space around me has shifted somehow. I am no longer in my own reality, but a different one, one where if I am not careful, I might get lost in. Nevertheless, I feel surprisingly whole. I'm ready for whatever awaits me on the other side. I'm all here. Don't lose yourself.

We step out of the elevator into the corridor, the same kind as before, grey and dreary. Moving along it, we then enter through a door into another corridor, this one nothing like the ones that came before it. The walls are finished in an off-white color with gold trim. The lighting is soft, and the floor is carpeted in brown with gold motifs. We're no longer in the servants' quarters. Like Mr. Freeman, the Excelsior has a hidden side to it as well.

"Come," says Martin, advancing down the hall, "this way."

I forgot he was here; he rarely ever speaks. I also hadn't realized when he let go of my arm, but funny enough, now that he has, I feel detached and will get lost if I stray too far.

I follow closely behind him, touring the halls until we meet

Mr. Freeman waiting outside the door of the penthouse. There's a loud babble of voices coming from behind the door. Is this it? Is this the party?

"Finally," says Mr. Freeman, coming up and drawing me forward, "I was beginning to get worried. I hope the journey here wasn't too much trouble."

"No sir, not at all," Martin replies.

I shift my eyes quickly at him. Easy for you to say, you weren't the one getting dragged around.

"Good, come along now," says Mr. Freeman, "they've been expecting us."

We step up to the door, Martin opens it for us. We appear on the scene of a luxurious party in the penthouse's lounge. The lounge is large and open, with the ceiling extending upwards to the second level of the apartment. A balcony runs along the top. In the center, a huge chandelier hangs, ornamented with crystals. I've never known them to be so vast in size. The room is full of guests, some dressed in black, the color of the Engineers, and some in the vibrant attire of the Secondaries, and all talking amongst themselves without a care in the world. And then there's me, the only one in white. At least I've managed to wear something nice. There are even a few Librivoxes wandering about in their grey uniforms, waiting on guests with trays of drinks and appetizers.

"Go with the other Protectors Martin," says Mr. Freeman, "we'll see you later." Martin leaves and goes into the kitchen. "Now, let's see. Where are they?" he says to himself as he begins skimming the room.

I stand here, my heart racing. I thought this was supposed to be a small party. I'm sure by now some people have noticed me. And how can they not? I hate to think that I'm being whispered about by these Engineers, and of nothing nice of course. Slowly more and more guests have become aware of my presence. I can feel their eyes creeping all over me. I have never wanted to do anything more desperately than to sink into the floor. What have I gotten myself into? Why am I here? I don't belong here. Then again, I don't belong anywhere, but especially not here. I'm not nervous anymore, I'm angry. Why did he bring me here, just to be gawked at? If I'm going to make it through the night, I have to be willing to put my anger aside and ignore the thought of what everyone here must be telling each other. Why should I care what they think of me anyway? They're not good people to begin with, so maybe it's a good thing that they hate me.

I look up, taking in my surroundings. In the middle of the room, underneath the chandelier, is a small seating area: four bright orange leather sofas arranged in a circle, with a table in the middle. On one side, a large bar spans the wall of the room, and a few billiard tables. Outside on the terrace, they've set up a dance floor, which is currently full of other guests. On a thinly raised platform tucked away in the corner of the room, a band provides music for the party.

It all looks so fun, and even under the right circumstances, I would've even liked to join in on the excitement. But as of now, I can't, given the choice.

I look around some more, but this time, on my second viewing of the room, I shift my focus instead on what the Secondaries are wearing. For the most part, Secondaries have a very bizarre sense of fashion. Not a single one of them looks alike, either in style or pattern. Granted the opportunity to wear what one likes, they've taken full advantage of it.

Some wear outfits made of chrome or metallic materials, foil dresses composed of silver and gold, and holographic fibers—the iridescent kind that changes colors in the light. And some adorned in spangles or sequins.

Then there are the less flashy outfits, the ones made of lacework, mesh, or gauze; large puffy clothes made of faux furs printed with stripes or spots. And yet somehow, these outfits manage to look just as elaborate and complex as the rest. And then there's the use of color—an essential element in the design of these outfits. A stark contrast to what they force the Librivoxes to wear with their grey uniforms. Secondaries aren't assigned a specific color, as long as what they wear is neither white nor simple. The only noticeable advantage to this is that you'd never mistake one for the other. But even in their constant pursuit of trying to look different, they all somehow end up coming across as the same.

But it doesn't stop at the clothes. There are also the cosmetics; it's what tie their outfits together. Some have faces painted in luminescent or neon makeup, sprinkled with glitter, or bedazzled with rhinestones. And all glistened with oil, to give the skin an unnatural shine. And hair, either dyed or bleached, with too many styles to name. I should think most of them actually wear wigs as opposed to their real hair. Some have their hair knotted with tinsel and slicked back with gel and glitter, rolled up, puffed out, tied back, and—then I see her, the woman with braided hair. I take another look to make sure, and it's her alright, and for a moment, all other thoughts disappear. It's been nearly half a year since I last saw her. Does she even remember me?

"Evette darling, over here," Mr. Freeman calls out, signaling her to come.

So, he knows her, the woman with braided hair. Evette, this is her name. Was this her way of contacting me, has Mr. Freeman brought me here just to see her? Then he really must be an Unthinker after all. She looks up, smiles, and begins to walk towards us. She's wearing a short luminescent lavender dress, sequenced, with a high neck and long sleeves. Her face sparkles with glitter. If she didn't have her braids in, I might not have recognized her.

She comes closer, blood rushes into my cheeks. I didn't think I'd ever see her again. But now she can tell me all about the resistance. I've been in the dark too long. But as she approaches, I notice something in her face. Within a small fraction of a glance, she flashes me a piercing stare, intensified by her shimmering silver eyes: a look of dread. It only lasted less than a second, but it was enough to shake me to my core. She remembers me alright, but she isn't the one I'm here to meet. She didn't expect to see me again, and of all places, I must have caught her completely off guard.

"Hello, darling," Mr. Freeman says, kissing her on the cheek.

Are they? No, he's too old for her, and she's too young. Though I doubt that would stop an Engineer.

"Where's Meltzer and the others?" he says.

"They're sitting out on the terrace," says Evette, "I'll go get them for you."

"Thank you," he says.

She turns, heading in the direction of the terrace. As she passes, she casts me a quick side-eyed glance. "What the hell are you doing here?" she is saying in her head.

"What do you think?" Mr. Freeman says, "I bet you've never been to a place like this before, have you?"

I glare up at him. I feel as if I've been tricked. Once again, my expectations have not been met. So, what then? Have we really come here to meet his friends?

"No, sir," I say, "no, I haven't."

When Evette returns, she's accompanied by three Engineers, two women, and one man.

"Thank you Evette," says Mr. Freeman, "you can go now."

She says nothing, but simply nods, then leaves. I try to watch which direction she heads in, so that afterward, if there's time, I can speak with her privately, but my attention is quickly pulled away.

"I'd like you to meet my colleagues," says Mr. Freeman, drawing out one arm in front to introduce them, "this is Ms. Vivica Kohen, head producer of Apocalypse Now. Dr. Seneca Sinclair, who's head of public relations. And this is Mr. Mark Meltzer—"

"Whose line of work you are not at liberty to disclose Frank," says Mr. Meltzer.

"We've heard many interesting things about you," says Dr. Sinclair, shaking my hand.

"Oh," I say, quite surprised that I've been spoken about behind my back. I don't really know what things Mr. Freeman can possibly say about me, there's not much to tell; and with what little there is to, why tell it in the first place?

"Why don't we sit while we discuss it, shall we," says Mr. Freeman, leading us to the ring of sofas. As we walk, I try to look around to see where Evette is, but she must have disappeared into another room because she's gone again.

Chapter 27
Victim.

Mr. Meltzer and Ms. Kohen sit together on the sofa opposite me, across the center table, flanked by Dr. Sinclair and Mr. Freeman in the armchairs—Dr. Sinclair on the left and Mr. Freeman on the right—and all facing me as I sit awkwardly on the remaining sofa alone. I'm fortunate to have my camera with me, or else I wouldn't know what to do with my hands.

Once we're all settled in, there's a short delay in the conversation, as if they're all deciding in their minds who should be the one to speak first. Mr. Meltzer is the first to break the silence, but just as he begins talking, another Engineer suddenly approaches and plops himself down in the empty space beside me, pulling everyone's attention, including mine.

"Well, well, what do we have here?" he says playfully through his deep voice. He's talking about me. "Oh, let me guess, did Frank drag you into this? This has his name written all over it."

His witty attitude is quite a pleasant surprise. I never would've thought an Engineer could behave like this, it's very becoming.

"Please, Bryan, do you mind?" says Mr. Meltzer, as if this sort of thing was a usual occurrence, "we were in the middle of a serious conversation."

The Engineer named Bryan shoots Mr. Meltzer an annoyed look as he takes a sip from his drink. The man has shaggy grey hair, a scruffy beard, and is wearing heavy cologne, which, combined with the smell of alcohol on his breath, violates my nose with such a harsh scent. The top half of his button-up is open, with strands of chest hair peeking out from underneath.

"You know I've noticed that you guys never seem to invite me to one of your little meetings," says Bryan.

It occurs to me now that something about him feels oddly familiar. I think I recognize him from somewhere.

"Now's not the time Bryan," says Mr. Meltzer, "if you want to stay, then be quiet."

"Don't worry," he says, with a burp, "you won't even know I'm here."

It's strange, really, the more he drones on, the more I can't shake the feeling that I know him somehow, or at the very least know *of* him. I think it has something to do with his voice.

"This is very important Bryan," says Dr. Sinclair, "we can tell you all about it later, but right now, it's best if you go."

"You know, telling me that only makes me want to stay even more," he says, swirling his drink in the air.

"Listen Bryan," says Mr. Meltzer, "if you don't leave now, I'm going to call your supervisor, I think it's about time they find a new replacement."

"You know I'm beginning to think I'm not welcomed here," he half whispers to me under his breath, "say, how about you and I blow this joint; I know a place down in the Fourth Sector where we can really party."

And then it clicks. Is it really him? I look into his face, beneath that mess of hair of his. It is. No wonder I thought he looked familiar. He's the Operator, or rather, he is his likeness and voice. I hardly recognize him with all that extra fuzz on his face, but the more I look, the more I see it now. This man, the face of the Operator? This is both deeply amusing and sad. Everyone thinks he's the one in charge of the whole city.

"Ignore him please," says Mr. Meltzer.

"Could you keep your voice down!" Bryan yells back, "can't you see you're making the boy nervous?"

"Can you for once in your life act like an Engineer?" says Mr. Meltzer.

"What? Am I not allowed to wonder why you dragged over some poor Primary all the way over here, and for what, another one of your crummy schemes?"

"You've had too much to drink Bryan." Says Mr. Meltzer.

"Alright, you know what, I'll go," he says, "but only because you guys are being mean." He gets up, but before he leaves, he turns to me one last time and says, "be careful with them. You don't know what you're getting yourself into," and storms off.

"You'll have to forgive us," says Dr. Sinclair, "he's usually less… attentive."

"Forget about him," says Mr. Meltzer, "let's just get this over with before he decides to come back."

In all my life, I never would have thought.

"Now, I'm sure as you know by now," says Mr. Meltzer, "there's been a sudden rise in abduction cases occurring throughout the city in relation to Unthinker terrorist attacks, and we believe that you might have some information that could possibly help benefit us in our work to eradicate these brain jobs, once and for all."

I say nothing but stupidly stare back, not knowing what to say. There's too much to unpack, and all at once. I was not prepared for this. They all seem to notice my confusion, and Dr. Sinclair quickly steps in to speak next.

"Frank told us there was an incident that occurred about a week ago in the exclusion zone during a rescue mission," she says, "and you were there to witness it: a hostage situation. And we were wondering if you could tell us more about it?"

"What?" I say, even more bewildered.

Slowly, I'm beginning to understand why I'm here, but every time I think I have an idea of what this all might be about, a new piece of information is revealed, and suddenly I find myself asking a different question—one even more baffling than the last. How many layers does this mystery have?

"We apologize for bringing it up," she says, "we know how hard it can be to talk about these sorts of things, and I promise you, we wouldn't want to ask you about this unless it was important to us." She leans in, "please, can you tell us what happened?"

I begin going over it in my head, thinking of the right way to respond. What do they expect me to say? My focus is suddenly drawn behind Dr. Sinclair, where I spot Evette sitting in a velvet armchair at the other side of the room, glaring at me covertly, trying to get in on the conversation.

I've almost forgotten—now there's another problem, one that I haven't had to worry about, that is, until today. But unlike my other problems, all that it requires of me is to not get caught, but now not just for my sake, but for Evette's as well, because now I know her name.

A name alone is such a trivial thing: merely a title for one's own self. But for an Unthinker, it holds more power than this. It can also be a death sentence. As an Unthinker, if you're caught knowing the names of other Unthinkers still on Circuit, they'll beat them out of you first, before coming for them next. You might be able to resist for a little while, give up a false name or two, but only for a little while. Eventually, everything will come flooding out, one way or another. So, for now, the knowledge of my name remains only known by me.

You're going to need to lie, I tell myself. This won't be easy, so you're just going to have to start making things up as you go.

"I—I don't remember much from that day," I say. This isn't true, I remember every second of it, the memory replaying itself in my head. It's hard not to forget. "It all happened so fast," another lie. It felt like time had slowed down, or as if I had been severed from it altogether. I felt numb. "I'm not sure what you want me to tell you," I say, "I was frightened, frightened that she would get hurt. I can't even begin to describe what it must have been like for her."

I'm angry with myself now, for doing this. But in the moment, what choice do I have? I should never have come; I had that choice.

"Oh, but you must," says Mr. Meltzer, "you must have some idea of what it was like. You did meet with the victim, after all. How did that go? Did she have a chance to speak her mind?"

He's very direct with these questions. He doesn't bother trying to hide his motives behind some false idea, unlike Mr. Freeman. He has nothing to hide.

"She was... disturbed," I say, a bit unsure of myself, though I don't know why. This was the first true thing I've said since we've started, "that sort of thing does something to a person. I'm sorry I couldn't be of more help."

I hang my head in shame, but from everyone else's view, they must think I'm mournful. Does Rachel know what she's being used for?

"We understand," says Dr. Sinclair. She turns, looks at Mr. Freeman, he returns the look and nods in agreement, then she turns back again at me. What is she about to divulge? "You see..." she pauses, "we came to the conclusion that if we could find a way to make the victim's story sound upsetting enough, we would publicize her traumatic experience and use it as a form of leverage against these terrorists."

Why not make something up? That's still an option. Nothing's stopping them from doing it. Usually, when it comes to a situation like this, their first thought is to lie, and then if that doesn't work, they might tell the truth, or just lie again. But I suppose they have no need to lie, not this time, since somebody is already doing the lying for them. They can't truly believe they're the good guys in all this.

"Not enough attention has been brought about these abductions," Ms. Kohen says, "only what's been said in the news, and we hoped that with Ms. Rachel's story, she could shine some light on the subject, since she's the only person who's been rescued."

Not enough attention? What more could they want?

"We've had our monthly Purges," Ms. Kohen goes on, "our Pacifications, but we still lack something in the matter, something on a personal level. The news of her rescue has already garnered so much attention, and that was only the beginning. We'll have her guest speak at Purgings, host Peace Parades, attend Prisoners' Pacifications. She could even get a chance to be on television. We intend for her story to get as much publicity as it can. It will inspire people. We need the whole city to know her pain so that it can also become theirs."

Now I'm scared for Rachel, and what this means for the resistance. They're all insane, every last one of them. No matter how many times they hide behind those stupid smiles, they're all crazy.

I look up once more at Evette, but she's gone. I begin looking around frantically, searching for her, ignoring where I am. Where did she go? Why did she leave? She couldn't have gone far.

"We want to give you another chance to speak with her," says Dr. Sinclair, apparently not having noticed my sudden change in behavior, "if what you say about her current mental state is true, then I'm not sure how long it will be until we can begin to set our plan in motion."

"Those psycho-terrorists must've really messed with her mind," says Mr. Meltzer.

"It's getting late," says Mr. Freeman, "I think it's time for you to go now," he says to me, "I wouldn't want to keep you here any longer than needed. You and I will continue this discussion tomorrow back in my office." He begins writing something on a small piece of paper, then flags down a stray Librivox and gives it to him. The Librivox leaves off in the direction of the kitchen, where I assume he will return with Martin.

And just like that, I feel myself slipping away, like waking up from a dream that I don't wish to wake up from. I don't want to be pulled back into my reality yet. I'd only just got here, and I thought maybe I could get a chance to speak with Evette or, if not that, send a message. Five minutes is all I would need. A minute, ten seconds, I'd do anything just to have a moment to speak with her. Words can't describe how alone I feel right now. I was alone then. Before this, there was no one else to talk to. But this is worse, because now that I finally have someone to talk to, I still can't.

As I stand here waiting for the Librivox to come back with Martin, another Librivox approaches, this one holding a metal serving tray, and on it, a single glass of champagne. He walks directly up to me, presents the drink, offering it like he would with any other guest. Is he allowed to do this? Am I allowed to accept?

I was going to decline, and I would have, if it weren't for the fact that partially tucked underneath the base of the glass, I notice a small white folded piece of paper: it's a note. My eyes widen. It must be from Evette. Who else? She had the Librivox bring it here. That's the thing about the Librivoxes, even after all they've been through, having been silenced and stripped of their status, it doesn't deter the fact that some might still retain the will to rebel.

I look up at the Librivox, and our eyes meet. He's shaking. He's scared half to death. He hints at the paper, signaling me to take it. I give a slight nod.

You might not know it yet, but the Librivoxes are among the most dangerous kinds of Unthinkers to the Engineers. They're the only ones who have even the slightest amount of power to prove that things don't have to continue the way they are now, because, to the Engineers, they're walking contradictions. If only they had their voices.

Even with so much taken away, the position of a Librivox does have its advantages. They have easy access to places that no one else has. You'll never see one walking about on the street; they have their own tunnel system underneath the city and between buildings and districts. They're supposed to be kept hidden away, out of the public eye. The Engineers don't like to bring much attention to their existence, which can come in handy. They've been known to be very good at smuggling things. To an Engineer, they are nothing more than an afterthought. No one would think twice about them or suspect a thing. They can't even speak. Silent but deadly.

I take up the glass, put it to my lips, and with one quick motion, pour all the drink into my mouth and swallow. The champagne has an unusual, unfamiliar taste, but a flavorful one at that, though I can't quite place it. The best I can come close to describing it is it tastes as if my tongue was never meant to come close to tasting something even remotely like this.

I place the empty glass back on the tray, and as I pull my hand away, I carefully yet swiftly slide the note off, concealing it underneath my fingers. Then wiping my mouth, I slip the note down past my palm into the sleeve of my coat. I do this within a matter of seconds and without hesitation. Martin returns, and the Librivox leaves.

I don't know what's in the note, or whether Evette intends for me to read it now and have me write back to her later. In my younger years at Surrogate, I would pass notes like this to other children in secret; whenever Mother Sylvia wasn't looking, we would write to each other this way, our little hands stretched between desks, hoping to share our own thoughts for a change. We would do this for a little while until other children started reporting it, and we'd stopped altogether; you already know what would have happened to us if we were caught doing it. We learned at a young age not to trust anyone. If that's the case, then I don't have enough time. I need to think of something quick.

"Martin, would you kindly escort him safely back home to his Habitat," says Mr. Freeman, "and don't forget the other thing."

Martin nods and grabs my arm.

"I'd like to go to the bathroom," I say rather suddenly; this was all I could think of. They all look up at me, slightly surprised, as if they only expected me to speak unless spoken to, I can see I've caused a disturbance. "If I may," I add.

"You may," says Mr. Freeman indifferently, "and then you can go."

As we leave, Mr. Freeman begins to go into a spiel about how he thinks they can instill better security measures for Primary citizens, but I don't get to hear this as Martin escorts me away.

We enter the penthouse kitchen through a double-hinged door. There are more Librivoxes here, and some stare as I pass, but by this time, I've gotten used to it. There are also a few Protectors here, sitting down in a small waiting area.

I enter the kitchen bathroom, lock the door, pull down the toilet seat lid, and sit, my body trembling from the neck down to my chest, though not from fear, but excitement. I've been waiting for a moment like this for what felt like forever. I was beginning to think the time might never arrive, and out of all the other things, this seemed the easiest to wait for. But once this is over and done with, there's still a lot more to come, and with those, they'll be even more challenging. Time is my enemy, but it is also my friend. At least there's one thing out of the way. I pull the note out, unfold it, and read.

Freedom Tower
8:30
Purging day

I say nothing, but sit motionless, reading the words over in my head. She wants to meet with me. After all this time, I finally get to speak with her, with someone. I am not alone. I toss my head back, shut my eyes, take a long deep breath, and breathe out. "Thank you."

I stand up and lift the toilet seat lid. I look down once more at the note in my hands, now slightly crumpled and softened from the sweat. I won't be needing it anymore. It's simple enough to remember, and why risk having it? I drop the note into the toilet, watching the ink from the paper begin to slowly fade away, and flush. It's gone; nothing left now but the memory.

It's strange how time never truly stops. With every second that passes, nothing ever exists just as it is, we have to keep moving. It's these moments that make me feel like time doesn't exist. I exit the bathroom, Martin seizes my arm, and we walk.

There are many things I still don't know and probably never will, but I'm fortunate to know as much as I do now.

VI

Assimilate

Chapter 28
De-file.

I sit silently, facing forward, in the back of Mr. Freeman's car, gripping tightly on my camera as it rests in my lap. You're alright now, you did it, you made it back safe, back to your own reality.

My body sways with the motion of the car as we veer into my district. The streets are empty. It's late, too late, everyone in my Habitat is asleep by now. I glance over at Martin. He's sitting in the opposite corner of the car, stiff and stone-faced, his hands clasped firmly around his knees, concentrating all his energy on his posture. He's a Protector alright, a man always on the defense. He looks like he's about five seconds away from defecating on the spot, and I have to catch myself from laughing. I roll my eyes. If he was alone, would he still try to appear intimidating, or is he doing this all for show? Either way, it's stupid. I can't imagine what kind of training Protectors must undergo to garner such obedience. Luckily, the end of the night is drawing to a close, and so is my time with Martin.

As we approach my Habitat, the car slows down, then stops. The chauffeur gets out and opens the door. I lean forward, and as I get up, I notice movement in the corner of my eye. I turn to Martin. He has one arm drawn out towards me, and before him, in his hand, he's holding a file. The muscles in my neck begin to tense up, I can feel a small lump forming in my throat; saliva fills my mouth. I look down at the file, then up at him, his face still blank and unresponsive. I swallow my uneasiness, reach out my arm, and take it from him. Is this what I think it is? I read the name printed on the file, a woman's name. Is it my mother's? I look up at Martin, but his stare offers neither confirmation nor denial. I quickly exit the car and enter my Habitat.

I arrive at my apartment, unlock the door, and step inside. I slowly close the door behind me, being mindful of how loud I am. It shuts with an audible click. I turn the corner from the doorway and see Curtis in bed, asleep. I'm surprised he didn't wait for me to return before deciding to go to bed. I was expecting him to be standing in the doorway as soon as I entered. I even prepared what I was going to say, but I suppose he was too tired and decided it wasn't worth the trouble. Work and Thought Blockers can do that to you. I take my shoes off and make my way across the room to my bed, watching Curtis, hoping he doesn't wake from the noise. When I come to my bed, I quietly place my shoes beside it and sit, my back to him, the file hidden from view.

I notice the emptiness of the file, the weightlessness of it in my hands. Is this real? I was hoping for there to be more. But this is all that's left. Of course, I shouldn't have expected much. They don't bother keeping that many records of people like this anymore, even ones from so long ago. Most of them had either been destroyed or De-filed: deliberately hidden with the intent that they would get lost or forgotten, since they were classified as "unimportant."

Nowadays, all they do is discard of their records at the waste facility, along with their human counterpart. I'm surprised Mr. Freeman managed to recover anything on her at all. I'd only just asked him a few hours ago.

I should feel happy, or at the very least content, for obtaining such secure files, but what I feel instead, is dread.

Now that I have it in front of me, in my hands, I don't want to open it. But isn't this what you wanted? You can't say no now, or else you'll never truly be able to live with yourself. She could still be alive, there's still that chance, a slim chance, but a chance nonetheless. But it's not worth the trouble of getting my hopes up. I know why I'm scared, and why I don't want to open it, it's because I already know what's inside. I take a proper hold of the file, untie the string which fastens it shut, and open it. The first thing I see is a note from Mr. Freeman:

This is as much information we could salvage on her, all other records were destroyed.

- F

So, this really is all that's left. Moving on to her records, I notice these papers have seen some age. The pages now are an ivory color, and their texter is soft. No one's touched these documents in years; I'll have to be gentle with them then. The first few pages are just the usual status files, a fingerprint sheet, and her Recall registration card. There are photos of her, like that of mug shots. The photos are not in color, and are a bad quality, but I can still make out the brown hair and brown eyes. Her eyes are big, and her face looks older than I remember, but the basic features are mostly the same. Time has warped all things, even memories.

There is something odd about her appearance, something uncanny. Though these are pictures of my mother, she is nowhere to be found in these photos. She has left herself entirely. Maybe if the photos were in color, I could see something of her, not just the still image of her body caught in rigor mortis. But it's her, nonetheless. I refrain from looking at the photos any longer, they're too much to bear.

I read her name over again; her name of course is something I will keep to myself. But what I can tell you is that at that time she'd still been allowed to have a surname, instead of a Cryptogram. Although Secondary Cryptograms are different from ours, the fact of the matter is that they haven't lost the use of their surnames—the ones inherited from their fathers. The difference between Primaries and Secondaries is that we don't have fathers, at least not to the Operator.

I never knew my father; at any rate, it's forbidden. Once a woman becomes pregnant with her impregnator's child, she is forced to lose all contact with him. That's one thing, no matter how hard I try, I know I'll never find: my father. This is the only time I'll ever mention him, not that I'm upset about it, but I find no use in speaking about him, especially now. As far as the Operator is concerned, he doesn't exist.

This surname, however, would have come from my grandfather.

The next set of documents is her case records, everything they've got on her from the Recall Clinic, and so on. There's not much to explain, but I'll give you a brief outline of her file. The records say she was admitted to the Recall Clinic, having been charged with attempted kidnapping, and refusal to surrender her child, where she was later declared an Unthinker, and Purged to the mines. The rest of her case records haven't been updated since. Even after all they've done, this bit of knowledge gives me hope.

Finally, I come to the last document in the file, a singular slip of paper. I take it up and hold it out before me in my hands. At first, I'm unsure of what I'm looking at, I've never seen one of these before, only heard. Everyone would eventually get one, but after a while, the Operator decided to stop issuing them to people, following it was found there was no use in having them anymore. But my mother received one before the decree to go without them altogether had been sent out. It takes me a moment until I realize what it is. What I hold in my hands is her death certificate.

Something quick and sharp sinks within my chest, weighing me down, then a burst of heat and chemicals flare throughout my body, seeping into my nervous system. Inside me, a bomb's been set off. I have to catch myself to sit up. There's a tightness in my throat, a sharp burning sensation, it's suffocating me, I can't breathe. I open my mouth, and something slips, a broken piece of speech. I cover my mouth to stop the noise from escaping. My body begins to tremble, and my eyes fill with tears. I drop the paper, gripping at my chest.

I'm in shock. I kept telling myself that she was somehow alive, but I already knew my mother was dead. I didn't need a piece of paper to tell me this, and still, here I am. So, she really is gone after all, and for a moment, I'd been given a hint of possibility, just a hint, but even that was too much hope. I just wanted so badly to know. It was my way of giving me closure, I needed proof, I thought it would make me feel better, because I had nothing. But it didn't work, because in the end, she's still dead.

Chapter 29
Freedom Square.

Curtis and I drift along the sidewalk, my hand tucked in my coat pocket, fiddling with the watch. The air today is at peak humidity. Any day now they'll turn on the filtration, but until they do, the mist will slowly settle itself in, filling up as much space as possible, lining the city in a cool vapor. The edges of the world turn into a sort of haze, you can't tell where it begins or where it ends.

"You know, I was surprised when you insisted on leaving the apartment early for the Purging," says Curtis, "lately, you haven't been showing too much appreciation for these sorts of things, I was beginning to get worried."

I tend not to put too much thought into what Curtis says anymore. I don't blame him for the way he is. All I can tell myself is that it's not his fault. But I can't help but think that maybe one day he'll be the reason I won't escape. I can't argue with him about anything because I know if I show even the slightest hint of criticism, he'll report me to the Operator as soon as possible. Whenever he speaks, all I can do is nod my head in agreement. I like to keep our conversations brief; that, or I try to find a way to quickly change the subject.

"Have I done something to bother you?" he says rather abruptly, "or does this have something to do with your previous roommate?"

My focus snaps back to the sidewalk in front of me. Did he seriously just ask me that? There's no way we're doing this right now, the absolute gall of him.

"What are you talking about?" I say quickly, trying to act naive.

"It is about him, isn't it?" he says.

He's still pushing it? I guess I couldn't go on ignoring him forever.

"You're afraid if we get close," he continues, "I'll end up disappointing you like he did. I never considered what it must've been like for you. You must feel pretty ripped off, to have had an Unthinker as a roommate. But I promise you, I wouldn't break your trust like that. I'm nothing like those brain jobs."

Oh, so that's what he thinks is going on? Well, if you look at it that way, I guess it makes sense. But do I really want to go through lying about Finn again, and to Curtis of all people?

"Forget about him," Curtis goes on, "don't give him the authority over your mind to keep tormenting you like this. You'll see, years from now his existence won't mean anything to you."

I think I've heard enough.

"No," I say, playing up to him, "it's not that."

Curtis looks at me confused; this is the first time I've ever told him he was wrong about anything. He turns forward again, and we walk together in silence. Suddenly he steps in front of me, stops. "Then what is it?" he says sternly, "because I've tried being patient with you, but you're just so stubborn, tell me, why don't you want to talk to me?"

I glare at him, and we just stare at each other as he waits for my response. He has some nerve to think I'd ever want to be friends with someone like him; his personality alone is enough reason to stay away.

I roll my eyes. "Just hurry up," I groan, dragging him by

the shoulder, "or we're going to be late."

The roads and buildings are coated in a thin layer of dew, giving them a glossy, sleek finish as the nearby lights from drones, flickering neon signs, and television screens reflect off them. Large water droplets trickle down from the firmament, the vast maze of wires and cables that act as the city's nervous system. My hair is greasy from the fumes, and my face sticky. I'm all damp beneath my coat from the sweat.

We come to the checkpoint leading into the next district and get in line, one behind the other. When it's my turn, I show the Protector my card, he scans it, signals me to walk forward. I go through the metal detector when the alarm suddenly goes off, and I jump from the noise. One of the Protectors on standby quickly aims his machine gun at me, charges it, making a sharp metallic click. I freeze as his flashlight shines in my face, causing my eyes to dilate.

"Lift your hands and don't move!" shouts the Protector through his mask. My heart pounds inside my chest. I spread my arms out, and another Protector comes up to me, this one holding a hand-held metal detector, and begins waving it over me. I stand motionless, staring at the Protector through his tinted goggles. Finn told me if a Protector ever pointed his gun at me, to look at him in the eyes, that he might hesitate to shoot, leaving a small opening for a chance to escape. Not like I would get far.

As the Protector scans past my left pocket, the metal detector alerts him that it's sensed something. I'd forgotten to take out the watch.

The Protector reaches into my pocket, takes up the watch, and begins curiously looking at it. "What kind of weapon is this?" he says.

"It's a pocket watch," I manage to stammer out.

He stares at the watch for a moment, then back at me. "Don't forget to empty your pockets next time," he says grudgingly, handing back the watch, "now move along." I put the watch back in my pocket, grab Curtis, and continue walking.

"Why'd you bring that stupid thing with you?" he says.

Of all the things, that's what he's worried about?

"Just shut up," I say, "and keep walking."

The clock tower was still in operation in the early fifties but was shut down sometime after my admittance into Surrogate and has long been dormant ever since, its hands forever stuck at six o'clock. Yet, even when I was young, I could still remember the square had always been left untouched by the rest of the city, apart from Purgings. My guess is that no one ever went there, since that's where they used to publicly beat and execute Secondaries who tried to defy social order back in the earlier days of Apocalypse, when the world seemed so different, yet somehow the same.

All things considered, there had been a brief moment in time when life was what one may have once called *ordinary*. Not perfect by any means, but better compared to everything else. When I was a child there were no Purge Rallies, no Prisoners' Pacifications. We'd thought things were finally getting better, oh how wrong we were. Though on looking back, there were many signs, many warnings, for what was to come. You'd think we would learn from the past, but no. Time seems to be moving backward somehow, and from the looks of it, it doesn't appear to be slowing down.

How I'd do anything to go back, and relive the life I'd lost; I have to correct that, I did not lose my life, it was stolen. But I can't go back, those moments are gone now, and I'm stuck here. The past casts a long shadow over this city, and I'm caught, right in the middle of it.

So that's it, Primaries avoid coming here, I suppose out of respect for Secondaries, aside from days like today, because today there is a Purging. Oh, how times have changed.

There are far more people here already than I had anticipated; it won't be long now until the whole square is full. I know I can't go in through the front of the clock tower, too many people will see, so I'll have to enter through the back from the alleyway.

Curtis and I merge with the crowd, all of us moving collectively as one through the rapidly narrowing space, working together to funnel everyone through the security check. As soon as we're deep enough in the crowd that we can't avoid rubbing shoulders with someone else, I slow down, trying to be discreet, before coming to a complete stop. Curtis continues without noticing, and I watch as he gets further out of view. I'm waiting for him to be far enough away that I can't see him, nor he see me, and what I'm about to do next. When I finally lose complete sight of him in the crowd, I simply turn around and casually walk away.

I know what I'm doing must look suspicious, traveling against the movement of everyone else. But right now, I can afford to, supposing I'm able to keep myself from attracting any more unwanted attention. I try to keep a composed attitude, making sure to avoid any eye contact. So far, I've managed to hold a straight face, but inside, I feel like I'm going to break down at any moment.

When I make it out of the crowd, I keep back and stay close to the walls of the buildings, trying my best to blend in with the background. As I come nearer to the next alleyway, I slow my pace, straighten my posture, and when I am certain no one is looking my way, I veer into it as naturally as possible, like a car on a motorized track, hoping that no one's noticed or took suspicion.

Without looking back, I follow along the passage until I come to the first bend, then continue in the path leading around to the back of the tower. As soon as I turn the corner and am out of sight, I break into a sprint and begin hurrying down the passage. My body immediately registers this sudden change in heart rate as a sign that I'm in danger, and I go into a panic, nearly slipping several times on the wet floor as I run. I begin to sweat, my heart racing. Am I being followed? Did someone see me? Are those my footsteps I hear, or someone else's?

I come to a fork, stop, and peer my head around the corner, down the passage that breaks off into the square. The people there have their backs turned to me, they won't see me. I continue down the other passage until I arrive at the back entrance of the clock tower. I'm surprised at how much my feet hurt; our shoes aren't designed for running. I step up to the door, turn the handle, it's unlocked. Just as I'm about to pull it open, a sudden thought comes to mind, and I stop. I begin to look around at my surroundings. I recognize this place. I've been here before, once, a long time ago, with my mother. It was on that day, when she'd brought me here to see the clock tower for the first time, she pulled me in here. At the time I didn't understand why she did that, but I know now that she was trying to hide us from the Psi-Ops. I think I should go inside. Now's not the time to reminisce about the past. I pull the door open and go in.

The inside of the tower looks like it was midway through reconstruction before it was abandoned. They'd gutted its insides, hollowed it out, and left behind only the exoskeleton. There's some scaffolding along the walls, paint cans on the floor, plastic buckets, drop cloths. The empty walls have been covered in a plastic wrapping marked with caution tape. Some of the windows are plastered with old newspapers, and the ones without glass installed are draped with frosted vinyl sheets. There's a cage elevator, but the power's been shut off. I make my way up the stairs to the third floor, the steps making slight cracks beneath my feet.

The top of the tower is dark, illuminated only by the outside light coming from the square. It's better this way, easier to hide.

So, this is where me and Evette are meeting, it's not much, but it'll do. I wonder how long until she'll be here. I check my watch, I'm half an hour early. I guess I'll just have to wait here until she arrives. Suddenly I hear footsteps behind me, then a voice:

"What are you doing here?"

Chapter 30
Clock Tower.

I turn to see a woman standing amidst the shadows. She steps forward, emerging into view, her face sparkling in the light. It's Evette. She must've been hiding behind one of the support beams. She's wearing an elegant lavender fur coat, with a matching hat, and arm muff. It amuses me to see her all dressed up like this, she looks like she just came back from a party, which might actually be true. Every time I see her, she has on a new outfit, each one vastly different from the last. I wonder what she'll wear next.

She comes closer, glaring at me with her shimmering silver eyes. Beneath the layer of rhinestones that adorn her face, her skin glistens in a liquid-smooth glaze. I realize that her under-eye makeup has gotten all runny, with what's left now a wet, sparkling mess of purple glitter. Has she been crying? No, she hasn't. It's just been smudged from the mist. There's a reason we Primaries don't often wear fabric clothing, apart from the heat, it's the air, it's too damp. Our clothes would get soaked within minutes of walking outside. The fur on her coat has already begun to clump together in knots. She must not be familiar with how humid Primary districts get. Then is she really from the same district as Mr. Freeman? It's a good thing she's got her braids in, or else her curls would get frizzy.

"Didn't you hear me?" she says, "I said, what are you doing here?"

"What do you mean?" I say, "you told me to—"

"I told you to come at 8:30," she says, walking up to me, "in case one of us was being followed. I only just got here a few minutes ago myself. What if someone saw us both come in here?"

"Don't worry," I say, "I wasn't followed."

"But how can you be sure?" she says in a concerned voice.

I wasn't anticipating this being how we'd start our secret meeting, but I suppose it's best to get these sorts of things out of the way before we go any further.

"I—I don't know," I say, "but I'm sure I would've noticed."

"Well, maybe someone didn't follow you," she says, "but someone tried to follow me."

Hearing this, I feel a sudden heightened sense in my awareness. I haven't been fully conscious of my surroundings until now. I'm alert.

"What?" I say, "are you sure?"

She turns away from me, and thinks for a moment. "He must have been a Psi-Op," she says, "it's alright though. I managed to lose him down in the Fourth Sector, but by then, he'd been following me for half an hour."

It's this last remark that has me feeling even more worried than before. Slowly I'm beginning to doubt whether I should have come here. And now, a new fear has been added to my list of things to watch out for.

"Are you sure you lost him?" I say seriously.

She turns back and looks at me. "Yes," she says, "he was easy to spot out. I would've noticed if he were still on me."

Even as she says this, she still manages to keep her composure. This assurance in her voice helps release some of the tension within me, just enough to make room for a bit of faith.

"But why would you have a Psi-Op?" I ask.

"Who knows?" she says, "maybe they're looking for someone who matches my description, which is unfortunate. There aren't that many women out there whose style is as unique as mine."

I look on, confused. Is she making a joke? She can sense my uneasiness, that's for sure. I give a nervous laugh, but I still can't shake off this anxious feeling of mine. Perhaps it's too early to start making jokes. Suddenly I'm reminded that I must warn her of our dilemma. The guilt of knowing had slowly built up inside me. To think that it might be all my fault, that I would be the reason she couldn't escape.

"I have to tell you something," I say.

She looks at me. "Yes?" she says, "what is it?"

I wasn't planning on telling her now, I didn't want to worry her. But I also didn't want her to find out before it was too late to do anything about it. Sooner or later, I'd have to tell her, so why not now?

"I know your name," I say.

She looks at me, and her expression changes from calm and collected to a look of horror. "How—how do you—"

"It was at the party," I say, "when Mr. Freeman called you, he said your name: Evette."

"Stop!" she says, dropping her arm muff, "don't say it." She puts her hands to her forehead and begins pacing back and forth, breathing heavily all the while. Even through her panic state, she still manages to keep herself from making too much noise.

Out in the square, the speaker for the Purging has begun reciting his speech, talking in his usual overzealous, overenthusiastic voice. He would do just as well without the microphone.

"I need you to try to forget it," she says, "do you hear me!"

"I can't just forget it," I say.

"Well, I don't know," she says, "just try."

"Listen," I say, "why don't I tell you my name?"

She lifts her head from her hands and looks at me. "Don't!" she yells, "are you insane? Why would you want to do a stupid thing like that?"

"Because it isn't fair to you," I say.

"Life's not fair," she says, "but that doesn't mean you get to throw it away. You have a better chance of escape than me, don't waste it."

She reminds me of Finn, the way she seems to know how to handle a situation under stress, and how protective she is. She's right of course, about chances, and not wasting them. Why risk it?

"I'm sorry," I say.

She takes a deep breath. "It's fine," she says, "it's not your fault. We're just going to have to find some way to keep you from getting caught."

We say nothing to each other for a few moments, hearing only the echo of the speaker's voice reverberating through the air. "We're going to get out of here," I say, "I don't plan on dying in this place. When we get out, then I'll tell you my name."

The crowd outside cheers.

"What did Frank invite you for anyway?" she says, "I mean, what was so important this time that he had to bring someone to the Excelsior?"

"You say that like he's done it before," I say. "How do you know Mr. Freeman? Are you and him… you know, together?"

"God no!" she says, offended at the notion. "I—he's—don't worry about that. I just know him. And yes, he has done it before, many times, usually with other low-ranking Engineers. But never with the ones you met with, that was a first."

"So, I'm not the only one," I say, "but what about the others before me? What would he want with them?"

"He's known for being very good at getting information," she says, "he is the editor-in-chief of the newspaper after all, it's his job. When Engineers want to know something, they flock to him for information. He's organized his own personal team of Psi-Ops which he secretly subcontracts. They collect the information he needs, through whatever credible source they can find, and he brings it to the Engineers, which in your case meant you. He does this to make himself look more powerful in front of the other Engineers.

"Does that mean I have a Psi-Op?" I say.

"Well, if you have a Psi-Op," she says, "he's long gone now, probably lost him in the crowd. Sorry to say, but you Primaries all look the same. But still, you can't be too careful."

"Then that's how he knew about what happened that day in the outer city when they captured Rachel," I say, "that's what Frank brought me to the Excelsior to talk about. He and those other Engineers are planning to use her as some sort of victim performer."

"That's sickening," she says, "poor woman." She turns away, clutching herself as if the thought makes her nauseous. "And all because of those stupid Exterminators," she says, turning back towards me.

Another cheer from the crowd.

Evette walks over to one of the windows and peers her eye out through a tear in the vinyl sheet. "I've never seen one of these up close before," she says, "in my district, all the Secondaries there tune in to watch the Purging. They enjoy hearing about Primary affairs. To them, it's like watching a telepro."

This is exactly how I expect them to see us, for those of them who do, our pain to them is their medium of pleasure. It is their life's work: demonize the people at the bottom, and force them to fight among themselves, so those at the top can gain more power in the end.

"I had no idea this place existed until a couple of weeks ago," she says, "and to think, we're right under their noses. They'd think no one would risk it, and on a Purging Day no less."

"I guess that's why it's the perfect place," I say.

Evette turns to me and just stares. "How do you do it?" she says, "how do you survive being a Primary?"

Although I've been asking myself the same question for years, the strange thing about this is that I already know the answer. The only trouble I have now is trying to convince myself that it's enough of an explanation. I can't help but think that there's more to this answer.

"A lot of faith, I guess," I say, "and a lot of patience."

"Is that really all?" she says, stepping away from the window.

I think for a moment and consider all my little habits, all the arbitrary rituals I do to keep myself from going insane. And then I remember my audio logs.

"Well, no," I say, "that's most of it, but there is this one thing I do that helps a lot. I have this tape recorder you see, and every once in a while, when I can't seem to hold in my thoughts any longer, I'll document them in audio logs. Sometimes it's just ideas, and other times I recount my day."

"How nice," she says, smiling, "someday, you'll have to let me hear those recordings."

The tone of the conversation has drastically shifted, now would be a good time to tell a joke. "But I've run out of tapes," I say, "the last time I recorded an audio log was about seven months ago, and I haven't managed to find any since."

"You've got that many thoughts, huh?" she says, giving a small laugh, "well, I'm sure I can bring you one next time we meet. I can ask our Librivox."

"Thank you," I say. This brings us to the end of that conversation, which calls to mind a question I've been meaning to ask. "Evette, how do you think you became an Unthinker?" I say, "I mean, Secondaries are the least likely to become one. They've been brought up in such a way that seems nearly impossible to, yet here you are."

"Don't you mean how did I become *desaturated*," she says mockingly, "well, I guess they just missed some of us. No, but seriously though, when I was six, my grandfather was an Engineer. Of course, at that time, the world hadn't immediately devolved into what it is today, and you can thank him for that. He did everything he could to delay the inevitable. He was the first of his kind. Back then, when the war had ended, he fought to break the cycle of hate that caused all this in the first place. He wanted change, and I mean real change. He wanted to destroy the box history placed him and everybody else in. He was the smartest man I knew. Of course, the other Engineers didn't like that. They got rid of him," she pauses, "how about you? How do you think you became an Unthinker?"

I wasn't expecting her to ask me this question. I should think the answer is obvious enough. Most cases of Unthought are of that found within Primaries, and yet in comparison to the rest of Apocalypse, I am a rare specimen. However, on thinking it over again, it makes sense that she would ask this question. All she's ever seen of what Primary life is like is what's been shown on television, which isn't much, but isn't how it is for everyone. She has no idea what it's really like. I suppose that goes both ways.

"My real mother tried to run away with me," I say, "the day she was supposed to surrender me to Surrogate. At the time I didn't know what was happening. When they finally caught us, they took her away. They told me she was dangerous, but I knew it was a lie. After that, things slowly began revealing themselves. I realized the way things were headed, and here I am now."

Outside in the square, the speaker has just finished his speech, and the Purging has begun. A loud chorus of distorted screams and cheers start up. Just the sound alone of the crowd is frightening enough. You'd never guess what was really going on if you weren't there yourself.

"So, what about the resistance?" I say in a louder voice, as all this time we'd been whispering, "any news?"

"I haven't heard much," she says, "things have been slow lately, but that can only mean they're working on something big. Listen, we'll need to be leaving soon, but before you go, I managed to get in contact with someone else through the televox. I told him all about you, and he wants to meet with you. He's one of yours, a Primary, so it'll be easier for you and him to talk. He's been doing this longer; he knows more than me. If you have questions, he can help you, take this," she slips me a folded piece of paper, "it's instructions on where to meet him. Memorize it, and then destroy it."

We hear the crowd cry the usual chant of: "PURGE! PURGE! PURGE!" and then one last final scream, which means the Purging has come to an end. But soon, they'll begin the rioting. This is also around the time they cut the cameras for the live feed.

"Let's meet again in a month from now," she says, "same time, that way I can tell you what's been going on in this place."

"Alright," I say.

"If you can't make it next month," she says, picking her arm muff off the floor, "we'll have to wait another month until we can see each other again." We hear the sounds of broken glass coming from downstairs. They've begun throwing things through the windows, and the Exterminators won't be long either. "Let's go before those no-brainers decide to set the building on fire." We head downstairs to the ground floor, towards the back door.

"Goodbye… *Compos Mentis*," I add without thinking.

"Goodbye," she says, "*Compos Mentis*," and we depart.

Chapter 31
Thought Blocker.

It's early in the evening, the part of the day when time begins to slow down. All that's left to do now is wait for the day to come to an end. Curtis has already returned home from work, as well as most of the people from the Bureau. Ever since coming back from the Purge Rally last week, he's begun to distance himself from me, rarely speaking anymore. I think he's finally given up trying to be friends, took him long enough, I did make it fairly obvious from the start, but he wouldn't let up. I hope that from now on we can just stick to being roommates.

Today I have that meeting with the other Primary—the one that Evette had arranged for me through the televox. I don't know what else to call him by, the Primary. I have no name for what we are in relation to each other. We are contacts of a sort, proxies perhaps. We may even go as far as to call ourselves confidants. I won't lie and say I haven't been thinking about it. I caught myself whispering the word a few times today already, I've just been so anxious. After tonight, there's only one thing I hope to have the opportunity to call each other by, and that's "friends." But as of now, he is a stranger, and I to him. I suppose in the end it doesn't really matter what we call each other. To the Operator, we are simply co-conspirators.

The thought of having a fellow Primary Unthinker as a friend hasn't entered my mind in a long time. I'd nearly abandoned the idea, as well as a few others. You learn to let go of some of your ambitions, the ones too heavy to carry, too hard to burden, to focus on the ones you have left. But it's alright now. It all worked well in the end, though for some, not for others. If only, if only. If only what? What do you suppose you could have done? You didn't know. You can't keep blaming yourself for what happened. I thought you were over this. It's not like you can do anything about it now. It's too late, Finn is gone. There's nothing you can change. All you can do now is learn from it. I don't plan on making the same mistake twice.

If it were up to me, I would've chosen to have had this meeting while Curtis was still at work, so that he wouldn't know I'd be going out. But there wasn't any way for me to reschedule, and I wasn't going to walk around for hours waiting until it was time to meet. So I decided not to make a big deal about it and just leave at the time we'd agreed upon.

Curtis is sitting in bed, listening to his new radio, the sound set to low volume, holding it up to his ear. He knows I get annoyed when he has it too loud. I'm sure the minute I walk out of the apartment, he'll jump out of bed and turn on the television. As I'm getting ready to leave, Curtis listens on with an annoyed look on his face, but I already know that whatever's annoying him has nothing to do with what's on the radio. He's been like this ever since he came home from work. What is it now? Did something happen in the Records Department again? I'm tempted to ask him what's the matter, as he's rarely ever like this, and for so long. But if I do, it might encourage him to start speaking to me again. If he's still like this when I get back, then maybe I'll consider asking him. But for now, I'm just going to pretend I haven't noticed. Maybe he's just trying to get my attention.

Taking up my clear vinyl briefcase, I start towards the door.

The air in my district is much clearer today, I won't need the umbrella. As I go to unlock the deadbolt, I hear Curtis suddenly call my name.

Are you serious? I stop and step back out of the doorway. "Yes?" I say.

He shuts off his radio, places it beside him, and begins staring me down. So, I'm the reason he's been annoyed.

"When was the last time you took your Thought Blocker?" he says.

I try not to show surprise in my face. I'm shocked he's even asking me this question, and so directly. Why would he probe me about this? Did I do something wrong? I can't recall having done anything that would've raised suspicion, not since leaving him at the Purge Rally, but I'd already told him I got lost in the crowd, and he didn't seem to argue against it. Maybe he suspects the reason I haven't been talking to him is because I'm an Unthinker and has been holding on to this theory for some time. Whatever it may be, he's beginning to catch on.

"During lunch hour at work today," I say calmly, "why?" For some odd reason, I feel offended, as if he hadn't the right. Me, an Unthinker? Never. Maybe I'm angry at myself for having allowed an opening for suspicion, and after all my efforts. Why him? Why now?

"Did you take any from your bottle today?" he says.

What is he getting at? "Yes," I say, "this morning."

"I'd like to see you take another," he says.

He knows I've only just picked up my new prescription last week, and I've already flushed this week's set of pills down the toilet, so he shouldn't be asking me this.

"And why would you want me to do that?" I say.

"Because I don't believe you," he says, flatly.

I look at him, angry now. "I already told you I took one today," I say sternly. This isn't the first time we've had this discussion. Back when he was first assigned as my new roommate, he asked me why he'd never seen me take my Thought Blocker before, and I flat out told him I think it's disgusting when people watch me do it. So, what's his problem now?

"There were eighty-four tablets in your bottle two days ago when I counted," he says, "and when I counted how much there was this morning, the amount hadn't changed. Do you mean to tell me that if I ask you to count how many there are now, it won't be the same number?"

My heart skips a beat. A tight knot forms in my throat. So that's it, he's been counting my pills to see if I've been taking them. But the question of "why" still stands. However, he only thinks I haven't taken them these last two days, but that's still enough to report me to the Operator. I have to be very careful how I answer him.

"No," I reply, "you're making a very serious accusation. Now listen. If I let you count how many pills are left in my bottle, the number will be the same, but I did take my pill this morning, as well as yesterday and the day before that. But those pills that I took didn't come from my bottle. You see, I don't like to go through my bottle so quickly, I would hate to run out when it's least convenient. What if I need to take it and can't get one in time? So I often ask around the Newsroom to see if anyone can spare me some of theirs as a precaution. Do you understand now?"

I'm surprised I even managed to come up with this excuse so quickly. To be honest, I don't think it's a very solid excuse, but at least it's a reason. Though I don't expect Curtis to agree, he goes through his pill bottles at twice the average rate. He's addicted to that stuff. But that doesn't matter. It just needs to sound believable, coming from me.

He squints his eyes at me, gives a sideways glance. He's not quite convinced yet. "If that's true," he says, "then how come you've never asked me to give you one before?"

"Because—because—" at this, I have a sudden bright idea, "because I know if you start sharing with me," I say, trying to sound sympathetic, "you'll have to go through the hassle of ordering a new prescription every week from then on."

Curtis understands he's already under enough stress having to visit the apothecary every three weeks, instead of the standard monthly visit to fill his prescription. Now just imagine what more of a pain it would be to make sure he doesn't run out all the time. He's terrified of Unthoughts. This is what they get for using fear as a form of manipulation.

"Trust me," I continue, "I'm doing you a favor… but if it makes you feel better, I'll take a pill from you, just this once." Before Curtis even has a chance to respond, I walk over to the refrigerator in the kitchen, take out a pouch of filtered water, walk back, and stand in front of him. "May you give me a Thought Blocker?" I say, laughing inside my head, holding out my hand.

He waits a moment before moving, reluctantly, as he's begun to question himself. Too easy. He sighs and finally gives in to defeat. For now, this seems to have eased his suspicion of me. After this whole ordeal is over, and I'm in the clear, it won't be for a long time until he tries something like this on me again. I've left him frustrated with himself, proven wrong once more. He's even begun to doubt his own reasoning, to him, it has not been so reliable. Eventually, he'll just start ignoring his skepticisms altogether. Serves him right.

He grouchily gets up, takes up his briefcase, unbuckles the strap, and begins rifling through it. After a moment, he finally pulls out his nearly empty bottle of Thought Blocker. I nearly burst out laughing. This is too perfect. He pops it open and regretfully hands me a pill. I take it and deposit the pill into my mouth. Then putting the pouch of water to my lips, I pretend to swallow, carefully slipping the pill through the rim into the water.

When I'm done, I open my mouth to show Curtis I've taken it. He says nothing more but returns to his bed and continues listening to his radio. I leave without saying goodbye, to further demonstrate how annoyed I am with him for wasting my time, the pouch of water still in hand. I'll have to throw one pill away every other day from now on, instead of the usual five or six every week, in case Curtis ever decides to start counting my pills again. I have to take extra measures with him. Out of everyone else, he's come the closest to De-psyphering me.

Chapter 32
S.O.S.

Twenty-five years I've lived, and like a child, I still retain the instinctive urge to talk to myself out loud, even in the presence of others. When I still had space on the cassette tapes to record my audio logs, this sort of thing wasn't a problem, because by then, I had no reason to seek the need to satisfy my thoughts, as I'd been doing that through my recordings. Though I wouldn't exactly call it a "problem." I don't mind the habit, and in fact, I'm actually quite fond of it. The amount of freedom that speaking one's mind holds is enough to make life here bearable. But under these circumstances, it is a problem, because of how dangerous it can be when left untreated. Now even I'm talking about it like it's some disease, there's a reason they use that analogy so often.

But it's true, ever since I used up my cassette tapes, slowly, I've had thoughts, thoughts I normally wouldn't think about, even when in the comfort of my own apartment, begin to surface from my mind, in the form of speech. Once I even had to check myself after noticing that I was doing it. I was pretty startled by it at first, because of how sudden and unexpected it was, and how long it took before I realized what was happening. It only lasted a few seconds, but even that was too much. It's silly to think that the simple act of talking to myself might just be the thing to get me Recalled.

Sometimes there's no getting around it. When the mind is so full of thought, one can't help but satisfy the need to express them. I'm running out of mind.

I move along the pavement, not as casually as I do when going on a walk, but with an air of purpose—one hand in my pocket, still fiddling with the watch, and the other firmly clasped round the handle of my briefcase. I didn't need to bring my briefcase with me this time; we'll be meeting at one of the automats in Liberty Plaza, not somewhere I would need it, but it would've looked strange to be seen walking without it. With it, I at least look like I'm off on some affair: official business. No matter how minor the task may be, people don't do anything for themselves anymore, only for the Operator. I also decided not to bother with taking the metro today. Not that it's busy or anything, but I'd much rather enjoy the walk, and the distance from my Habitat to Liberty Plaza isn't that far either, so I've no reason to worry about being late. There is also the other thing. It doesn't seem obvious to the common Unthinker—the mind will find solutions only if it is looking for them—but if you haven't found out about this yet, I'll share it with you now. The more often you're seen walking about, instead of taking the metro, either by Protectors or other Primaries, the more you can work on slowly building a good name for yourself.

Apart from the Psi-Ops, there are people who make work of reading other people's behaviors. It's a well-known practice. People are always watching each other, looking out for any signs of rebellion. Granted that I stay out of trouble, just walking can build a good name for myself, like an unofficial merit system.

You're more likely to be dismissed as a suspect, less likely to be brought in for questioning, and overall become more trustworthy on account of good comradery.

But it can take years to produce results one might even

remotely consider satisfactory. And ideals change all the time, so they can never be fully pleased with how you are at any given moment. You'll always have to do better, better at being worse. As long as you're willing to play the part, even so far as to regularly attend and participate in social events, then maybe one day you'll become indistinguishable from the real thing. I've been trying nearly all my life, and I still can't manage it. Although, Finn was always very good at doing this, even when he was young. But no one can ever be free from suspicion. Everyone is a suspect, some more than others.

As I make my way through the plaza towards the escalator, I spot out of the corner of my eye a small gathering of a sort, marching together in perfect unison. Without looking, I know this is an assembly line of children out on their usual day trip. They're crossing through the bottom of the atrium to the other side. I step up onto the escalator, begin to ascend. We're not supposed to look at the children or come near them. The children are instead meant to observe us and what it's like to operate in the city. It's to prepare them for when it comes time for them to leave Surrogate. These trips are the only time children are permitted to be out in public, heavily guarded of course. I take the risk and look.

These children are no more than eight years old. They walk in two lines, parallel to one another, the lines slightly off balance so that the children aren't standing exactly side by side, and tethered to a rope that runs down the middle. Protectors stand guard, two at each end, while their Mother stands at the front, leading the whole procession, directing with her sign.

The children wear their matching white ponchos so that they look something like little chess pieces. Pawns. I used to be one of these children, once, a long time ago, and a curious one at that. This group of children, however, doesn't seem to care much about anything that goes on around them, instead choosing to keep their eyes fixed on their Mother.

Already, I've been staring too long. But just as I'm about to look away, I sense a hint of movement from among the group, and my eyes happen to meet with those of a little girl's.

She gazes up at me with her large round eyes, then fully lifts her head towards me, and smiles. For a moment, I'm unsure of what to do, but quickly settle down and manage to return the smile. Then without skipping a beat, she looks forward again as her Mother begins to speak, and they all swiftly file off into another corridor, and out of view. The way they travel together, with the Mother in front leading her children, reminds me of how baby ducks are by nature said to recognize their mother through imprinting and follow her wherever she goes. I can't believe I still remember that. Only, nothing about this form of imprinting is natural.

I arrive at the automat, where we planned to meet. He's supposed to be sitting alone at one of the tables along the balcony overlooking the atrium. This is so that it'll be easier for us to speak without anyone noticing.

Before I get in line to receive my food, I do a quick scan of the tables first to see if I can try to spot him out. I don't want to make the fatal error of mistaking somebody else for him. There aren't many people eating alone, and of the people who are eating alone, only one is sitting at a table against the railing. From what I can see, this man has black hair, an umber complexion, and looks to be around the same age as me. The note didn't mention his appearance, but he is in the right seat, so this must be him. Now to get my food. Once I collect my tray of individually prepacked items, I slowly begin to make my way towards the man, reading his demeanor as I go. Perhaps there's something about him that will tell me whether or not this is really him. I get closer, and nothing seems to be out of the ordinary. He looks like every other person here. Could he be the wrong one? As I come within a few feet of the man, I start seriously doubting if this is him at all. This has to be him.

I place myself in the seat behind him, our backs to each other, as he'd instructed me to do in the note. Now to wait for a signal. I sit, staring at the tray before me, preparing my food, making sure not to start eating anything until we begin talking; that way, if someone is watching, it will only look like we're eating with our mouths open. A minute passes, and he still hasn't given the signal. I'm sure he would've done it by now. What's taking him so long? Just then, I hear something hit the ground beside me and look to see what it is. He dropped his bottle of Thought Blocker, the pills spilling all over the floor. The man crawls on his knees and begins hastily picking them up and putting them back in his bottle. This must be the signal.

"Here," I say, getting down on the ground to assist him, "let me help you."

"Oh, thank you Acolyte," he says. When we finish picking up the last of the pills, he reaches out his arm to shake my hand. "Thank you again Acolyte," he says.

As I reach out my arm to shake his, I look down at his hand and notice he's missing a finger. He must've gotten it removed back in Surrogate. I look up at him, and he looks back at me, then we smile at each other. It's him alright.

"You're welcome Acolyte," I say, and we shake.

We return to our seats and begin our short series of broken whispers, taking small pauses between each reply.

"I can't believe it's actually you," he says, "the famous white dove."

I take a bite of my food.

"The… what?" I say with my mouth full so that it only looks like I'm chewing. This is how I plan to speak to him as we advance through the conversation, taking every chance to answer, and I assume he does the same.

"Don't you know?" he says, "it's what we call you. You're very popular among the resistance. We all heard what happened. How by some miracle, you managed to deliver the plant after the Psi-Ops shot the original courier." A small group of people begins to pass by, and he pauses, waits, and continues speaking, "you can't imagine how much trouble it would've put us through if you didn't come along. You were a Godsent."

This bit of news surprises me. I don't know why, but to hear about the resistance having acknowledged my existence seems so surreal. It adds a level of humanity to something I'd previously thought not to have any. Until now, I've only ever been thinking of the resistance as something almost imaginary, even though I know for certain they are not. But now that I have this information—that it's not only I who am thinking of them, but that they are also thinking of me, and have been for some months now—it seals in the idea that they are people too.

"I didn't know that," I say, "so, what else can you tell me?"

"Well, what do you want to know?" he says, "I can also get information for you if you like, though it might take a while to get."

"Can you tell me anything about what they're doing to get people out?" I say.

"I can," he says, "but I can only share with you what I'm allowed to. They're keeping a tight lock on that sort of information. Only a few people know what's really going on. They call themselves the S.O.S.

"Is there any way I can get in direct contact with them?" I say, "I want to help."

"Not a chance," he says, "the only way you can get to them is to go Sub-Circuit yourself, or know people close enough to get you there. But I definitely wouldn't risk doing that. Once you're Sub-Circuit, there's no coming back. Besides, you saw what happened to Rachel."

I was hoping he would tell me there was at least some way I could go into hiding, if only they'd help me. But I see now that this question was only driven by selfish motives. Everyone wants to escape, but only a few can afford to.

"Though, what I can tell you," he continues, "is that the S.O.S. is planning something big, and that it'll be sooner than you think."

"That's great," I say, "is there at least anything I can do from here?"

"Nothing at the moment," he says, "the televox would tell me if they need someone to pick up a job. I can ask around though, but as of right now, it's best if we wait until they release something new."

"I'm sick of waiting," I say.

"Tell me about it," he says, "but if they do need anything, I'll let you know."

"Thank you," I say.

We take a brief intermission to eat as usual before we start speaking again. "Have they discussed any plans to break people out of the mines?" I finally say, wiping my mouth with the back of my hand. I ask this because I'd been thinking of Finn.

"Not that I've heard," he says, "why? someone you know got Purged?"

"Maybe," I say, "I'm not sure where he is, my old roommate. He got Recalled about seven months ago," then a bright idea enters my mind, "can you find out what might've happened to him? His name's Finneas 1-138. Can you remember that?"

"I'll try," he says, "but information like that is hard to get. It might take a couple of weeks,"

"I'm fine with that," I say, "as long as you can get it before anything happens."

"Any more questions?" he says.

"Just one," I say, "does S.O.S. stand for anything?"

S.O.S. used to be a distress signal of a sort, or at least that's what Finn told me. I never really knew to what degree of truth those Undocuments he used to read held, S.O.S. seems like an odd choice. But if the resistance is using that as their name, then maybe they did hold some semblance of truth after all. In any case, he told me it didn't stand for anything, just that it was universally used. Some people used to think it meant "save our ship," or "save our souls," but here I think it could mean something else.

"It's an acronym," he says, "for the *Seekers of Sanctuary*."

We stop talking and take this as our sign that it's time for us to leave. I hear him behind me starting to collect his things. I still haven't disposed of my Thought Blocker, so I'll wait till he leaves to pretend to take it.

"See you next week," I say.

He gets up, walks past me. "Till then," he whispers without looking, "*Compos Mentis*."

He didn't tell me his name, nor I him, for our protection of course. But for the sake of this story, I will give him one, that he shall not remain nameless, like so many others. From now on until the end of this story, or his, I will call him Darien.

Chapter 33
De-psypher.

I'd like to imagine Finn is at rest, finally at peace. In this world, I'm led to believe in anything, even the most inconceivable notion, if it means I can go on living. But there's something difficult about this. I desperately want to believe in it, and God knows I've tried. I want to believe in it because I refuse to believe in anything else. Because what I can't imagine is Finn, in the mines, working himself to death, still suffering for my sake, and after all this time, while I've been here.

Yet out of everything I've dealt with, this has been the most difficult to endure. It's come to a point where I can't even trick myself into believing it, that I refuse to believe in anything at all. It's taken a long time to finally admit this. I've been meaning to have this talk with myself, but even at the slightest moment of confrontation, the guilt prevails. The memory of him can only live on if there is someone who will remember, but I have willingly chosen to forget. By resorting to erase you from my memory I have ultimately become like everyone else. But it's not for the same reasons, I remind myself, this is not a Peace Parade. No matter how many times I give in to the guilt, in the end, I know it's for the best. It's time to let him go.

But it'll only be for a little while, I tell him, if he can hear me. Just until Darien can tell me what's become of you, if you've become of anything. I'll finally have that closure, though I can probably already guess what he's going to tell me, and once he does, I'll know for certain. But, if I must be certain of anything, anything at all, it's that I'm never going to see you again.

I'm summoned to Mr. Freeman's office. Today I've been assigned to meet with Rachel at the hospital again, though what the specifics of this job are I'll know soon after the briefing. It's been about a week since I last spoke to her, which is longer than I expected, seeing how desperate Mr. Freeman was to arrange this job, but I'm curious to know how she's doing. I suppose it's only taken this long because they wanted to give her time to recover. I'm lucky to have even been given the opportunity to see her again. Hopefully this time I'll be able to help her.

I arrive outside his office. Martin steps aside, opens the door for me, and I step in. Mr. Freeman's sitting at his desk, filling out the usual paperwork.

"Oh good," he says as I come in, "you're here." He quickly finishes off whatever document he'd been working on, then reaches into his desk drawer and pulls something out. "I've got a new job for you today," he continues, getting up from his desk to give me the object, "and out of all people, I think you'll find this one very exciting."

A new job? But I thought everything had been arranged for me to see Rachel today. Has something more important come up then?

"This has been a long time coming," he says. "After all these years, the Operator has finally granted us special access to provide inside coverage of Neo Synapse."

I look on with a vacant expression, my mind unable to process his words, when, out of nowhere, the news suddenly comes crashing down on me all at once. "What?"

"I know, right?" he says, grinning. "Though today's

assignment is only supposed to be a test. It's to gauge how the public will react, so we're starting off with something small. There's going to be a live therapy session in the facilities Enrichment Center, and I need photos. Here's your pass."

As he puts the pass in my hand, I spot, within a fraction of a second, the sheer look on his face as he casts me a long smile, his stare piercing deep into my soul, before quickly turning away. I freeze for a moment, replaying his smile over in my head. It wasn't his usual fake smile. No. Something about it felt frightenedly genuine.

"In a few minutes," he says, walking back to his desk, "a Protector will escort you down to the parking garage, where you'll be picked up in a car with Meltzer and two other Engineers. You remember Meltzer, right?"

I give a nod.

"Try taking a few snapshots as well," he adds, "that'd be helpful. You've got the day off tomorrow, so don't forget to leave your camera. Oh, and one more thing, while you're gone, it's best if you don't speak to anybody unless someone addresses you first."

"Yes sir," I say, still trying to piece together in my head everything that's going on. I look down at the pass in my hand, which has been printed and personally made for me. Something about this doesn't feel right. If he's been planning this trip for some time, he could've just mentioned I wouldn't be going to see Rachel. Now that I think about it, he hasn't talked about her in days. He was so keen on this assignment, so why the sudden lack of interest? I have to find out what's going on.

I look back up again at him. "Sir," I say, "I thought I was going back to the hospital, you know... to talk to the witness."

"Oh, that," he says, casually as if he forgot, "no, there's no need for that anymore. You won't be going back there anytime soon."

"Why not?" I say. The muscles in my neck begin to grow tighter.

"Because she hung herself," he says, "three days ago."

I don't move, I don't even blink. So that's it. Rachel's gone.

With what little freedom she had left in her, if you can call it that, she used it to leave this world by her own hand. And this whole time I thought she was still alive. My mind can't handle this news right now; this is too much to bear. My legs are about to give in. I hastily regain control of myself, enough so that nothing from inside will show; meanwhile, Mr. Freeman just stares at me, awaiting my response. If I don't say something back, anything, I'll give myself away.

"What?" I say, trying with all my strength to battle my emotions, "why would she do that, sir?" this seemed the most genuine thing to ask without sounding too concerned.

He squints at me and looks on with suspicion. Has he seen right through me, something in my face?

"You don't have to pretend in front of me," he says, "you and I both know very well that she was never abducted."

I feel the color seep from my face, and I go white. Has he known? All this time? Does he know I'm an Unthinker? He couldn't have. What is he trying to tell me?

"Sir?" I say, now visibly disturbed, my voice shaky and short of breath.

"I suppose now we'll have to write something," he says, too calm for comfort, "make something up. I've been brainstorming a few ideas for a headline. How does this sound: *Psycho-Terrorist Break into Hospital, Murders Protected Witness.*"

I don't understand. Why is he talking to me like this? Is he an Unthinker, or not?

He takes up a cigarette from a little metal case full of them and puts it to his mouth. Then, with the other hand, holds up his lighter, flips it open, and lights the cigarette. He takes one long breath in, holds it, and blows out, the smoke lit up in strips as the light from the partially open blinds behind him shines through.

"Or we can just not write anything," he says, opening his desk drawer and taking out a file. "It's not like anyone will wonder what happened to her. What do you think? Wouldn't that be better?" He opens the file and pulls out a piece of paper. My eyes widen. It's the photo I took of Rachel. He brings the lighter forward, holds it to the corner of the photo, and sparks the flame once more. The photo immediately catches, and he carelessly tosses it on top of his ashtray. The flame clings around the edges, slowly eating away at the photo, blackening and curling as the fire gradually closes in on Rachel. It isn't long before it joins the rest of the cigarettes as just another pile of ashes.

I don't hear the question; instead, what I hear is: "It's finally nice to meet you."

Mr. Freeman watches me, and I just stand there; I use the word "there" and not "here" because I'm not here. I have left my body and have transcended to an alternate state of consciousness, where the voice of my thoughts is so clear. Run, it's telling me, run as fast and as far away from him as possible. But I can't, I'm fixed in place. I won't move. I've lost control.

I was wrong, he's not an Unthinker. But he's not like the other Engineers either. He's something far more dangerous. He understands exactly what he's doing, and he enjoys it.

"You may go now," he says, smiling.

Instantly, I return to my body, and, as if voice-activated, turn around, knock for Martin, wait for him to open the door, and leave.

Today, I've finally met the real Mr. Freeman.

Chapter 34
Neo Synapse.

I'm being escorted down to the parking garage by a Protector. The parking garage is only authorized for Engineers and Secondary personnel. Primaries have no reason to go down there, seeing as we're not permitted a car. As I'm being escorted, I can't help but think that any moment now, once we arrive at the garage, there the red truck will be, waiting in all its wonder. And by then, I'll know it means I've come to the end of this story. But as soon as we step out, there, as Mr. Freeman had said, is the black cruiser of the Engineers, with Mr. Meltzer and two other Engineers waiting beside it.

If Mr. Freeman knows I'm an Unthinker, then why hasn't he reported me already? No one, and especially not an Engineer, would even think twice about it. Then again, he's not like other Engineers, as he's just proven. So, what then, is he just going to let me go? I doubt it. I can never tell what he's really up to, not until he decides to reveal it himself. He must see something in me then, something I don't, if he's so unmoving to even care to report an Unthinker. Or it could just be that he doesn't see anything in me at all. He's too important, too high in status, that it would bring him no satisfaction to see me Recalled, so why even bother. That's how little he sees in me; I am beneath him. But being him, I don't think this is good enough of a reason either. He's hiding something. Could I be looking at this all wrong? Whatever it might be, the situation has changed. I no longer live, safely hidden behind the confines of my false persona. And Mr. Freeman, whether intentionally or not, has infiltrated it. What he'll do, I don't know. Only time will tell.

He could try to blackmail me, threaten me, it wouldn't be the first of its kind; you hear about these things. Though he'd only do it to see me in anguish, not for any personal gain. He alone holds my very existence in his hands. You know, it only takes one opening for someone to bleed out to death. Will it be long, slow, and agonizing, or will it be sharp and quick, yet all so brutal? It's all up to him now. I have lost control of the situation. Then again, that was never something I had control of, only myself, and not even that's enough to call free will. It all comes down to him—nothing to do now but wait.

The two female Engineers break off from their conversation as we approach, but Mr. Meltzer is the only one to acknowledge me.

"Hello again," he says, reaching his arm out to shake mine.

"Sir," I nod, shake his hand, trying my best to hide any signs of distress.

"I was glad to hear you would be the one accompanying us on this trip," he says, "and not some stranger."

I'd never admit to this on any other occasion, but in a way, I'm glad to see him too. Just the thought of being alone in a car with three Engineers sounds unwelcoming enough, with them ignoring me whilst silently judging me the whole ride. But since Mr. Meltzer's here, I feel the drive there and back won't be as awkward. So yes, I am glad to see him too.

"You couldn't have arranged for him to get a separate ride?" says one of the other Engineers.

"Quit your complaining," says Mr. Meltzer, "it wouldn't make a difference. They won't start the live session until we're all there. Speaking of which, shall we get a move on."

One after the other, we enter the car's passenger compartment, each taking our respective seats: Mr. Meltzer and I on one side, and the two Engineers—who are visibly annoyed with our arrangement, as the Protector will reluctantly have to sit in the driver's compartment away from us—on the other. The car exits the parking garage, and we begin our drive.

From when we first entered the car until now, I'd meanwhile been looking out the window to avoid having to engage with the Engineers' conversation, when suddenly I hear Mr. Meltzer from behind address me.

"I was sad to hear when our *friend* at the hospital had to be discharged early," he says, he's talking about Rachel. "I'm sure Frank told you?"

Sad? What does he mean by sad? Could he actually be sorry for Rachel? I didn't expect him to feel anything towards her, let alone sympathy. But maybe he isn't as heartless as I thought.

I turn my head to look at him. "Yes," I say, my voice a little raspy, "I—I heard."

I couldn't save her. I should've done more to help her. I should've tried harder. Why couldn't she just listen to me? You saw what she was like, it wasn't her fault. Apocalypse had long gotten to her before you ever met. There was nothing you could do.

"I was hoping she could have more time…" he continues, now irritated, "enough to… to let her in on our plan, before she had to go."

I spoke too soon. Why do I even bother? It was stupid of me to assume so highly of him, to think an Engineer would care for someone else other than himself. But they can't all be like this, can they? Surely there must be some, if they haven't already been caught, like Evette's grandfather: an Engineer Unthinker. I smile at the thought, partly because it seems so ridiculous, but also because if it were true, it would be a minor defeat for the rest of them. Even if there was only just one, that would be enough to make me believe anything's possible. If there is someone like this, despite everything they've done, then it means they're not as impenetrable as they appear. And that humanity, in some form or another, can still exist among people who have none, and all is not lost. But as of now, I can't say for sure if anyone like this exists. One is such a lonely number.

"Oh well," he adds, "somebody else will come along, I'm sure. We'll just have to wait and see."

I take back what I said earlier, about being glad to see him. I think I would prefer the silent judgments over this.

For the remainder of the drive, I sit silently, staring out the window. Despite my surroundings, I can't help but wonder what it must be like living in Neo Synapse. Not much is known about what actually goes on in there. But if you listen carefully, you can hear things, whispers. If there's anything we would whisper about, it's about that place, and that goes for everyone. Everyone wants to know, but only a few can manage, and soon, I'll be one of the few. What a privilege.

By now, everyone's heard the stories: electroshock therapy, lobotomies, mutilations, things of that sort. But those are just rumors, planted by some unnamed provocateur with the intent of igniting intrigue. *Apocalypse Now* barely even reports about that place, I suspect it's to make it feel all the more mysterious. This is the first anyone's going to get a taste of what really goes on in there. And to think, I must be the first Primary ever to go in and come out in one piece.

Don't be so sure of yourself. We haven't even arrived yet.

Very soon, we come to the first gate, the road before us leading down a large tunnel, similar to the mines' access roads. The driver gives the Protector our passes to check us in. He types our numbers into the Cyber-Op terminal, gives them back. Then the Protectors on standby conduct a quick inspection of the outside of the car, as well as underneath, before finally waving us through.

The road goes on for a long way, deep in the earth, isolating us from the rest of the city. For a mile or so, the car drives without stopping, down the long stretch of tunnel, only able to see a few meters in front with the use of the headlights. Eventually, we reach the next gate, repeating the same procedure as before, before finally convening in a small parking garage.

We get out of the car and make our way towards the entry vestibule, where the doctors stand waiting for us. They welcome the Engineers, everyone taking turns shaking the other's hand, while I stand back and watch. Among the group of doctors, one man catches my attention: a tall, pale, thin man with uneven skin, hollow cheeks and sunken temples. This is Dr. Nimdok, head doctor of Neo Synapse. I wouldn't forget a face like his; I don't think anyone could. I saw him at that press hearing last year where he showcased the Ataraxia's obedience to the Operator. I wonder what ever happened to that guy. Sebastian, was it? They never mentioned his name in the news again after the Purging—probably killed himself, or eventually succumbed to his injuries as a result of their gruesome experiments.

I'm not really sure if I'm supposed to introduce myself or not, but as they all begin exchanging greetings with one another, I make a last-minute decision to keep back, and out of view. Besides, I'd rather not get too close to Dr. Nimdok. As it stands, he's quite unpleasant looking. I make myself useful and begin taking snapshots of them as Mr. Freeman had suggested. It's best I play it safe until I can figure out what role I have in this little game of his. Once the doctors and Engineers are properly acquainted, we enter through the security vestibule and into the lobby.

The lobby, as far as I can see, is surprisingly very average looking, like that of a hospital, except that it isn't busy, and in fact, we're the only other people here apart from the Protectors on post. This isn't what I had pictured in my head.

We come to the security check. But before we're allowed any further, we first must go through the proper screening. They search our things, have us walk through a metal detector, and are now about to perform a simple pat down, beginning with the Engineers. The Protector executing the pat down barely even touches the Engineers before quickly moving on to the next. I'm the last to be searched, but before the Protector can get to me, another Protector comes up and orders me to go with him. Confused, I follow him, noticing the doctors escorting the Engineers past the security check without me. What's going on?

He brings me to a small room, which is grey and dimly lit, the only light coming from a little metal lamp hung from the ceiling. On the floor in the middle of the room is an X marked in yellow, where the Protector orders me to stand and face forward. I hesitate for a moment, still wondering what I'm even doing here, but quickly do as I am told, fearing what might happen if I don't. Is this where he's going to perform the pat down?

I stand awkwardly in the middle of the room, fiddling with my fingers, getting more impatient with every second. The Protector waits by the door, facing forward, his hands clasped at the front. If he was going to pat me down, he would've started by now. Placed against the wall in front of me is a table, and on it, I see a wire basket, a thin flashlight, and what I think is a box of tissues. What are these for?

After a minute of waiting, I finally summon up the courage to ask the Protector what I'm doing here. But before I even have the chance to open my mouth, I'm interrupted by the sound of the room's metal door swinging open with a heavy latch. A man in a dark grey suit swiftly enters and goes directly over to the table, the door shutting behind him with a forceful slam. He pulls a pair of white latex gloves from the little box and slips them on, making an elastic snap. He turns to me, torch in hand.

"Alright," he says calmly, "remove your clothes for me."

The voice of my thoughts goes quiet. I can hear my surroundings, the silence of the room so loud. I must've misheard him; did he just tell me to remove my clothes? No, he couldn't have.

"Wha—what?" I say, in a low voice.

He looks at me, furrows his brow, sighs. "I've been authorized to conduct a detailed cavity search," he says with a disgruntled look on his face, "hurry up and remove your clothes."

I tense up. Here and there my muscles contract from the

stiffness, as if being given tiny jolts of electric shock. They're taking no chances with me.

"Remove them now," he says, "or we'll be forced to take them off for you."

Quickly, I nervously slip off my jacket, then undo my tie, the Protector confiscating my garments as I remove each piece at a time. Next, I unbutton my shirt, fumbling to pull the buttons out, getting several of them fastened in the holes. I eventually manage to take off my shirt, leaving me naked above my waste. Already I'm uncomfortable, and I'm only halfway through. Moving down to the lower part of my body, I start to untie my shoes, desperately pulling at the laces and almost ripping them out. I pull off my socks, give them to the Protector for inspection, the cement floor cool against my feet. I unbuckle my belt, pull it out from the belt loops, and unzip my pants. I lift each of my legs out, one at a time, feeling a chill draft pushing up against the hair on my thighs. I didn't think it would ever come to this.

It's such a simple thing to say: "It'll never happen to me." I can live my whole life so comfortably and carefree, thinking that somehow I've become invincible, that the world cannot hurt me. Then when the world does finally decide to strike, once it's found me, I'll be caught off guard, overcome with shock, seized of all prior understanding. I'm not invincible, I've just been lucky. No one ever makes it out in one piece.

You'll feel as if your whole world has been shattered. Something that was once there is now gone. Or you'll feel a sense of betrayal, misplaced trust. And the worst of it all is that there's no recovering from that. The moment you try to retreat to your old way of living, you'll always have that lingering thought in the back of your mind that at any moment when life feels safe again, pain and suffering will be waiting for you just around the corner. No one is immune to the terrors of this world. You should know that by now. I suppose I just needed to remind myself.

I stand, partially naked, in the middle of the room, only in my underwear, the Protector and officer waiting for me to take it off. Slowly, I reach down, but stop, trying to compose myself.

I don't want to do this, I want more time, to prepare, but I know I can only stall for so long. I'm already here, so I might as well get this over with. At this point, I go into hiding, retreating into my thoughts—the only place where I am truly untouchable from the world.

Chapter 35
Enrichment Center.

The cavity search is over. It was an eternity in there. I longed for it to end, for it all to end. I didn't see any other way that I could possibly escape. My only hope for freedom was to stop existing. Then in an instant, I was back, and it was over like it never happened. To be suddenly ripped out from infinity like that was beyond anything the human mind could comprehend. All I can remember is being nowhere. But I know for a fact that I was in that room, and I know what happened to me. I just can't remember—not mentally, only physically: muscle memory. I felt the way as one does when one wakes up knowing he or she had been dreaming, though unable to recall of what. A quick flash of an image, too warped to make out. The words of a voice I can't register. And then the touch of cold latex, I haven't forgotten that. The rest is incomprehensible, blurred out of my memory. I don't even remember putting my clothes back on.

Now I'm being escorted by the Protector, back down the hall from which we came, and into the lobby. Then into another hall we go, where Dr. Nimdok and the Engineers stand waiting in front of the landing doors for the tram. When they notice me approaching, Dr. Nimdok comments about my late arrival to the rest of them, which I don't hear, prompting laughter. I don't say anything, and decide just to ignore them, half because my mind's too groggy to care, and half because I know I'll get into some sort of trouble if I do. Dr. Nimdok scans his keycard on the scanner, whereupon the landing doors slide open with a heavy clattering, followed by the car gate. We enter the tram, take our seats, and begin our uncomfortably long ride down to the Enrichment Center, the car shaking alternately as we descend.

In comparison to the lobby, the tram system isn't in as good a condition. It's dark and dingy and very noisy, the fierce hum of the electric motor rocking the car up and down as the tram moves further along the track. Outside, the tram's motion alarms blare nonstop, accompanied by their whirling yellow lights, the combination quickly making me nauseous. It may not be as clean, but it definitely makes up for it by adding another layer of security to the facility. The shaft is divided into separate modules every ten meters, with gates that open and shut as we move between them, limiting access to only two modules at a time. I thought we would've reached the bottom by now, but it seems to go much further down than I'd anticipated. Each time we approach another gate, I think to myself this has to be the last one, only for it to open and reveal another section. How deep does it go?

The tram finally comes to a halt. At last, we've reached the bottom. We step off and come to the entrance of the Enrichment Center. We emerge at one end of a long empty corridor, lit by burning white fluorescent lights. The walls and floors are tiled in white porcelain, with many doors all around. Across the ceiling, thin pipes run along it, air ducts, electrical wiring. Several colored lines are painted on the floor, each seemingly leading to a different section of the facility. Everything looks so clean, so sterile, and yet there's something unsettling about it. Nothing in here looks exactly the way it ought to, like a parody of a hospital, or a distorted memory of Surrogate—a setting so imaginary, it can only exist in dreams.

The only trouble is, I am a wake, and this is no dream.

We come to the reception area and are greeted by a different set of doctors, along with a few nurse assistants. But most notably of all, waiting among them is the Mother. It never crossed my mind that there would even be a need for one; it seems odd, to be assigned a Mother whilst undergoing treatment. But the longer I think about it, I suppose it's only natural for them to do it this way.

While everyone else starts talking to each other, I step away, off to the side, and begin fiddling with my camera. After a minute or two of awkwardly tinkering with the lens, I stop, look up, and take in my surroundings some more. It's the apparent eeriness of this place, its dreamlike quality, that gives off a great air of familiarity, like having a memory of a place that doesn't exist. Something about its conscious design, juxtaposed with its surreal allure, creates in my mind a sense of cognitive dissonance. Someone—or something—far beyond the realms of human comprehension built this place intending to pass it off as manmade.

Though if I were to picture what Neo Synapse would look like in my head, it ought to look exactly like this. I feel as if I've somehow slipped out of my own plane of existence, out of my own time, and into an alternate dimension—one where I do not belong, nor am welcome. My very presence here is a mistake, and in fact impossible, by all standards of reality. I should not be here, and yet here I am.

"I didn't know the photographer would be a Primary," a sudden voice close to me says.

I look up, and my eyes immediately meet with hers: the Mother. She's standing right in front of me. How did she get so close without me noticing?

"You must feel quite special," she says jokingly.

I feel the sudden urge to pull myself away from her, because of how uncomfortably close she is to my face, but quickly stop myself, for fear of offending her.

"Yes, absolutely," I say, trying to act courteous, though without coming off as too excited; I need to act like I know my place.

She's an older woman, with a tightly pulled back face, which is pink and round. She has brown hair, brown eyes that—because of how close she is to me, I can see through the lens of her glasses—have very prominent veins and signs of cataracts. Overall, she's a relatively small woman and, oddly enough, has a noticeably welcoming demeanor. But from experience, I know that looks can be deceiving.

We don't say anything to each other, and she begins examining my facial features, her eyes moving up and down across my face. "What were you thinking of just now?" she finally says. She's a Mother all right.

"I was just thinking of how lucky I am," I say, "to be allowed the honor of coming here."

"Yes, what a rare sight this is," she means me, "you're the very first Primary I've ever seen to walk these halls."

This isn't entirely true. Every test subject ever admitted here is a Primary, or was once, and will be one again after assimilation.

"Forgive me, I'm Mother Peabody," she says, and we shake hands. "Well, I hope when you leave, you can go back and tell your fellow Acolytes all about your experience here. I'm sure they'll love to hear whatever they can about this place."

"Yes, I certainly have a lot to tell," I say, giving her an awkward smile to hide my discomfort.

We overhear the Engineers and doctors finishing up their conversations and know they're about ready to head towards the observation room.

"Time to go," she says, excitedly.

Everyone else leaves, returning to their posts, while the Engineers and I are escorted away. We continue down the corridor, turning one corner after the next, the only audible sound coming from our footsteps and the faint hum of the bulbs.

Is this worse than the mines? Worse than death? People who are sent here also die, but not in the same way, not physically. I try to imagine what I would be like, who I would become, if I were sent here, and had succeeded in my complete assimilation.

It seems almost impossible to picture myself, to be changed in such a way—so completely, so absolutely. I wouldn't be myself at all, and in fact, I would be an entirely different person. If I am merely my thoughts, then I, in this current state of consciousness, would no longer exist. I would simply disappear, be forgotten. And in my place, there'd be someone else, another man. He'll have my face of course, along with my body, though he'll go by another name. But he—whoever he is—won't try to escape, he won't try to resist, and he won't be me.

Some people can be so resilient to things, at least in their own minds. I know I used to be. I once believed I could do anything, anything at all, as long as I put my mind to it, but that was a long time ago. Back then, I never would've believed in this, but now there's no denying it; if I were admitted here, I would not survive.

The odd thing is, even after coming to terms with this, I don't find myself imagining this being my fate, not exactly. I suppose I was always so stubborn. But this is just an idea: what if somehow, some part of me could survive the procedure, leave a piece of myself behind, just enough in the hopes that maybe someday I can return—become whole again. He would have to be stored securely away, hidden deep within the innermost parts of my psyche, lest he be found by the new persona, and forced out like the rest of my old self—fade away altogether, wherever forgotten memories go. But that is the least of my worries. I fear a fate far more terrifying than this.

What I believe is that there are two forms of consciousness that make up a person's being, there is the unconscious state, and the conscious state. The unconscious part of me is in charge of managing all things within my body: my breathing, heart rate, blood pressure, hair growth, and everything else the other half of me can't. He works in the background of my existence.

The conscious part of me works directly in tandem with the things around me and my environment: my speech, movement, reactions, thought processes. He is the forefront of my existence.

Supposing one of them didn't work, I wouldn't be able to function properly without the other. If my body is active but has lost the use of the mind, I'll go into autopilot. I'll be gone, and all that will be left is a walking sack of muscle memory. And if my mind is active but has lost control of the body, I'll enter a catatonic state: paralyzed, unable to move, but aware of everything around me.

However, none of these outcomes is what I fear either.

For the most part, the pair never have any direct contact with one another, and are separated in every respect, all except one. The only possible instance where both states of consciousness can ever cross paths with one another is through their shared perception of the senses. And what's more, this metaphysical link between the two is what I've determined as being me.

Now comes the other thing: what if something were to go wrong during the process? What if whatever part of myself I attempt to preserve won't be enough to bring me back? What little of me I'll have stowed away in the cavities of my mind will be too weak to do anything on his own. My body will simply become an empty vessel for the new host to pilot, conquering the brain. While I go into hiding, deep within my subliminal, consciously aware of every action, yet powerless to do anything on my own but witness the horror of being trapped in a body that is no longer mine—forced to watch from behind these eyes, as I'm under the control of something else, something *Unhuman*.

But I'll never be found out; I'll never be erased. I'll just be left alone, and only then, become truly untouchable, as I patiently wait for the day of my return—a day that will never arrive.

This is what I fear.

Chapter 36
Test Subject.

After walking for some minutes, we finally come to the door of the observation room and go inside. It's dark in here, there are no lights on. There is, however, a large two-way mirror on the wall at the front of the room which is covered by a curtain on the other side, its thin fabric allowing small traces of light to peek through, just enough to see our way.

In the middle of the room are two rows of chairs, five in each row. The floor of the room is at an incline towards the back, so that the second row of chairs is slightly more elevated than the first, and all facing forward towards the window. It's like a theatre. The Engineers take their places at the front, spreading themselves out, while I sit in the back, getting the whole row to myself.

"How's the experience been for you so far?" says Mr. Meltzer, turning back to me, "we run quite the operation here, don't we?"

"It's—intriguing," I say.

I can't really say I know what to expect to happen during the therapy session. I've been so distracted by everything else that's happened today, I really haven't given it much thought. So, what, are they just going to bring out the test subject and have Dr. Nimdok and Mother Peabody talk to him for half an hour? That doesn't sound like something they would do, especially here; it seems too simple. There must be something more to this than they're leading on.

Just then, the curtains draw back, light floods my vision. I squint, shade my eyes, allowing them to adjust. I have a clear view of the room now, but I don't understand. The room is empty. The only thing in it is a single grey leather chair, like those at barber shops or dentists, hooked up to an electric panel connected to a throw switch. Along the chair, loose leather straps dangle from it. A metal headpiece wired up to an electrode hangs above. Just looking at the chair, I can feel my stomach begin to turn, the acids slowly starting to bubble over, leaking into my throat. I resist the urge to vomit. It's nauseating, the way it just sits there in the center of the room, so deliberately. Its notable vacancy adds to its frighteningly alluring effect, as if inviting someone to take a seat.

What is this?

After a minute or two, a low buzzing goes off in the room, then Dr. Nimdok bursts through the door. He comes to the window, stands behind it, looks at us through the glass. Quickly, I ready myself to take a photo, the whole time wondering where this is all going. They haven't told us everything.

"Good evening, ladies and gentlemen," says Dr. Nimdok, his voice faintly muffled through the intercom speaker, "I'm sure you've all been eagerly waiting for us to begin our demonstration, and for that reason, I regret to inform you that you have sadly been mistaken."

I move the camera away from my face, looking on with confusion. What is he talking about?

"There isn't going to be a live therapy session today," he says. He pauses, takes his glasses off, cleans the lenses, puts them back on again, "but this is instead an execution."

I don't understand. Is this a joke? He has to be joking, right? Why would they go through the trouble of bringing us here just to have us witness an execution? I glance at the Engineers, but to my shock, they seem more intrigued by this sudden announcement than surprised. This is no joke; this is really happening.

"All of our test subjects are given new names upon admittance, as to our custom, this is to symbolize the destruction of the old being and the beginning of a new persona. Though this test subject in particular, who's been given the name *Thomas*, doesn't seem to like his."

While Dr. Nimdok speaks, a nurse comes into the room from behind him, pushing a cart of what looks like surgical instruments, and begins setting up some of the equipment.

"We've been having trouble with him for a long time, ever since he was first committed," he continues, pacing slowly back and forth, "these are just some of the things he's done while under our care, and their repercussions.

"He secretly stopped taking his daily medication. And so, from then on, we've been injecting them in the form of a suppository.

"There was a time he thought he could abstain from eating his food, but we certainly couldn't allow that, so we've been force-feeding him through a tube up his nose ever since.

"He continues to act violently, and once even managed to bite one of the nurse's ears off. And that's just scratching the surface.

"But what has brought us to this decision is worse than anything we could have ever imagined. He, along with a small group of other test subjects, orchestrated a plan to escape this facility. And in their attempt, the other test subjects were pacified, he was the only one who survived. Now, this incident occurred about a month ago, and he's been in solitary confinement ever since, along with receiving his daily beatings. But after some consideration, we have come to the conclusion that his behavior can no longer be tolerated. He's actually the sole reason why we had this pacification chamber installed in the first place."

Dr. Nimdok turns to the nurse and whispers something to him. The nurse quickly finishes whatever he's doing and exits the room. Then he turns to us again and continues speaking. "He thought he could outsmart us; he is the most cunning out of all of our test subjects." Shortly after, we hear the low buzz of the door unlocking. The nurse enters, holds the door open. Then Mother Peabody walks in, hands neatly clasped, her heels clicking against the tile floor, followed by two nurses, both very large men. And in between them, they're dragging something, a man, holding him from under his arms. This must be the test subject. I've been so caught off guard, and still trying to grasp the situation, I almost forget to take a picture. I lift the viewfinder to my eye, aim the camera, and snap a photo.

Then I notice something, or rather, the lack of something. The test subject, he's missing an ear. And then it hits me, like a bullet, piercing through my chest.

It can't be.

"Subject 1-138 Thomas," says Dr. Nimdok, "Ex-name: Finneas."

In an instant, every part of me ceases to function, and just like that, my body shuts down. This happens so abruptly that for a moment, I'm left completely breathless from the shock. No air can escape my lungs, and my vision goes blurry. I nearly collapse into my seat before having to manually assume control over my body.

At last, I start to breathe, short but deep gasps, my lungs desperate for air. I'm too loud. I cover my mouth to suppress the noise. Everything's fuzzy. Tears trickle down my face. I begin blinking profusely to clear my vision. Suddenly pain swells up in my chest, a burning soreness from muscle contraction, combined with a surge of chemicals rushing through my bloodstream.

Finn's been here all along. I thought he was dead, but he volunteered for the assimilation program, the possibility never even crossed my mind. I'd hardly recognized him; it was the missing ear that gave it away. He's got bruises all over his face: yellow from old ones that have begun to heal, and purple from the new ones they've recently inflicted. He's also got a black eye. I don't want to think about what his body must look like underneath his uniform.

His head is shaven, with visible rough patches of blond hair. They must've done it recently, and with a straight razor, because his scalp is bleeding. I don't think he's awake, and if he is, he's not moving. He hangs limp, a bundle of flesh and bones.

The nurses fling him onto the chair, like a sack of meat, and begin the strenuous process of fastening him in, strapping him by the arms, legs, head, and waist, and making sure to pull tightly on the belts, Finn grunting with every tug. Once they're done, they recline the chair, and the nurses step off to the side at attention, like Protectors. Dr. Nimdok stands over Finn, who's still half asleep.

"Wake up Thomas," he says calmly, "we have visitors."

Finn twitches a bit in an attempt to come to, but can't. He's too weak, too beat up, even to open his eyes. Suddenly Mother Peabody rushes over from the other side of the room and slaps him hard across the face. Finn lets out a sharp cry and opens his eyes.

"He told you to wake up," she says sternly.

Slowly he starts to regain consciousness until he can keep himself awake. He tries to look around, to get a feel for his surroundings, but he can't, his head's fixed in place.

He could've ended this seven months ago, ended his suffering, when they first gave him the choice, yet he chose this instead. He thought he could escape. All that time for nothing, he's back to where he started, but now this time, he has no choice. Now it ends here.

"I hope your time in the White Room has given you the opportunity to reflect on your actions Thomas," says Dr. Nimdok, moving closer towards Finn and standing over him, "because it will be the last time you ever will."

Finn says nothing, keeping his focus on him.

"When you first arrived here," continues Dr. Nimdok, pacing slowly back and forth, his hands behind his back, "you were very obedient and always willing to comply. At the time, you were one of our most well-behaved test subjects. It was only later did we find out that you were lying to us in hopes that we might release you under the guise of a false assimilation report. You tried to fool us into thinking that your treatment was working. But, when we finally confronted you about it, you did not confess to it, not right away. Do you remember that? It took time for us to get the truth out, and when we finally broke you, you made no attempt to hide your true intentions, and you did not hold back. From that day on you became very defiant, and we did everything we thought was best for you at the time. After that, we sought to make it our number one goal to cure you, and everything seemed to be going well. We suspected nothing. We thought you had finally begun to make progress. That was until your recent incident. What happened Thomas? Why did you lie?"

Finn waits a moment to answer, sighs. "Because I thought we could escape," he mumbles, his voice tired and raspy.

Dr. Nimdok moves back to standing over him. "And look where that got you," he says, "do you have any idea what you did? You led those other test subjects to their death."

"No! You murdered them!" Finn whimpers, beginning to cry, "you murdered them!"

"They trusted you Thomas, and you failed them," says Dr. Nimdok, not shouting or angry, but in a calm, still voice, "did you honestly think you would escape; you knew they couldn't, and yet you let them die."

"I didn't," Finn says, "I didn't."

Dr. Nimdok moves slowly towards him and gets up close to his face from the side. "Look at me," he says, "and tell me, did you really think you could escape from us?" Finn stares at him, wide-eyed and teary. "I asked you a question Thomas," this whole time he's been speaking to Finn in an almost soothing, comforting voice.

"Yes," Finn pants out, "yes, yes."

Dr. Nimdok pauses, lets out a small laugh, then turns his head to Mother Peabody, who shares in his amusement. He takes a moment to compose himself before speaking again. "You're a good liar Thomas," he says, drawing back, "I'll give you that," then he reaches over to the cart of surgical instruments, runs his fingers over them, and takes up a pair of pliers.

"What are you—what are you doing?" says Finn. Dr.

Nimdok doesn't answer, but proceeds to clamp the pliers' jaws onto one of Finn's fingernails and pull.

Finn screams out in pain, telling him to stop, thrashing himself to get loose. The nurses on standby don't even look at him. They know he can't get out. He can't even move his head. Mother Peabody comes over and covers his mouth with her hand to muffle his screaming, which has become a deep excruciating cry, Finn still convulsing in the chair. I squirm in my seat, holding my hand over my face. Dr. Nimdok, undisturbed by the screaming and shaking, continues to tug away at it, as Finn's finger starts bleeding, until finally, he rips the nail completely out from its root. He lets the fingernail drop on the floor beside him and places the pliers back on the cart.

"If you proceed to lie to me one more time," he continues, "I'll have your tongue cut off, and make you eat it." Finn's cries are so strong his screams have gone silent, groaning in agony. "Now tell me, do you still think that you ever had even the smallest chance of escape?"

"I—I don't know," he says: he's just about lost his voice.

"Then tell me Thomas," says Dr. Nimdok, "if you didn't know, then why did you put yourself and the lives of those other test subjects at risk?"

"Because—because—" he doesn't finish his sentence.

"You can't tell me?" says Dr. Nimdok. He then turns to address us through the glass. "You see, this is exactly the kind of thinking that we've been trying so hard to eradicate. He was willing to have other people die, and for what: nothing. These thoughts kill people, and they still can't seem to understand that. We just don't want to see people die anymore. That is why we need full obedience. We have no right over what we should think. Our minds belong entirely to the Operator, and no one else."

"Because I wanted to be free," says Finn.

Dr. Nimdok turns back. "Free?" he repeats, "we've already offered you everything necessary for freedom, and yet you still refuse Thomas. Thomas? Thomas," he repeats to himself, "why, you're not Thomas at all. No. You're Finneas, aren't you? Finneas is the one who let those test subjects die while their minds were still sick; they will never know what it's like to be truly free. And Finneas is the one who will be held accountable for their deaths, by paying with his life."

Suddenly, the nurses at attention spring into action and begin by fastening belts with wet sponges between the metal contacts on Finn's legs. Then they adjust the chair to an upright position and strap the metal headpiece on his head. With his voice nearly gone, he pleads for them to stop until they cover his mouth with a leather harness, and his cries become muffled.

I have a better view of his face: his eyes are wide open, bloodshot, with veins protruding from his forehead. Because of the way he's positioned, it's like he's looking straight at me, but he isn't. He's looking into his own reflection on the other side of the two-way mirror.

"You know Finneas, if you never tried to escape," says Dr. Nimdok calmly, "we would've never suspected you were still lying to us. Why, you might've even been released. That's how well of a liar you are." He moves in on Finn, leans over him, and pushes down on his arms. "The metal contacts on your legs and head are capable of producing 2000 volts of power, with enough energy to cause every muscle in your body to contort so severely your bones will break from all that force. Your eyeballs will burst out of your skull. Your very flesh will suddenly begin to tear itself apart, and all your blood vessels will burst. Then your skin will start to burn, and within a matter of seconds, you'll be blackened to a crisp. If I'm going to remember anything about you at all, it's what you're going to smell like being fried from the inside out. Oh, and you might even defecate yourself in the process.

"Try not to be afraid," he says, moving away from him, "you brought this on yourself, remember? But it's all right. It's not like anyone will care. No one will remember you; you have already been forgotten. Who would want to remember someone like you? Why, you are not even human. You resemble something of a human yes, but you've never been a human a single day in your life. You are an *Unhuman*, you are a shape, a formless being, you are not even alive, and what's more, you have never lived."

Dr. Nimdok walks away from him, stands beside the electric panel, and places his hand on the switch. "You'll feel the pain of every jolt of electricity streaming through your body," he says. He doesn't pull it, he doesn't count down, but waits, looks directly into Finn's eyes as he weeps in the chair. Finn breathes heavily through his nose, due to the harness over his mouth, his chest rapidly expanding, and eyes stricken with horror. I make some attempt to look away. Is he going to pull it?

He continues to stare, unmoving, then suddenly, just when I think he's not going to do it, he pulls the switch. It makes a heavy screech, then the sound of a loud machine starts, the flow of electricity giving off sparks as the circuit closes, causing the lights to flicker. I haven't looked away. Even with Finn's mouth covered, he lets out a horrific scream. I scream too, but it's drowned out by all the noise. But that's all that happens. The metal contacts don't give off any electricity. What's going on?

Though muffled, Finn screams and screams, his face red, bawling uncontrollably. Dr. Nimdok comes close to him, bends down, so that their eyes are leveled. "You have been mistaken," he says, "something that has never lived cannot be killed. You cannot die. You would simply cease to exist. My job is to give you life. One day you will live, you will become human, and then you will be allowed to die."

Mother Peabody walks over to him. "You are not leaving this place anytime soon," she says, smiling.

"From now on, no more lies," says Dr. Nimdok, "this is just the beginning, and by the end of it, you will be free."

Finn is just as confused as I am, his eyes quickly shifting back and forth between them, before finally passing out. He goes limp, lying slumped in the chair. Then Dr. Nimdok turns to us one last time.

"Ladies and gentlemen, this concludes the legal execution of subject Finneas, and commences the inception of Acolyte Thomas, a new persona."

The session ends, and the curtains close.

VII

Compos Mentis

Chapter 37
Exodus.

Mother Sylvia told us that all bad things in Apocalypse happen because of us. "We locked them out; we were safe in here, protected, while they were out there, suffering from the radiation. We refused to let them in; they had to break their way in just to survive, but their torment didn't stop there. We saw them as lesser than us, because of their sickness, because of something we did to them.

"We tyrannized them for years, in ways you couldn't even imagine. It's only recently that we've managed to rectify most of our past crimes, completely dismantling every measure set in place against the Secondaries that had suppressed them from achieving human status. But it takes more than that to sufficiently make up for what we've done.

"As a form of atonement, it is now our duty to ensure we abide by the new balanced structure, to keep us from resorting back to our former selves. It is through the outweighing of our wrongs that we can truly show our commitment in redeeming ourselves. But always remember this, no matter what we do, it will never be enough."

I remember that alright. I also remember knowing full well that this hadn't been the fault of any of these children, and yet we were the ones being held accountable. No one should be held accountable for the past faults of our precursors, but everyone, in some form or other, is responsible—responsible for doing better, better than the last. And I mean everyone. But they don't understand that.

That's all it is really. It's just bad people fighting bad people, and good people getting caught in the crossfire. If only we spoke up, if only we realized sooner, if only we knew what the world would be like—if only.

Instantly seized from my sleep, by body breaking out in a cold sweat, I awaken to the sudden growing sense of dread steadily approaching. I check my watch, it's 1:50. The Exodus I took early today is finally wearing off. I won't be able to go back to sleep. I forgot how good Exodus is at disguising pain, as well as everything else. But it's all coming back. I can't let it take hold of me again. I won't.

I quickly get out of bed, go into the bathroom, and take a seat. When we left Neo Synapse, I didn't think I would make it home. The entire time I was contemplating doing certain things, committing certain acts. I still am, although not as strongly. What's worse is that it feels like I never left. I'm still here, trapped in Neo Synapse, watching Finn mentally raped all over again. At least with the Exodus, it won't feel as real. Now everything will seem like it's only a dream—a very vivid dream.

I take out my ExoPen, steady myself first, then quickly jab it firmly into the center of my thigh. I hold it there for a few seconds, waiting for it to completely administer the Exodus. After a moment, my muscles begin twitching from the rushing stimulation. I already feel much better. I put the pen away and let myself rest for a few minutes, allowing the drug to set in. My mind grows hazy, and my body begins to float as I become weightless.

After a while, I get up from the toilet, wash my face. I look awful. I know it's not right. But neither is what they're doing out there. I just couldn't take it anymore; Finn would understand. But then I remind myself that he wouldn't, all he would say to me is: "How can you forget what happened after that night? Or did you try to erase that too, like how you tried to erase me?"

I shake my head. Shut up. I can't deal with this right now.

Without Exodus, everything just feels so lifeless. It sounds strange, but I feel like I should be dead. I don't belong here. By keeping myself alive, I'm actively defying the will of death. But I won't be able to keep him waiting for much longer. Any day now, and he'll come to claim what's rightfully his.

I leave the bathroom and see Curtis in bed, sound asleep. I hobble slowly over and just stare at him, watching his chest fill with air, then deflate. He looks so calm, so peaceful. What if I were to slit his throat? Or smother him with a pillow? I'm bigger than him, and he wouldn't be strong enough to fight back. I've considered the notion more than once: killing Curtis, but never has the desire been so strong before. Why should he get to live after I'm gone? It's embarrassing to think that he has a better chance of survival than me; it's not fair. If I die, I'm bringing him with me.

My eyes suddenly shift their attention to Curtis's neck; the way he lays, leaving it exposed like that, it's so enticing. It's the perfect opportunity. Then, without a moment's pause, I find my hand has somehow found itself now around his neck. I don't know how it got there. But soon, my confusion quickly turns into amusement. I press my thumb down, only using a little force at first, before quickly turning to both hands to squeeze his throat. What am I doing?

Curtis's eyes burst open. I instantly release my hands and stand back in shock. Curtis immediately sits up, tending to his neck.

"What—are you doing!" he coughs out frantically.

I don't react in any way, but stand, staring mindlessly at him, a little embarrassed actually. He continues yelling at me, waiting for a response, but I don't hear him. Eventually, all I can work up the will to do is give an awkward: "I'm sorry," then simply turn around and go back to bed.

I'm sorry.

Chapter 38
Late.

It's the next day, and things between Curtis and I have never been more awkward. So far, he's managed to go the whole day without saying so much as a word to me, not even to ask about last night. Until now, he's kept himself mostly busy with his radio, listening to the broadcasts with his new ear speakers, while I've chosen instead to occupy my time solving a crossword puzzle in the newspaper. Does he think I was sleepwalking? He has no reason to suspect otherwise, unless he thinks I've gone insane, which is true. If I were really insane, would I even know it? I scared him. I scared me too. Looking back on it now, I want to laugh. You worried yourself over nothing. See, everything's alright, though I can't say the same for Curtis. He must be horrified. I wonder what he's thinking right now. Whatever it is, it's nothing compared to the fear I feel every single day.

Today I'm meeting with Darien at the automat; it feels like it's been forever. Last week I was going to ask him to reschedule the hour so that we could meet at an earlier time, but I forgot. Now Curtis is going to wonder where I've been going out on these evenings. He doesn't need another reason to accuse me of going behind his back to conspire against the Operator, he already has enough of those. Let me see now, what's a six-letter word for rat? I can think of one word: C-U-R-T-I-S.

"Is there something bothering you?" says Curtis.

I look up, somewhat startled. "No," I say, trying to act natural, "why—do you ask?"

"It's just that you've been acting strange lately," he says, trying to hold back what he really means.

"Oh," I say, "how so?" he must think I've lost my mind.

"You don't look well," is all he says.

"Oh, don't worry about me Curt," I say, "I couldn't sleep last night, that's all," I fake a smile. He stares at me, afraid to speak, but I continue the crossword puzzle.

"Have you been having Unthoughts," he says.

I gaze back up at him. He has a worried look on his face. He's hoping, yearning, willing that I don't say yes.

"No," I say a little sternly.

He waits a moment before speaking again. "They can help you," he half whispers, "it's not too late. You can report yourself. You wouldn't get into any trouble."

I get up, sit at the edge of my bed, my body facing him. "I said I'm fine." We stare at each other for a while until he can't take it any longer and is the first to look away. I trust now he'll get it in his head to stop pestering me. But I can't stay. I need to get out of here.

"I'm going out to refill my prescription," I say, slightly jovial, to show that I'm over and done with the previous conversation, "I'll be back later." He finally gives up and continues listening to the radio.

I get ready and start for the door. As soon as I'm out of view, I take a moment to breathe. What are you going to do with him? We may as well stop pretending to be nice to each other. I say "we," like he's ever been nice to me. Then again, I haven't been nice to him either.

At the apothecary, I give the apothecarist my prescription

order. As she turns around to refill my bottle with this month's Thought Blockers, I notice from behind the counter, off to the side, a box of ExoPens. The apothecarist's back is to me, now's your best chance; but do I really want to? For a few moments, I manage to hold myself back from doing anything, but she's taking too long. You won't get caught. She's too focused on counting the pills. Alright then, just be careful. After checking that no one else is around, I quietly lean up over the counter, balancing myself as I reach out my arm and manage to grab two packets. That wasn't so hard now, was it? Curtis is right. I'm not well.

When the apothecarist is done, she returns to the counter and starts recording my order in the Cyber-Op terminal.

"Oh, and can I also get a packet of ExoPens?" I add. I think I'm going to throw up.

Before heading to the automat, I stop by a public bathroom and enter a stall, where I quickly begin unwrapping one of the ExoPens. This is your last dose for today. Do you hear me? At this rate, there won't be any of me left. In my hurry to open the packaging, I accidentally drop the pen from its wrapper, and it falls straight into the toilet. Great. I stare at it disappointingly, knowing full well what I must do next. I reluctantly reach down for it, wincing a little, and after trying my best to dry it off, jab myself in the arm with the needle. It's only water, I tell myself.

I should have known by this point I was losing myself, but in the moment, I just couldn't care. Oh how fast you have fallen.

The air is warm today, thick with moisture, and yet the streets seem busier than usual. They must be having a sale today on portable oxygen tanks. A Mother and her assembly line of children are out on their routine walk of the city. I spot the same girl I saw last week standing among them, but she doesn't see me as I pass. Mother Sylvia once mentioned she had a daughter, but that she disposed of her at the Organ Banks; it's a common practice among Surrogate Mothers.

"It wasn't an easy choice, but it was the right one," she said, "I knew from the very beginning that I would regret nursing a daughter. I was generous enough to let her stay as long as she did, not that it much mattered in the end. Though I'm sure they found a good use for her at the Organ Banks. Now I have an even more important responsibility."

I was surprised how unbothered she was when she used the word "daughter." It isn't common practice to refer to an Unchild in such terms, instead choosing to use the word "it." The use of such language helps to dehumanize those children who've fallen victim to a Harvesting, it absolves the mother from the act. But since she did, she must've known what happened, what she did to her own daughter.

I take my tray of food and, as calmly as I can, make my way to our designated meeting place. Though as I come closer, I realize Darien isn't there yet. I shouldn't have come so early. If only Curtis wasn't still home, then I wouldn't need to wait outside in public. I sit down and begin preparing my meal in the ordinary fashion, really taking my time with it, before I can't hold off any longer and start eating. I'll have to chew slowly then. I don't want to be halfway through my meal by the time Darien shows up, or else we won't have the chance to talk as long. Has it really only been a week? It feels like I've lived a whole other life since then. Another day of this, and I don't think I would've lasted. Just sitting here has given me an immense amount of relief, better than the Exodus. I'm going to tell him everything that's happened with Rachel, as well as what's going on with me and Curtis. I also need to tell him he can stop looking for Finn's records, because I already know.

Minutes go by, and he still hasn't arrived. It's not long before I suddenly realize he might not be coming. This doesn't feel right, Darien should've been here by now, I wonder what's keeping him. I check my pocket watch: half an hour late. I can't stay here much longer, I'll need to be going soon. I don't mind waiting a couple more minutes. At this point, as long as I catch a glimpse of him, remind myself that I'm not alone, then maybe it'll be enough to help me last till next week. But if not, I don't think I'll even live long enough to see next week.

I stare down at my tray. By now I've nearly finished all my food. He's not coming, is he? I begin looking around, hoping that at any moment, his face will emerge from somewhere suddenly amongst the crowd. Now I'm worried. What could've happened to him? It could just be nothing, right? Something else must've come up, unless, what if he's been caught? But if that's true, he could've told them he would be coming here to meet me, at this exact place, waiting at this exact time, with someone of my exact description. There could be a Psi-Op watching me right now.

Just then, I hear the footsteps of someone coming nearer and the sounds of shuffling directly behind me from the seat being taken. Is it Darien? I can't tell, I was too distracted. I slowly, yet hesitantly, turn in my chair, to get a better look. He's a man, his back is to me, from behind I can't tell if it's Darien or not. I lean over the side to see his face, but he quickly takes notice of me and turns around to see what I'm doing.

"Hello Acolyte," he says, "can I help you?"

"No," I say, "no, sorry." It isn't him, and of course it isn't, he wouldn't be this late, not of his own will.

I get up, a little awkwardly, trying my best not to go into a panic. I take my tray and what remains of my food and toss it into the recycling. I've become so paranoid I forgot to pretend to take my Thought Blocker. What are the chances that someone saw me throw it away? It's too late now, just focus on trying to get out of here. But if a Psi-Op is following you, you need to get rid of it first. Where do I go then?

I descend the escalator towards the bottom level of the plaza, again and again resisting the urge to glance over my shoulder. Sometimes they'll send out more than one. How many could there be? It's hard to tell, the plaza is swarming with people, could be anyone. They're everywhere, I can't get away.

Suddenly, everything in my head goes quiet, the voice of my thoughts broken by the sound of someone close by calling out a woman's name.

"Jessica," she says. I turn to look. It's a woman. She's trying to talk to the little girl in the assembly line. She gets closer. "Jessica, remember me? It's mommy." What in the world is she doing?

A Protector quickly steps in between her and the rest of the children. "Get back!" he yells, aiming his machine gun at her. We're supposed to pay as little mind as possible to the children, but everyone around has stopped to watch.

"Please, Jessica, don't you remember me?" the woman says. The little girl looks on, frightened, and so do the rest of the children.

"Mommy?" is all she mumbles.

"Mommy loves you Jessi—" the Protector takes one step forward and shoots her in the gut. At this, the children begin screaming and are quickly herded away by the other Protectors.

Their Mother then comes forward and stands before the groaning woman on the ground.

"She isn't yours anymore," she says, in the same arrogant voice the Mothers all seem to share, "you surrendered her under my care, and now this is how she'll remember you."

The woman tosses about the floor, blood leaking from her mouth and stomach, too in pain to get up. It's not long before the Recall Officers appear and drag her away.

Chapter 39
Hclp.

Stranded on the edge between madness and reason, I suddenly find myself standing alone outside the old man's antique shop. I don't even remember how I got here. With the little control I had left, I somehow managed to drag myself over here. I suppose I just needed to get out of there quickly, and this was the only place I could think of. It's all I have left. Where else could I have gone?

I step up to the door, pull the handle, but it doesn't open. Is it locked? I look up. The shop's closed. It can't be, not now. I try the door handles again, violently shaking them to get them open, now using my foot to pry it with. Frantically, I begin banging loudly on the door, but the old man doesn't answer. He must not hear me then, that's it. I need to get in; there's only one thing left to do. Without hesitating, I pull my arm back and, in one quick motion, smash my fist through the door window. I reach inside, fumbling to find the lock. There's a click, and the latch releases. I got it. I hurry inside and quickly shut the door, feeling the excitement rising within me. I stare back at the broken window. I did it, I actually did it.

"What did you do!" I hear a voice cry behind me. I turn around to see the old man standing in the middle of the doorway with a bewildered look on his face. He stares at me for a moment when his gaze suddenly turns into a look of horror, pointing at something below me. That's when I notice what sounds like something dripping on the floor next to me, and I realize how wet my fingers have suddenly become. I lift my arm to see what's the matter, and my smile slowly fades away. Scores of deep gashes run along my hand, from my knuckles up to my forearm, shards of glass embedded in my skin, and all dripping red with blood.

What have you done.

Upstairs in the old man's apartment:

The old man hurriedly shuffles about the room, grabbing as much supplies as he can, before rushing back to his bed, where I sit, anxiously waiting for him to tend to my wounds.

"I'm sorry I broke your window," I stammer out, "I shouldn't have come here."

"Are they looking for you?" he asks, cleaning the blood off my arm.

"What?" I say, "no, I… I just really needed someone to talk to." I feel I've reclaimed just enough control over myself to keep my mind from escaping like that again. The last time something like this happened, I wasn't so lucky.

"Is that what this is about?" he says, "well, I suppose I can't blame you. It can get awfully lonely sometimes."

"Yes," I say, realizing how sympathetic he is, "I just didn't know where else to go."

"Well, now that you're here," he says, "what is it that you wanted to talk about?"

"I uh…" What can I say? It's all so much. Where do I even start? "Well, to begin with," I say, "I've been having a bad day… actually, I've been having a bad day for a really long time. Nothing seems to be going right for me, or anyone for that matter. Everything is falling apart. I don't know what's real anymore. I'm afraid I'm losing myself. I don't know how much of this I can take. I just want it to be over." As I say this, the very fear I've been trying to hide from all day begins to creep up on me again. "I'm sorry. I shouldn't have brought this on you."

"It's alright," he says, "I know how you feel."

At these words, the severity of what the old man must've had to endure all these years suddenly begins to weigh on me. He's gone through this far longer than any of us have, and yet he's still here. "How do you do it?" I mutter.

The old man pauses, looks down, his eyes mournful. "I've lost family, friends, watched millions killed. I've stood back and witnessed the collapse of mankind. I pray you never have to feel what I've been through. I can't tell you how many times I've lost hope, but somehow, miraculously, whenever I think it's the end for me, I always seem to find it again."

"Oh God," I say, "how did you ever survive in this place?"

"You've got so much to lose," he says, "but I've already lost everything, everything except faith that we'll get out of here one day, and I'll get to see the surface again. You see, I wasn't born in Apocalypse. I was born on the surface. I don't remember it much, but it exists, waiting for me. And it's waiting for you too. Just know that for you, things can still get better."

Tears roll down my face, and I turn away. "Better?" I say, "I don't see how anything can get better," I turn back to him, "but I'd still like to try."

He's just about done bandaging up my arm. "Go home," he says, "get some rest. You still have a long way ahead of you."

"Thank you," I say, "here, take this. I don't trust myself enough to get rid of them later, so I'll do it now," I pull out the rest of the ExoPens and hand them to the old man. "Oh, and there's one more thing." Out of all the questions I've been meaning to ask him, the answer to this has been the one I've wanted to know ever since I first heard those words uttered to me. "I was thinking… have you ever heard of the phrase, *Compos Mentis?*"

His face lights up. "I have," he says, "many times."

"Does it mean anything?" I say.

"It's an expression," he says, "it means to have control of one's mind."

Chapter 40
Escapade.

When I finally got home, I found the apartment empty. Curtis must've grown worried waiting and gone out looking for me. My mind was in such a haze from the Exodus that as soon as I laid down to shut my eyes, the next thing I knew, I found myself walking through Liberty Plaza—but I'm not alone. My real mother is here too. We're on another one of our outings. It's been so long. I look up at her, and she's smiling, and then I realize it, this isn't a dream at all. But how is this possible? Have I managed to travel back in time to when she was still alive? We continue walking, and all seems well. This is real, isn't it? I hold on to her hand tighter, afraid I might lose her, and time around me seems to disappear. Hours it feels like, I don't want this to end. Then suddenly, she begins to fade. I look at her and tell her not to let go, but who I see instead is Curtis standing over me, yelling at me to wake up. I'm jolted awake almost instantly, back to the present. I'm in my apartment, I'm twenty-five years old, and my mother is still dead.

"Get up," says Curtis, "come with me."

"What is it?" I say, dazed.

"Just hurry up and get dressed," is all he says.

Curtis leads on as we advance the sidewalk, trying to keep pace with him, as well as with myself. I'm not fully awake yet, I don't think I will be for the rest of the day. I feel like I'm sleepwalking. I've been shut out of my head, or better yet, locked in. I've lost control. I didn't even yell at Curtis for dragging me out of bed unexpectedly, neither did I object to coming with him on this walk, I simply went along. I suppose it was revenge for waking him up last night. As for Curtis, he's been awfully quiet. I don't think he's even said a word to me since we left. Either that, or I'm too disoriented to realize he's been talking to me this whole time.

"Where are we going?" I work up the effort to ask.

Curtis says nothing at first, but turns his head back slightly, showing the tiniest hint of a grin, then looks forward again. "It's just a little further ahead," he says.

After a few minutes, we suddenly break off down a back alleyway where we see a group of people holding a Peace Parade. They've managed to construct a large bonfire in the middle of the alley from old junk and debris, a dome of rubble ignited into flames. The red Recall Wagon and fire truck are also present. Is this why he brought me out, to come to a Peace Parade, what else did I expect? But before we go any further, Curtis stops, stands there, his back to me, then: "Why didn't you tell me your Deliverer tried to abduct you when you were a child?"

I take a moment before answering. "What did you say?"

"I know what happened," he says. He turns around, "how she tried to run away with you but got caught."

I stare at him, confused. Does he mean my real mother? How does he know this? Unless, he couldn't have. He reaches into his coat and pulls out a file. He shows it to me. It's my mother's.

"I found this hidden under your mattress. Did you really think I wouldn't find out? How did you even get this?"

Is he serious? This is why we're here, to talk about my mother? "Why can't you just leave me alone?" I say.

"I'm trying to help you," he says, "she's the reason why you've been acting this way."

"You don't know anything," I say. I go to turn away.

"I know that even after her death," he continues, "she still has a hold of you, doesn't she? She's never once let you go. But I think it's time you finely break free from your Deliverer."

"My… what?" I say, a little peeved.

"Your Deliverer," he repeats, "the woman who gave birth to you."

"You mean my mother," I snap at him.

"Your Mother?" he says, "what are you talking about? Your Mother is Mother Syl—" he pauses, thinks for a moment, then scoffs, "I don't believe this. You still refer to your Deliverer as your mother, and even after what she did to you? Now I know why you've been so attached to her all these years after she betrayed you. You need to understand, she's not your mother anymore, she never was. She's nothing to you, she was sick, and you, are an embarrassment."

Don't waste your energy on him, he's not worth it.

"So, what are you going to do with it," I ask, "are you going to burn it? Throw it into the fire?"

"Not me," he says, "you. You're going to throw it into the fire."

"Why," I say, "why are you doing this?"

"Can't you see she's driving you insane?" he says. "You can't go on like this. It's pathetic. You need to forget her, it's the only way," he steps forward, holds out the file to me, "cast it into the fire, erase her, once and for all."

I snatch the file out of his hand, look down at it, trying to think of what to do. This is by far the worst thing Curtis has ever done to me. He searched the apartment, trying to find something incriminating against me, and tricked me into coming with him to a Peace Parade, just to force me into forgetting about my mother. I can't believe I'm saying this, but even after everything he's done, what I find most frustrating of all is, for once in my life, I think he's right. I mean, he's wrong about me feeling betrayed by my mother for trying to run away with me, and yet his solution still holds. I'm ashamed to admit this, but I've considered it, because I know, in the end, what must be done. I can't continue to keep her here with me anymore, not if it hurts me every time I'm reminded of her. I need to let her go. But do I really mean that? I look back up at Curtis, nod my head. "Alright," I say, "alright, it's time I move on." I can't tell if the pain of keeping her here is worse than forgetting.

Curtis's face lights up with excitement. For once, he approves of my decision. He steps aside for me to pass. I slowly walk up, begin to make my way through the crowd of onlookers as other people take turns throwing things into the fire. Am I really going through with this?

It's my turn now. I step up to the fire, my skin hot against the flames. I look down at the file once more. I'm sorry mother, this isn't how I wanted it to end, you deserve better than this. I'm ashamed of myself, I'm not worthy of being your son. You knew if you got caught what would happen, you died trying to save me, you couldn't give me up. But in the end, I've decided to save myself by giving you up instead. This is the true betrayal. You would've fought till the end if it meant keeping me, but I'm not strong like you. And then I think, maybe this isn't betrayal, maybe you would've wanted this after all, to risk your life all over again just to save me one last time. Only now you're not just risking your life, but all that's left of you. I surrender. Goodbye, mother. I love you.

I hold the file out in front of me and toss it into the fire. Some of its pages come loose and are slowly consumed by the flames. The thicker pages begin to crumple themselves up, coming alive in their last moments as they twist about, before soon fading into nothing but ash. I didn't notice when I started crying. I can't believe I did that.

Curtis comes up beside me, and quickly pulls me away. "It's alright," he says, "you did what was only necessary. You still have a long way ahead of you, this is just the beginning. From now on, I'm going to have to help you find your way, since your failure of a Mother couldn't."

At the sound of these words, something ignites within me. I stop walking. Curtis turns to see what's the matter.

"What is it?" he says.

My head hangs heavy with the voice of my thoughts, trying to break free from the prison that is my mind. "You're wrong," I mutter, "she didn't fail me. I failed her."

He looks back at me, worried. "Are you feeling alright?" he says, moving closer.

Suddenly, something comes over me. It all happens so fast. I seize him by the throat with both hands, slam his body against the side of the fire truck, and begin strangling him. Curtis tries his hardest to fight back, staring up at me with a look of pure horror.

In our struggle to overpower the other, we begin knocking each other around until we both end up crashing into a bank of trash cans, where I manage to pin him down by the neck and begin choking him. I can feel his heartbeat, his face quickly growing red. I don't believe it; this can't be happening. Curtis stares back at me, his eyes bursting out of their sockets, his throat burning. I can feel the blood rapidly pulsating beneath his skin. I didn't think I had it in me, but now that I'm here, I can't stop. I've gone too far. I must finish this. I push down on his neck harder, his head sinking amongst the garbage bags, gasping for air. He starts gripping me, hitting my arms, trying to get me to let go, but it's not working. He opens his mouth to scream, but all that comes out is a gurgle of noise. I've wanted to do it for so long. Pressure builds in my head as if I too am being strangled. My arms go numb from the tension, my veins bulging out. Curtis starts convulsing frantically trying to break free. His time is running out, it'll be over soon. Both of our pulses rise together, beating as one. I can't breathe. When suddenly, something sharp and quick hits me on the side of my head, then everything goes white.

Chapter 41
Recall Clinic.

If you've ever experienced memory loss, then you understand what it's like to wake up with that helpless feeling, knowing your mind has been violated, and by forces far beyond our conscious control. It's difficult to fathom that something like that is even possible. How can our minds be tampered with in such a way that our memories can be erased, just like that? It awakened me to the true nature of how we comprehend this world. Our consciousness exists as a mere projection of reality; what our minds perceive may not always be as they appear. The information from our senses to our brain is just as easily susceptible to being damaged, and sometimes even by our own hand. So no matter how hard I try to remember, I still have zero recollection of the night Finn came home to find me on the floor, overdosed on Thought Blocker.

When I eventually woke up, I could sense right away that my body had gone through something, and yet my mind was not there to witness it. Finn tried to explain as well as he could remember what happened after he found me, and from there, it's sad to say, I could easily guess what events must have transpired leading up to that moment. Life in Apocalypse had finally taken its toll. I had fallen, deep within an inescapable void of despair. I was home alone and had grown impatient waiting for Finn to come back from work. I didn't know where else to turn. I began taking Exodus, little by little at first, but I eventually lost control. I had taken so much Exodus that I was rapidly entering a Mental Escapade. By this point, I was probably still cognizant enough to realize what a huge mistake I had made, and regretted my decision, but it was too late. My mind was steadily going into escape, and there was nothing I could do to stop it. I had to act quickly, so I did the only thing I could think of. I took my bottle of Thought Blocker and swallowed as many pills as I could, which happened to be all that was left of the bottle. I thought if I was quick enough, I could prevent the psychosis before it caught up to me. And my plan worked, too well it seemed.

When Finn found me on the floor of the apartment, he told me he thought I tried to kill myself. I can't even imagine what he must've felt in that moment when he realized what I did. I know he must've gone through all kinds of mixed emotions, but even that didn't stop him. He was able to get most of the pills out, but the rest had already taken their effect. I was in a coma for the next two days, but in the meantime, he was able to cover for me. I had never felt so ashamed in my entire life. Maybe it would've been better if he had just left me to die.

Some things never change.

Present day:

I'm not sure how long I was out; I must have locked myself up somewhere deep within my subconscious, somewhere so far down, it would take some time before I could pull myself back out again. I don't even remember waking up. Suddenly I'm sitting in a room that is not my room, in a bed that is not my bed. The room is small, white, nothing about this place looks familiar, though without being told, I already know where I am, and what I'm doing here: this is the Recall Clinic, and I have been Recalled.

Was getting myself Recalled the only way I could sober up? There's nothing left to hide behind, no more smoke screen, it's just me. Now whatever I feel, whether I choose to ignore it or not, will be real. People can be Recalled for many reasons and are released the next day, though, to be Recalled for being an Unthinker, it is but a prelude to an inevitable death. Though now that I'm here, this isn't what I thought being Recalled would feel like. I've pictured this moment my entire life, imagined myself in this exact scenario, and yet, what I feel is not fear, but relief. The weight has finally been lifted off my shoulders. All I can think about now is not having to hide anymore, not having to run, not having to dread the day I get caught. I've passed the point of no return; I might as well make the most of it.

This place is much cleaner than I thought. I imagined it more depressing in my head. There's the bed that I'm sitting on, which hangs attached to the wall. Over to my left are the toilet and sink, and above the sink, a mirror. There's the door to my cell, and of course, no windows. The room is brightly lit, there's no way to tell what time it is, not without my pocket watch.

My face feels sore. I get up, hobble over to the mirror. The mirror isn't made of glass, but a sheet of steel which has been highly polished. I stare at my reflection and begin taking inventory of everything I see: brown eyes, short brown messy hair, a swarthy complexion. They took my clothes and gave me a plain white shirt and boxers to wear. There's a cast on the bridge of my nose. I think it's broken, or was. Three stitches on the left side of my forehead—that must've been where I felt them hit me before knocking me out—a brownish-purple bruise under my right eye, and, from what I can see, several other marks all over my body. I don't remember taking any punches from Curtis; he wouldn't have had the energy to do any of this, not after what I did to him. Recall Officers tend to get carried away with doing their job. They must've tackled me and beat me with their batons, not realizing I was already unconscious. If it wasn't for my injuries, I would've thought I made the whole thing up, I still can't believe what happened.

Curtis will suffer minor trauma to his throat, nothing too severe. He's probably already back at the apartment. I wonder if I've been replaced by now. They're quick with that. Curtis and his new roommate will get along just fine, nothing like the way we treated each other. He'll want to tell him all about me, and I know exactly what he'll be saying: "He attacked me, he just snapped, I don't know how I couldn't have seen it coming, I guess I held out too much hope for him. It's obvious now he was sick, it's scary to think what could've happened when we were alone, I was just lucky enough to come out alive. Every last one of them, they're all the same, psychotic lunatics. They deserve to suffer."

I know whatever it is I'm being accused of isn't true. On all other accounts, I should be innocent, but not according to them. My crime is being sane in an insane world. Even with everything that's happened to me, all the torture, and all the pain, I still can't help but ask myself if maybe I do deserve this after all.

Mr. Freeman did this on purpose, didn't he? This is why he didn't report me, he planned this all along. He knew what seeing Finn would do to me. Though he isn't entirely to blame, I did fall for it after all. Well, Frank, you got what you wanted.

So, what happens now? I suspect it won't be long until they begin the interrogations. The Psi-Ops will make quick work of me, make sure I don't leave anything out, and they don't leave anything in. They'll have me dissected, cut open. My mind probed and prodded. My insides gutted out, squeezed dry. Evette, what'll happen to you? I let you down. You'll have to go into early hiding now because of me. That's if you've already found out I'm gone. Knowing you, you'd find a way. I should've left something behind, some sort of marker, a sign to be remembered by. I don't want to be forgotten, erased by a machine. And the old man, I let him down too. I don't know what he saw in me.

Compos Mentis. Compos Mentis. Compos Mentis.

"Do you know where you are?" I hear a voice say to me.

It takes some time for my eyes to adjust. There's a woman standing in front of me, a doctor. That's funny, I didn't hear her come in. How long has it been?

"I said, do you know where you are?" she repeats.

"Yes," I say.

"Do you know why you're here?" she says.

Is she being cynical? I can't tell. She's too calm.

"Because I attacked my roommate," I say, "so they think I'm an Unthinker."

"Are you?" she says.

"Yes," I say, "are you here to interrogate me?"

She hesitates to speak. "You had a Mental Escapade," she says, "we ran some tests on you, and we found high traces of Exodus in your blood, which means they know you haven't been taking your Thought Blocker. But I'm going to try to prove that you're not an Unthinker, we just need to come up with a convincing enough explanation."

Am I hearing her right? Why is she talking like that. "I'm sorry…" I say, "I don't understand."

She puts her hand on my shoulder. "I'm going to try to get you out of here," she says.

"You're going to try to get me out of here?" I repeat, bewildered. That's when I realize that I've seen her before: Dr. Savant. "I know you. You're that one doctor who went on Felix's show. They forced you to apologize to the audience because you questioned the Operator. I'm sorry for what they did to you."

This catches her off guard, but she's trying not to show it. "It's alright," she says, she takes a minute to speak, "so, can you think of any excuse why you wouldn't take your Thought Blocker."

"You don't have to do that for me," I say, "not that I'm not grateful for what you're trying to do, but I think I'd rather stay here."

"What do you mean?" she says, almost offended, "why wouldn't you want to go back?"

"Are you really asking me that?" I say.

"So, what," she says, "you think you're better off being

Purged or Pacified?"

"It's better than being out there," I say.

"You don't know what you're talking about," she says, "you have the chance to escape capture, and you're just going to throw it away?"

"I just saw a woman get shot by a Protector for trying to talk to her daughter," I say, "I've had plenty of time to think it over, and I've accepted my fate."

"This isn't right," she says, "people would kill just to have someone tell them they know a way to get them out. Don't you understand? You're giving up your future."

"If I can't even survive living in the present," I say, "what makes you think I can survive living in the future."

"At least you'd have a future," she says, "I won't be here much longer. Soon enough, they'll find a reason to get rid of me. That's what they do to Secondaries like me. But until then, I want to help as many people as I can. Don't you see, I'm already dead, but I'm not going to let that stop me."

I'm amazed at her resilience, even in the face of death. If only there was some way to guarantee my success, then I would let Apocalypse continue to torment me with every atrocity it had to offer, but there isn't. I'm afraid of it ending, ending with all my suffering amounting to nothing. There's only one thing truly guaranteed in life, and that's that there will be an ending.

"Before any of this started happening to me," I say, "I was ready to give my life to the resistance, but I've learned now I'm not a rebel. I'm not sure what I want anymore." Now I know how Rachel must've felt.

She sits down next to me, takes my hand. "Promise me you'll try," she says.

I turn to her and begin to cry. Someday I'm going to have to face reality. "I can't."

Chapter 42
Deliverer.

The next time I fell asleep, I dreamt of my mother again. These kinds of dreams I find are becoming more and more frequent, though remain relatively the same. We'll either be together alone, or when there are other people around us, we pay no mind to them. We hardly speak to one another; we just know what we're thinking. But always before the dream ends, she suddenly disappears, a reminder that I can't bring her with me when I wake up.

I awaken to the sound of the cell door opening abruptly. Dr. Savant rushes to my side. "What's going on?" I say.

"I'm sorry," she says, "I wasn't the one who authorized this. They didn't even tell me she was coming." As she says this, another doctor enters the room, this one escorted by a Protector and holding a clipboard, followed by the familiar sound of heels clicking as someone approaches. It isn't. She enters, steps forward, stops in front of me. It is. Mother Sylvia. How long has it been? Seven years give or take. She's aged quite a bit. Her face still holds that same maniacal expression. But what in the world is she doing here? We meet eyes for the first time in years, then suddenly, all the trauma I left behind comes flooding back. I panic, quickly draw back, and sit huddling in the corner, hiding my face.

"My poor child," she says, "look at you, all grown up." I don't say anything, partly out of shame but mostly out of fear. What is it about her that makes me feel like throwing up? "What's the matter dear? Don't you miss your Mother?"

I'm shaking, I'm going to black out. I hold myself, slow my breathing, and for a second, I see my real mother smiling down at me.

"You don't know how badly I do," I mumble. I hate that my real mother has been reduced to being labeled with the added prefix "real" instead of just "mother," the way it ought to be. Sadly, under the state of the current language, I'm forced into a position where I must alter even the simplest of speech just to clarify my point in the context of present terminology.

"As soon as I heard what happened to you," Mother Sylvia goes on, "I thought I might as well come and see you, since I wasn't there for you when you needed me most of all."

Suddenly, I catch another glimpse of my real mother.

"But that's not true," I say, surprised, "you tried your best to help me, to keep me safe."

"I didn't do a good enough job," she says, I hear her come closer, "I failed you."

How could I have been so selfish? I never had the opportunity to properly appreciate the sacrifices my real mother made for me. "No," I say. I turn around and fall on my knees before Mother Sylvia, keeping my head down as I cling to her skirt, "I was lucky to have you as a mother. You're the reason I'm still alive."

"I should've been a better Mother," she says.

"That's not true," I say, "you were a great mother. I wish I could've spent more time with you before we had to part."

"I'm sorry," she says, "I'm so sorry you went through this alone, my poor child."

"It's alright mother," I say, "it wasn't your fault. I'm the one who should be sorry. I've almost given up hope."

She's here, I know she is, my real mother, she's here with me now, I can feel her, she's come to say goodbye, and good luck.

My mother is dead, but she did not die in vain.

I was officially exonerated a few days later. After the initial visit with Mother Sylvia, the other doctor who was there determined I stopped taking my Thought Blocker because I allowed myself overtime to become upset with the reality that Mother Sylvia wasn't there to take care of me anymore: "It checks out with the witness's statement," he said, "the poor boy just missed his Mother," the witness being Curtis. The night I attacked him he gave a statement where he mentioned just before my escapade, he made a remark about Mother Sylvia, which is what incited the hysteria. Only what really happened was that when I heard Curtis speaking badly about her, I couldn't help but think of my real mother.

As I checked out, I asked the man at the reception desk about Dr. Savant, but he said there were no longer any records of her in the system. So, they decided to get rid of her after all. I'm glad I got to meet her when I did, I wish I could've thanked her for trying to help me. She did help me.

Before I left, they gave me sleeping pills to help me get back on a regular sleep schedule, since I had lost all sense of time while in the Recall Clinic. After everything was certified, all I had to do was to take my Thought Blocker. I only pretended to take it of course, throwing it away as soon as I walked out the door.

I'm going home now. There's a Purging today. The streets are busy. I was only there for a week, and so much has changed. The world seems so different. I've never really acknowledged it, but in some ways, I'm luckier than most. But how could I feel lucky? Well, I'll tell you. So many people would've wanted the opportunity to come back, and to think I almost turned it down. I should've been more grateful. Gone are the days when life in Apocalypse seemed merely a burden. I'm not only living for myself anymore, but for the sake of those who couldn't. I have to survive for them, it won't be easy, but I'll do whatever it takes.

I almost forgot about Curtis. Will he be angry with me because they let me come back? I'm sure he thought he'd never have to deal with me again. Things will definitely be awkward between us, more than they have been. Even if he is annoying and could potentially report me to the Operator, I still can't help but feel sorry for him. He must live such a miserable existence to think the world is out to get him, when in fact, it's quite the opposite. I can only hope that one day he'll see how wrong all of this is. I didn't think I'd ever find myself pitying someone like him, but it's true. At least I know I still have some humanity left.

I open the door and step inside. I was only gone for a few days, and already things like walking into my own apartment feel nostalgic. Curtis hasn't left yet. He's listening to the news as he gets ready for the rally.

"Hello," I say as he approaches, but he walks right past me, "look I… I'm sorry I caused you so much trouble. I can't tell you how hard it's been on me to know I hurt you."

He goes over to the television and turns up the volume. This is going to be harder than I thought.

"If you never want to speak to me again," I say, "I understand. I let myself fall into such a lonely place that I became so caught up in my own problems, there was no escape. Please believe me. I don't want us to be like this anymore. Can't we just get along?"

He gives me a side-eye glance, sighs, and turns off the television. "I'm sorry too," he says, a little defiantly, though he's obviously trying, "you're not the only one to blame for this mess, if I didn't try to be so controlling over you… when you were clearly lost, I might've been able to prevent all of this from happening." I'm shocked he's even considered apologizing, let alone forgiving me. "For now on, I'm going to try to be more patient with you. I see now I could've treated you a lot better."

"Thank you," I say.

Chapter 43
Evette.

We leave for the rally a little later than most. Now once we get there, it'll already be crowded. As we walk, all I can think about is seeing Evette. If I'd gotten out even a day later, I would've had to wait another month to see her again. I hate the feeling of not being with her, every minute we spend apart from each other, I think of her as being dead, and I'm just waiting to find out. Or as if she's slipped out of reality, only existing for the few moments I get to spend with her, before disappearing again. Only of course this isn't true, she has her own life, her own problems, and she's more than capable of taking care of herself. Then again, our situations are very different.

Just like last time, I manage to sneak away from Curtis through the crowd, down the alleyway, towards the clock tower. I reach the back door and go inside. I quietly make my way up the stairs to the third floor, and out of the darkness, I see Evette, and she sees me. She's wearing a mauve iridescent vinyl vapor coat, a black holographic mesh top over a purple lace brassier with a matching garter belt, and heeled boots. Her face is adorned with violet sequence, which shimmers in the dark, though none shine more beautifully than her shimmering silver eyes. This time she came prepared. Her last outfit didn't do so well, given the climate.

Before I have any time to react, she rushes into my arms and hugs me. "Thank God you're alright," she says. I notice her shaking, "I wasn't sure if you were coming or not. I heard what happened."

"I'm sorry I scared you," I say, quite taken aback, "it was all my fault."

"Did those brain butchers hurt you?" she says, examining my face.

"No," I say, "no, I'm fine, though the Recall Officers could've been more gentle with me."

"What were you thinking?" she says, hitting me in the shoulder, "you could've gotten yourself killed."

"I know," I say, "don't you think I know that?"

She pulls herself away and looks at me. "What happened to you?" she says.

I breathe in. "Just know that I'm alright now," is all I say. There's a brief moment of silence between us. She is the first to speak.

"Did you hear what happened to Rachel?" she says, "those stupid doctors pumped her up with drugs to help with her mind, but it only drove her insane, and she killed herself."

"I heard," I say, though I don't mention I didn't know it was because the doctors drugged her. Although she did hang herself, to know she didn't do it on purpose took some of the pain away, that maybe her story wouldn't have always ended with her body dangling from a ceiling. Why is it that we're driven to these kinds of ends? Not long ago I would've ended up the same, all drugged up and in search of an escape. The only difference is, I was the one who drugged me.

"If they cared at all for her," she continues, "they wouldn't have tried to dose her up."

"Apocalypse brings out the worst in everyone," I say, "even good people." She may not have done it herself, but she still suffered. "He's gone, you know," I say, "the other Primary you had me meet with, he's gone. He didn't show up the last time we were supposed to, so I figured he got caught. He's probably one of the prisoners getting Purged right now."

"What are you talking about?" she says, "he didn't get caught. He went Sub-Circuit."

"What?" I say.

"A lot's happened since we last saw each other," she says, "he's now a member of the S.O.S. Last I heard, he's part of a team of new recruits working on getting other people out."

All this time, and I thought he was just another victim claimed by the Operator, but no, he actually got out. I can't say I'm not jealous, but I'm more relieved he's not dead. He's still out there, somewhere, hiding out in the abandoned parts of the city.

"But what about us?" I say, "why aren't we helping?"

"That reminds me," she says, "they've been looking for someone to pick up a package, it's currently on route to our next courier. The guy's the owner of some antique shop in Liberty Plaza. Have you heard of it?"

"I know him," I say, "I can pick it up for them." I suppose it's only natural that the old man has been helping the resistance this whole time.

"Great, I'll let them know," she says.

"What's in the package?" I ask.

"All the records on the abandoned utilidors and power tunnels," she says, "files, maps, blueprints, you know, things of that sort. But if you're going to pick it up, it has to be done tomorrow."

"That's fine," I say, "I can pick it up after work."

"Alright then," she says, "let's meet in a week from now, then you can give me the package. Oh, and before I forget, here," she reaches into her purse and takes out a cassette tape, "I remember what you said last time, how you ran out of space for your recordings. One of the sides is used though, so you'll have to tape over it if you want to record something."

I take the cassette from her, examining it. I can't believe she did this for me. "What's on it?" I ask.

"Mostly music," she says, "Unmusic to be exact. Apparently the woman who owned it last used to collect songs that were considered too dangerous to listen to. You might even like some of them."

"Thank you," I say.

Outside in the square, the Purging has begun. I go up to the window, peer my eye through one of the holes in the vinyl sheet, and watch as they force the prisoners out between the two crowds, down the fenced pathway.

"What are you thinking of?" she says, noticing how quiet I've become.

"I should be there," I say, "getting Purged to the uranium mines."

"Why do you say that?" she says, confused.

"I don't know," I say, "it feels wrong for me to have survived as long as I have, like I've cheated at life somehow."

"That's what they want you to think," she says.

"I just think it's unfair that I have to watch them get Purged, while I've managed to last this long without getting caught."

"If it bothers you so much," she says, "then why don't you go down there and join them?" I turn to her, and we both laugh. "I didn't get a chance to mention it last time," she says, "but you know all that stuff about generational birth defects? Well, it's all made up."

"What do you mean?" I say.

"Why do you think they have them mining uranium in the first place?" she says, "they put it in everything, in our food, in our water, in our makeup, it's all contaminated. We're poisoning our own people to keep up this lie that we're victims of the past, when now we're only victims of ourselves. The original genetic disease died out years ago. Whatever symptoms are occurring today are purely artificial."

I don't even give a reaction; this sort of thing doesn't surprise me anymore. Somehow, I feel like I knew this all along. But how could I? Finn never mentioned it to me, and I certainly couldn't have figured this out on my own. I guess it just seemed like something the Engineers would do. Only in Apocalypse.

The conversation has gone silent, now comes the moment I've been dreading.

"Listen… there's something I need to tell you," I say.

She throws me an anxious look. "What is it?" she says, hesitantly, she can hear the seriousness in my voice. She's not going to like this.

"Mr. Freeman knows I'm an Unthinker," I say.

She stares at me, trying to process this news. She opens her mouth as if she's about to speak, but she doesn't.

"He's known for a while," I continue, "I don't know what he's planning, but it doesn't seem like he wants me gone all together… at least not yet."

"What are you standing here for!" she finally blurts out, "if he knows you're an Unthinker you need to go! We have to get you out!" she turns away, thinking, "I can get in touch with someone, but who knows how long it'll take to arrange an escort."

"There's no need to rush," I say, "I'm not in any immediate danger."

"That doesn't matter!" she says, turning back to me, "you don't know how far Frank is willing to go!"

"What? How do you—" suddenly I realize what she means. "He knows you're an Unthinker too," I say, not as a question, but as a matter of fact. "So he's the one who's been sending Psi-Ops to follow you."

She stands there staring, not just at me, but at the scene in her mind of what Mr. Freeman could do to me—to us. "He can make life here very difficult for you," she says, her voice trembling.

"Who is he?" I say.

"He's my uncle," she says.

"What else?" I say.

She holds her gaze. Her stare is so sharp, it can cut the air between us like a blade. "He's a monster," she says.

Mr. Freeman's only just found out about me, but he's known about Evette far longer. It must be absolute hell.

"We'll get through this," I say, trying to comfort her, "I survived his first attempt on me, don't worry."

"If he finds out about us, who knows what he'll do," she says, she begins to cry, "I can't lose you—"

Suddenly, I notice a glint of light at the edge of my vision coming in through the window. But before I have the chance to look, Evette starts towards me, puts one hand around the back of my neck, covers my mouth with the other, and thrusts me against the wall, out of view from the window. We hear the sound of the drone buzzing just outside, carefully scanning over every opening in the tower. We quietly watch as the searchlight darts about the room, peering through the holes in the plastic sheet, visible by the dust particles in the air, like hundreds of tiny broken beams of light.

After a minute or two, the drone finally moves on, leaving us both in a state of deep shock. We hold each other in our arms, staring into the other's eyes, not saying a word. The longer I stare, the heavier the truth begins to weigh on me: after tonight, we might never see each other again. Evette slowly pulls herself away from me, fear growing on her face. She knows it too. I've never wanted to be with anybody more than I do right now. We find ourselves suddenly moving in on each other as our lips join together. Evette is the one to act first. She retreats into the darkness as we both begin to undress ourselves, removing our clothes, one piece at a time, until there's nothing left.

She stands in the open, her shadowy figure mysterious against the darkness. But there's something wrong; she doesn't want to move. She begins to hug herself, then slowly steps forward, out into the light. My breath escapes me. Out of all the things to be unprepared for, how could I have ever prepared myself for this? Once the realization of what I'm looking at finally hits me, I have to stop myself from drawing back in surprise. I thought they were tattoos. My eyes linger on her, scanning over every inch of her body. She knew there was no way I wouldn't notice them. When she finally accepts the reality that I've seen them, she looks down at herself as well, her braids falling over her face.

Legions and legions of black scars score all across her dark skin, from her shoulders down to her thighs. The scars are like a physical manifestation of her body slowly being corrupted by Apocalypse—a virus gradually destroying her from the inside out. Not only has the pain scarred her mind, but her body as well.

It must be absolute hell.

That evening we joined in the exchange of our human desires, our bodies becoming one. We were told that a relationship like ours could not exist, or else it would destroy everything the Operator worked to accomplish. Let's hope that we'll live long enough to see that happen.

I lie next to Evette in the damp cool air of the room, basking in the warmth of her body on my bear skin. I turn to her, and I tell her my name.

VIII
Package

Chapter 44
Promoted.

I'm sure you've been wondering why I still talk about the Operator as though he truly is who everyone claims him to be, even after I've proven that he's nothing more than a fraud. The Operator may not be real, but there are very real people behind him who are responsible for running this operation. It is this amalgamation of thinking minds who are the ones really in charge: the Engineers. Together, they are the Operator.

Today will be the first time I've gone back to work since this whole mess started. I was only supposed to be on break for a few days, but I ended up being gone for a week instead. I didn't know this until afterward, but once the Bureau was notified that I'd been Recalled and put under investigation, I was actually fired. But to my surprise, just before Dr. Savant disappeared, she took it upon herself to try to fully reinstate me back to my old position, and she succeeded. All of this took place while I was still in the Recall Clinic, so I had no idea she'd done this. She was able to help me after all. Though, after today, I'll find out whether this was of benefit to me or a disservice.

We step out into the atrium, welcomed by that familiar shift in the atmosphere; however, this time, my body barely even reacts to the clean air. The air in the Recall Clinic is kept surprisingly well-ventilated, so I guess I'd gotten used to it.

Curtis and I head to our respective departments. I step out of the elevator, walk down the hall, enter the Newsroom. As soon as my presence is known, I sense a clear disturbance in the air. I can feel the tension rising around me. It's strange coming back here; it's very unwelcoming, and I mean more than usual. Everyone here must've heard by now what happened to me. They're probably all thinking that the doctors made some mistake. How could they allow me to keep my job in the Bureau after what I did? I lift my head a little as I walk, a faint smirk growing across my face. You're not going to get rid of me that easily.

As I walk down the center aisle, I steal a glance behind me, up at that looming office window. What's going to happen to me now that Mr. Freeman knows I'm an Unthinker? He's decided to keep me here after all, but what does that mean for me? When I came back from Neo Synapse that same day to develop the photos, Mr. Freeman was in a meeting, so he had his assistant come pick them up from me instead. He must be anxious to see what's become of me ever since.

As I approach my cubicle, my heart suddenly lodges into my throat. A Protector is waiting beside my desk, not Martin though, a different one. Has he been replaced? He stares at me as I come nearer, trying my best to remain calm.

"Come with me," he says, directing me to step in front of him, towards the upper level stairs. Mr. Freeman's been awaiting my return. Alright Frank, I'll play along with your sick game for now.

We walk up the stairs, along the balcony, straight for Mr. Freeman's office. My chest is pounding. This is one of the reasons I didn't want to come back, but I'm ready now. I'll take whatever he's got in store for me. The Protector steps forward, stretches out his hand, and opens the door. Oh God, please don't let me suffer too much.

As I step into the room, it suddenly dawns on me that all the lights in his office are on. I've never seen the room all lit up like this before. I consider this, as well as the new Protector, but before I have time to fully piece it together, I enter and am met face to face with an Engineer I've never seen before. He's slightly taller than me, heavily built, with dark, slicked-back hair, and an inflated face.

"Come in," he says, "Enzo, shut that door." I enter and seat myself in the client's chair.

Where's Mr. Freeman?

"I'm Mr. Takahashi," he says, a little surly, "I've taken over Mr. Freeman's position as the new editor-in-chief. Before Mr. Freeman left, he went to considerable lengths to tell me a bit about you. It appears you left quite the impression on him."

I sit quietly, listening to what he has to say. Mr. Freeman told him about me?

"I'm going to let you know just this once," he continues, a little aggressive now, "I don't care that he thought you were someone special, but when you work for me, I expect you to know your place. No extra privileges, understood?"

"Yes, sir."

Mr. Freeman told him I was special? Why does he always have to talk to people about me?

"And about your little incident," he says, picking up a piece of paper from his desk, "it says here that you had a Mental Escapade and attacked your roommate. Personally, I would never tolerate such behavior as an excuse for absence, but the Recall Clinic did deem you fit for reinstatement; and after all the things Mr. Freeman said about you, I wanted to see for myself what you were made of… and perhaps, maybe make Frank eat his words. But if you so even think about misbehaving while under my employment, I won't waste any time finding a new replacement, understood?"

"Yes sir," I say.

"Good," he grunts, "now that that's out of the way, it's time for your first assignment. There's going to be a statue unveiling in Liberty Plaza, as a monument to the Operator. The unveiling will be at ten thirty. Now I trust you know by now how to do your job, so get to it."

"I just have one question sir," I say, almost without thinking.

He lifts his round head and glares at me with a look of half surprise and half anger. "Yes, what is it?" he says, his face growing red.

With everything I've been through, I don't feel even remotely intimidated by this man. "Where's Mr. Freeman now?" I say.

He scowls. "Why does it matter? Do you miss him or something?"

I just stare at him, willing him to tell me, even through his irritation.

"He was promoted!" he eventually bursts out, "now stop wasting my time and get to work!"

"Yes sir," I say.

I get up, leave his office, back to my cubicle. So, Mr. Freeman's been promoted. I don't know how to feel about this. For one, I don't have to deal with him anymore. In theory, it sounds great, but it makes me wonder why he would let me get off so easily. He'll find another way to reach me, I just know it; he can't possibly be done with me yet. Mr. Freeman can always find a way to beat my expectations. I guess he would rather have me here in the meantime, until he can commence whatever plans he has in store for me.

I can hear him now. "It's not your time," he says, "there's still plenty more I want you to see." For the first time, I know what he's thinking. I, and those like me, are the reason he does the things he does. He takes pleasure in seeing us suffer. I can't help but think if maybe one day he'll make me wish I'd been Purged instead.

Chapter 45
Lockdown.

I pack my things and head back down to the lobby to sign out. After the unveiling, I should see if I can stop by the antique shop to pick up the package, though I'll have to drop it off at my apartment first before returning. But will I have enough time? If I'm late, Mr. Takahashi might notice. No, perhaps it's best I stick to waiting until after work to get it, as long as I get it today, that's all that matters.

I join the queue, making sure to have my card ready, but after a minute of waiting, and the line having moved not once, I look around to see that none of the other lines have moved either. Something's stopping us from leaving. Several minutes pass, all of us growing ever more impatient. A few people have taken to complaining when, without warning, the emergency alarms suddenly start blaring throughout the entire Bureau. All round we hear shouts as the Protectors begin directing us to return to our departments. I hurriedly go back the same way I came, noticing everyone around becoming deeply on edge. What in the world is going on? I've never seen the Bureau in such a panic before; even I'm beginning to get anxious.

I manage to return to the Newsroom just as they make the announcement that we'll be going under lockdown. I hardly have any time to process this, it's all happening so fast; I never thought anything like this was even possible. They've trapped us in here. No one goes in or out. But why? What's going on? Is it the resistance?

All work has ceased, and talks of a possible psycho-terrorist attack in the Bureau have rapidly spread throughout the department, the thought of which has incited varying reactions amongst the other workers. Some have broken down into full on hysterics, fearing that the resistance will succeed in overthrowing the Bureau. Others are confident enough in the Protectors' ability to stop them, and are glad that the resistance would be stupid enough to try, saying they may as well have just turned themselves in. Then, unsurprisingly, there are those just itching with excitement about the attack, hoping to use it as yet another excuse to cause panic among the public by spreading more lies.

Amidst the commotion in the Newsroom, I manage to slip away from the conversation, retreating yet again into the darkroom—the only place I can ever truly be alone with my thoughts. I lock the door behind me, making sure to turn both the safelight and *Darkroom In Use* sign on. If I'm going to be locked up in this place, I may as well use my time wisely. I pull a chair out and climb onto one of the developing tables, the one beneath the ceiling panel behind which I've hidden the Bible. I push up and begin feeling inside for it. It isn't long before I suddenly realize the Bible isn't there. My heart instantly drops. No, it can't. I must've hidden it behind a different panel. I reach my arm deeper into the pitch-black recess of the ceiling, sweeping my hand back and forth, to cover more range. It has to be here somewhere; did someone take it? My fingers suddenly press up against something, and for a moment I'm relieved. But as I grab hold of the object, I quickly realize this isn't the Bible. I slowly pull my arm out to see what I have in my hand. It's an envelope. What is this doing here? And where's the Bible?

I climb off the developing table, trying to come up with a

fitting explanation for how this could possibly be happening, though I know perfectly well there is only one person who could be responsible for this. The envelope is small but thick, and is full of what feels like a stack of letters. I open it and pour its contents out onto the table. In the red of the light, it takes my eyes a second to realize what I'm looking at, when suddenly I feel as if a bullet has torn through my chest. Staring at the horrific sight before me, I frantically begin spreading the papers across the table for a better look. My eyes widen. This can't be real.

They're all photos of me—hundreds of them. Walking out in the city, waiting in the metro station, strolling around Liberty Plaza, having lunch at an eatery, and even some of me in the Bureau. Evette was right, Mr. Freeman's had someone spying on me this whole time. I can't say I didn't suspect it, but this, this is insane. The photos appear to have been taken over the course of these last few months. Suddenly, another wave of panic fills me, and I begin rifling through the photos, praying I won't find one with me and Evette. After several minutes of looking, I feel a slight weight lift off me. Good, he still has no idea. But he could just as easily have found out.

I loom over the table, staring down at the farewell gift Mr. Freeman left for me, my face tightening with rage with every minute that passes. This was a threat. He wants me to know that he's still in control, wherever he is. He thinks he can scare me, but I'm not going to break that easily. I don't know whether it's bravery or sheer stupidity, but this whole event seems to have sparked something inside me. I'm done putting up with his games.

At once, I spring into action. I grab one of the developing trays, and quickly make work of sliding the photos into it and scattering them into the processing sink. I can't risk throwing the photos away; there's too many, someone might find them. Cutting them up wouldn't be helpful enough either. No, I'll have to make sure not a single trace of them is left. Once I finish depositing all the photos into the sink, I go over to the chemical closet, unlock it, and begin searching among the glass bottles until I find it—a bottle marked: "Concentrated Sulfuric

Acid."

Everything is prepared. I step forward, standing over the processing sink, holding a rag to my mouth. I force myself to take one long last look at the scene before me, searing this image into my memory so I don't forget who and what I'm up against, then carefully begin pouring the liquid. Upon contact, the acid reacts immediately. It slowly begins melting the film at first, dissolving it into a dark sludge, fumes rising from the ooze. I step back, holding the rag tighter to my face as a putrid odor emits from the gases. The rag isn't as effective as I'd hoped. As soon as the foul smell hits my nose, I begin retching uncontrollably before hawking up a wad of phlegm to the floor beside me. The mass of melted photos suddenly begins breaking down even more, far beyond its physical matter, bubbling and expanding into a thick tar-like mass of hissing pus. This reaction lasts less than a minute before finally stopping. Slowly removing the rag from my mouth, I stare down at the sink—the place where the photos once remained now resides a sizzling black abomination.

All this time I feared Mr. Freeman would make me regret not turning myself in, but in the end, he's the one who's going to regret ever letting me live in the first place.

Chapter 46
Curfew.

Hours passed until we were finally allowed to leave. We remained under lockdown for nearly the entire day. Afterward, the Operator declared an early city-wide curfew, so everyone was ordered to go directly home without detour. I'd lost all chance to pick up the package. What could've possibly scared the Operator to react so drastically? Curtis came home a few minutes after me. We immediately broke into a conversation about everything that had happened.

"I asked around," he says, "some said they found a bomb."

"A bomb?" I say.

"It could be," he says, "others said one of those terrorists had snuck in somehow, and tried to assassinate an Engineer. Can you imagine? Someone else said they were trying to break into the Operator's control module to hack his computer servers."

"Well, what do you think happened?" I say.

"I don't know," he says, "but… there is one thing," he lowers his voice, "after the lockdown, I overheard some of the other Record Keepers saying that we're permanently shutting down the Library of Unbooks."

The hairs on the back of my neck stand on end. "Really, what for?" I say, trying not to sound worried.

"It's too much of a security risk to keep them," he says, "they don't want that kind of information falling into the wrong hands, so they're just going to get rid of them. Let's hope they'll hold a giant book burning."

Those books are the last of their kind. If they destroy them, then there won't be anything like them left. They'll have all gone extinct.

"Yes," I say, "let's hope."

I lie in bed, pretending to be asleep. It's only been an hour, but now's as good a time as any. Before Curtis took his Thought Blocker, I slipped a few of my sleeping pills into his water while he was in the bathroom. Even as he began to feel drowsy, he didn't suspect a thing. I'll be back before he wakes up. He won't even know I'm gone.

I get out of bed, quietly put my shoes on, and make my way towards the door. I can't believe I'm going through with this, but I made a promise, the resistance is counting on me. I have to get that package.

I slowly open the door and peek my head out into the hallway. It's empty. I quietly step out and start towards the stairwell, trying to remain composed. I go inside, quickly shut the door behind me, and begin to descend to the first floor. Suddenly from above, I hear the sound of a door opening echo through the stairwell. People are coming. I stop, too scared to move. They're going to catch up if I don't run. I try my best to keep quiet as I hurry along the stairs, staying as close to the walls as I can. As I come to the ground level, I hear the people stop on the landing directly above me, and then their footsteps fading away as they enter the hall. I take a moment to relax. That was too close. I can't let anyone see me. Maybe I should've tried to come up with an excuse, in case someone recognized me.

At the base of the stairwell is a back exit door that leads directly into the alleyway. Everyone always leaves through the main entrance, so I never gave it much thought to go out this way before. After making sure there aren't any alarms, I push open the door, stepping out into the cold. I should've dressed better, but at least I won't be as visible. I've never been back here before, but I should still be able to find my way.

I creep along the darkened streets, taking refuge amidst the shadowy corners of Apocalypse, navigating through the alleyways along the city, only using the roads if it can't be helped. Every few minutes, I'll stop to take cover behind a newsstand or in a telephone box when a patrol car or drone cruises by. This is by far the most insane thing I've ever done. The streets look eerie, completely empty like this. It's so quiet. I never realized how open everything is. There aren't many places to hide, but for the most part, the mist already provides me with just enough of a layer of invisibility to get by.

I'm nearly there. For the next few blocks, I continue without stopping. It should be all clear from here. As I draw closer to the plaza's entrance, a patrol car suddenly turns onto this street, its large double searchlights sweeping back and forth across the road like high beams through the fog. I look around for somewhere to hide, but it's moving faster than I thought, I don't have enough time. I risk it and take cover behind a mailbox. It's not big enough, they're going to see me. I watch as the left searchlight glides along the edge of the street, rapidly closing in on my location. I'm trapped. My heart explodes slowly in my chest, and my throat swells with chemicals. I shut my eyes and prepare for what's about to happen.

"Over here, we got one!" the Protector says through the speaker. Instantly my blood turns to ice at the sound of his voice. "Come out with your hands up!"

"I didn't do anything, I swear!" cries another voice, this one not coming from the speakers but from someone else.

I open my eyes, quickly coming to the realization it wasn't me who they spotted. I look up in shock. Cast against the wall of the building in front of me is the shadow of the mailbox, as well as the outline of me trying to hide behind it, caught directly in the beam of the searchlight. I slowly begin to peek my head out from behind the mailbox. On the other side of the street is a man, a Primary, holding his hands up, standing in the mouth of an alleyway, caught directly in the center of a large spotlight. He looks absolutely terrified. His clothes are filthy, and he's covered in sweat stains. He must've been trying to hide behind the trash cans in the alleyway, but he's too large. No wonder they saw him first.

"Don't move!" says the other Protector as he gets out to arrest him, aiming his taser gun.

"Please, don't hurt me!" he whimpers, then he glances towards the mailbox, and his stare locks onto me. I see the fear in his eyes as he understands this is the end for him, then I hear the loud blast of the gun as the metal prongs pierce into his skin. He lets out a sharp cry as the surge of electricity streams through his muscles, his legs quickly giving out. He drops to the ground with a heavy thud, groaning like a wild beast as he convulses on the floor. I don't see what happens next, because after the two Protectors go to collect his body, I take my chance and make a run for it, not looking back.

Chapter 47
Sacrifice.

I make it to the door of the antique shop, breathless and exhausted. It's unlocked. I hurry inside, and shut the door behind me, holding a sharp stitch at my side. In the semidarkness, I see the old man sitting at the counter hooked up to his oxygen tank, reading a book.

"I knew you'd come," he says through his mask, "here, let me just get it for you," he reaches beneath the counter and pulls out the package, which is wadded in a thick plastic wrapping. "What's the matter?" he says. He sees my frustration.

"I just saw them take another guy," I say, "I was hiding, so they didn't see me. He was scared out of his mind." I can't tell if I'm crying or if it's just the sweat trickling into my eyes. "Why… why does it have to be this way?" I say, "how could we let them do this? You're old enough to remember. Tell me, how could we give our freedom up for this? How could humanity be so stupid to ever allow anything like this to happen? Tell me!" my voice rising to a shout.

He looks on, startled. I didn't realize where my emotions were taking me. I see now this question had struck him somewhere painful.

"I'm sorry," I say, "I—I didn't mean to—"

"It's true," he says, "I was there, so I'm partly to blame. I didn't speak out when I could have. I was afraid."

"No, I didn't mean it like that," I say, "none of this is your fault."

"It may as well be," he says, "it's funny how a little sacrifice can go a long way. Even a single voice can change the world."

"But even then, there's still the problem with the ones who have the power," I say, "they wanted this, to be in control, it's power that's the cause of all our problems, not you."

"No," he says, "power is not the cause of all our problems. Power alone would not have led us to where we are now, not even the desire for power. It's corrupt power that does it, power in the wrong hands, and we gave it to them. It's what caused the nuclear war in the first place. It's why those poor Secondaries were tyrannized so long ago. And it's why society is what it is today. Evil begins where truth ends."

"But humanity is going to take it back from them," I say, "won't we."

"That's a fine thought," he says, "too bad I won't be there to see it."

I look up at him, confused. "Why wouldn't you?" I say.

He pauses and prepares himself to speak. "The Psi-Ops came by and told me I had a week before they would come and take me away. They think I'm a risk to them because I'm old; I've seen too much."

My lungs go empty of air. "What?" I say, "when was this?"

"Seven days ago," he says.

We stare at each other, the look of defeat on both of our faces.

"They explained to me how it worked," he goes on, "told me it wouldn't hurt, said I'd be asleep when they do it, that I wouldn't feel a thing. They told me I had behaved well enough, followed the rules, kept my mouth shut. You've at least earned the privilege to go in peace, they said. But it's not just me. They're rounding up all the remaining Surfaceborns still on Circuit. Not that there's many of us left, they just don't want to bother waiting any longer for us to die out."

This must be why Evette told me I had to pick up the package today. "Can't we get you out?" I say, "we can send someone. It's not too late."

"It's alright," he says, "the Recall Wagon will be here early tomorrow morning. Besides, there's no use in risking someone else's life just to get me out."

"But you can leave," I say, "you've waited this long. You can finally go home."

"It's too late," he says, "I've already told them not to send anyone for me."

"You—you can't give up," I say, finding it more and more frustrating to change his mind, "you deserve this more than anyone else. There must be something we can do."

"I'm not giving up," he says, "but if I am giving up anything, I'm giving up my spot to you."

"What are you talking about?" I say.

"When it comes time for the resistance to start making advancements in their plan to begin a second wave of rescues," he says, "they've already decided to take you with them. I'm no use to them. I couldn't even offer help to the world when it needed it most, so what good could I do? But you, you've already proven you're of more worth to them than I ever was. Don't be like me, don't stand back and watch your world burn, do something before it's too late."

"But you can still help them," I say, gnashing my teeth out of anger.

"I am helping them," he says smiling. He glares at me. So that's it then, he's made up his mind. "As my last effort to offer any help in this world, I give you my chance for escape so that you may live. I've already lived. It's my time to go now," he says my name.

I drop to my knees in anguish. "I'm so sorry," I say, crying, "I'm so sorry that you had to live through all this."

"Don't be sorry," he says, "believe it or not, I chose this life. Besides, you'll see me again someday. Till then, let me be an example to you, of how not to become me."

He helps me back on my feet, and we hug.

"But before you go," he says, walking back behind the counter, "I'd like you to have something," he reaches down and pulls out a little metal box. He opens it and takes out a gun. "It might come in handy," he says, holding it out for me to take. I don't know what to say. I take it, along with the package. They're never going to stop hunting us, not until they've killed every last one.

"I promise I won't let you down."

Chapter 48
Audio log No. 29.

It's the next day, early in the morning. The mist has thinned throughout the night. He's washing his face, afterward, he combs his hair, maybe even trims his beard. Now he's getting dressed. He's in his best suit. He had to get it out of storage. He wants to feel comfortable. He's downstairs sitting in his rocking chair, his eyes closed, listening for the sound of the truck approaching. He's not using his oxygen tank; he doesn't think he needs it anymore. He hears the truck just as it pulls in, then the doors slamming and the footsteps on the front stairs. They don't knock, they don't even come in. The Protector stands holding the front door open for him. He gets up, and hobbles through it. No words need to be exchanged. As he walks out, he takes one last look at the shop, before he steps up to the back of the truck. Its double doors stand open, inviting him in. He's too weak to bring himself up, but the Protector is considerate enough to help him. He thanks him and takes his hand, struggling at first to lift himself, but after managing to get one foot in, is able to enter just fine. Some time passes, now he's in a chamber, lying on a leather gurney, no longer in his best suit, but in a polyester shift, a needle feeding into his arm. He's not scared, he's not panicking, he's calm. The doctor comes in, administers the anesthesia. He slows his breathing. He thinks of the surface, picturing the sun, remembering how warm it felt on his skin, as he slowly drifts off to sleep, at which point he's already gone.

You know, I ought to apologize for telling this story. If I ever made you cry, or scared, or angry, or any other of those things. It was never my intention to make you feel one way. I could apologize, but then again, you chose to listen to me in the first place. You could have stopped anytime; I'm merely sharing my experiences. What's interesting is that, even with so much already said, there were some things I had to change or even cut out completely. I did this for both my and your sake. There was just too much violence, too much suffering. At the very least, I had some consideration for you. I would never want anyone to experience the things I've had to endure. Though you can still find traces of their existence, these abandoned moments. They reside in the background only now as mere afterthoughts. They aren't hard to find, as long as you go looking for them. Though if I am to apologize for anything, it's that I could have done a better job of sparing you the pain, I am sorry for that.

And so then, the story continues.

I made it back to my apartment at around 1:40, by then I was exhausted. I didn't need sleeping pills. Though before I let myself dissolve into bed, I made sure to hide the package in the vent above my desk.

It's the following day, evening has already arrived. I sit at my desk, preparing to begin the newest entry in my series of audio logs. I unwrap the cassette tape Evette gave me, insert it into the recorder, making sure to place it empty side up. I shut it, pull the receiver to my mouth, hit record.

"Audio log number 29," I say, "hello again, it's… been a while." It's like I'm talking with an old friend whom I've fallen out of touch with, and don't know how to act around anymore.

I've forgotten how to be myself. "So, where do I even begin?" I laugh, "I'd like to start off by commemorating this log to everyone who couldn't be here, and not just those who are dead. After my time in the Recall Clinic, I made a promise to you and myself that I wouldn't give up no matter what. It's because of you I find the will to keep living," already, the tears start to form. I stop, remind myself that I don't have time, and after clearing my throat, I continue. "Tomorrow I'm meeting with my contact in the abandoned clock tower in Freedom Square. I'm dropping off a package. I haven't opened it myself, but the package is said to contain files on the city's abandoned utilidors, my guess is the resistance wants to use them to move about the city more freely. There have been talks about a possible Peace Parade taking place somewhere near Freedom Square at around the same time, so I was thinking of telling Curtis that I wanted to go as an excuse for leaving. If he ends up coming with me, I'll just have to figure out another way to lose him once there, which shouldn't be too hard. Peace Parades tend to be very crowded."

It takes me a moment to realize how naturally I've returned to doing one of these recordings. I finally feel like my old self again. There's a reason I find pleasure in doing this, it helps me so much to keep my thoughts in check. "I'm sorry," I laugh into my hand, "it's just that, it's been so long since I last made one of these, I forgot how much I enjoyed doing this. It's because of my contact that I even had the chance to make this recording. She's the one who gave me the cassette tape that I'm using to record this very message, so thank you to her." Now comes the other thing. "This is sort of strange to confess. I wasn't sure at first if it was even possible for me. I never thought this was how it would happen, and now that it has, there's no denying it: I've fallen in love with a Secondary." Blood rushes to my face. "She's a very smart woman, and she's very resourceful. But most importantly, she feels the same way about me—" there's only one thing stopping us, "but we can never be with each other," I say, "not while we're still here." I stop, struggling to understand what exactly it is that I'm trying to say, and whether or not I want to say it. "I was afraid to fall in love, and more afraid to fall in love with someone like her, because now I can't afford to lose her." Every possible thing that could happen to her begins to play out in my head. "I wouldn't be able to live with myself if anything happened to her, but…" I pause, "but I realize now that I'd rather feel this way for the rest of my life if it means doing everything in my power to keep her safe. Evette, we are going to get out of here together. *Compose Mentis.*"

I stop the recording and just sit silently for a few moments. After a minute, my face begins to feel sore. I've been smiling all this time; I don't think I've ever felt happier. It's true then, I'm going to escape this place.

I look back at the cassette and remember how Evette mentioned that its previous owner managed to save some of the music she recorded. I've got nothing else to do. I eject the cassette from the recorder, turn it to its other side, insert it back into the tray. I shut it, rewind it, and press play.

Chapter 49
Temporal Interlude.

The time has come to set my plan in motion. I thought it all out yesterday. When it would've come time for me to leave, I wouldn't have been able to take the package out from the vent, not without Curtis seeing me. So, before he came home yesterday, I had to put the package in my briefcase, as well as make sure to keep him from finding it all day.

"Are you sure you don't want to come?" I say.

"No, it's alright," says Curtis, "you go ahead. I've got things I need to do first." I don't attempt to push him any further, as I'd prefer it if he didn't come along, but I didn't want to appear dismissive of him altogether.

I leave my Habitat. As of present, I find myself overwhelmed with a profound sense of optimism. I've survived through so much in this life, and I know there are more challenges to come. But I can't help but feel proud of myself for making it this far, and for once, everything feels like it's going to be alright.

The walk to the clock tower will be slow, so I'll have plenty of time in between for myself to just think. I value these moments, I've noticed all the best thoughts seem to come about when you're in the midst of something, or when you're about to go to sleep. But even then, I have to be careful, it's dangerous to do your thinking out in public, one can always get lost in one's own thoughts. Someone might catch me staring, smiling at nothing: space out. It's happened before. One of the many symptoms of having Unthoughts. What should I do then? "Clear your mind," Mother Sylvia once said, "all that thinking will give you a headache."

I cruise through the fog-ridden streets, a solitary white figure shrouded by vapor and hot neon. I understand now this war is not one we wage against a body, but one within our own minds. When I was young, I used to feel like as time moved on, I somehow got left behind. I was stuck, living in a forgotten present, while everyone else conformed to the desires of this world with ease. Something was wrong with me, and I needed help. For a long time, that's what I'd been led to believe, and not by accident. Then I discovered I wasn't alone.

So many times, I could've walked by someone, seen them passing by on the street, and never even knew it—someone just like me. Back then, if you had told me this, I never would've believed it—not only in your existence, but in the revelation that there are far more of you than I could have ever imagined.

I'll be coming to the checkpoint soon. When they ask what's in the package, I plan on saying it's just something I'm bringing to the Peace Parade to burn. They wouldn't go through the trouble of reading through it.

After a block, I reach the checkpoint, only, there aren't any Protectors stationed at it. That's strange. I suppose they decided not to keep it in operation for the Peace Parade. But why would they just abandon it like this? I slip past the checkpoint and continue walking when, out of nowhere, two large yellow trucks tear through the middle of the street, their sirens blaring. They've called the Exterminators.

I stand and look on in confusion as they speed by, before watching as they turn off in the same direction as the square.

For a moment I can't move, when a sickening feeling fills my stomach, knowing something is wrong. I break into a sprint, following after them, fearing the worst. As I come closer, the sounds of a thousand screams fill the air, all crying out in a violent barrage of terror and rage. Is that the Peace Parade? I turn the corner, and what I see next is complete and utter chaos.

A riot has broken out in the square, people everywhere scrambling to escape. Left and right, rioters are plucked from the street. The Exterminators have already started fumigating the area, fueling the panic even more as clouds of toxic smoke come rolling in. Then there's the clock tower. A blazing fire tears through the middle of it, with large flames lashing about in a frenzy. Huge plumes of black smoke roll high up into the air, covering the firmament behind a film of dark soot. Swarms of drones buzz overhead, their searchlights tracing the ground below in beams of light, trying to capture as much footage of the mayhem as possible.

I stand back and watch in horror as all of this unfolds before my eyes. This can't be real. Suddenly, the ground starts to tremble beneath my feet as the clock tower slowly begins to collapse in on itself, leaving nothing but a heap of stone and rubble.

IX
Escape

Chapter 50
Sub-Circuit.

In the moment, all I could think to do was run—run and not look back. Don't. Don't you dare stop now. I need to get home. But I can't go on any longer. I'm going to pass out. I come near an alleyway and stop in to rest and catch my breath. Oh God, what do I do now? Where do I go from here? How could this happen? And where's Evette? Was she in the tower when it fell? What if she got trapped in there when they started the fire? Stop it. She could've made it out before that. She would've had plenty of time. Please, God, tell me she made it out. Tell me she's alright. How will I even find out? She was my only connection to the televox. I can't even get in contact with them to find out where she is.

A fire truck goes zooming past the alley, the sound of their sirens snapping me out of my shock. You need to breathe, or you'll go into a panic, do you understand? Calm down. Now, first order of business, get back home, it's all you can do right now.

I get up and continue running.

*　　*　　*

As I step up to the door, I can hear from inside my apartment the sound of the television; Curtis is watching the news about the riot. I step inside, shut the door behind me. I turn around and notice the television isn't on at all, and that the voice I've been hearing this whole time is, in fact, my own voice. I walk in, Curtis is sitting at my desk, listening to one of my recordings. I glance up at the vent. It's open. He removed the grill. I come closer and that's when he finally notices me. Instantly, he jumps from his seat, quickly reaches for something on my desk, and points my gun at me.

"Don't move," he says. He looks hysterical. "Don't move, or I'll shoot."

I stop, hold my hands in front of me, as if this would do anything to stop a bullet.

"I knew it!" he says, "why couldn't you just turn yourself in?"

"Curtis, please, I can explain," I say.

"No!" he says, "so many times I tried to help you, but you were just too stubborn to listen," tears well in his eyes, "I'm going to give you one last chance. Give yourself up now."

"I'm not going to do that Curtis," I say. I'm feeling surprisingly brave for someone with a gun pointed at him. "You can stop trying to convince me that I'll ever want to become like you. You're only trying to convince yourself."

He's shaking. "You could've been worth so much," he says, "what a waste."

I can't let my irritation show. I have to act first if I want to get out of this unharmed. "Curtis, listen to me," I say, "the resistance can get us out."

"Shut up!" he says, "I'm done listening to what you have to say."

"They have a plan," I say.

"That's a lie!" he says, "there's nothing out there!"

"But there is," I say, "we can leave."

"You're not going to trick me like how they tricked you."

"It's true," I say.

"Stop it!" he says, "the earth is dead! We killed it!"

"No! It isn't!" I say, "they brought back a plant. I saw it

with my own eyes. I held it in my hands. It was alive."

"Why should I believe you?" he says, "I heard what you recorded on those tapes. Everything you've ever said was a lie. You've never once told me the truth."

"The truth?" I say. I've had enough of this, "what do you know about truth? All of your so-called truths are manufactured. Every single thing you do, say, and think is decided by someone else. Truth doesn't exist here."

"I hope you know you're going to rot down in those mines," he says, "waiting for those terrorists to come and save you."

"I'd rather be down there for the rest of my life," I say, "if it means not spending another day of it up here with you."

He looks at me, and I look into his face, and we both know what's about to happen next. I get myself ready. He repositions his aim, points directly between my eyes. I don't blink but stand my ground, staring straight down the barrel. Time moves slowly as I watch his finger bend back and pull the trigger. It clicks, but it doesn't shoot. I let out an exhausted sigh. The moron forgot to take the safety off.

In one swift motion, I lunge towards him, reaching straight for the gun. We struggle over it, trying to rip it out of the other's hands, before it suddenly slips between our fingers and lands on the ground a few feet from us. We instantly throw ourselves to the floor, scrambling to get it first. I grab it, quickly switch it off the safety, turn to face Curtis. He throws himself on top of me, grabs my wrist, shaking my arm to get me to let go. I fire one, two rounds, hoping one of them will land, but end up missing both, the bullets hitting one of the panes in the end wall window. Shards of glass sprinkle the floor. I fling the gun to the other side of the room, and as he gets up to go after it, I grab his leg and drag him back to the ground. I climb over him, try to hold him down by the throat, but he quickly turns to me and spits in my face. As I smear his saliva out of my eyes, this gives him enough of an escape to get back on his feet. I cling to his pants as he pulls away, clawing my way up, until we both have a hold of each other and begin slamming one another about the room. I bash his head against the floor and pin him down by the throat once more.

As I start to strangle him, my entire body tenses up, trembling all over. I clench my jaw to keep myself steady, drool leaking down my chin. I begin to hyperventilate. My arms go sore, my fingers begin to cramp, the sweat dripping from my face. I don't want to go through this again. I press down on his neck tighter, putting my whole weight into it. The sound of my heart drums in my ears as Curtis chokes on his dying breath. I start to scream. His tongue begins to swell up in his mouth, his face rapidly turning a grotesque purple, vanes bulging from his forehead. I begin to cry, and immediately release my hands. I watch as Curtis goes into an uncontrollable coughing fit. Shaking on the glass covered floor, he crawls into the corner away from me. I get up, turn around, and stumble over to my desk, nearly about to pass out. I lean against it as I try to catch my breath. Then from behind, I hear Curtis scream. I turn around to see him charging at me with a shard of broken glass. I grab his wrist just as he stabs me in my shoulder, and a cold pain travels down my arm. I hold him off as we struggle to overpower each other, blood dripping on the floor. I manage to push him off me, and as he tries to swipe at me once more, I stoop, and in my rage, shove him as hard as I can. In an instant, he falls back, crashing through the shattered pane, and out the window. Not even a second later, I hear the heavy thud as his body slams against the concrete below, ending him once and for all.

I sit motionless on the floor, staring into nothingness, when from out of my surroundings, I suddenly notice a familiar ticking sound. I look up and see at the other end of the room my pocket watch lying open on the floor in front of me. It had fallen out of my coat. I never realized just how loud it was. I awkwardly pull myself to my feet, make my way across the room, crouch down, and pick up the pocket watch. I turn it around. The glass cover is cracked, but other than that, it still works. It's 9:00. Any minute now and they'll be coming for me. I shut it, put it back in my pocket, then I hear the footsteps as they come inside. I couldn't even last a week, and already I'm being Recalled again. I didn't expect to be returning to the clinic so soon. I turn around to see just who I expected, a Recall Officer, but only the one. That's strange. I never knew them to work alone. I've only ever seen them operate in groups of three or more. He steps forward and calls me by my name. I realize he's waiting for me to respond.

"Yes?" I say, too exhausted to even get up.

He comes closer. "I'm here to escort you and the package to the safe house," he says, "Evette is waiting for you."

I must've hit my head at some point in the struggle. I've begun to hallucinate. "What?" I say.

"I'm here to get you out," he says, flatly. He begins looking curiously about the room, noticing the blood and the glass. "Are you alright?" he turns to me.

I don't hesitate. "I just killed my roommate," I say, "I pushed him out the window."

He thinks about this for a moment, then says, "we should leave now, before they come for you."

I nod. "Alright," I say. I get up and begin to pack my things. I grab the package, my cassette tapes, and the gun. We leave through the back exit into the alleyway, where his red Recall Wagon awaits. He opens the back doors for me.

"The clock tower was just a diversion," he explains, "we only have a few hours to get you out, so we need to hurry."

I can't bring myself to believe what is happening right now. I'm still convinced this is some hyper-induced hallucination, and that once this is all over, I'll eventually wake back up in the Recall Clinic, with no way to get out now. But I don't care. I step up to the back doors, and climb in.

Chapter 51
Hostel.

I sit in the truck's box compartment, the motion of the car rocking my body side to side in my seat, feeling the vibrations of the tires beneath my feet as we drive on. This is it, no turning back now. As of today, the only life I knew no longer exists. This is your one chance. If they catch you now, it's over.

Even though my situation has drastically changed, I feel no different on the inside. I should be excited, but not yet. It's still too early to tell. I don't intend to hold off my excitement until I know for sure that everything will be alright, or else I'd be waiting forever. I just have to have faith that for now, all is well.

I feel the car begin to slow down before coming to a stop. I hear the officer get out, then in another moment, he opens the doors.

"Come on," he says, "this way." I step out and emerge into another alleyway.

"Are we out of the main city?" I say.

"Not yet," he says.

I follow him through the back door of one of the buildings. We're in a hostel. The further we go, the more I realize it's abandoned. Using his flashlight to light our way, we walk upstairs and continue down the hall until we come to the door of one of the rooms. He opens it, and I step inside. It's empty. I was expecting to see Evette, or at the very least someone else in the resistance, but no.

"You told me you were taking me to see Evette," I say, turning to him, confused.

"She'll be at the next safe house," he says, taking off his hat to wipe his forehead, "she's probably already there. But I have to go now. Stay here and be quiet. I'll come back for you in an hour."

"Wait, where are you going?" I say.

"I have to check if I'm all clear to keep moving," he says.

"Why can't I come with you now?" I say.

"Because it's too dangerous," he says, "the Psi-Ops have probably figured out our plan. They'll be looking for us. Here, take this," he hands me a glowstick, "if you hear anything, hide, I won't be too long." He leaves, and shortly after, I hear the truck pull out of the alleyway and drive off.

I crack the stick to activate the chemicals, lighting the room in a green glow. This is one of those dead parts of the city. Other than the occasional patrol car or drone, there's hardly any movement. The only disadvantage to this is that I've been left in near complete darkness. I move the glowstick around the room, scanning its light over the furniture as tiny dust particles flit about the air. In one corner there's a kitchenette and dining area. Next to that is the living space for the television: a broken center table, a sofa, an armchair, but no television. I find the bathroom, but there's no door. At the other end of the room is a pair of empty wire bedframes, where a large chunk of ceiling has collapsed on top of one, with small pieces of broken drywall strewn about the floor. This building is falling apart.

I place the glowstick on the floor in the middle of the room and walk over to the armchair, trying to brush off as much dust from the cushion as possible. I sit down, laying my head against the armrest. It hasn't yet registered in my mind that this is actually happening. This all just seems too good to be true. It's frustrating. I should be happy, or at the very least scared, scared of the thought of being caught after all this time. But I feel neither of these things. If I knew for sure that tonight was the night I would escape, I would be overjoyed. But I don't. That goes to show how much I've become accustomed to my plans failing—maybe not so much as failing, but never playing out as I expected. If there's one thing I've always come to expect, it's that my expectations, no matter what, will never be met.

I sit in the armchair and begin to shut my eyes as I let myself sink back into the void of my head, and everything goes dark.

Out from the void, I hear someone calling my name, and I feel myself being shaken awake. I open my eyes. I'm sitting in my mother's lap.

"You fell asleep while I was reading to you darling," she says, "I know you had a long day," She carries me in her arms to the kitchen, where she makes me something to eat, before tucking me into bed. "Good night darling," she says, kissing me on the forehead, "I love you."

Why would I ever want to forget this? All the best memories I have are of her.

I wake to the sound of a door slamming from somewhere in the building, echoing through the empty halls, and I suddenly remember where I am. Next comes the heavy footsteps as someone races through the hostel straight for my room, getting closer and closer. I jump from my seat just as the Recall Officer from before bursts through the door, shining his light directly at me.

"We need to go now!" he says. He grabs my hand and begins dragging me out into the hall.

"Why, what's going on?" I say.

"They know you're here," he says, "the other safe house has been compromised. Everyone there's been Recalled."

"What about Evette?" I say.

"They caught her too," he says, "there's nothing we can do. She's gone."

I stop, trying to process this news. That can't be right. She couldn't have been caught. She was fine just a few hours ago. Evette will find a way out. She has to. We were supposed to escape together. She can't end like this. Tears begin to fill my eyes.

"What are you doing?" says the officer.

"We have to go help them," I say, grabbing his arm, "we have to do something."

"Stop it," he says.

"We have to go after them!" I yell, desperately tugging at him, "we can't just leave them!"

"I said stop it!" he shoves me against the wall.

"Please, I'm begging you!" I cry hysterically, "you can't let them take her away from me!"

"Listen to me," he says, "she's gone. We have to keep moving. They're already on their way. Do you want us to get caught too?"

I turn to him, unable to speak. I shake my head.

"Come on then," he says, "I know another safe house we can hide you at."

In my state of mind, I become detached from myself. Like a fail-safe switch, my psyche separates from the body, going into autopilot. From here on, everything becomes blurry, suddenly coming face to face with the truth, before disappearing into nothing: I'm never going to see Evette again.

Chapter 52
Safe House.

Slowly, I begin to return to my body. But now that I'm back, I find it isn't how I left it. Have I been gone that long? What's happened to me? It feels like every fragment of my being was suddenly taken apart, and then, in a rushed attempt to restore me, crudely put back together again. No part of me remains spared. All that I am now is a botched replica of my former self. After today, I'm never going to be the same.

The truck stops and the officer opens the door. "We're here," he says.

I don't get up right away, but remain seated, looking off into nothingness. He doesn't try to rush me, but stands holding the door open, waiting for me to get up. I don't want to keep him, so after a minute or two of fighting with myself, I finally get up from my seat. I walk like I've just woken up from a month-long coma, which perfectly describes how I feel. I'm still getting used to being back in a body, a body that is not mine.

I step out and look around me. We're in another alleyway.

We enter one of the buildings, and I quickly realize it's a Habitat, though it isn't as nice as the ones for Bureau employees. So, the safe house is in here?

"Try to be quiet," he says, "and stay close to me." We walk until we come to the door of an apartment on the second floor. He knocks, no answer. He knocks again, and this time there comes a slight shuffling from inside. We wait. After a minute or so, the door unlocks, and a woman peeks her eye through the opening. The officer says something to her under his breath. She glances at me for a moment, looks back at the officer, then shuts the door to undo the chain lock. She opens it, and we hurry inside.

"Make yourself at home," she says to me, "I'll just be a minute."

I look around her apartment. She hasn't risked turning the lights on, the room is divided up into smaller sections: the kitchen, the dining room, the living room, the bedroom, and then there are the doors for the closet and bathroom. I take a seat over on the sofa, facing away from them, while the woman and officer stand by the door to talk. I hear him begin explaining to her everything that's happening. I sit, twiddling my thumbs, wrestling with my situation. Evette has been caught. The Psi-Ops are out there looking for me. I still have a chance to escape.

Suddenly, the hairs on my arm stand on end. From out of my surroundings, I hear, just audibly, a slight creaking sound and quickly spot movement at the edge of my vision. I look up to see that the closet door is now open just a crack. I lean forward in my seat, peering through the opening, but it's too dark to see anything. I wonder what could've made it open like that—a draft, maybe. If I'd been thinking any louder, I probably wouldn't have even noticed.

"Are you alright?" says the officer, now standing next to me.

I look up. "Yes," I say.

"I'm going now," he says, "I'll come back for you later. Will you be fine here?"

I nod. "Yes," I say, "I'll be fine."

"Alright," he says. He leaves, and the woman goes to lock the door behind him.

"Here," she says, "let me take a look at that," she means where Curtis stabbed me in the shoulder.

She guides me into the bathroom, has me sit on the toilet, and opens my shirt. She begins to dress my wound. "What happened to you?" she says.

"My roommate stabbed me," I say, "he tried to kill me."

"You're lucky," she says, after taking another look at it, "this may not be that bad, but it could've been a lot worse."

She's not wrong. I haven't even realized it, but I could've died.

"Hold still now," she says, "this is going to sting a little." She begins by disinfecting the area, then cleans the wound, and has now moved on to adding the stitches.

"So, I hear you're getting out," she says, "how does it feel?"

"Well, to tell you the truth," I say, "it's a lot to handle."

"The officer told me what happened," she says, "I'm sorry about her. You know, there's always a chance she can still get out, at least she won't be Purged or Pacified."

I suppose she's right. Even though Evette's been caught, they won't kill her. The resistance can still rescue her. In the meantime, she'll just have to try to survive in her new life as a Librivox. But how many years will she have to wait?

"Thank you," I say, "for letting me stay."

"It's no trouble at all," she says.

She finishes by bandaging up my shoulder, when from outside the bathroom, we hear something fall in the other room. There's somebody else in the apartment. We both become alert.

"Stay here," she says as she gets up, "and whatever you do, don't come out."

"Wait, where are you going?" I whisper.

She closes the door behind her, and after a moment, I hear more sounds, followed by whispering. What's going on?

I get up, move slowly towards the door, my heart ripping through my chest. I press my ear against the door, then quietly crack it open. I can clearly hear her talking to someone in the next room. I step out and turn to see her sitting on the floor in front of the closet, which is now fully open. I come closer and see who she's talking to. It's a little boy. She has a son? He sees me first and is surprised. The woman turns around and doesn't know what to do.

"It's alright sweetie," she says to her son, "this man will be staying with us for a little while. Say hello."

"Hello," he says.

I wave at him. "Hello," I say, surprised.

"Are you hungry," says the woman to her son, "here, how about I make something for you to eat." She gets up and goes over to the kitchen. As she passes me, she turns to me and hints at her son. She wants me to keep him company.

He stands up and moves towards me. "You're bleeding," he says, "does it hurt?"

"What? No," I say, "not anymore. Your mother made it all better." This is silly, I think. I don't know how to talk to a kid.

"What's that," he points at my pocket. The chain from my watch is hanging out.

"Oh, that," I say, "it's my pocket watch, see," I pull it out to show it to him, "would you like to hold it," he nods, and I give it to him. "Do you know what that's for?" I say. I can tell he finds it very interesting.

He shakes his head. "No," he says.

"It's how people used to tell time," I say, "it's kind of hard to read because it's broken, but right now, it says it's 1:09."

He puts it up to his ear. "Why is it making that noise?" he says.

"It's so you know it's still working," I say. He gives a slight giggle, then starts clicking his tongue to imitate the ticking noise.

I could cry. He's one of the only few children in Apocalypse completely unadulterated by the Operator.

"Do you want to play with me?" he says.

"Of course," I say, trying to hold back my tears. He smiles, grabs my hand, and leads me to the closet, where he pulls out a small box of homemade toys.

"Here," he says, "you can be him," he hands me a

humanoid figure made from tinfoil, "we're on a mission to find the missing thimble."

"How did it go missing?" I say.

"I lost it," he whispers.

"Come and eat," says the woman from the other side of the room, "food's ready."

"Are you coming?" he says.

"Sure," I say, "let me just talk to your mommy first, alright?"

He gets up, goes to the dining table, and begins eating his food. I go into the kitchen, where his mother is washing the dishes.

"Why didn't you want me to find out you had a son?" I say.

"I thought it would be safer if you didn't know," she says, "I told you to stay in the bathroom."

"I'm sorry," I say, "how old is he, by the way?" I know he must be at most four years old, but I'm much more concerned about why she hasn't tried to get him out sooner. From the looks of it, his fifth birthday must be any day now. Why risk waiting till the last minute?

"He's six," she says, "six and a half."

"What?" I say, "how—how is that—"

"After he was born," she says, "I had help forging his records: a stillbirth. To the Operator, he doesn't even exist."

I watch him from the kitchen. He looks small for a six-year-old. That's amazing. I never thought being erased by a machine could be a good thing. He can live a life free from the war over his mind. I think of what my life could've been like if my mother had found a way to do this with me.

"Has the resistance contacted you yet," I say, "about any plans to get you and your son out?"

"They did offer to bring us with them a few months ago," she says, "but I told them not to worry about us for now. I just don't think it's safe yet."

"Oh," I say, a bit confused.

"You won't believe how hard it was the first couple of years," she says, "to leave him alone all day, afraid that if he'd cry, someone might hear him."

"Must've been tough," I say.

"It was horrifying," she says, "every day I'd come home expecting to see the Psi-Ops waiting for me at my door."

"He's an adorable boy," I say, with a hint of pain in my voice.

"You know what's funny," she says, "he looks just like his father," she laughs.

I give a smile, but find I can't bring myself to laugh with her. This is no joke. "How long do you think until they find your son and take him away from you?" I say.

She stops scrubbing. "What?" she says, unsettled.

"How long are you going to keep putting him at risk?" I say, "you might never get the chance to escape again. Why waste it?"

She looks away, ashamed, and begins scrubbing faster.

"Come with me," I say, "we can get you out, you and your son."

"I can't," she mutters, "it's too dangerous."

I come closer. "You can't keep him hidden forever," I say, "what if something happens to you? They'll find him, and you won't be here to protect—"

She slaps me across the face.

I touch my cheek, turn back to her. "I'm trying to look out for you," I say, unfazed, "I'd hate to think what they might do to him."

She looks at me, then down at her hands, her face slowly turning red. She begins to cry. "I'm sorry," she mumbles through her tears, "I'm so sorry. I didn't mean to."

I go to hug her. "I know," I say, "it's alright."

The Recall Officer should be here any minute now.

"Alright sweetie," says the woman to her son, "are you sure you have everything? Because once we leave, we're not coming back."

He nods his head.

Someone knocks at the door. The woman quietly goes to answer it. It's the officer, and she lets him in.

"It's getting more dangerous to move," says the officer as

he rushes in, "we have to go now if you want to get there undetected."

"We're ready," I say, "let's go."

"What are you doing?" he says.

"They're coming with us," I say.

"I was given strict orders," he says, "I can't bring anyone they're not expecting."

"What? But we can't just leave them," I say,

"Please, you have to take us with you," says the woman, but he pays no mind to her plead.

"Either you come with me now," he says, "or I leave you here and take the package their myself."

I shake my head. "No," I say. I reach my hand into my briefcase.

"I don't have time for this," he whips out his baton, steps forward, and makes a grab for my briefcase—but immediately stops. The woman lets out a horrified gasp and shields her son with her hands. I stare down at the Recall Officer, my arm stretched out before me, pointing my gun directly in his face. I didn't know what else to do. It was either this, or leave them behind.

"I said they're coming with us."

"Please," says the woman, "you don't have to do that."

"Shut up! You'll thank me later."

"You're insane," says the officer.

"I don't want to have to kill another person today," I say, "doesn't one seem enough to you?" The Recall Officer glares at me. He's more angry than terrified. We are outwaiting each other, but I am unmoving.

"Fine," he says grudgingly, "but you're responsible for what happens to them."

I don't move, but keep the gun pointed at his face. I want him to understand he is on my time, not his.

"Thank you," I say, slowly lifting the gun away, "now, get us out of here."

Chapter 53
Elevator.

All three of us sit in the back of the Recall Wagon. Opposite me the woman holds her son by her side. We haven't said a word to each other since we left her apartment. We're nervous, we're on the verge of something big, we can feel it. There's no telling what's going to happen from here on out. Now that we're so close, there aren't many possibilities left, our options are waning, the world's closing in on us. We're approaching the end, but the end of what? The end of the Operator's torment, the end of our life in Apocalypse, the end of our lives?

The truck comes to an abrupt stop. The woman and I look at each other. We listen as the officer exits, slams the driver's side door, comes around to the vehicle, unlocks, and opens the back.

"You need to get out, quickly!" he says.

"Why? What's going on?" we've stopped in another alleyway.

"I've just heard on the scanners they've got Protectors and

Exterminators both patrolling the area. I'm not authorized to be here. This is as far as I can take you. You have to continue alone on foot. There's an abandoned hospital a few blocks away, there's a freight elevator in the basement, it goes directly down to the utilidors, the S.O.S. will be waiting for you, use this key."

He hands me a key. "Thank you," I say. I shake his hand, "*Compos Mentis.*"

"*Compos Mentis,*" he says, "go, now!" he gets back in his truck and drives off.

We waste no time. I quickly pick up the boy, put him on my back, and with his mother, we begin running down the alleyway.

My mind is racing now. We haven't got much room to make mistakes. How long will our luck last? Keep it together. We're almost there.

In no time, we find the hospital and manage to break our way in through one of the back exit doors. The building's red emergency lights are on. We take the stairs down to the basement and emerge into a set of dusky concrete block corridors. The elevator is somewhere down here in these tunnels. We hurry, turning down one hall after the next, searching desperately for the elevator. We're really going to make it out, aren't we?

Running, we spot the elevator a long way off at the end of one of the passageways. This is it. We race down the hall towards the elevator, when from behind a corner further down, we see the beam of a flashlight approaching. They're already here. We draw back, and just as the Protector rounds the corner, we hastily take refuge behind the nearest door. Had he not been busy talking on his two-way radio, he would've seen us.

We stand pressed up against the wall of the storage closet, listening as the Protector inspects each room as he passes. I get my gun out. It won't be long before he reaches us next. There's no way all of us can outrun him now. If we even try to leave, he'll catch one of us for sure. We're trapped. I look at the woman. She holds her son in her arms, shaking and tearing up.

The boy too is beginning to cry. She turns to me, and the sheer look of terror on her face fills me with despair. Every fiber of my being collapses into my chest. We're not going to make it after all. It's been over twenty years, and still, the same old scene plays out again and again: a mother and her son torn apart, with no way of an escape. Time has come full circle. This is all my fault. They're going to suffer at the hands of the Operator, and it's all because of me. I'm the one who brought them here, and I'm the one who's going to get them out.

"Here, take this," I give her the key and my briefcase with the package inside, "I'll distract him while you and your son make a run for the elevator."

"No," she cries, "I won't go without you."

"You have to," I say, "just leave the key before you get on. Do not wait for me." I hug them both goodbye, taking one last look at them before turning away.

I step up to the door, wrap my hand around the handle, breathe in. I fling it open and make a run for it back up the hall from where we came. The Protector's flashlight suddenly locks onto me, and he shouts for me to stop. Just as I turn the corner, I hear the piercing sound of a bullet tearing through the air. It misses. I keep running, and by some miracle, manage to gain enough distance away from him. I hear him calling for the other Protectors on the radio as he gives chase. I turn off down another corridor, then stop for a moment to hear if he's still following. I silently wait behind the corner, listening for his footsteps. I hear him coming. He stops partway down the hall. I get my gun ready, but my hands are shaking too much. Come on, you can do this. I watch as the light passes a few times in my direction. He doesn't know which way I went. After a moment, I hear him go down a different passage. I patiently listen as his footsteps slowly fade away out of earshot, making sure he's really gone. I can't be bothered to waste any more time, soon this place will be swarming with Protectors.

I quietly attempt to make my route back towards the elevator, the sound of my heartbeat drumming in my ears. It isn't long before I start to hear the distant shouting of more Protectors, their voices echoing in the darkness. I need to hurry.

I find myself once again in the connecting corridor that turns off towards the elevator, but I'm not alone. There, I see a Protector's flashlight cast against the opposite wall as he moves down the hall in my direction. I stop just behind the corner, thinking I might be able to find some other way around, when, from behind me, I see more lights in the distance slowly encroaching from another corridor. I'm surrounded. I was hoping it wouldn't come to this. I watch as the beam of light in front of me grows larger the closer he gets, gliding back and forth as he scopes where the joining passageways break off to either side. I have to time this just right. I watch as the light hovers in my direction for a few seconds then moves towards the other side. Do it now. I emerge from behind the corner, drawing my gun. But I'm a split second too late and I'm suddenly met with his flashlight shining in my face.

Shots ring out.

I feel the bullet rip through my body, clean and effortlessly. The Protector's neck bursts open in an explosion of blood, and red splatters on the walls and floor. I drop to my knees, holding my stomach. I look down at my hand, it's covered in blood. I don't understand. I'm not supposed to die here. Coming from every direction, I hear a stampede of heavy boots rapidly closing in on my location.

I rise back onto my feet, my energy slowly withdrawing from me, gasping for air. Don't even think about giving up now. I stumble my way to the elevator, dragging myself along my legs. There's the key on the floor. Dizzy, I pick it up and quickly shove it into the call station keyhole, and call for the elevator. Inside I hear the hum of the motor running as it pulls the car. Violently hitting the button, I look back down the hall as the Protector's lights rapidly come into view. They're going to get here before the elevator does. I act fast, and start frantically shooting down the hall before any of them can round the corner, trying to keep them at bay. I suddenly spot a few yards away an unused fire extinguisher hooked to the wall along the corridor and direct my aim at it, and after a few missed shots, manage to hit it. It explodes with a loud pop as the compressed air escapes the canister, instantly creating a wall of white dust. The Protectors begin angrily shouting at each other. Finally, the landing doors slowly rattle open, followed by the car gate, and I step inside. The Protectors take this moment to return shots down the hall, even through the smoke screen, but they're too late. I hit the button for the utilidors. The elevator shuts and begins to descend. I can't hold myself up any longer. My legs suddenly give out, and I stumble back against the wall of the car, falling to the floor. I look up at the ceiling, hot tears streaming down my face, swallowing lungfuls of air. Fear escapes me, and I finally welcome peace. I did it.

I've had a long night, but I think I can rest now. I don't have the energy to cry. Perhaps this isn't the end after all, but the beginning of a new story. Mother, Evette, Finn, Mr. Freeman, Curtis, Dr. Savant, Rachel, Darien, woman with red hair, old man. Everyone else in this story has moved on to their new story, either in rank or status, in life or death. And so, my time has come. I have begun my descension. It's so cold. I'm losing too much blood; the taste of iron floods my mouth. I shut my eyes, and let the stillness take me.

And to you who have loyally followed along this story, I thank you for listening. Maybe one day, we will finally tell each other our names, and learn to use them. It's only a matter of time. But for now, I will sleep, and when I wake up, it won't be in a world where even the knowledge of one's name means death, but a new world, because I am free.

Thank you, God, for giving me the gift of storytelling.

www.ingramcontent.com/pod-product-compliance
Lightning Source LLC
Chambersburg PA
CBHW020054310726
48970CB00002B/308